MR PERFECT

SINISTER IN SAVANNAH BOOK 2

AIMEE NICOLE WALKER

Mr. Perfect (Sinister in Savannah Book Two)
Copyright © 2020 Aimee Nicole Walker

aimeenicolewalker@blogspot.com

ISBN: 978-1-948273-19-0

Photographer © Christopher John of CJC Photography
www.cjc-photography.com

Cover art © Jay Aheer of Simply Defined Art
www.simplydefinedart.com

Editing provided by Miranda Vescio of V8 Editing and Proofreading
www.facebook.com/V8Editing

Proofreading provided by Judy Zweifel of Judy's Proofreading
www.judysproofreading.com
Also Jill Wexler and Michael Beckett

Interior Design and Formatting provided by Stacey Ryan Blake of
Champagne Book Design—www.champagnebookdesign.com

To the scrappers who never lose sight of their dreams, even when they seem unattainable. Chin up, shoulders back, and straighten that damn crown. You are enough.

MR PERFECT

SINISTER IN SAVANNAH BOOK 2

CHAPTER 1

A shrill sound woke Felix from a deep sleep. What was it? The neighbor's vicious peacocks shrieking in the bushes outside his window again? No, that wasn't the right noise. By the time it sounded again, Felix was wide awake and fully aware of what had woken him.

A phone.

To most, a ringing phone in the dead of night was a bad thing. To a reporter, it was the sound of opportunity and possibility. Would this be the story that brought them fame and notoriety? Any reporter who claimed not to want those things was full of shit. They either were lying to themselves or just everyone around them. Felix was many things, some of them unpleasant, but self-delusional wasn't among his attributes or flaws. He knew who he was, what he wanted, and what it took to make it happen. He didn't lie to himself or anyone around him.

It was the only way to live.

Felix retracted his right hand from beneath his pillow. He reached for his phone but connected with a second pillow where his night-stand should've been. Wait a minute. He was on the wrong side of the bed. That alone wasn't enough to induce panic, but the sleepy voice answering the phone from his normal side of the bed was.

Oh God.

The events of the evening assailed him—one earth-shattering, technicolor image after the other. It wasn't *his* phone ringing. He wasn't even sleeping in *his* bed.

Fuck. Oh fuck. What have I done?

CHAPTER 2

Two weeks earlier…

"He's a sanctimonious prick, and I can't stand him," Felix growled into his phone as he pulled into the parking lot at work. He'd once dreamed of a grander position than the lead investigative reporter for a midsize market newspaper. *Savannah Morning News* was supposed to be the first stop on a huge adventure, but Felix was still here thirteen years later. He was happy. Scratch that. Happiness was as foreign a concept as living on Mars. Felix was content. Right?

"Of course," Reanna, his best friend since college, said, yanking his focus back to their conversation.

"I don't like your patronizing tone, Ree," Felix shot back.

"I haven't had enough coffee to deal with your bullshit, Fee." She was the only person on the planet he'd let get away with calling him such a ridiculous name. Ree and Fee—two peas in a pod. Felix had been the poorest kid and Reanna had been the only black student in their journalism program at Emory. They attended the university on scholarships and grants, while most of the kids were there on their parents' dimes. They never let Felix and Reanna forget it either. Felix was bitter then, and he was bitter now. Ree had fared much better than he, and deservedly so. She was the best person he knew.

"You're the one who called me," Felix reminded her.

"To wish you a happy birthday, not to get started on your old grievances against Jude Arrow."

The Straight Shooter. Christ. The moniker infuriated Felix more than he should permit. "I'm not the one who spoke *his* name."

Ree snorted. "I just asked if you've run into him since he moved to Savannah."

"He's living here?" Felix asked, feigning stupid. Oh, how he wished he didn't know the back-stabbing bastard was living in Savannah. Felix didn't believe ignorance was bliss in any situation besides this one. Knowing Jude lived here and worked for Channel Eleven only stirred up trouble he couldn't ignore.

"This is me you're talking to. There's no need to pretend." Warmth and compassion suffused Reanna's voice. "Have you seen him?"

"No."

It felt like he'd been holding his breath every day for six months waiting to run into Jude someplace. A small part of his brain had expected Jude to seek him out and take another swing at the apologies Felix had refused to accept in college. Felix didn't need to be a smug bastard, although he was the smuggest of them all, to expect Jude to know he worked for *Savannah Morning News*.

It was equally unbelievable another investigative journalist, even one who specialized in another medium, hadn't heard of the *Sinister in Savannah* podcast Felix had formed with his two friends, Jonah and Rocky. Hell, the trio had recently appeared in an interview for the morning show Jude's network produced. Jude had most likely known but made no attempt to seek out Felix, and that's what pissed him off the most. Irrationally so, since he'd told Jude on graduation day to never speak his name again, let alone talk directly to him.

Ree's sigh was as thick as the humid June air hovering over his beloved city. Felix knew what she was going to say, or at least what she wanted to say. Holding on to his grudges seemed unhealthy to her, but they fueled Felix to push harder, kept him hungry and in fighting form. Felix never again wanted to be the butt of anyone's jokes, or the emotional punching bag for bullies, and he refused to spend another day in poverty.

He might not be wealthy, but Felix was far removed from the always-hungry kid with the hand-me-down clothes from Goodwill. Some days it felt like his childhood was a different lifetime ago or had belonged to someone else entirely. Whenever he started to forget, Felix made himself remember by pulling out his school photo from second grade. Staring at his hollow eyes in the gaunt, dirty face would ground him.

Felix remembered getting himself ready for school as best he could without running water, food, or clean clothes. Hell, sometimes they didn't even have electricity. Even if his mother had stayed sober long enough to buy food with her monthly stipend, it would often spoil when the power company disconnected their service for delinquent payments.

On that picture day, he'd picked his favorite shirt up off the floor and put it on, even though he'd worn it the day before and knew his classmates would tease him mercilessly. Felix had held his head high and pretended their barbs hadn't landed.

The scrawny kid with the haunted eyes wasn't the only thing Felix noticed when he looked at the old photo. He saw determination in the straight posture and squared shoulders. He'd wielded that fortitude like a shield, deflecting as many jabs and poisonous barbs as possible. His strategy worked. Most of the bullies had lost interest in picking on a kid who hadn't given them the reaction they'd wanted. Todd Dartmouth was the only one who'd made it his personal mission to singlehandedly destroy Felix's spirit, but he never could. Not on picture day in elementary school when he'd teased Felix about the shirt. Not in high school when Todd recognized the jeans Felix wore were a pair Todd's mother had donated to Goodwill when the knees started to wear too thin. Not ever.

"I know, Ree," Felix finally said. Because he did. There had to be healthier ways to stay hungry than clinging to the most hurtful times in his life. "Enough about me. My life is as boring as watching paint dry."

"You and your podcast friends were interviewed on *Good Morning America*. You find that boring?"

"No," Felix said. He loved every aspect of producing *Sinister in Savannah*. As much as he loved the content, his favorite part was the brotherhood he'd formed with Rocky and Jonah.

"The podcast is going great, and 'Ride the Lightning's' success has blown us away," Felix said. The story of the 1982 murder of a drag queen and the coerced confession that followed thirteen years later had become an overnight sensation.

"But?" Ree prompted

"Something is off or missing. I can't quite put a finger on it."

"Maybe you need to get laid."

Felix was in the middle of a particularly lengthy dry spell. Was that it? "Or maybe a man turns thirty-five and starts seeing the world differently."

"Is your biological clock ticking too?" Ree teased. She and her husband, Stephen, had been trying to get pregnant for over a year. The last time they'd spoken, Ree mentioned looking into fertility specialists and adoption.

"That's all you, gorgeous. Have you and Stephen reached a decision?"

"We have," she said after a pause. "I know people think we're crazy, but we decided to seek help from a fertility specialist."

"Why would anyone fault you for doing everything you can to become pregnant? Whose business is it anyway?"

"Our families are just worried about the expense," Ree replied.

"Are you asking them to pay for it?"

Ree laughed. "Of course not, but we will have to take money out of our retirement accounts, or refinance the house, and there are no guarantees it will work."

"It definitely won't work if you don't try. I could lend you the money," Felix offered.

"I love you with all my heart for offering, but I can't accept. You have no idea how much money I'm talking about," Ree said. "I won't even know how expensive it will be until after Stephen and I have completed all the exams and screenings."

"I did some research when you brought it up a few months ago. I've heard enough about the process over the years to know it's expensive. I love you, Ree. You want a baby, and I want to see it happen."

Felix didn't make the offer lightly. His biggest fear was to make a mistake that would send him back to an impoverished existence. He had looked into the eyes of rapists and killers during interviews and hadn't hesitated to ask tough questions. Felix had been threatened with violence when he got too close to someone who hadn't wanted their misdeeds exposed. None of those things disrupted his sleep or caused him to break out into a cold sweat. Recalling the hollow sensation of an empty stomach was enough to trigger nightmares and insomnia for days, if not weeks. Felix knew what it was to covet something so much that it took over your life. He was able to help, and he would, if Ree let him.

"It sounds so shallow," Ree said softly. "There are so many babies out there who need a good home. Stephen and I have so much love to offer them. We made a pact. We'll give the fertility thing a try for a year, but we are going to adopt regardless of the outcome. If I don't get pregnant, we'll begin the process right away. If I do get pregnant, then we'll adopt in a few years."

"You and Stephen will make amazing parents. Let me help you."

"No way. I appreciate your kindness. It means more to me than you'll ever know."

"Anything for my best girl. The offer still stands if you change your mind."

They chatted for another fifteen minutes until Felix spotted the rookie journalist pulling up in front of the newspaper. The kid rubbed him the wrong way. No one was as perfect as this kid pretended to be—always dressed impeccably and never in a bad mood. Felix called bullshit. Minerva, the paper's editor and his immediate boss, ate it up, though, so Felix was careful what he said about Jimmy Alsop.

"Felix, honey, you're growling," Ree said. "Are you thinking about Jude again?"

"That damn do-gooder rookie writer just pulled in. I see him checking his hair in the mirror, and I just want to stomp over there and mess it up."

"So mature."

Felix laughed. "I didn't say I was proud of the urge. Isn't it enough that I recognize it and don't act on it?"

"It's a good start."

Felix watched the twentysomething man get out of his car with a bakery box and walk quickly to the front of the building. "I better get in there before Jimmy starts measuring my office for the replacement furniture he plans to install once I'm gone."

"You think he's gunning for your job, huh?"

"I know so."

"It won't do any good," Ree said. "Minerva loves you."

"Until someone shinier comes along," Felix replied. "Today is not that day, and that's all I can be sure of really."

"True. I love you, Fee. I can't wait to see you this weekend." They'd made plans for Felix to drive to Atlanta to celebrate the big three-five.

"Love you, and I'm looking forward to seeing you too. Give Stephen my love."

"Will do."

Felix disconnected the call, turned off his car, and headed inside. *What surprises will darling Jimmy have in store for me today?*

It didn't take him long to find out. He'd strung a colorful banner across the break room that read: Happy Birthday Felix!

Jimmy had his back to the door and didn't know Felix had arrived. The rookie removed brightly decorated cupcakes from the pastry box and arranged them on a three-tiered display thingy. He completed his task and stood back to admire or assess his work. Felix wasn't sure what he wanted to do more: eat one or shove it in Jimmy's face. The rookie reporter adjusted the pale green cupcake at the top by moving it a few centimeters to the right. "Now, it's perfect."

"Except you missed the comma between birthday and my name."

"Oh!" Jimmy gasped. He spun around, placing his hand over his heart. "You scared me."

"Sorry about that." Felix wasn't. "What's going on here?"

Jimmy laughed nervously, gesturing to the banner. "I figured it was pretty self-explanatory."

"Okay. I can see what's going on. Maybe the better question is: why are we having a celebration for my birthday? I've worked here for thirteen years, and I've never had a birthday party."

"Maybe that's due to your prickly attitude," Jimmy countered.

"I'd believe that if I was the only one who hadn't received a banner and cupcakes before you came along."

Jimmy blew out an exasperated breath. "Can't you allow someone to do something nice for you?"

With the exception of his friends, people didn't do things for Felix unless they wanted something in exchange. "No."

Jimmy narrowed his eyes and crossed his arms over his chest. "Don't you think that says more about you than it does other people?"

"Maybe, Jimmy. It still doesn't explain why we're starting a new tradition with me. Why not Maureen from classifieds? Her birthday was two weeks ago. No cupcakes. No banner. Holton's birthday was last month. No cupcakes. No banner. So, again, I ask: why me?"

"James."

"Excuse me?" Felix asked

Jimmy rolled his eyes. "My name is James, and sometimes people call me Jamie. No one calls me Jimmy."

"No one?" Felix asked, quirking a brow.

"Okay. My mamaw still does. Everyone else calls me James or Jamie."

"I've been calling you Jimmy since you arrived," Felix countered.

"And I've corrected you each time."

"Yet you make a banner and bring in cupcakes for my birthday. Why?"

Jimmy sighed as heavily as Ree had. Felix understood. He was exhausting, especially when something didn't add up. Felix had been downright rude to Jimmy from day one, and yet the kid set up a little birthday party. Felix smelled a rat.

The younger man ran a hand through his perfectly styled hair, messing it up and somehow making it look even better. "You don't like me, and it bothers me."

"I don't know you," Felix countered. "If you want to succeed in this business, then you better find a way to squelch your people-pleasing tendencies. You'll burn out in a year. You need to write the unvarnished truth about whatever story you uncover and not pull your punches just because someone might not like it. I've been an asshole to you since the day we met. I don't deserve cupcakes and a banner, even one with incorrect punctuation." Jimmy groaned and covered his face, and Felix felt bad about embarrassing him. Sort of. "Even though you shouldn't have gone to the trouble, I have every intention of stuffing one of these cupcakes in my mouth."

"Yeah?" Jimmy asked, sounding hopeful.

"Absolutely. Thank you for the cupcakes and the banner."

"Even though I forgot the comma?" Jimmy asked.

"Yes, Jimmy."

The young reporter rolled his eyes. "You're sticking with Jimmy, huh?"

Felix smiled as he crossed the room. He snagged a strawberry cupcake off the display and said, "Absolutely. James is too formal, and Jamie is too…" Felix waved his empty hand around in the air as he searched for the right word. "I don't know. It just doesn't fit."

"Fine," Jimmy groused. "Happy freaking birthday."

"There's the spirit," Felix said as Jimmy stormed out of the room.

Felix ate his cupcake in three bites, then went back for a second. Maybe Jimmy wasn't so bad.

Felix's morning was busy, which meant it went by so fast he couldn't dwell on the speech he was scheduled to deliver at The Rotary Club's luncheon. He had aced his public speaking and debate classes, so that wasn't what made his palms sweat during the drive across town. It was his ulterior motive for accepting the opportunity in the first place. There was a certain Rotarian he wanted to speak to, and the ordinary methods of scheduling an appointment hadn't been successful.

By the time he arrived for the meeting, the sun was high in the sky and scorching the earth. Felix parked the car, then put on the tie and grabbed the blazer he'd brought with him. Christ. It had to be a hundred degrees with the humidity, and the gentry still insisted on wearing formal attire for Rotary meetings. The business-casual craze hadn't made it to Savannah yet.

Once he was satisfied that his tie was straight, Felix turned off the car and quickly headed across the parking lot. He had every intention of drinking his weight in sweet tea during lunch. He reached the vestibule inside the building and skidded to a halt when he saw the sign for the event. It read: The Rotary Club is proud to present Felix Franklin and Jude Arrow.

"Fuck me sideways," Felix murmured.

"That's a position we've never tried."

CHAPTER 3

T he familiar deep voice was the psychological equivalent to an electro-magnetic pulse bomb, short-circuiting the wiring in Felix's brain and shutting down his systems, one by one. Felix's vision dimmed first, then his hearing dulled, and his chest became tight from the trapped air in his failing lungs.

Nope. He will not get the best of me.

Felix closed his eyes and counted to ten. Then he did it again before slowly reopening them. Felix turned to look into the sapphire blue eyes of the only person he had allowed to break his heart. Damn, the man looked even better in person than he did on TV. *Bastard.*

His nemesis wore a charcoal gray suit with a pale green shirt and a paisley tie that would've looked dorky on anyone but him. Felix could tell by the way the fabric hugged Jude's broad shoulders, trim waist, and thick thighs that he hadn't bought it off the rack at a department store as Felix had with his suit. *Fancy bastard.*

"Jude." Felix's grim voice lent no doubt about his feelings toward the man.

The corner of Jude's mouth twitched as if he were fighting off a grin. He must've won the battle because his lips stilled after a moment. "Hello."

"Hello?" Felix asked, his voice rising on the second syllable. Why had the word pissed him off so much? How else was Jude supposed to greet him? Hiya? Howdy? It shouldn't have rankled him, but it did.

Jude raised an immaculately groomed, raven eyebrow. "I would've added your name, but you forbade me from ever speaking it again." When Felix didn't have an immediate comeback, Jude grinned. "You do remember the scene you made on graduation day, right?"

"I remember the *conversation*," Felix corrected.

It wasn't like he had stormed the stage, shoved the dean out of the way, and blurted out his demand through the microphone. Jude had called out his name after the ceremony as Felix strode across the quad's lush green grass for the final time. He'd been full of mixed emotions. Pride for his accomplishment. Anxiety over landing a job and putting his degree to good use. Sadness from knowing he would never see Jude again, though he'd never voice that truth out loud to anyone. He'd turned to face Jude, a spark of hope catching fire inside him. All Felix had needed to hear from the man were two words: I'm sorry.

Instead, Jude had said, "I want to make things right between us."

Crossing his arms over his graduation robe, Felix had asked, "Why now?"

"Felix, you act as if I haven't approached the conversation over the past four years. You're the one who hasn't wanted to talk about what happened."

"Wrong again," Felix had said. "I'd tired of hearing you deflect and deny what you did. I wanted you to apologize for deceiving me."

Jude's cheeks flushed red with anger. "I won't apologize when I haven't done anything wrong. You were looking for reasons to push me away and grabbed hold of the first opportunities that came along. Why is it you can be so objective in every situation except for ones involving me?"

Felix shook his head. "If you don't know the answer to the question, then we have nothing to talk about. In fact, do us both a favor and never speak my name again. Pretend you never met me because I'm going to do everything in my power to forget you exist."

Staring into Jude's eyes now, it was impossible to forget the hurt he'd witnessed on graduation day. Felix had to forcibly remind himself of what a master liar and manipulator Jude had always been. His nemesis took two slow steps toward Felix, violating his personal space. He could've retreated a few steps, but fuck anyone who believed he would. Jude took a deep breath, his nostrils flaring. Then he leaned his head closer, giving Felix two options: pull back or meet that delicious mouth halfway. He held his ground instead, waiting to see how far Jude would push.

"I have a newsflash for you, Ace. I've said your name many times over the years. Sometimes so powerfully there's no way in hell you didn't feel the rumble, regardless of the miles separating us. I'll let you decide exactly what I was doing during those moments." Jude straightened up but didn't step back.

Felix swallowed hard but didn't say anything. He couldn't. His mouth felt like someone had shoved a wad of cotton balls inside it. Felix's tongue felt too heavy to move. Luckily, he was saved from responding when the Rotary president, Neal Jade, stepped into the vestibule.

"Great," Neal said, his booming voice echoing off the walls of the small space. "Both our guest speakers are here. They're about to serve lunch, so come on in and get comfortable."

Felix was as far removed from comfortable as he could get. The only thing that would make him feel better would be to turn around and walk out of the building. It wasn't an option. Not only did he refuse to give Jude the satisfaction of running him off, but he couldn't blow his opportunity to corner an elusive man who could be up to something unethical at best and highly illegal at worst. Felix's gut told him there was a story there, and he had to pursue it. That thought freed his tongue.

"Perfect," Felix said. "I appreciate you allowing me to speak to the club today."

"It's our pleasure. Savannah is lucky to have such esteemed reporters as yourselves."

"Honored to be here, Neal," Jude said.

"Follow me, fellas," the club president said before turning around and heading back inside the hall.

Jude followed, halting only long enough to lean in once more. "Happy birthday, by the way."

Felix wasn't surprised Jude remembered, but he was shocked Jude admitted he did. Felix remained in the vestibule for a few moments to gather himself while Neal and Jude walked deeper into the room. When people noticed Jude, they immediately broke off their conversations and rushed to greet the annoyingly handsome man. Felix squared his shoulders and approached the cluster of people surrounding Jude. He expected some of them to show him equal attention but only received a few smiles and some clipped nods, so he continued toward the head of the room, where a table was set up for the Rotary officers and the guest speakers. Neal Jade's nameplate sat in the middle of the table and place cards for Felix and Jude sat on either side of it. Thank fuck Felix wouldn't have to bump elbows with Jude during the meal.

Felix was careful to keep his expression neutral while insidious bile-like bitterness burned a path up his esophagus and threatened to choke him. Once he reached his seat, he took a long drink of water to wash it back down. He was tempted to wipe his mouth with the back of his hand to give Savannah's finest the show they expected from him. No matter how hard he worked or how many accolades he collected, it would never be good enough for people like them.

He would never be good enough.

A small part of Felix had expected a slight shift in attitude after the *Sinister in Savannah* podcast took off, especially after the appearance on a nationally syndicated morning show. Nope. The good people of Savannah still chose to fawn all over Jude Arrow. Why? Felix knew Jude's physical appearance drew people in, and there was no ignoring his charisma. A shiver rolled through him as he recalled the exchange in the vestibule and the flash of heat he'd seen in Jude's dark blue eyes.

Felix took another sip. Then another.

Jude's magnetism didn't just pull at Felix; it grabbed him by the balls. Time and time again, Felix's gaze drifted to his nemesis and the crowd circled around him. A short, paunchy man said something his nemesis must've found hilarious because Jude tipped his head back and laughed heartily before clapping the man's shoulder. Felix remembered all too well the strength and tenderness Jude's hands exuded.

"I have a newsflash for you, Ace. I've said your name plenty of times over the years. Sometimes so powerfully there's no way in hell you didn't feel the rumble, regardless of the miles separating us."

Oh fuck. No matter how hard Felix tried, he couldn't stop imagining Jude stroking his cock and calling out his name while coming. Even though Jude was probably just trying to get a rise out of him, he couldn't deny the words reached him on a visceral level. As if Jude sensed Felix's gaze, his enemy turned his head and looked into his eyes. Jude's lips slowly curved into a devilish grin, telling Felix he knew precisely where his mind had gone. *Evil bastard.* Felix needed to look away, but he couldn't. Maybe he just didn't want to.

"Excuse me, sir. Can I get you something to drink other than water?" The soft feminine voice broke the hold Jude had on him. Felix looked over to his right to where a young server stood with a pitcher of water in her hand.

"Sweet tea, please," Felix said.

"Sure thing. Would you like more water also?"

Felix glanced at his glass and was surprised to see he'd drained it. "I would. Thank you."

She refilled his glass, then set the pitcher on the table and pulled out a pad from her apron pocket. "Your entrée options today are blackened sea bass with seasoned rice and broccoli, fried chicken with mashed potatoes and gravy, or vegan lasagna. Which would you prefer?"

"I'll go with sea bass, rice, and broccoli. Thank you."

The we-love-Jude club broke up as soon as the Rotarians noticed the waitstaff coming in to take orders. It seemed like they loved their stomachs even more than they did the wolf in a tailored suit. While they ate, Felix quietly observed the people and conversations around him. The first thing he noted was a lack of diversity. More than half of Savannah's population was black, yet only one of the black business owners was in attendance. Where was the representation? There were no Hispanic or Asian members either and only a scattering of women throughout the room. The sole purpose of Rotary was to bring business and professional leaders together to further goodwill and peace around the world. In this room, it seemed that the most significant section of Savannah's population wasn't invited to the table.

Neal Jade spent most of the time kissing Jude's ass during lunch, but Felix didn't mind as it provided him the opportunity to alter his speech on the fly. He'd originally planned to talk about investigative journalism in the modern era, but he had something more important he wished to discuss. Neal only spoke to Felix when he informed him that Jude would be speaking first. What? He wasn't saving the best for last? How shocking.

Felix planned to tune Jude out so he could map out his new speech but found himself sucked in once more by the bastard's charisma, hanging on to Jude's every word like all the other attendees. It wasn't so much what Jude said because his speech was safe and dull. Jude's superpower was in his delivery.

Some things never changed.

Jude's voice was silky and polished with the perfect amount of timbre. He entertained with self-deprecating humor as he talked about some of his more memorable investigations from his days in Atlanta. The audience gobbled it up. Not Felix. He fought the urge to roll his eyes. Then he pondered the same question for the hundredth time since Jude moved to Savannah: why had Jude Arrow given up a lucrative career in Atlanta to move to a much smaller market in Savannah? Felix smelled a story, and he was going to get the answers. He could make a few calls and send out a few feelers, but he would prefer to torture the information from Jude.

"Now it's time for me to hand the microphone over to a tenacious reporter whom I've had the privilege to know for many years now. Please give a warm welcome to Felix Franklin."

The Rotarians clapped heartily, but Felix wasn't foolish enough to think they were cheering for him to take the podium. Most of the audience's attention stayed riveted to Jude even after he returned to his seat. That wouldn't do.

Felix stood straight and proud behind the lectern and decided to speak from the heart. "The biggest threat facing Savannah citizens right now is complacency." That got some heads turning in his direction. "What kills economic growth and progress? Complacency. What stifles the human spirit? Complacency. What encourages unrest and hatred?" Felix leaned a little closer to the microphone and lowered his voice. "It's okay if you want to shout out the answer with me." He nodded at the audience and said, "Complacency." He was happy when a few of the Rotarians said it too. "What breeds mistrust of law enforcement agencies and politicians?" He bounced his hands up and down to encourage them. "Complacency," he and half the room said. "Complacency is invisible and usually silent, but it's deadly. How do we prevent it?"

Felix looked around and was pleased to see he'd captured everyone's attention. Some members looked uncomfortable or pensive, a few looked pissed, but most at least appeared to be interested in what he had to say, including the person responsible for Felix accepting this speaking gig. This was why Felix never took the safe route. He wanted to reach people on a deeper level and give them another way of seeing things.

"Some of you look really uncomfortable right now. You might be wondering what the hell I'm doing up here, or how I earned an invitation, or perhaps you're trying to guess what I'm going to say next." Felix chuckled, then smiled at the group. "Good luck with that last one." The members laughed at his attempt at self-deprecation, even the pissed ones, and it encouraged him to charge forward.

He spent the next fifteen minutes challenging the Rotary Club members to push outside their comfort zones. Felix urged them to get to know people that didn't look like them, worship like them, and love like them. "Stand up for others when you see them being abused or oppressed, especially by those who are supposed to protect them. Complacency is a powerful foe. It might be invisible, but it is *not* invincible. Compassion. Empathy. Education. Those three things will clobber complacency in every battle. Choose your weapons wisely, folks, and let's go to war. Thank you for your time."

Felix was pleased with the warm applause he received as he made his way back to his seat. His eyes locked with Jude's who clapped along with the members and Rotary officers at the head table. Jude's heavy-lidded gaze gave Felix all kinds of ideas. He stowed them away until he was alone.

After Felix returned to his seat, the club president leaned toward him and said, "How would you like to become a Rotarian and head up a steering committee to increase the diversity of our group?"

Felix was rendered speechless. He had expected Neal to be angry over his bold assertion that the group was lacking in any way. Once he recovered from his surprise, he had to decide if he had the time to take on the responsibility. The hectic demands of his job at the paper and his podcast commitments left little personal time to do things that made him happy. Who was he kidding? Work and having a purpose brought Felix more joy than having free time to get into an argument with an idiot on social media. This offer was the kind of opportunity he'd been waiting for, and he'd be foolish to pass it up. Not to mention hypocritical. *Do as I say and not as I do.*

"I'd be honored, sir," Felix said, extending his hand to Neal. "Can I call you later today to discuss it in further detail? I'd stick around after the meeting, but I have an important commitment."

"Absolutely," the older man said jovially before rising and returning to the podium.

Felix hoped Neal wouldn't take too long to wrap up the meeting, especially since he told him he had another commitment, but Southern gentlemen never seemed to be in a hurry to do anything. Anticipation to corner his prey grew with each passing second until Felix was practically vibrating. He studied the man surreptitiously so he didn't draw any unwanted attention to himself and tip his hand.

When Neal finally adjourned the meeting, his quarry rose from his seat, nodded to those around him, and began heading toward the exit. Felix had two choices: do the same or wait for another time to approach the man. Persistence was his virtue, not patience. Felix also swiftly rose but turned to face Neal, who was nearing the table.

"I'll be in touch this afternoon, Neal."

"Sounds great. Looking forward to it."

Felix followed his prey, excitement building with every step.

"Felix," Jude called out behind him. "Can I have a minute?"

Felix nearly stumbled when his name rolled off the devil's forked tongue. *Damn him.* He pretended not to hear Jude and increased his pace. This might be his only chance, and he wouldn't lose it.

Felix cleared the building and sighted his prey once more. Fortune was smiling down at him because someone had stopped the elusive man before he could slip away.

I got you now, Mr. Perfect.

CHAPTER 4

Felix knew better than to interrupt the conversation his target was conducting with the exuberant Rotarian. Instead, he stood beneath a shade tree not too far from where Cameron Spencer, The Auto King, had parked. He settled for observing the exchange—something reporters were exceedingly good at. You could take many cues from a person's body language or the way they treated others when they didn't realize anyone was watching.

The two men were a study in contrast. Cameron Spencer was a striking man with thick, perfectly groomed blond hair and a tanned face that made his smile look even whiter. No way on God's green earth were his teeth naturally that bright or perfect. Had to be porcelain veneers. Spencer was tall, broad-shouldered, and trim, where the man who'd waylaid him was the exact opposite in every aspect. At first glance, Felix saw two friends catching up on old times. Cameron grinned down at the shorter, older man whose lips moved a mile a minute as he gestured wildly. Upon closer scrutiny, Felix noted the tiny furrow in The Auto King's brow, his rigid posture, and his darting glances toward the direction he wanted to go. What about this man made someone like Cameron Spencer feel uneasy? Maybe it wasn't the man but the delay itself that was irking him. If so, Felix was going to grab the man by his discomfort and give it a good twist.

The older, paunchy man mimed reeling as he talked, leaning back like he had a massive fish on his imaginary line. Was he sharing a fishing story, or was he in sales like Spencer and had landed a large client? Then the man held his hands up in front of him, spacing them a good eighteen inches apart. Definitely a fish story. Spencer guffawed and slapped the man on the shoulder hard enough to make him stagger step to the right. Frat boys had their bro hugs, and businessmen had their bro slugs.

Spencer's jovial features screwed up into disappointment as he took a step toward his vehicle, then jerked his head in the direction too. Felix didn't need to hear Spencer's voice to know he was politely ending the conversation. The short man nodded and smiled at The Auto King, but his frustration was obvious. Spencer slugged him again, then pivoted and started walking toward his car.

It's showtime.

Spencer pulled his cell phone from his pocket and looked down at the screen as he crossed the parking lot, which meant he hadn't noticed Felix leaning against the trunk of the tree just five feet from his car.

Felix waited until Spencer was only a few feet away before stepping from beneath the shade tree. "Excuse me, Mr. Spencer. Could I have a moment of your time?"

Spencer's body jerked to a sudden stop. He snapped his head up and locked his gaze on Felix. Spencer's eyes widened, and his mouth popped open in a silent gasp. Then his surprise turned to annoyance. Spencer narrowed his eyes and pressed his lips together into a flat line. As if someone flipped a switch, The Auto King flickered to life right before Felix's eyes. Spencer smiled radiantly, and the creases in his forehead smoothed out. It all happened so fast, but Felix had glimpsed genuine alarm in the man's dark eyes before he cleared his expression. Interesting. Who did Cameron Spencer fear?

"Mr. Franklin," Cameron said jovially. "I think your speech was great, and I couldn't agree with you more."

"Thank you, Mr. Spencer."

The Auto King gestured to his car. "I wish I could stick around and chat, but I really need to get going. I'm already late for a meeting." He started walking to his car without waiting for Felix to respond. He'd at least given the other man a cursory moment to talk about the whopper he'd caught at the lake. Why not give Felix the same courtesy?

Felix stepped forward too so that both men reached Spencer's car at the same time. "I'm afraid I must insist on a moment of your time, Mr. Spencer."

"Mr. Franklin, with all due respect, I find your mannerism rude. If you'd like to speak to me, you can call my assistant at the dealership and make an appointment."

"I've tried. Five times, to be exact. That was after speaking to every manager in the place from the service department to the general manager. I'm going to have my say right now and give you a chance to do the right thing."

Cameron quirked a blond brow, crossed his arms over his chest, and chuckled. It wasn't a humorous sound, but a dismissive one. "Are you threatening me?"

"Does the truth scare you?" Felix countered.

Spencer heaved a sigh as he glanced at his watch. "You have five minutes, Mr. Franklin. Not a second more."

"Great. I only need two," Felix replied. "I bought a brand-new Ford Fusion from your dealership four years ago. It was my first new car, so of course, I bought one with all the bells and whistles as well as the extra protection plans your dealership offered me. I made sure I had gap insurance, so I wouldn't get screwed over if I totaled my car. I also bought an extended warranty to provide bumper-to-bumper protection against mechanical malfunctions once the factory warranty expired. Are you familiar with those programs?"

Spencer hitched his chin higher. "Of course."

"The transmission went out on my Fusion three months ago, and I've tried every conceivable way to get your dealership to honor the extended warranty they sold me. All I've received is the runaround, including from you."

"Mr. Franklin, I assure you, I wasn't made aware of your attempts to speak to me."

Felix chuckled, mimicking Spencer's dismissive tone. "You'd have me believe your personal assistant failed to give you the message on five occasions?"

"Veronica screens my messages, and yes, that includes her making judgment calls about which ones to give me, and which ones to delegate to someone else in the dealership."

Felix couldn't argue with the logic. If he owned several dealerships, he'd need someone to run interference for him. Spencer had to receive dozens of calls each day that would be best handled by someone in sales or service. "Mr. Spencer, I can appreciate the need for your assistant to screen your calls. However, I provided her with detailed information each time I requested an audience with The Auto King." Spencer scowled at his reference. *Good.* "I told her about the service department refusing to replace the transmission because they *claimed* I hadn't met the maintenance schedule recommended in the owner's manual."

It was utter bullshit. Where most people buy a new car on a whim, Felix thought about it for two weeks before he pulled the trigger. Even though the payment was well within his budget, he couldn't shake his fear that he was heading for financial doom by having both a mortgage and a car payment.

"Well, there you go," Cameron said dismissively, reaching for the car door handle.

"Not so fast, sir," Felix said firmly. "I did follow the maintenance schedule, and all services were performed at your dealership, but by some twist of unlucky fate, the records are no longer in your system."

"We did upgrade our computer systems last year, and we lost some of the records. It's regrettable and unfortunate," Spencer said.

"It is for some, but not me. I've saved every single receipt from your dealership, including those colorful printouts they gave me that explained exactly what they serviced and checked during my visits. I got out my nifty owner's manual and looked at the service recommendations. I met every single one of them. I am no longer willing to play games with your dealership, Mr. Spencer. I met the terms of the warranty contract, and I expect you to meet yours."

Felix didn't tell Spencer he'd received an email from Molly Gregg, a customer who'd had a similar experience with The Auto King when she tried to file a gap insurance claim after totaling her car. He also didn't share with Spencer the woman had done a little digging and discovered that the company issuing gap policies, Indemnity Gap Protection Plans, was owned by the same parent company that extended the warranties, Platinum Auto Protection.

Molly initially took her concerns to Felix's nemesis, but Jude hadn't been interested in pursuing her claims. Felix sure as hell was. Not only did he have a personal stake in the outcome, but Felix believed the extended warranties and gap policies were nothing more than scams. It wasn't illegal or unethical for The Camelot Corporation to offer both services to dealerships, but Felix found little information about them on the internet. While the companies were licensed in the state to operate a business, their websites were generic and unprofessional. Felix had found a consumer website that encouraged their members to share experiences that would either encourage or discourage others from using service providers. There was no shortage of people claiming The Auto King screwed them over. Where there was smoke, there was fire.

Spencer pasted that phony smile on his face again. "Mr. Franklin, it sounds like your frustrations are justified, and I do apologize that my dealership has let you down. We do value each of our customers and want them to return when they shop for their next car. We've gotten off on the wrong foot here this afternoon, and I take full responsibility for it. I truly am late for a meeting, but I would appreciate the opportunity to make things right with you. Would you consider meeting me at the dealership around four this afternoon?"

Felix was surprised by the man's swift turnaround, but he wasn't fooled by it. Felix pasted a phony smile on his face too and bro slugged The Auto King. "Absolutely. I appreciate it. I'll bring my file of service records with me."

"You do that," Spencer said, sounding like he was fighting off a grimace.

Felix smiled genuinely at the man as he stepped back. "I won't keep you another second. See you soon, Mr. Spencer."

The Auto King nodded, then opened his car door, slipping inside without another word.

Felix felt triumphant as he watched Spencer drive away. He would get his transmission fixed *and* figure out what the snake was hiding.

"Felix."

His good mood evaporated as he turned to face Jude, who was barreling toward Felix with a purposeful stride that matched the determined expression on his face. Felix's first instinct was to run, but he wouldn't give Jude the satisfaction.

"Why did you ignore me inside?" Jude asked when he stopped in front of Felix. "I know damn well you heard me call your name. I saw the way your body stiffened."

"Which time? Inside the meeting hall or just now in the parking lot?" Felix quipped. "You broke the rule, either way."

"Felix. Felix. Felix," Jude replied snidely. "It was a stupid rule, and one I never agreed to, anyway. Why did you ignore me to chase Cameron Spencer down in the parking lot?"

Felix wasn't surprised Jude had figured it out, but then again, Felix hadn't tried to conceal his intention. "It's none of your business, Jude. Go on back to your station before the sun melts your hair mousse."

Felix pivoted and headed across the lot to where he'd parked his ancient Jeep Wagoneer. He'd bought Woody just out of college, and he'd never once let him down. Jude's dress shoes slapped rapidly against the pavement as he followed Felix.

"Don't tell me you're buying Molly Gregg's claims," Jude said.

Felix didn't stop until he reached his car. Then he turned and faced Jude once more. "I don't know what you're talking about."

"Bullshit. Mrs. Gregg told me she was taking the story to you when I refused to dig further into her allegations. Considering how much you hate wealthy people, I'm not at all surprised you jumped all over it."

Felix's jaw hurt from clamping it so tightly. He took a deep breath and forced his body to relax. "I do not hate wealthy people. I do resent when those people amass their fortunes by illicit gains or by stepping on the little people. My conversation with Mr. Spencer has nothing to do with this Molly person. If you must know, The Auto King's dealership is trying to screw me over. I won't have it."

Jude lifted a raven brow. "You approached him in the parking lot after a Rotary meeting to air your grievances? Why not call his dealership and request a meeting?"

Felix threw his head back and laughed. Then he bro slugged Jude much harder than was necessary. "It's so funny you think I didn't try that already. Nice to know you still think so little of me. Piss off, Jude." Felix opened the car door, but Jude leaned around him to close it again.

The maneuver brought their bodies close together, and Felix could feel the heat rolling off Jude's body. Rather than step away, Jude remained there and chuckled. The rich, throaty sound made Felix's traitorous heart gallop. "Don't try to bullshit a bullshitter, Felix. You think I can't recognize your tells after all these years. You think you're onto a big story. You want it so bad you can taste it."

Jude's breath ghosted over Felix's neck. He couldn't prevent the goose bumps from popping up all over his body, but he could fight off his urges to shiver and lean into Jude's heat. Not now. Not ever again. *Liar.*

"You don't know anything about me, Jude."

"You're wrong, Felix." Jude took a deep, shaky breath. "You didn't ask why I wanted to talk to you after the meeting."

"I told you already. We have nothing to discuss. Step back so I can get in my car. I don't want to cause a scene and embarrass The Straight Shooter in front of the good citizens of Savannah."

"We have a lot to talk about, but I guess I'll let you discover that on your own," Jude said.

Felix turned around to square off against him, but Jude had already started to walk away. "What's that supposed to mean?"

Jude turned around and walked backward. "Oh, no. I tried talking to you like an adult, but your stubborn ass wasn't having any of it. You'll find out soon enough," Jude casually said before turning back around.

Jude's stride was purposeful, and his posture spoke of a man who was utterly confident in his own skin. Or a man who had the upper hand. What had he meant when he said Felix would find out soon enough?

Felix hated surprises and had a bad feeling he wasn't going to like whatever secret Jude was keeping. It went against his nature to retreat, but he got inside his car and fired his old faithful to life, knowing it would irritate Jude that he hadn't taken the bait.

Felix would get the last laugh when he uncovered Cameron Spencer's secret and exposed The Auto King, aka Mr. Perfect, as nothing more than a common criminal.

CHAPTER 5

"Felix, Minerva is looking for you," Jimmy told him before he could reach the sanctity of his office. "She said it's important."

He held up his hand to acknowledge the rookie reporter without slowing his stride. Felix closed his office door behind him and retrieved a bottle of Tylenol from his desk. The heat and humidity, combined with the tension from his run-in with Jude, had given him a nasty headache. Felix stripped off his jacket and tie, then loosened the top button of his dress shirt. He pulled a bottle of water from his mini-fridge and chugged half of it to chase two tablets before going to see his boss.

Minerva Driscoll looked like Marilyn Monroe but had Nora Ephron's humor, Gloria Steinem's activism, and Barbara Walters's determination. Beyond her in-depth knowledge of publishing, Minerva had impeccable people skills. She knew how to get the best work from each reporter on her staff. She pushed when she needed to and backed off when a laid-back approach was warranted. She fearlessly sought the truth, no matter the personal cost. Felix admired her greatly.

He knocked on the frame of her open door. "You wanted to see me?"

Minerva glanced up from her computer and smiled. "I did. Come in. Happy birthday, by the way."

"Thank you," Felix said as he sat across from her desk. "What's up?"

"October is Crime Prevention Month, and I want to start making plans for the special features we're going to run."

"Already?" Felix asked. Minerva was always thinking ahead, but this was even early for her.

"You're familiar with Jed Akins, right?"

A sinking feeling began in the pit of Felix's stomach. "He's the station manager for Channel Eleven news."

"Yes," Minerva said. "Our two outlets have worked together on past projects as a cross-promotion type of thing."

"I'm aware." The paper had joined forces with Channel Eleven in the past to do segments on weddings, gardening, and barbecuing. *Savannah Morning News* saw an increase in subscriptions as a result, so it made sense that they'd continue to look for new ways to promote both outlets. *Fuck me.* Felix knew where this was going. Minerva wouldn't call him into her office to get his opinion on articles and promotional pieces that didn't involve him. Suddenly, Jude's urgency to chat made sense. "What kind of projects did you have in mind?"

"Well, that will be up to you and Jude Arrow to decide. You're familiar with The Straight Shooter, right?"

"I've heard of him," Felix said casually.

Minerva's right brow arched upward. Maybe some of his hostility had seeped into his tone. "We thought it would be best if our two ace reporters met soon to discuss possible segments."

"You're leaving it up to us to decide?" Felix asked.

"Obviously, Jed and I will have final approval before anything is recorded, written, aired, or published. We just thought the two of you should meet and brainstorm ideas a bit."

He wanted to say hell no, but he wouldn't refuse Minerva. She'd stuck her neck out for him too many times to count, and if this is what she wanted, he would find a way to make it work. "When?"

"They're expecting you tomorrow at noon."

High noon. How fitting.

"I'll be there," Felix said with a firm nod.

Minerva smiled happily. "I can't wait to see what you come up with."

Felix stood up and returned her smile. "I'm sure it will be great." *If it's like college, I'll come up with all the ideas while that glory hog takes all the credit.* Felix tilted his head toward the door. "I need to give Neal Jade a call. He's asked me to become a Rotarian and head up a steering committee to bring diversity to their club."

Minerva nodded. "He asked you, a white man, to do this? Not a woman or a person of color?"

Felix chuckled. He'd been so flattered by Neal's suggestion and distracted by his eagerness to speak with Cameron Spencer to absorb the irony in the invitation. "Thanks for pointing it out, Minerva." She winked. "You know who'd do an excellent job?" Felix asked.

"Shut your face and get out."

Felix laughed all the way back to his office. The conversation with Neal was brief, and the man was grateful Felix had pointed out the folly in his suggestion. "I'm part of the problem."

"Don't be too hard on yourself, Neal. Someone had to point it out to me also." *Maybe Felix wasn't as* woke *as he thought.* "We do better when we know better," Felix said. "Thanks again for letting me speak at your meeting today."

"I'd love to have you back," the Rotarian said.

"I'm just a phone call away."

After they hung up, Felix scanned past articles he'd written during Crime Prevention Month. He wanted to show up prepared for his meeting with Jude the next day, and it was apparent that his nemesis had a head start on coming up with ideas. Felix wouldn't trot out something he'd already done. Afterward, he got out a notebook and started making a list of various topics they could discuss from self-defense to the latest technology to prevent home burglaries. The list felt lame and lackluster, but it was a beginning.

Felix checked his watch and noted he had less than an hour before his appointment with The Auto King. He grabbed the Fusion's service records file from his bottom drawer, logged off his computer, and headed out of his office. Several people wished him a happy birthday, which he appreciated even if he found it a little odd. No one had cared about birthdays until Jimmy showed up. Thinking about the rookie reporter re-minded Felix of the birthday treats in the break room. He made a quick detour to snag another cupcake on his way out.

The heat and humidity punched him in the face as soon as he stepped outside. Jesus. Why did he live in the South when he hated the humidity so damn much? Because he hated the idea of cold winters, snow, and ice even more than the sultry Savannah summers. He devoured his cupcake before it melted and made a horrible mess on his dress shirt.

Felix arrived for his appointment fifteen minutes early. As soon as he climbed out of his Wagoneer, two salesmen started converging on him from opposite ends of the car lot—one on foot and the other on a golf cart. Felix began walking faster, and they sped up too.

"Good afternoon, sir," the man on foot said as he got closer. He had to practically jog to keep up with the golf cart's pace.

"It's a great day to buy a new car," the one driving the cart said.

If time weren't an issue, he'd string the two eager beavers along and pit them against each other. He wasn't in the mood, and it was just plain mean, so he held up his hand. "Not in the market, fellas. I'm just here to see Mr. Spencer."

"Oh," the man on foot said, sounding winded.

"Have a good day," the golf cart driver said as he performed a U-turn.

A blast of frigid air washed over Felix when he stepped inside the showroom. He couldn't help but stop and appreciate the reprieve from the stifling heat. The Auto King's floor layout was like the other dealer-ships he'd visited when shopping for his new car. There was a smattering of desks placed strategically around the ample open space, so they didn't detract attention away from the shiny vehicles on display. Felix had to admit it was an effective setup because his eyes were immediately drawn to a burgundy, luxury SUV he did not need but suddenly wanted.

To the left, a glass wall separated the finance department from the showroom. It allowed the bullshitters to keep an eye on the floor so they didn't miss a potential sale. Nervous buyers got to see how hard the sales-man and finance manager worked to secure their deal. Felix remembered sitting in the hot seat at the salesman's desk and studying the faces of the men in the fishbowl for clues as they reviewed the application and made phone calls. Going into the process, Felix knew he had excellent credit, sufficient income, and a good down payment. There was no reason for any bank to turn him down, yet the bitterness he couldn't always suppress had risen to the surface. He'd hoped for the best but braced himself for rejection. Felix's fear had been for nothing, but he could remember it so vividly.

The glass room reminded him of a bullpen in a police station, except the suits currently chatting at the dealership weren't trying to solve a crime. They might have been engaging in them, maybe even unknowingly.

In the far-right corner in the back of the showroom were the service counter and a waiting room for people to hang out while their cars got serviced. The dealership provided free coffee and muffins throughout the day, and there were several vending machines in an alcove behind the seating area. A few customers sat around watching a twenty-four-hour cable news channel, which was the equivalent of unknowingly having their brains sucked out. Objectivity in journalism wasn't dead yet, but it was definitely on life support. Finding impartiality was hard, and practicing it was even harder in the current polarizing political climate. Speaking the truth garnered many enemies, so it was a good thing Felix had no problem being the bad guy.

"Good afternoon, sir," a deep voice said from his right.

Felix looked over as a tall man stood up from his desk and buttoned his suit jacket. Couldn't Spencer allow the guys to wear polo shirts in this kind of weather? Then again, it was cold enough to hang meat in the showroom. Felix smiled and held up his folder. "I have an appointment to meet with Mr. Spencer."

The salesman's smile faltered. He released his jacket and sat back down. "See the black glass door on the other side of the service desk?" Felix nodded. "That's where the executive office is located. Betsy at the service desk will need to buzz you in, so go see her first."

"Thanks," Felix said.

Betsy wasn't at the counter when Felix arrived, so he entertained himself by reading the posters on the wall, which touted how much

Spencer valued excellence, honoring his principles, and servicing his customers. There were dozens of plaques bestowing high honors such as Businessman of the Year and Top Ford Dealership in Georgia. Other accolades were reserved for the vehicles themselves, such as their safety and durability. Then there were the team photos of various youth teams the dealership sponsored over the years. Felix was making a second pass over the display and quickly losing his patience when Betsy finally appeared.

"Well, hon, you should've rung the bell. I wasn't aware anyone was at the counter."

"Bell?" Felix asked, looking pointedly at the bare slab of black marble.

She glanced down at a spot where she expected it to be, then shook her head. "Oh, damn. One of the service guys must have stolen it again. They think it's funny, but I don't."

"Assure them that your customers don't either," Felix replied. "My name is Felix Franklin, and I have an appointment to see Mr. Spencer at four. A salesman told me you'd have to buzz me back through to the executive offices."

Betsy narrowed her eyes. "His assistant didn't inform me about the meeting."

"It's a recent addition to his calendar."

She held up a finger and picked up her phone. "I still have to double-check."

"I understand," Felix said calmly.

"Hey, Roni," Betsy said into the phone, "I have a Felix Frank—" Betsy's eyes darted up to meet Felix's as she listened to whatever Veronica had to say. "Okay. I'll send him back."

Felix nodded at Betsy and headed toward the black glass door. When he reached it, a mechanical lock audibly disengaged. Felix pulled open the door and stepped into The Auto King's opulent space. Publicly, Cameron Spencer had often eschewed the royal moniker given to him. He would pretend to be an average Joe who'd built up his empire by rolling up his sleeves and getting to work. Any person who walked into his private office space would see that his humility was phony.

The commercial-grade tile gave way to gleaming hardwood floors with an elegant area rug woven with purple and gold wool—two colors associated with royalty. In case the visitors didn't get the connection with the hues alone, they only had to look at the center of the rug to see the royal crest of a magnificent gold lion and a shield. Beneath it was a banner bearing The Auto King's credo: Excellence. Service. Honor. This was the real Cameron Spencer. The cars had their showroom, and The Auto King had his.

A petite woman stood up as he approached her desk.

"You must be Veronica," Felix said, extending his hand. "We've spoken several times."

She shook his hand, then said, "Yes, I recall."

Veronica's stiff posture, dry tone, and brittle gaze caught him by surprise. He understood why Betsy's eyes darted up to his. Whatever Veronica had said on the phone had most likely been unflattering. During their past conversations, Felix had never raised his voice or said anything to earn her disdain. And she'd never once let her professionalism slip. What had changed? Had Spencer taken his frustration with Felix out on her? Or had he reprimanded her for failing to do her duties?

"Mr. Spencer is waiting for you," she said, gesturing to the gold double doors at the rear of the space. *Was this guy for real?* "Can I get you something to drink?" Veronica asked.

"No, thank you," he replied before crossing the room and opening the doors.

The luxury of the outer room only intensified in Cameron Spencer's private space. Felix stood silent, hoping he wasn't gaping at the purple velvet walls with gold trim and accents. He'd never seen anything so tacky in his entire life. One end of the room had a gleaming, black walnut conference table with gold brocade chairs surrounding it. Above it hung a crystal chandelier that you'd expect to find in a formal dining room in a palace. *Christ.* Felix thought of the money wrapped up in the lighting fixture alone and nearly cringed. How many starving kids could Spencer feed with the money he put into his office décor?

Felix's eyes landed on Spencer, who sat behind a behemoth desk made of the same black walnut as the conference table. The sucker had to be twice the size of an ordinary desk. Was Spencer compensating for something else being too small?

"Felix," Spencer said, his jovial voice sounding like he was greeting a long-lost friend. "Come on over. Would you like Veronica to get you something to drink?"

"She already offered, and I declined. Thank you." Felix sat in a purple leather chair across from Spencer's desk. "I know you're a busy man, so I'll keep this brief." Felix reached into the file and pulled out the stack of his receipts. Then he grabbed the copy of the service schedule he'd made from the owner's manual.

Spencer reached for his phone. "Let me get Roni to make copies for us."

"No need," Felix said. "I have backup copies. These are for you."

The Auto King pulled his hand back and rested it on the armrest of his executive chair. "Of course, you have copies," Spencer said. "An ace reporter such as yourself would have his ducks in a row."

"First, a computer upgrade wipes out my original records. I'm almost afraid to see what happens next. A hurricane? Fire? So, my backups have backups if you catch my drift."

"Hard not to," Spencer said dryly.

Felix pulled out another stack of papers and laid them on top of his receipts. Spencer stared down at them with a puzzled expression on his face. "Those are printouts from consumer sites created for people to share excellent experiences or warn others about horrible ones. If all your promo posters hanging on the service department wall are true, you'll be upset to discover that Spencer Auto Mall falls into the latter category. I redacted their names or any identifying information, including the website addresses, to protect their privacy."

Spencer picked up the printout and started reading it. Felix quietly watched as The Auto King flipped page after page. After he finished, Spencer set the documents on his desk. The Auto King ran a finger over the bridge of his nose for a few seconds before lowering his hand. "It seems I have a bigger problem than I realized. Thank you for bringing it to my attention."

"You're welcome," Felix replied. "I'll just leave my receipts with you to go over with your service department. I'd like to have a phone call within twenty-four hours. After months of getting the runaround, I don't think it's asking too much."

Spencer rose swiftly from his seat and grabbed the paperwork off his desk. "There's no need for delay, Mr. Franklin. Come with me."

Felix followed Spencer through the showroom and out to the service department bays. He nearly groaned out loud when he saw Todd Dartmouth, his nemesis from school, standing behind the desk. The man looked older than the last time Felix had seen him, but not much else had changed. Todd's thick hair hadn't thinned, he hadn't gotten fat, and his broad shoulders weren't sagging. Too damn bad. Todd's eyes widened with recognition when they landed on Felix. Then he volleyed his gaze between Spencer and Felix until the two men reached him. He only had eyes for The Auto King at that point.

"Good afternoon, Mr. Spencer," Todd said, sounding like Wally's douche bag buddy in *Leave it to Beaver*.

"Hello, Todd."

"I'm surprised you know my name, Mr. Spencer. I just started here a few weeks ago."

"I know all my employees," The Auto King boasted. Felix wanted to roll his eyes but managed to refrain. "Is Bill available?"

Bill Whitman was the service department manager. Felix had had the unfortunate experience of dealing with the moron on several occasions.

"No, I'm sorry, Mr. Spencer. Bill left for the day. His daughter is having a baby."

"That's fantastic news for them," Spencer boomed as if he actually cared. "I'll give Bill a call at home later. In the meantime, I need your help, Todd."

Spencer put a hand on Felix's shoulder, and it took everything in his power to keep from shrugging it off.

"Of course, sir. What can I do for you, Mr. Spencer?"

"This gentleman is Felix Franklin. I'm sure you've heard of him,

Todd. He's an investigative reporter and one of the hosts of the *Sinister in Savannah* podcast that everyone is talking about."

Todd looked at Felix again. "I know who he is." Felix was impressed that Todd kept a sneer off his face and hostility out of his voice.

"There's been a terrible misunderstanding. Mr. Franklin's transmission went out on his Fusion through no fault of his own. He purchased an extended warranty when he financed the car." Spencer held up the stack of receipts. "He's kept up his end of the bargain, and we're going to honor ours. I want you to order a new transmission this evening and make arrangements with one of our tow truck drivers to retrieve Mr. Franklin's car tomorrow morning. His extended warranty guarantees him a rental car or a loaner from our lot." Spencer turned to face Felix. "You can have your pick of brand-new cars to drive from our dealership. There's no need to involve a rental car agency in the process. We'll deliver it to your home when we pick up your Fusion."

"Any car?" Felix and Todd both asked.

Spencer chuckled. "Yes."

It was on the tip of Felix's tongue to refuse the offer, since he had his cherished Woody Wagon, but fuck that. Vehicle transportation was included in the warranty, and Spencer owed him this much for jerking him around. "Thank you."

Spencer nodded. "It's the least I can do. I want to make things right with the others too." Felix knew Spencer was referring to the angry customers dragging his ass on the consumer site. Felix had purposely printed off the most unflattering comments.

"I can make a post inside the site informing them to contact the dealership," Felix offered.

"Please do," Spencer said. "I'll let Bill know to expect the calls and to set up a process to make sure each claim is thoroughly investigated." Then he looked at Todd. "Can you get the process started for Mr. Franklin? I want to be sure he's not inconvenienced further by waiting for Bill to return."

"Absolutely. You can count on me, sir."

Spencer turned to Felix and extended his hand. "We got off to a rough start, but I appreciate you bringing your situation, as well as the others', to my attention."

Felix gripped the man's hand and shook it. "Thanks for your time, Mr. Spencer."

"What's the address for where we need to pick up your Fusion and drop off the loaner?" Todd asked, interrupting them. He wouldn't want to listen to Spencer praising Felix's character.

"I'll leave the two of you to get things going. Let me know if there's more I can do," Spencer said, as he walked away.

Felix rattled off his address to Todd, then turned to the side so he could observe Spencer. The man had surprised him, which didn't occur often. Spencer stopped at the entrance to the showroom, where a hand sanitizer station was set up and pumped three squirts into his palm, vigorously rubbing his hands together before proceeding into the showroom. Was the guy a germophobe or was touching Felix the part Spencer found offensive?

Todd laughed, pulling Felix's attention back to his childhood bully. The man sneered at him just like the time in the gym locker room in high school when he'd flung a sweaty piece of fabric at him. "Are my hand-me-down jeans and shoes enough, or do you want my used jockstraps too?" he'd taunted.

Todd leaned across the service desk and said, "I don't care how much fame you have; you'll always be trash."

"Says the man who's too stupid to realize his boss only knows his name because it's stitched on his shirt," Felix said, trying hard not to show that Todd had struck a nerve.

He could've said so much more, such as pointing out that Todd's football scholarship hadn't gotten him far in life. The NFL hadn't formed a line outside his door to draft him like he'd expected, and according to the latest gossip, Todd had recently separated from wife number four. Felix could've remarked on those things, but he wanted to believe he was a better person. At least on most days.

Todd looked down at his shirt and seemed to deflate a little before Felix's eyes.

"I've decided which vehicle I want you to deliver to my house to-morrow morning." Felix pointed to the showroom. "The dark burgundy SUV caught my eye, and I'll look fabulous driving it."

The badass vehicle would take the sting out of being made to feel like invisible bacteria on someone's hands. Cameron Spencer wouldn't get rid of him so easily. He'd temporarily been distracted by the man's willingness to make things right, but Felix would not be distracted or deterred by a fake, over-bright smile and a flashy new SUV.

"But that Lincoln costs eighty thousand dollars."

"Mr. Spencer said any vehicle, and that's the one I want. Do I need to go back to his office and speak to him again?"

"No," Todd bit out angrily.

Felix crossed his arms and quirked a brow. "No, what?"

"No, *sir*," Todd groused.

That's more like it.

CHAPTER 6

Felix had stopped letting people make him feel dirty a long time ago, or so he'd thought. The inferiority complex he'd battled his entire life had him by the balls and wouldn't let go. He couldn't forget the memory of Spencer needing hand sanitizer after shaking his hand, or the sneer on Todd's face when he witnessed it. Felix had gained the upper hand in the end, but it was a hollow victory.

Hollow. Empty. That's precisely how Felix felt when he stopped at the grocery store to pick up snacks for the podcast production meeting he was hosting at his house.

This is the worst birthday in the history of birthdays. Even worse than the time he dug out stale cupcakes from the dumpster behind the grocery store.

Felix was more disgusted by his internal pity party than he was with the actual circumstances that spawned it. He wasn't a whiner; he was a doer. His ability to objectively analyze the situation and turn it to his advantage appeared to be broken. Not broken. More like it had a low battery. What Felix needed was a night with friends to eat junk food, chat about righting injustice, and recharge.

"Felix."

He froze in the act of reaching for a bag of tortilla chips.

You've got to be kidding me. This guy again?

Felix lowered his arm, then turned and met Jude's sapphire blue eyes. He raked his gaze over Jude's body. He'd changed into casual clothes. Jude looked more delicious in a navy blue Atlanta Braves T-shirt and faded denim jeans than any man had a right to. The fit of the shirt was perfect. It clung to his broad shoulders and impressive pecs without looking tacky or showy. Jude's jeans were the kind of faded effect you get from many years of washing and wearing instead of the distressed look designers charge an arm and a leg for.

Damn, he looked good. Felix could separate the man who'd become a stranger from the boy he'd known when Jude wore suits. But in casual clothes... Felix's brain got snagged on memories of falling in love for the first time, followed by the most painful betrayal he'd ever known. Felix grabbed on to the last thought and held on for dear life so he wouldn't do something stupid.

"Are you following me, Straight Shooter?"

Jude cringed. Why? Was it the use of his ridiculous moniker, or was it Felix's accusation? "Don't call me that, please. Not you."

"Because I know it's bullshit?"

Jude pressed his lips together in a firm line. "It's too impersonal for the history we share."

Felix opened his mouth to respond that their reasons were one and the same. Because of their shared history, Felix knew Jude's nickname was a lie. It wasn't what came out though. "You didn't answer my question. Are you following me?"

"No." Jude lifted a red basket filled to the top with various grocery items. Then he nodded his head to Felix's basket, which so far only held a jar of salsa. "Looks like I was here first. Are *you* following *me*?"

Felix snorted. "You wish."

"Actually, I do," Jude said. "I guess by now you've had a conversation with your editor about Crime Prevention Month."

"I have."

"I'd like to clear the air between us so we can enter into this partnership free of old baggage."

"Would you now?" Felix asked.

Jude nodded. "I would. Are you honestly going to say you wouldn't prefer to bury the hatchet?"

"I'd *love* to," Felix replied. "I just don't think you'd appreciate where I'd like to bury it."

Jude heaved a long-suffering sigh. The kind parents give when their kids have worn them down after a lengthy battle. He wasn't quite ready to throw in the towel yet. "Why don't I go back to the meat counter and grab another ribeye? I will make you dinner, and you can air out all your grievances against me."

Felix shook his head. "I already have plans."

"It's your birthday. Of course, you'd have plans."

Felix didn't celebrate his birthdays; he never had. He also had no desire to correct Jude's assumption.

"Look, we don't have to be best friends to work together," Felix said. "We'll establish ground rules and adhere to them and keep our focus on the projects."

Jude's shoulders slumped, and his gaze fell. Felix almost felt terrible, but his nemesis rebounded quickly. The shoulders returned to their proud carriage, and those assessing blue eyes met Felix's once more. "I'm sorry." Jude took a shuddering breath. "I should've led with those words years ago. Maybe things would've turned out differently."

Felix's throat went dry. The things he wanted to say caught there, forming a lump he had to swallow down before it choked him. "Thank you."

Jude looked like he wanted to say more, but he nodded and walked away without another word. Felix told himself not to watch him go, but his eyes were drawn to him. Some things would never change, including the urge to call out to Jude. He couldn't—wouldn't—let the man take another swing at his heart. Felix forced himself to refocus his attention on picking out snacks. He added tortilla chips and barbecue potato chips to his basket. Unable to stop himself, he turned his head and looked for Jude again, but his nemesis had already left the aisle. It was for the best, even if it didn't feel like it.

He thought about the steak dinner all the way home and regretted not picking a few up to grill for himself and the fellas. Pizza didn't sound nearly as tempting as it had a few hours ago.

When Felix arrived at home, he was surprised to see Jonah's and Rocky's vehicles already in the driveway. What the hell were they doing there so early? Even more strange was that neither man was in their car. Felix went inside and found Rocky, Jonah, and Avery setting platters of food on his dining room table. Not long ago, the battered table had been their makeshift recording spot until they converted a spare bedroom into a studio.

"What's all this?" Felix asked, raking his gaze over fried chicken and all the trimmings.

"Happy birthday," Avery said, stepping forward and hugging him. Felix returned the affectionate gesture.

Jonah had sure hit the jackpot the day his aunt Ellen decided Avery would make a good intern for the big guy. Not only did they make a fierce cybercrime-fighting team, their personalities perfectly complemented one another. Jonah was quiet and broody, and his boyfriend was sunshine and sass. Felix was glad Jonah had stopped fighting his feelings for the younger man. It was only a matter of time before they took their relationship to the next level.

Avery pulled back and smiled up at him. "I hope you don't mind that I tagged along with Jonah."

"You're his better half, not some tagalong," Felix said. "You're part of our team and always welcome."

"Thank you," Avery said as he returned to Jonah's side.

"So, which one of you numbskulls broke into my house?" Felix asked. Jonah and Avery both pointed to Rocky. "Figures. Really, Major?"

The private detective glared at him. He hated when Felix used his first name. "I'll let you have that one because it's your birthday."

"Who told you it's my birthday?"

Rocky snorted. "You know what I do for a living. Once I found out you went digging through my background, I returned the favor. Then I let the big guy know, and he said we should throw you a surprise party."

Felix looked at Jonah, who just shrugged. "I didn't encourage Major here to pick your lock and let us inside when you weren't home." Jonah looked at Rocky. "It's invasive."

"It's not your birthday, so you don't get to call me by that ridiculous name," Rocky told Jonah. It was hilarious his friend thought Rocky was a preferable name over Major, but to each their own. "Pawing through his jockey shorts is invasive. Setting up a birthday buffet is nice," Rocky continued.

"Who pawed through my underwear?" Felix asked.

"No one," Rocky said. "I was just making a point."

"You arrived before he had a chance," Avery quipped.

"Come here, you little brat," Rocky said, hooking an arm around Avery's neck and rubbing his knuckles over the smaller man's head.

"Did you have a rough day?" Jonah asked, pulling Felix's gaze away from Rocky's antics.

"It was full of surprises. Some of them good, and some of them not so much."

Rocky released Avery and studied Felix. "What happened?"

Felix sighed. "I'm not sure where to begin."

"The beginning is good," Rocky suggested.

"Let's make our plates while the food is still hot," Felix suggested. "Then we'll do story time."

They loaded their plates with chicken, sweet potato casserole, biscuits, black-eyed peas, fried green tomatoes, and coleslaw. Felix was deeply touched by their thoughtfulness, which he told them after he inhaled half the food on his plate. "Maybe birthdays aren't so bad after all."

"You're too young for a midlife crisis," Rocky said.

Felix elbowed Rocky. "Idiot." To Jonah and Avery, Felix said, "My hang-up with birthdays is a conversation for another day. Today's events are far more enthralling." Felix started with his run-in with Jimmy and finished with the showdown with Todd after Spencer embarrassed him. He knew his cheeks were red because his face felt like someone had set it on fire.

His friends sat quietly for a few seconds before all three of them started talking at once.

"Who the hell is this Todd joker?" Jonah wanted to know.

"You got Spencer on the ropes now," Rocky said.

Sassy Avery waggled his brows and said, "Personally, I'm a big fan of forced partnerships in the workplace."

They looked at one another and started laughing. Felix's friends began talking over one another again but swapped topics as if they'd rehearsed it.

Rocky crossed his arms over his chest. "You want me to rough Jude Arrow up?"

"Do you think Spencer was being sincere about making things right?" Avery asked.

Jonah put his arm around Avery's shoulder and pressed a kiss to the smaller man's temple. "No one forced me to work with you."

Avery turned his head and looked at Jonah. "Like you'd tell Ellen no."

Felix had always liked Ellen Rigby, even if her position with SPD, first as chief and now as the police commissioner, occasionally put them at odds with one another. She was brilliant, astute, and formidable. Jonah wasn't likely to tell her no, but she wouldn't suggest something that wasn't in his best interest either. Avery was the best thing to happen to Jonah, so kudos to Aunt Ellen.

Felix held up his hand to get their attention. Once all eyes were on him, he said, "One at a time." He turned to Rocky first. "No, I don't want you to rough anyone up."

"I'm serious, Felix," Rocky said. "I don't know what this asshole has done to you, but I know it's bad if you've held a grudge for so long. You're the fairest person I know. Want me to get dirt on him so we can run him out of town?"

He recalled the genuine joy he'd seen in Jude's eyes both times they ran into one another and the humility in his voice when he apologized, even though it was too many years too late. Those things unsettled Felix in ways he wasn't prepared to unpack just then. "No," Felix replied honestly. "I want to see how this plays out."

He faced Jonah and Avery. "I assure you that my working relationship with Jude Arrow will not result in an epic love match like yours.

And as for Spencer," Felix said, shrugging his shoulders, "I'm going to hold The Auto King to his word. I'll post my experience in the chat room with a message for disgruntled commenters to contact the dealership. The only thing I know for sure right now is that his executive office is the grossest display of wealth I've ever seen."

"Golden throne?" Avery asked.

"I didn't see the executive bathroom, but I wouldn't be surprised," Felix said with a wink. Grateful to have the attention shifted away from him, Felix took his time describing the private space in great detail. By the time he finished, they'd cleared their plates and were eying the peach cobbler Marla had baked for him. "Anyone save room?"

The guys moaned a collective "no."

They decided to save the dessert for later and moved into the studio down the hall. They weren't scheduled to record an episode, but Felix had found some great executive chairs at a consignment shop. Their planning sessions sometimes lasted for hours, so the soft leather was much more comfortable to sit on than the wooden dining room chairs.

"Let's start with the latest information about Bo Cahill," Felix said. "I want to lean harder on the governor to give Bo a full pardon."

"Do you think we can pull it off?" Rocky asked, leaning forward. "No one is claiming Bo Cahill didn't kill Vanderwahl, not even his family."

"Bo's case was botched in so many different ways," Jonah said. "First of all, he should've never been charged with first-degree murder. The prosecutor didn't even attempt to prove the killing was premeditated, and the judge let him get away with it. Bo Cahill shot the sheriff's son. Bo should never have been held in the man's prison, nor should he have been tried in the same county where the sheriff presided. The lawman would've been on a first-name basis with every judge. There was no way he was getting a fair trial."

"Bo didn't receive competent counsel either," Felix added. Then he opened Bo's file and pulled out a stack of documents. "Agnes sent these to me. They're copies of the phone records showing how many times she called the sheriff's department for help when Vanderwahl started harassing her. She'd also called other municipalities and even the state police looking for someone to intervene on her behalf. Not even one of the worthless assholes stepped up and helped her." Felix took a calming breath. "You've all seen the photos taken of Agnes after the assault, as well as the medical reports. Bo's attorney didn't enter any of this into evidence at trial. I think we have a strong enough case to get the governor to overturn the conviction."

Rocky smiled. "I think we need to raise some more hell."

"I'm in," Jonah said.

"We will start by revealing these facts on our podcast and follow it up by pursuing a posthumous pardon," Felix said. "Are you guys free on Thursday night to record the episode?"

"Works for me," Rocky said. "What about you, J?"

Jonah nodded. "We'll be here."

"Now, we have to shift our attention to Mr. Perfect. I'm not sure what to make of all this. I need to learn everything I can about The Camelot Corporation. Their office is located in Atlanta. I'm going to check it out when I head down to visit Ree this weekend."

"What's with Rocky's face?" Avery asked. "Is that his Joker impersonation?"

Felix looked over and laughed. Rocky wore the biggest grin he'd ever seen on the man. "Cat who ate the canary," Felix remarked. "You've found something big, haven't you?"

Rocky nodded. "A birthday present for you."

"Well, damn," Avery muttered. "We didn't bring a gift."

Jonah chuckled. "I don't think it's a physical present."

Rocky waggled his brows. "My sources in Atlanta got their hands on a list of Gentleman Jack's members. Guess whose name is on it?"

Felix's mouth fell open, and his heart started racing. "No way."

Rocky nodded. "Happy birthday, my friend."

"What's Gentleman Jack's?" Avery asked.

"An elite sex club catering to all appetites," Jonah said.

Avery crossed his arms over his chest. "How do you know about the place?"

"Honestly, I thought it was just a legend," Jonah replied.

"I procured two private invitations," Rocky said. "Mind if I tag along to

Atlanta with you? We can check out the club and The Camelot Corporation's office when you're not visiting with your friend. What do you say?"

Felix cupped the back of Rocky's head and briefly kissed him square on the mouth. "Best gift ever."

Rocky winked. "You're welcome."

They spent another hour going over additional podcast plans for future episodes. Felix offered to share the peach cobbler with them after wrapping up the session, but his friends claimed they were still stuffed.

"There's a carton of vanilla ice cream in the freezer," Avery said. "Marla thinks of everything."

"Should I transfer the cobbler to another dish so I can wash hers and send it back with you?" Felix asked.

Jonah laughed. "She's expecting you to return it in person once you're finished."

"Won't take me long," Felix said, planning to put a big dent in it as soon as his friends left.

They exchanged goodbyes, then Felix ran to his kitchen and scooped up a big serving of cobbler. He put it in the microwave to warm it up a bit while retrieving the ice cream from the freezer. The aroma of cinnamon, butter, and peaches wafted in the air.

Meow.

Felix set the carton of ice cream on the counter and looked down as his cat, Pulitzer, who rounded the corner and strolled into the kitchen. He wore a pissy expression on his face that made Felix smile. He bent over and scooped up his furry beast. "You could've come out. The fellas would've liked to meet you."

Meow.

Pulitzer sounded indignant as he stared at his human servant through narrowed green eyes. Felix scratched behind the tabby cat's ear until the beast began to purr and rub his head against Felix's chin.

"You're not so tough." Felix leaned forward and kissed the top of Pulitzer's head, recalling the nostalgic feelings Jude stirred inside him at the grocery store.

Maybe the cat wasn't the only one whose hiss was worse than his bite.

CHAPTER 7

The rumbling tow truck backed into his driveway at an ungodly hour the next morning. Felix figured the timing was purposely done to annoy him, but he'd been up for hours. By the time the driver rang his doorbell, Felix had already seen to Pulitzer's needs, run four miles on the treadmill, showered, and made breakfast. The joke was on them, or so Felix thought, until he opened the front door and saw the trash littered all over his front lawn. Someone appeared to have upended a garbage bag, or two, in the grass.

"Looks like you pissed someone off," the driver said dryly. The name stitched onto his shirt identified him as Skeet. Was that his real name or a nickname? Short for Skeeter, perhaps?

Gee, I wonder who I pissed off?

Felix refrained from rolling his eyes and shrugged instead. "Sure seems that way, but I'm used to it by now. People don't like it when you expose their criminal behavior. Dumping trash in my yard is kind of immature, don't you think?" Todd would have to try a lot harder to rattle Felix.

The tow truck driver turned his head and spat a dark brown glob over the side of Felix's porch. "They're just making a point, I reckon."

Felix heard another vehicle approach and glanced up to see the burgundy Lincoln SUV coming down the road. He had been prepared to fight the dealership over his request but wasn't upset he got to reserve the energy for his meeting with Jude later. "I suppose you need the keys to the Fusion."

"There's less likelihood of damage if I shift the car into neutral rather than just drag it onto my rollback with the winch," the man replied dryly.

"That's the avenue I want to take, then."

Felix's fixation with never being poor again was eclipsed only by his obsession for caring for the things he'd accumulated. He'd never had a fucking thing that was just his growing up. All his clothes and shoes had belonged to someone else first. When Felix was able to buy anything for himself, he went overboard trying to keep it in pristine condition. It was one of the reasons why he refused to let the situation with the Fusion go. The service department manager telling him he had failed to care for something he treasured so much was a kick to the ribs after he was already down.

"I'll be right out. Let me just grab them for you."

Before Felix could close the door, the person driving the Lincoln stepped out of the SUV. Fucking Todd Dartmouth.

"So, this is your place, huh?" Todd looked around, as if the fucker hadn't already been there to dump trash in his yard.

Felix knew his simple ranch house wouldn't look like much to most, but it was everything to him. He'd purposely looked for a house on the outskirts of Savannah, so he could get more property and privacy for his money. As much as he loved the convenience of living smack dab in the heart of the city, he'd have gotten half the house and a tenth of the yard. He equated it to a buy-one-get-one sale at the grocery store. Who didn't want twice the merchandise for the same amount?

When Felix saw the listing for this single-story brick home on two acres in the Wilshire Estates, he knew it was his forever home. The property had been overgrown from neglect, but all Felix saw was potential. He fell in love with the wooded lot and the large detached barn in the rear of the property. For a kid who grew up in a trailer park with homes practically stacked on top of one another, the place was a palace. He wasn't deterred by the labor-intensive work the house needed; he was inspired by it.

"Home sweet home." Felix closed the door long enough to retrieve the Fusion's fob and ignition key. When he reopened the door, Todd had joined the driver on the porch. The two of them were murmuring, and Todd wore a shit-eating grin on his face. He thought he got something over on Felix. Again.

He was wrong. Again.

Felix raked his teeth over his bottom lip to keep from laughing at Todd. He'd never turned the cheek when it came to the bully. Felix just found smarter ways to get even and make Todd's life hell. Like the time in high school when he'd overheard the bully bragging about skipping school and stealing the absent notices out of the mailbox before his mother got home from work. Felix imitated the principal and called his mother at work to ask if Todd was okay since he'd missed so much school. Since he'd also known Todd's girlfriend was pulling the same stunt, Felix had made sure her older brother found out about it. He'd had a tough time hiding his smug joy when Todd had showed up at school the next day with a busted lip and a black eye. To make it even better, Todd had ridden the bus to school because his parents took his car keys away.

"Here you go," Felix said, jangling the keys to catch the men's attention. The tow truck driver snatched them from his hand, then turned and walked down the porch steps. Felix shifted his focus to Todd. "You have keys for me?"

The bully narrowed his eyes for a few seconds. Did he really think his childish antics would get a rise from Felix? After an awkward pause, Todd placed the keychain in Felix's outstretched hand, careful not to let his fingers touch Felix's, of course. "I'm supposed to go over the features on the SUV to make sure you're comfortable with it."

"That won't be necessary," Felix replied. "I can figure it out." Modern vehicles resembled airplane cockpits with all their bells and whistles these days, but Felix was confident he'd be able to operate the SUV. He only needed to figure out how to turn on the radio and air-conditioning.

"Suit yourself," Todd said before turning and walking away. He climbed up into the passenger side of the tow truck and shut the door.

Felix remained on the porch, supervising Skeet as he loaded the

Fusion onto his rollback. Felix was prepared for the dealership to find opportunities to get even with him for giving them a hassle, but he wouldn't make it easy for them to pull off.

"Have a great day," Felix called out right before Skeet climbed into his rig. The man turned and spat another glob of tobacco juice into the yard. Felix could see Todd smirking at him in the side view mirror and barely suppressed the urge to flip the man off.

Once they drove away, Felix donned rubber cleaning gloves, then retrieved a rake, a shovel, and extra-large lawn trash bags from his garage. He raked the trash into a pile before shoveling it into the bags. It didn't take long, but Felix spent the time to his best advantage—plotting revenge and coming up with a strategy for handling Jude.

Afterward, he went inside and showered for a second time. It didn't matter that he'd worn rubber gloves, Felix still felt dirty. He spent an additional fifteen minutes figuring out what to wear. Silly, but necessary. He didn't want to look like he was trying too hard. Felix ended up choosing his favorite denim button-up shirt, khakis, and his favorite brown ankle boots. Everyone said the faded denim paired well with his amber eyes, but he just liked how soft the fabric felt against his skin. Felix knew for a fact the khaki pants hugged his ass exceptionally well, and he'd be a liar if he said he didn't want Jude to notice.

Next, he studied his appearance in the mirror. Should he shave his dark brown stubble or leave it? He wanted the look that best said, "I don't care what you think." Felix left the scruff, added some product to his damp brown hair, then got the hell out of there before he lost another forty minutes to inconsequential wardrobe decisions. No matter what he wore, Jude would look at him like he was a snack, and Felix would like it.

How was that for honesty?

The rest of Felix's morning improved immensely, starting with his drive to work in the super lush SUV and discovering another reporter had snagged Jimmy to assist them with a project. Too soon, it was time for him to head to the news station to meet with Jude and his station manager, Jed.

He stepped into the restroom to check his appearance once more, chiding himself for his foolishness the entire time. Felix found Minerva waiting for him in the hallway. She had her signature extra-large tote bag on her shoulder and sunglasses resting on top of her head.

"Ready?" she asked as she turned and walked away.

"You're going with me?" he asked, falling into step with Minerva. She hadn't said so the day before. Had she detected his reluctance to work with Jude and was ensuring things went smoothly?

"I'm just tagging along for the free lunch," she quipped. "Okay, maybe I want to supervise the photo shoot."

Felix skidded to a stop. "Photo shoot?"

Minerva stopped too and looked at him with wide eyes. "Did I forget to mention that part?"

He wasn't falling for her innocent act. It worked like a charm on most people, but not him. Felix shook his head. "You didn't mention they were feeding us either, but I was willing to let it go. I consider it a welcome surprise. But a photo shoot? Come on, Minerva. You didn't do this with the other cross-promotional segments."

"Lower your voice," Minerva hissed as she hooked her arm through Felix's and resumed walking. Felix could either go with her or make a scene. There really was no choice here. "The others will hear you, and I plan to blame Jed for the extra attention given to you and Jude."

"What's going on?" Felix asked when they cleared the building.

Minerva stopped and looked up at him. "The other reporters offer great value to the paper, but none of them have your star power. Have you ever looked at yourself in the mirror?" He knew he wasn't unattractive, but that could be said about tons of people. "It's more than your looks though. Your intelligence and passion for making things right just add to the total package. People are drawn to you like a magnet, Felix."

Unfortunately for him, it was usually the wrong kind of people. Trouble with a capital T.

"And Jude," Felix said. "I'm sure his appeal factors into the decision."

"He's not unfortunate looking," Minerva said coolly. A girlish giggle bubbled out of her, totally ruining her casual vibe. Her eyes widened, and she slapped her hand over her mouth.

"For fuck's sake, Minerva. You're acting like you just belched." Felix was so charmed by it that he momentarily forgot his irritation with her.

"In business, belching is much preferred over giggling. I've battled the dumb blonde label my entire life. I've learned to stifle my laughter, cloak my sense of humor, and mask my intelligence just so people would take me seriously."

Felix smiled. "I don't think less of you because you giggled."

Minerva smiled. "Thank you."

"Now, why don't you tell me the real reason you're going to all the trouble of a photo shoot to promote this joint venture? Besides my dashing good looks and cleverness, that is."

"You're going places, Felix."

"Come on, Minerva," he said, shaking his head.

"I'm serious. Your talent is too big for this market. It's only a matter of time before HBO, Oxygen, or the ID channel comes along and steals you away from us." Minerva sighed. "As your friend, I'm so proud of you and excited to see where your beautiful brain and passion for justice takes you. As your editor, I want to benefit from your brilliance for as long as I can. New subscriptions to our paper have tripled since you started your *Sinister in Savannah* podcast. Tripled! That's unheard of in this day and age."

"Minerva, I'm flattered by your high praise, but I'm not going anywhere. Savannah is my home, this is where my friends are, and I love working for you. I'm totally fine with you getting good usage from whatever notoriety I have. God knows you've had my back since day one. Just be upfront with me going forward. I hate surprises."

"Unless it's during an investigation," she countered.

God, he loved uncovering a juicy scoop. "Those are the only good surprises."

"You have yourself a deal."

They ended up driving separately to the news station, which worked in Felix's favor so he could get his riotous emotions under control. He'd spent way too much time replaying and analyzing Jude's apology. While he wasn't an expert on speech or body language, Felix was seldom wrong about his impressions. Jude had seemed genuinely sorry.

The question was: what, if anything, did it change? Nothing.

Liar.

Rather than calming his nerves, Felix had worked himself into a higher frenzy by the time he arrived at Channel Eleven. Sweat dotted his upper lip, and his torso felt damp. *Christ.* The last thing he needed was sweaty pits for the encounter. Felix could blame the summer heat, but Jude would see straight through him. That was the crux of the problem.

Where'd the intrepid reporter go? It was a photo shoot, lunch, and a planning session. No big deal.

Minerva tapped on the driver's side window. Felix turned off the SUV and got out. "Did I make a big mistake here?" she asked after they began walking toward the entrance.

"No."

Minerva hummed. "I let my investigative skills get rusty when I became the editor. I'm missing something, aren't I?"

"Jude and I have a complicated history, but it won't interfere with us working together. I promise."

She stopped at the door, pushed her sunglasses on top of her head, and studied Felix. "Are you sure?"

No. He wasn't sure, but he said, "I'm positive."

Minerva continued to assess his expression for a few seconds before she nodded and opened the door. Felix was grateful for both the chilly air-conditioned climate and Minerva accepting his word without pushing for more details.

The friendly receptionist greeted them and said Jed would be out soon to get them. Rather than sit next to Minerva, Felix studied the photos of the various anchors hanging on the wall. It was fun to see the evolution of hairstyles and fashion over the years.

"Minerva," a jovial voice said from behind him.

"Jed," his editor said happily. "It's so nice to see you again."

Felix turned around and locked gazes with Jude, who stood beside his station manager. While his foe's body language spoke of confidence, Felix saw a glint of uncertainty in Jude's dark blue eyes.

56

Minerva made introductions between Jed and Felix. The station manager was friendly and welcoming, and his handshake was firm.

"I guess there's no need to introduce you to Jude," Jed said.

"No, there isn't," Felix replied, hoping he sounded friendly. He looked at his nemesis and nodded. "Jude."

Jude raised a dark brow. "Felix."

Minerva and Jed exchanged a confused look before studying their ace reporters.

"Was this a big mistake?" Jed asked.

"No," Felix and Jude said at once. Neither of them so much as blinked.

Minerva laughed nervously, which snapped Felix out of his combative mood.

"Everything is fine. Right, Jude?"

"Peachy," Jude replied.

Felix chuckled, then glanced at Jed. "I wonder if I can have a private word with Jude before lunch and pictures?"

Jed looked between the men and shrugged. "Of course. Jude, why don't you and Felix chat in your office." He turned to Minerva. "I have some ideas for the photo shoot I'd like to discuss with you."

"Sounds great," Minerva said, then followed Jed down the hallway behind the receptionist's desk. She glanced over her shoulder once. Felix winked to assure her before they turned out of sight.

He would not let her down. Jude had taken an enormous step the previous evening, and Felix needed to acknowledge it so they could try to move on and work together.

"My office is this way," Jude said, gesturing to the same hallway Jed and Minerva had disappeared down. Felix followed Jude to a space that was like his in size and style—masculine minimalist.

Jude sat on the edge of his desk and silently waited while Felix looked around the room. Stalling tactic? No. It felt necessary. What was he trying to find, anyway? Then it hit him. Felix was subconsciously searching for a sign of the boy he'd loved in the possessions of a man who was a virtual stranger.

His heart skipped a beat when he found it.

CHAPTER 8

The baseball autographed by Chipper Jones, the Atlanta Braves infielder, rested in its place of honor in a souvenir display. The baseball itself was still in great condition except for the smudge left by the slugger's bat. The Hall of Famer had hit the home run into the outfield seats, where an eager boy enjoyed an afternoon game with his father. The wooden souvenir base wasn't as glossy as it had once been, and the glass top was chipped in a few places, but Jude telling him about the special day was still pristine in Felix's mind.

They'd been assigned as partners for a freshman journalism project. Felix's roommate had been a strange one, and he tried to avoid him as much as possible. The library had been packed, so Jude suggested they go back to his dorm room because his roommate was seldomly there. Felix had already developed a major crush on the guy but had no intention of acting on it. He'd caught the dark-haired hottie staring at him often, but not in an offensive manner. Still, it made Felix feel like his skin no longer fit his frame. Felix wasn't even sure what to say to someone like Jude, who always exuded confidence. Felix had seen the baseball display case sitting on the shelf over Jude's desk and had asked about it.

Jude had told Felix it was such a rare occasion for him to have one-on-one time with his dad, who worked seventy-hour weeks. He had been thrilled to have his father's full attention, so the home run ball falling into his glove had been icing on the cupcake. Jude's father had been as excited as his son was and asked around to see where they might be able to go to get the ball autographed. They loitered around in the parking garage, where many others waited and hoped for the opportunity to meet their favorite player too. Jude had been impatient, but his father's good mood had never ebbed. Their perseverance paid off, and twelve-year-old Jude got to meet his hero and get the ball signed.

By this point in the story, sadness had crept into Jude's voice. Felix had known whatever Jude said next would be awful. Jude's father had died of a brain aneurism two weeks later. The souvenir case the ball rested in was the last gift his father ever gave him. The little gold plate on the base, now slightly tarnished, listed Chipper's name and jersey number on it, as well as the date and the distance the home run ball had traveled. The ball, trophy case, and the memory meant the world to Jude.

Felix wasn't surprised to see the baseball in a place of honor on the bookshelf along with the broadcasting awards Jude had received over the years. The only revelation was how rocked Felix felt by the memory. Not so much recalling the story itself, although it was sad, but what happened afterward.

For the first time in his life, Felix hadn't been looking out for himself. He'd wanted to make Jude feel better, but he was clueless about how to do it. No one in his life up to that point had taught him how to comfort someone. Then he thought maybe sharing something about his own father would somehow make Jude feel better about losing his.

"Kelly said my dad took off when he found out about me." Felix's confession had rolled off his tongue as casually as if he'd spoken the ugly truth daily.

Jude had wrinkled his forehead adorably. "Who's Kelly?"

"My mom," Felix had replied.

"Oh," Jude had said softly. There was so much weight in that one word. It hovered above them awkwardly for a few moments. "It's his loss, Felix."

That was the moment Felix's crush had begun blossoming into love. He'd let down his guard, and one confession turned into two and so on.

Sometimes, Felix spilled his secrets between kisses amidst tangled sheets as the two young men grew closer than either of them had been prepared for.

Jude cleared his throat in his small office, yanking Felix back to the present. "I don't want to keep Minerva and Jed waiting too long. They'll likely come up with more ridiculous schemes."

Felix forced himself to meet Jude's gaze. "Ridiculous? Like working with me?"

Jude snorted. "No. I'm looking forward to that part, but the photo shoot..."

"It's a bit much, isn't it?"

"Just a little," Jude replied. His lips twitched at the corner, looking like a nervous tic. Felix knew better. The man was fighting off one of the smiles that came so naturally to him. Or at least they used to. "So, you wanted to talk?"

Felix rubbed the back of his neck while he figured out what to say or how to begin. "Look, I just wanted to tell you that I appreciated your apology yesterday."

Jude grimaced.

"What?" Felix asked, his stomach starting to sour.

"I don't think my apology means the same thing to you as it did to me," Jude said sheepishly.

Felix felt his face heat as he seethed internally. "What the hell does that mean? Are you taking the apology back?"

"No," Jude said, rolling his eyes. "I'm trying to explain that I wasn't apologizing for what you think I was."

Felix just stared. Jude had rendered him utterly speechless.

"I wasn't apologizing for the crimes you *think* I committed against you in college," Jude continued.

What the fuck is happening here? Felix's face must've betrayed his confusion because Jude groaned and reached for him. Felix staggered out of his reach. "Then what *did* you mean?"

Jude heaved a deep sigh and lowered his arm. "I am sorry that you believe I betrayed you."

What? The question shrieked through Felix's skull.

"I'm also sorry I failed to earn your trust," Jude carried on obliviously. "If I had, you never would've believed me capable of betraying your secrets to our journalism class."

"Let's not forget how you stole my project idea for senior year," Felix added.

Jude groaned again. Any louder and the people in the building would get the wrong idea about what was happening behind closed doors. "Felix, I did not—"

Felix held up his hand. He didn't want to hear another lie from those beautiful lips. "Just shut up. I've heard enough of your fake apology to last me a lifetime."

"It wasn't a fake apology. It just wasn't the one you wanted to hear," Jude argued, crossing his arms over his massive chest. The move pulled his dress shirt tighter over his bulging biceps.

Goddamned sexy bastard.

Felix quirked a brow. "Okay, we'll call it a non-apology, then. How does that work for you?"

"A non-apology?" Jude asked. "What the hell is that?"

"When someone does or says something horrible to you, you call them out on their bullshit, and instead of saying, 'I'm sorry I hurt you,' the loser pops off with 'I'm sorry your feelings are hurt.' That is not the same thing at all. It's implying the person who's hurt is the one at fault. It's victim-blaming, and I hate it."

Jude clamped his jaw so tightly that Felix was surprised he didn't hear his teeth cracking under the strain. His nostrils flared as he worked to calm himself. After a long, awkward staredown, Jude relaxed his jaw and tersely said, "You're an idiot."

Felix chuckled, the sound filled with disdain. "You'll have to find harsher insults to throw me off my game, Arrow."

"I don't want to throw you off your game, Felix. I simply want..." Jude shook his head. "Never mind. I don't know what I was thinking."

The tension suddenly faded from Felix's body, leaving him feeling emotionally drained. "Let's just get through today, okay? Minerva has a lot riding on this, and I don't want to disappoint her."

Jude nodded. "It's obvious you think highly of her."

"She's never let me down. I can't say that about many people."

Jude flinched, making Felix momentarily regret the barb. "I can ignore the past and work together. Can you?"

"Absolutely," Felix said. So, he wasn't *always* honest. But this white lie wouldn't hurt anyone. He'd make sure of it.

Both men plastered phony smiles on their faces when they joined Jed and Minerva. Neither the station manager nor the editor was fooled, but they went along with the pretense. The catered lunch consisted of a variety of cold cut sandwiches and condiments, chips, pickles, potato salad, baked beans, and cookies. Simple but delicious.

Felix had been too angry to eat at first. *Fucking fake-ass non-apology.* Then he noticed Jude hoovering down his food like he didn't have a single care in the world. The TV reporter was all smiles and laughter as he chatted up Minerva. Refusing to be outdone, Felix set his frustration aside, ate his food, and made small talk with Jed. The station manager seemed like a really nice guy, who spoke passionately about his career in journalism. It turned out his gig as a station manager was relatively new, and Jed admitted he preferred chasing leads over crunching viewership numbers.

"Amen to that," Minerva said. She clanked her can of Diet Coke against Jed's Mountain Dew.

The photographer arrived with three assistants, a selection of wardrobe pieces and props, and more attitude than one person should have. "The name's Woodrow, but my friends call me Woody."

"Woodrow," Felix said, shaking the man's hand. The photographer quirked a ginger brow. What? He thought they were friends after a mere introduction?

Jude, the ass-kissing sycophant, smiled charmingly. "Nice to meet you, Woody."

"The pleasure is all mine, honey," the photographer purred. "Are we ready to get started?"

"We are," Minerva said. "Jed and I would like a simple photo shoot that stays true to what these reporters are about."

"Hmmm," Woody said, raking his eyes over Jude and Felix. He formed his thumbs and index fingers in mirroring L shapes to make a three-sided box. "Uh-huh," he said, moving the frame from Felix to Jude, then back again. "Intensity just radiates off them. Makes me wish I was shooting a completely different set of photos today."

Jed coughed, Minerva giggled nervously, and the reporters just glared at Woody.

"Okay. My remark was totally inappropriate. I apologize."

"Just to be clear," Felix said, raising his hand. "Are you apologizing for your actions, or for how we perceived your words?"

"Uh, for my actions," Woody said, slowly drawing out each word. He ping-ponged his gaze back and forth between Felix and Jude.

Felix turned to Jude, who looked mad enough to chew nails. "See. Woody knows how to issue a real apology."

"Christ," Jude said, stepping forward until only a few inches separated them. "Do you really want to do this now?"

Someone snapped their fingers, then Woody said, "Jasper. My camera, please. Right now."

Felix was too focused on Jude to pay anyone else much attention. Jude's sapphire blue irises had darkened to almost black. Felix knew he was either turned on or furious. Perhaps angrily aroused. "Yes, Jude. I want to do this right here, right now."

The sounds of a camera furiously clicking registered in Felix's brain, but he didn't dare turn his head to see what the hell was going on. Jude might view it as him backing down. No fucking way.

"I'm not sorry for what I said to you at the grocery store or in my office," Jude told him. "I meant it. I'm also not going to apologize to you for petty college bullshit."

"Fellas," Woody yelled loudly, intruding on their moment.

They both turned and looked at him. Felix knew he was scowling and imagined Jude's expression was similar. Minerva gasped, Jed clapped, and Woody snapped a photo before looking down at his camera.

"There's the money shot," Woody said proudly. "I'd hate to see these two coming for me if I were a criminal, dirty cop, or unethical politician."

Woody showed the digital display to Minerva and Jed. "What do you think?"

"That's a wrap," Jed said happily.

Minerva checked her watch and grimaced before retrieving her tote from the chair. "I'm so sorry, but I must get going. Walk me out, Felix?"

He nodded, then followed her out into the hallway. She stopped there and rounded on him instead of continuing outside.

"Are you sure you're up to this? It's not too late to call it off."

Felix surprised her with a hug. "Thank you, Minerva."

Her brow furrowed, marring the smooth skin with worry lines. "Why on earth are you thanking me? It's obvious how unhappy you are around Jude Arrow."

Felix took a deep calming breath. Then another. And one more for good measure. He could do this. He *would* do this. "For putting my feelings first. It means more to me than you know. I got my temper tantrum out of my system. I'm good to go now."

Minerva narrowed her eyes. "Are you sure?"

"Okay, I'm not quite good there yet. I'm better than I was before and getting closer to good by the minute."

She hitched her tote higher on her shoulder. "I trust you, Felix."

"I won't let you down," he promised.

Minerva studied him for a few more moments before nodding and walking away. Felix blew out a harsh breath before heading back into the room where Woody and Jed talked animatedly. Jude stood apart from them, leaning against a wall and scowling down at his feet.

"Jude?"

He snapped his head up and stared at Felix.

"Are you ready to start planning our segments?" Felix asked.

Jude nodded. He didn't say anything until they reached the privacy of his office. "We don't have to do this. I can come up with some lame excuse why it won't work."

"It's not necessary," Felix assured him. "Let's just hash out some ideas for Crime Prevention Month."

"Are you—"

"No, I'm not sure," Felix abruptly said, cutting Jude off. "I just know I need to try."

"Fair enough."

An hour later, they had an impressive list of potential topics and interviewees. Felix also had a vicious headache, which he attempted to ease by rubbing his temples. Recognizing the signs, Jude opened a drawer, pulled out a bottle of Advil, and handed it to Felix.

"Thanks," Felix said, shaking out two tablets and chasing them with a swig of Dr. Pepper. "I think we have a good start. We can work via email until we need to record the segments for your channel."

Jude nodded. "Fair enough."

Felix rose from the chair. "See you around, Jude." He'd made it to the door and had gripped the handle when Jude called out his name. Felix slowly turned and faced him.

"Why don't you ask me what's really weighing on your mind? Maybe you'll feel better."

Felix could've told Jude he was full of shit or reiterated the horrible ways Jude had betrayed him. Instead, Felix said, "Of all the markets you could've chosen when you left Atlanta, why'd you pick Savannah?"

Jude stared at him for so long that Felix thought he'd decided not to answer. Then he opened his mouth and said the one thing Felix would never have predicted. "Because you're here."

CHAPTER 9

Because you're here.

The words bounced around in Felix's head for days, only quieting when his brain was too focused on something else. So Felix stayed busy until he was too physically and mentally exhausted to obsess about them. The phrase had followed him into his dreams on most nights, and Felix relived the expression on Jude's face as the lie had slipped between his lips. If he hadn't known better, Felix would've believed Jude was telling the truth.

When fixating on the encounter was unavoidable, like during a road trip to Atlanta with Rocky, Felix found himself homing in more on Jude's body language after he'd told the lie than his actual words. Jude's posture had stiffened as if he'd braced himself. For what? Felix to hit him? Call bullshit at the top of his lungs? He'd been tempted to do both.

Felix hadn't done or said anything to Jude. He'd just left. Then again, the action had spoken louder than words ever could. It told Jude that Felix hadn't believed him, and he hadn't cared. Jude's declaration hadn't registered with him one iota.

Except it had. Felix's unspoken, one-word reply echoed through his brain every time he thought about the exchange. He hadn't said it in Jude's office nor had Felix uttered it at any other time. Voicing it would give Jude's words weight or meaning. Felix couldn't—wouldn't—allow him to have that kind of power over him. Not again.

"Wow," Rocky said from the passenger seat. "The rear seats are also heated and cooled. Usually, it's just the front ones. They even have their own temperature controls back there."

Liar.

"Seriously," Rocky said, holding up the owner's manual he'd started perusing.

Felix cringed. He hadn't meant to say that out loud.

"I'm not sure how effective having dual control temperature really is in such a confined space," Rocky continued. "If you set your control to sixty-five, and I set mine to seventy, then the air temperature in the car will be a variation of the two. It's not like there's a barrier between us to ensure your temperature stays sixty-five and mine stays seventy. I think it's an excellent gimmick to snag a buyer's attention, but in theory, it's just not practical. Now, if I could pick how I distributed my airflow independently of yours... That would be badass. I like air blowing in my face but hate it on my feet. Maybe you're the opposite."

"I wasn't calling you a liar," Felix bit out. "I've had this internal battle going on in my head for days, and part of it slipped out."

"Jude?"

Felix nodded.

"I noticed you seemed distracted last night when we recorded the podcast episode. I figured it might have something to do with him."

"Why?" Felix asked.

"I haven't known you long, but he's the only person who either sends you into a fit of indignant rage or makes you withdraw deep inside yourself like a turtle."

Felix sighed. "He does have that effect on me. Our meeting on Tuesday didn't go well. I'm honestly not sure I can handle working with him, even though I've assured Minerva I can."

"What happened?"

Felix told Rocky about the fake-ass non-apology confrontation in Jude's office, followed by the argument during the photo shoot. "We managed to buckle down and get some work done afterward, and I thought just maybe I could do this."

"And then?" Rocky prompted.

"He told me the biggest lie of them all." Felix swallowed hard. "I asked him why he'd chosen Savannah when he left Atlanta. He said 'because you're here.'"

"How do you know he's lying?"

Felix chuckled, but the sound was as hollow as a dead tree. "It has to be a lie."

"Because?" Rocky asked.

"Otherwise, it would mean..." Felix puffed out a frustrated breath. He didn't know because he refused to allow himself to consider what it meant. "Jude has lived here for months and never once approached me. I'm not hard to find."

"Until this week."

"We ran into each other at the Rotary meeting this week. He didn't seek me out."

"Or maybe he did," Rocky countered.

Felix glanced over at his friend, noting the sly grin on his handsome face. "You think he orchestrated my Rotary speaking gig?"

Rocky laughed. "Running into you at a public event where you're not likely to cut off his balls is smarter than showing up on your doorstep or calling you out of the blue."

Easier too. Jude called it working smarter, but Felix thought it was lazy. "You think Jude's the one behind the joint venture with the news station?"

"Could be," Rocky said. "You said it wasn't the first time the two media outlets worked together though."

Felix narrowed his eyes as the seed Rocky planted started to take root and spread. "Jude would be aware of the history." And use it to his advantage. Also lazy. "What was Jude's advantage? What had he hoped to accomplish with forced proximity?"

"Really, Felix?" Rocky asked. "Think about it."

Because you're here. Felix didn't want to think about it.

"What did Jude do to you in college to make you pretend to hate him so much?"

"I can't stand you, Major," Felix groused.

Rocky blew him a kiss. "About as much as you can't stand Jude Arrow?"

"Don't make me pull this SUV over and dump you out on the side of the road. It's a scorcher out there today, and we're still an hour away from Atlanta."

"You're not getting into Gentleman Jack's without me, so..."

Rocky had Felix there. "Fine. Jude told everyone in our journalism class that my mother was a trailer park whore."

"Bastard," Rocky said. "I can't believe he spread such vicious rumors about you."

"He's a duplicitous bastard, but he didn't lie about me." *Just to me.*

Felix had trusted Jude with a truth that hurt him more than any lie ever could, which was why Jude's betrayal sank deeper than Felix's bones. It felt like a permanent scar on his soul.

"Kelly did whatever it took to get by. First, it was to feed a drug habit. She sobered up by the time I was in eighth grade but finding a good-paying job with her reputation was impossible. She sheltered me from the truth for as long as she could. Kelly never brought the men to our trailer or exposed me to her lifestyle in other ways. You know how kids are though. Their parents hadn't hesitated to talk about the trailer trash at the dinner table, and my classmates had eagerly filled my head with the harsh truth about my mother."

"Fuck, Felix. I'm so sorry," Rocky said.

"It's okay. Kelly and I are in a good place now."

"How the hell did Jude find out? He's from Atlanta, and you attended Emory University there, right?"

Then, as if fate really wanted to fuck with him, a Jude Arrow promo came on the radio. Felix changed the station, wishing he could also steer the subject in a different direction. Instead, he said, "Yeah."

"How in the world had he known about your personal business back in Savannah?"

Felix sighed deeply. *I believed in him. I trusted him.* "I foolishly confided in him."

"You loved Jude," Rocky said softly. "It explains so much."

Felix tightened his grip on the steering wheel and his heart. "I did. He betrayed me."

"The son of a bitch better hope we don't run into each other," Rocky growled. "I'll fuck up his pretty face really good."

Rocky's loyalty made Felix's heart swell and fondness for his friend thickened Felix's voice when he said, "Aw, Major. I knew you liked me."

Rocky snorted. "Only every other day. I guess you're in luck today. Tomorrow, I might want to fist-bump Arrow instead of breaking his nose."

Felix laughed, grateful for Rocky's attempt at lightening the mood inside the luxury SUV. "Since it's my lucky day, does that mean you're buying lunch?"

Rocky reached over and ruffled Felix's hair. "Sure."

"Your destination is on the right in three hundred feet." By the time they reached Buckhead, Rocky had changed the voice for the GPS half a dozen times before settling on a British accent.

"I can pretend it's Henry Cavill," he'd teased. The computerized voice sounded nothing like the sexy man they both crushed on. Felix was just grateful Rocky had turned his attention away from his history with Jude and back to the Lincoln's features.

Felix pulled into the parking garage, then they checked into the Hyatt and headed up to their room.

"Which bed do you want?" Rocky asked.

Felix shrugged. "Makes no difference to me."

Rocky dropped his duffel on the bed closest to the door, so Felix did the same with the one closest to the window.

"I owe you lunch," Rocky said.

Felix smiled. "I know the perfect place. It's within walking distance." They took the elevator down to the lobby and exited out on Peachtree

Road. "See those two towers?" He nodded toward a complex with two beautiful skyscrapers and a parking garage sandwiched between them. "That's the Peachtree Plaza, which is Atlanta's version of the Chrysler Building. Several major corporations have their offices in one of those two towers. I believe there are also residential penthouses in the top for the Big Peach's wealthiest citizens."

"Please tell me they have restaurants too," Rocky said. "My stomach is trying to eat itself."

Felix laughed. "There are many places to eat in either tower, ranging from cafes to Michelin-starred restaurants." There were dozens of high-end stores to shop at and even a fitness club.

"I have a five-star appetite, but a two-star budget," Rocky quipped.

"I know just the place." Felix led him to a lovely bistro in the second tower. A hostess led them out to a covered terrace, where a server promptly dropped off menus and took their drink orders. Once they were alone again, Felix leaned forward and said, "Do you know who else claims this building as their corporate office?"

Rocky grinned. "The Camelot Corporation?"

"Exactly. The website for the Peachtree Plaza states they offer top-notch security for their buildings. They boldly claim many of America's most successful corporations call their building home, but they don't list who they are."

"It's understandable," Rocky said before taking a long drink of his lemonade. Then he reached into his shirt pocket and pulled out a pair of eyeglasses with black rectangular frames. Rocky slipped them on and tested the fit before picking up the menu and looking at his food options.

"Reading glasses?" Felix asked.

Rocky peered at Felix over the top of the menu. The harsh lines and dark color of the frames made Rocky's eyes look a lighter shade of blue. Felix was momentarily stunned by his friend's looks. It wasn't the first time, and it wouldn't be the last. Rocky was just so pretty, which seemed like such an odd thing to say about someone so ruggedly handsome. It was just the best way to describe the private investigator. He was fucking pretty.

Rocky adjusted them again as if he wasn't sure about the fit. "Yeah. I'm trying them out. What do you think?"

Felix bit back a snort. "Are you seriously fishing for compliments right now, Major?"

Rocky laughed. "Maybe assurances that I don't look like a dork."

As if. "You look okay."

"High praise, indeed," Rocky said, then smirked.

Their server came a few minutes later and took their orders. Rocky ordered a soup-and-sandwich combo with cookies for dessert, and Felix ordered a salad with seared sirloin steak and bleu cheese dressing. No dessert.

"I'm so grateful you don't plan on kissing me later," Rocky said once they were alone again. A hard shudder rolled through him.

The remark caught Felix off guard, and he nearly choked on his Coke. "Why did you say that?"

"Oh, was I mistaken?" Rocky asked. "If so, you'll need to brush your teeth thoroughly, floss, and gargle with mouthwash first."

There it was again, the feeling that Felix was dirty or unclean. He hadn't expected it from someone who'd come to mean so much to him. "What are you talking about? I have excellent hygiene."

"I know that, dumbass. I'm grossed out about the bleu cheese dressing. God, if one of those chunks landed in my mouth, I'd—"

Felix's bark of laughter cut him off. He was so relieved to hear it was an aversion to the food he'd ordered and not the idea of kissing Felix that had made Rocky ill. "You're safe from me, pal. You're not going to vomit, right? I can wave the server over and request ranch dressing instead."

Rocky shook his head. "I just won't watch you eat."

Felix tilted his head and leaned forward. "Is that something you're into? Will they satisfy your perversion at the club tonight?"

"You know," Rocky said, "I've never really thought about it. I reckon watching people eat certain foods might be considered erotic to some. Listen, if that kind of thing is in high demand, I'm sure Gentleman Jack's offers it to their clients."

"I have to admit, I'm excited to see what the place is like."

"Don't embarrass me, Felix."

"I won't, Dad."

The food was delicious, and Felix enjoyed Rocky's company even more. Sparks had flown when mutual friends had introduced the two men, but they were the wrong kind for romance. They'd butted heads until they had found common ground that bound them: love for true crime and hatred for injustice. Rocky, Felix, and Jonah went from helping Locke and Key, Savannah's top detectives, solve a serial-rapist-and-killer case to forming an investigative podcast together. It was a huge leap— one which was paying off in dividends Felix couldn't have foretold.

After their server cleared their table and Rocky settled the bill, Felix said, "I thought we could test their security measures and check out their directory. You know they have one."

The lobby of Peachtree Plaza Tower Two was immense and luxurious. Black marble flooring with veins of rose gold running through it stretched for as far as the eye could see. Felix couldn't begin to guess how much they charged for leasing office space. There was a long, sleek black counter against one wall where seven smiling people assisted visitors. Each of them wore matching black vests, white shirts, and peach and black ties—bow or traditional. Across from the counter was a seating area that included a floor-to-ceiling water feature that was both soothing and pretty.

Felix watched as an older woman handed her ID to the man assisting her. He looked at something on the computer, then gave the ID to her and a keycard like the ones a hotel clerk provides at check-in. The woman nodded before walking to the bank of elevators, where three security guards waited to check keycards or employee badges, whichever applied. After security confirmed the person had a valid reason for getting on an elevator, they moved through a metal detector operated by three more security guards. Only then were they allowed to ascend higher into the tower.

"We're not getting on one of those elevators without an appointment," Rocky murmured from beside him.

"Nope," Felix agreed. "Let's find a directory."

There wasn't one in the lobby of Tower Two, and Felix realized the security team on the first floor would provide visitors with directions. Once someone arrived at the appropriate level, there would be signage and personnel to assist them. They wouldn't just let people wander around aimlessly on those floors once they got up there.

Felix and Rocky found what they were looking for in the shopping mezzanine. The directory was tucked discreetly into an alcove near the entrance where the bathrooms and drinking fountains were located. Felix started to doubt his suspicions when he spotted The Camelot Corporation listed among the other businesses. It would cost an absolute ridiculous sum of money to rent a fake office in a building like this. Wouldn't Peachtree Plaza require some sort of proof that a corporation was legit before renting space? Not if you knew the right people. Cameron Spencer would have endless connections to resourceful people.

Felix raked his eyes over the names of the other businesses. Nothing stood out as promising until his gaze landed on the name of a law firm. After a quick internet search, Felix learned that Moxley, Benton, and Hearst was a global law firm with offices all over the world. Based on his past research, successful money launderers utilized international lawyers to help them establish bank accounts in foreign countries where they could stash their ill-gotten gains.

"I have a plan B." Felix turned his cell phone screen so Rocky could see what he'd discovered.

"I like it."

"I haven't said what it is yet."

Rocky winked. "I still like it."

Once back at their hotel, Felix called the number on the website. He scheduled an appointment with one of their attorneys but couldn't get in for five weeks. The delay annoyed him but it didn't come as a surprise. While he chatted with the receptionist, Rocky tinkered with his eyeglasses before picking up his phone.

Felix disconnected the call and entered the appointment for the meeting into his phone. He'd just hit save when he heard his voice coming from Rocky's phone. It was a snippet of the conversation they had at lunch.

Rocky let out a whoop. "Those spyglasses worked well. Nifty little fuckers."

Felix moved to sit on the bed beside his friend. He looked at Rocky's phone and watched the video he'd captured.

"Let me see those," Felix said. Rocky handed the eyeglasses to him, and Felix studied them carefully. "I don't see the camera."

"It's no bigger than a pinprick," Rocky said, pointing to the tiniest circle in the bridge of the frames. "The power button is on the right arm and the volume is on the left."

"That's why you kept adjusting your glasses. I just thought they were a shitty fit." Felix watched more of the video on his phone. "The clarity is amazing. I wonder how it will do in a darkened room. Say a nightclub."

Rocky grinned sheepishly. "We'll find out tonight."

CHAPTER 10

"**A**re you sure we can't wear jeans?" Felix asked as he cinched his brown leather belt that matched his dress shoes.

"Not if you want to get inside the club."

Felix glanced over and saw Rocky fastening cufflinks at the wrists of his gray dress shirt.

"Why are you staring at me?" Rocky asked, a smile tugging at his lips.

"Cufflinks? Who are you, really?"

Felix had kept his voice light and teasing, but he was dead serious. He'd learned a lot about Rocky when he'd checked into the man's background when Royce and Sawyer had recruited Jonah, Rocky, and himself for the clandestine Humphries investigation. The lure of setting a trap to catch the serial rapist and killer was high, but Felix had wanted to be confident he could trust the people on the team. He'd found nothing in Rocky's background that raised a serious flag. He also hadn't discovered an explanation for why Rocky owned cufflinks.

His enigmatic friend laughed, then put on his black suit jacket before strolling over to where Felix stood gaping at him. He leaned in and said, "I'm Batman."

Felix laughed and shook his head. He knew it was Rocky's way of distracting him from pursuing his original line of questioning. For

Rocky, Felix would let it slide. The man was entitled to secrets. "Am I Boy Wonder?"

Rocky's answering smile was ornery and dazzling. "If you play your cards right. Anything goes at Gentleman Jack's."

Felix slid his navy blue jacket on over his crisp white shirt. "So those cufflinks..." The teasing glint dimmed a little in Rocky's eyes, and Felix wondered again what mysteries the blond man kept buried in his soul. "Do they serve dual purposes? Your eyeglasses take videos? What do those little onyx things do?"

"Black diamonds," Rocky corrected. "And they open doors."

Felix knew Rocky wasn't implying the diamonds would shoot lasers and burn through steel. The fact that he owned them meant Rocky had connections to get him, and now them, into places that were closed to most people. An elite club that catered to illicit appetites, for example. Suddenly, the collar of Felix's shirt felt too tight, even though it was open at the throat since a tie wasn't required. He was the misfit kid again who hadn't owned the right clothes, lived at a respectable address, or hob-nobbed with affluent people.

"Are you ready?" Rocky asked.

Felix shook off his inferiority complex and nodded. Rocky's percep-tiveness shouldn't have surprised him. He was a private investigator, after all. Felix was still stunned when Rocky cupped the back of his neck and pressed a kiss to Felix's forehead.

"You clean up nice, Fee."

Rocky had caught the tail end of a phone conversation between Felix and Reanna once. She'd called him Fee before disconnecting, and Rocky's evil grin warned Felix that he'd whip it out at an opportune time. Felix had expected Rocky to use it during one of their quarrels or during a moment when Rocky wanted to get even with Felix. This was the op-posite of those occasions, and the tenderness made Felix's insides feel like wiggly worms.

"Don't you start with me, Major," Felix said, moving to pull away. Rocky tightened his grip, then leaned his forehead against Felix's.

"You are enough. Always have been, and you always will be."

Felix opened his mouth to speak, to deflect the intimacy between them with a joke. Nothing came out. Felix registered the acceptance and understanding in Rocky's eyes and was grateful his big mouth couldn't ruin the moment with his usual word vomit. Instead, Felix patted Rocky's smooth cheek and stepped away.

"I miss the stubble," Felix said, finding his voice. "You're almost too pretty without it."

Rocky laughed. "Don't worry, it will start growing back before we reach the club."

"Maybe we should've booked two rooms instead of a single with two beds," Felix said when they stepped into the hallway. "You might meet someone tonight and—"

"No."

Felix wanted to know the story he sensed in his friend's terse response. Rocky was one of the most flirtatious men he'd ever met, but Felix had never seen him act on it. Felix knew for sure that Rocky had turned down a date with the sexy nephew of a club owner he'd met when they were investigating Earl Ison's murder for their podcast. Rocky had remarked about the guy's looks and how nice Drew seemed during the few times they'd chatted but claimed he wasn't interested in dating. Whenever someone pushed for more information, Rocky changed the subject.

"I can stop at the desk and get my own room if you want to bring someone back," Rocky offered.

"No," Felix said with equal fervor. Felix knew his reason hinged on the complex emotions he still felt for Jude Arrow. Was Rocky's excuse different or the same?

What kind of man would grab Rocky Jacobs's attention so hard he couldn't let go? Felix hoped to find out.

Gentleman Jack's swanky location and tight security matched what Felix had anticipated. He knew there wouldn't be throngs of eager young people lined up behind a velvet rope outside the place. Felix wasn't even surprised when he noticed the telltale bulge of a shoulder holster beneath the bouncer's jacket.

Rocky handed the behemoth man what looked like two blank credit cards. Felix and Rocky had shined their cell phone lights on the black plastic, tipping them in every direction to find a trace of writing or something that indicated why the cards would get them inside the club. Felix had expected some type of holograph, but they found nothing. Big and bald held the opaque plastic beneath a scanner, and they finally understood when the soft blue light illuminated the club's logo, which was a jack of spades playing card. Their names and photos also appeared on the passes, only his said Clark Kent instead of Felix Franklin, and Rocky's said Bruce Wayne.

"Enjoy your evening, Mr. Wayne and Mr. Kent," the bouncer said, handing them back their cards.

Rocky gave the bruiser a brief nod, so Felix did the same.

"Mr. Kent and Mr. Wayne?" Felix asked once they were out of earshot.

Rocky winked. "Told you I was Batman."

The interior of the club was where Felix's imagination had steered him wrong. He'd expected hard-thumping music and sex acts everywhere his eyes landed. Instead, the atmosphere was mellow and surprisingly elegant. Felix tried not to gawk as his gaze roamed around the room. The posh black motif was only broken by green ambient lighting. Behind the bar was an enormous glass mosaic featuring the jack of clubs. Nearly every table was full, and there weren't many vacant barstools.

A statuesque blonde holding a tablet approached them. She wore a short black skirt, a white dress shirt unbuttoned far enough to show a tantalizing amount of cleavage, and a million-dollar smile. "Good evening, gentlemen. My name is Mercedes. May I see your cards?"

She accepted Rocky's card first and inserted the black plastic into a reader built into the tablet. It brought up his fake name, photo, and a list of preferences. When and how had he provided them? When could Felix get a closer look at what made the private investigator tick?

Mercedes handed Rocky's back to him, then accepted Felix's. He briefly wondered if Rocky had given him weird preferences as a joke, but this woman would be trained not to react if he had. She smiled at Felix when she returned the black plastic to him.

"Since this is your first time visiting, I need to go over a few rules and have you sign some documents."

"Documents?" Felix asked. Like some kind of medical waiver? Was he ensuring them that his heart was healthy enough to witness the proclivities in the club?

"A simple non-disclosure form," Mercedes said. "Guaranteeing our members' privacy is of utmost importance."

"Yes, of course," Felix said.

Felix understood why the vibe in this part of the club was calmer. This was more like an anteroom. The wickedly good stuff happened deeper inside the building. Anticipation thrummed through Felix as he and Rocky followed Mercedes to a booth. She placed the tablet in front of them, and Rocky took advantage of the moment to slip his eyeglasses on.

Mercedes went through the club rules, which covered things like no touching without consent, no filming or taking photos, which were things Felix expected to hear.

"We have four sections in the club, and you'll need to scan your cards to enter each one," she said. "This, as you can see, is the jack of clubs. The next section is the jack of diamonds, followed by the jack of hearts and ending with the jack of spades."

She described the services they could expect in each. Felix noticed the place started off mild and got wilder with each progression.

"Now, I need to explain something important," Mercedes continued. "Your invitations are for observing only. We can't allow anyone to engage with the club staff until they've been fully vetted. While you will be given full menus at each location, you'll only be able to partake in the activities that won't bring you into full contact with a staff member. To ensure your compliance, the cards we issued to you will not open any of the doors to private rooms."

"Fair enough," Rocky said. Felix nodded.

Both men signed the disclosure. Felix was so flustered that he nearly signed his real name instead of the fake identity Rocky had given him.

"Enjoy your evening, gentlemen," Mercedes said silkily, slipping from the table and leaving Felix and Rocky to their own devices.

"Do you want a drink before we get started?" Rocky asked, gesturing to the small square kiosk on the table.

Felix shook his head. He preferred to keep a clear head. "Go ahead if you want one."

Rocky swiped his card in the reader to wake it up and scrolled through the menu until he found the one he wanted. "A Manhattan sounds perfect."

"That's a strong one."

"To match your will," Rocky said. The man who brought Rocky's drink to him was tall, broad-shouldered, and flirtatious. "Thanks, darlin'."

Felix wondered if the waitstaff was chosen based on the preferences members, or potential members in this case, had provided. Rocky seemed to have a tough time tearing his eyes off the server's ass when he walked away.

Rocky took a sip, then coughed a little. "They sure as hell don't water down their drinks." His voice sounded raspy as if the liquid had left a trail of fire in its wake. "Good stuff."

"Sounds like it," Felix said as he discreetly scanned the room. He watched as a leggy blonde led a man at least twice her age through a door in the back of the room with a glowing cobalt diamond on the wall above it. "How much do they charge for a drink around here?"

"This cost me twenty-five bucks."

"Wow."

Rocky leaned forward, eyes narrowed, and studied Felix's face. "Do you know your eyes are the color of the Manhattan I just drunk?" He scrunched up his face. "Or is it drank?"

"You drank the Manhattan, and now you're bordering on drunk," Felix said. He was utterly charmed by this side of Rocky.

"I am not drunk," Rocky said, shaking his head. "It's just that I rarely drank. Drunk. Drink. I rarely *drink*." Rocky slumped into his seat a little. Uh-oh. "I might be a little drunk."

"And here I thought this place overcharged their members. Getting smashed for twenty-five bucks is a bargain."

"Just leave me here so you can investigate."

"Shh," Felix said. "No way in hell I'm leaving you here by yourself. There's no telling what kind of trouble you'd find yourself in."

Rocky laughed harder than the remark deserved. "Probably end up married again."

"Married?" Felix asked. "Again?"

"What happens in Vegas doesn't always stay there." Rocky leaned forward, then crooked his finger for Felix to get even closer.

"Any closer and I'll be straddling your lap."

Rocky let out a snort slash hiccup slash giggle that might've been the cutest sound Felix had ever heard in his life. "When I first met you, I thought just maybe you could be the one to make me forget him." Rocky shook his head. "The son of a bitch got under my defenses, grabbed my heart with both hands, and stole a chunk of it." Who? His husband? "God, I'm so stupid." Rocky folded his arms on the table and lowered his forehead to rest on top of them.

Felix ran a hand through Rocky's silky blond strands. "You're human, Major. We all trust our hearts with people who don't deserve them."

Rocky raised his head so fast that it startled Felix. "Whoa. The room is spinning."

"I bet."

"That Jude is a son of a bitch," Rocky said.

"Yes, but we're talking about you now."

"I don't want to," Rocky said, laying his head back down on top of his arms.

Felix caught the eye of the server who'd brought Rocky's drink. He waved the handsome guy over.

"Is everything okay?" he asked, casting a concerned look at Rocky, who gave the server two thumbs up without raising his head.

"My friend isn't much of a drinker but still chose one of the strongest cocktails on the menu. Could he get a robust cup of coffee? Otherwise, our night is over before it begins."

The younger man smiled. "Of course, coming right up."

"Just leave me here," Rocky said, his voice muffled. "Sebastian will take good care of me."

"Who's Sebastian?"

The server chuckled. "I am."

It was funny how Felix hadn't caught his name. Rocky sure had though.

"There's no way I'm leaving you here. We're going to get you sobered up, then we'll tour the club."

"How about something to eat?" Sebastian asked. "Maybe a nice burger and fries? There's a reason people flock to McDonald's after closing down a bar."

Felix would have to take his word for it. They hadn't eaten dinner yet because they hadn't anticipated staying at Gentleman Jack's for long. They didn't really expect to catch Cameron Spencer engaging in sex acts, but you could judge a person by who they associate with, which was Felix's aim.

"Make it two burgers and two orders of fries," Felix told Sebastian.

"Can I get you something to drink? A soda, perhaps?"

Felix ordered a Sprite and thanked Sebastian. He briefly worried about how much this was costing Rocky but got over it when the meal arrived. The burger was made from quality beef. It was juicy and cooked to perfection, and the fries were extra crispy with just the right amount of salt. Rocky showed signs of improvement as soon as he started eating and drinking the strongly brewed coffee.

They laughed and talked about everything except the elephant in the room—Rocky's confession. While Felix was curious as hell, he wanted Rocky to tell him willingly, not because liquor had loosened his lips. It was even possible Rocky would forget he'd confessed to marrying someone who possibly broke his heart.

"I can't believe I got all poetic about the color of your eyes," Rocky said.

Felix looked up from dunking his fry in ketchup. Rocky's body language was tense and pensive. His gaze was locked on a spot on the table between them. "I don't know what you're talking about."

Rocky lifted his head and just stared at him for a few seconds.

"Poems rhyme," Felix said.

Rocky laughed. "Not all poems rhyme, Fee."

"The good ones do, Major."

They were back on solid footing again, and all was right in Felix's world. Until he glanced up and locked eyes with Jude Arrow.

What the fuck?

CHAPTER 11

Jude's dark blue eyes looked as black as midnight in the dimly lit space. Jude's mouth hung slightly agape as if his jaw hinges had broken. Felix imagined he wore a similar look of surprise on his face, although Felix hoped he wasn't as obvious.

Just what the hell was The Straight Shooter doing in a sex club anyway? *Like you need to ask?*

"Oh no," Rocky groused. "I don't like that look."

Felix tore his gaze away from his nemesis and focused on his partner. Rocky's speech had resumed its regular cadence and tone, and his eyes glittered with their usual intelligence and mischief. Felix wouldn't hand Rocky the keys to the Lincoln anytime soon, but he was confident his friend was back to firing on most cylinders.

"What look?" he asked innocently.

Felix glanced back at Jude, who'd recovered from his shock and was heading in their direction. Felix's body tensed from head to toe, but he forced himself to melt back against the booth as if he had not a single care in the world other than getting laid. *It has been a really long time.*

"The one that says you've either spotted a ghost or a ghoulish human." Rocky leaned forward. "Who is it? Spencer?"

Felix shook his head.

"Some kind of monster who's about to kill us?"

Jude arrived at their table before Felix had a chance to respond. Rocky took his time raking his gaze upward until it landed on Jude's face. Rocky smirked, then dismissed Jude with a negligent shrug.

"Yep. A ghoulish monster."

Jude ignored the barb. "What are you doing here, Felix?"

Felix quirked a brow. "I'm pretty sure a hard-nosed, investigative reporter like yourself should be able to figure it out."

Rocky tipped his head to the side. "I bet someone else does all the investigating, and pretty boy here just stands in front of the camera and takes all the credit."

Felix looked from Rocky to Jude, curious to see how the blow had landed. Rocky's intuition never failed to surprise Felix. He hadn't even told his partner about Jude's penchant for taking ideas and credit that hadn't belonged to him. Guess Rocky was familiar with the type.

Jude showed no reaction at all; he just kept staring at Felix. After a pregnant pause, Jude shifted his attention toward Rocky. "I don't believe we've met."

"We haven't," Rocky said flatly and made no attempt to rectify the situation.

Jude extended his hand toward the PI anyway. "I'm Jude Arrow."

Rocky ignored the civil gesture and clasped his hands over his heart instead. The PI batted his eyelashes like a true Southern belle.

Dial it down a notch, Scarlett.

"*The* Straight Shooter?" Rocky asked breathlessly.

Jude retracted his hand and turned back to Felix. "What are you doing here, Felix?"

"I've come to fuck my cares away," Felix lied. He wasn't opposed to engaging in sex as a distraction, but not if he had to pay for it. That hit too close to home for him.

Jude's face was granite—hard and cold. He hooked a thumb in Rocky's direction. "With this guy?"

"Hey," Rocky said. "I detect a heavy note of derision. I'm a fantastic lay, I'll have you know."

Okay, so maybe Major wasn't fully back to his usual self. This version

86

was feisty as hell, and Felix liked it a lot. Felix casually crossed his arms over his chest so he wouldn't reach for Jude or thrash Rocky.

Jude practically vibrated with anger. Or was a completely different emotion riding him hard?

Riding him hard.

Felix wasn't sure what mortified him most: Jude thinking Felix had to pay for sex or the semi-erection triggered by Felix's errant thoughts. He made a living from writing words, so he knew how powerfully they could paint images. Couldn't he pick phrases that wouldn't elicit visions of hot, sweaty sex?

"Can we go somewhere and talk privately?" Jude asked. "Please."

"No," Rocky and Felix said at the same time.

Jude snapped his head in Rocky's direction. "I wasn't talking to you, friend."

Rocky slid from the booth and slowly stood up. Felix wasn't sure if the pace was due to the alcohol still in his system or because Rocky wanted Jude to know just how little he was concerned about him. Jude pivoted to fully face Rocky.

"I'm not your friend," Rocky said, a menacing growl creeping into his voice.

"Does that make you my enemy, then?" Jude asked, sounding as cool as a cucumber.

Jude took a step toward the PI, who balled both hands into fists. Felix knew he needed to act fast before this escalated further, and all three of them were thrown out on their asses. He slid from the booth and placed himself between the two men, squaring off against Jude with Rocky at his back.

"I'll give you five minutes and not a second longer," Felix said.

Rocky chuckled. "Bet he only needs two and a half at best."

"I'll show you—"

Felix placed both his palms flat against Jude's chest, halting both his physical surge and whatever words he'd been about to say. Jude's big body crashed into his, and Felix nearly whimpered out loud when he felt how hard Jude was...everywhere. Jude's nostrils flared as he placed his hands on Felix's hips as if he had the right. Jude doubled down by flexing his fingers, gripping Felix tighter. He knew it was his overactive imagination at play, but he felt branded.

"Time is wasting," he said to Jude. Then he turned to Rocky, pulling free from Jude's embrace. "There's no need for you to wait here for me. I'll find you when we're finished."

Rocky searched Felix's eyes, looking for any sign he should stay. Felix winked as if to say "I got this" when they both knew he didn't. Felix could tell Rocky wanted to say so many things, but he gave him an abrupt nod before turning and heading in the direction of the door with the blue diamond above it.

"Is he your boyfriend?" Jude asked from behind him. His voice was closer in Felix's ear than he was comfortable with.

Felix slowly pivoted, allowing him time to think up a satisfying response. There were so many options. He could lie and say yes, he could string Jude along and make him work for the answer, or he could tell him the truth. Each had merit, but he decided to take door number two.

"Is that really any of your business, Jude?"

Jude opened his mouth to respond, but Felix tapped his watch.

"You're almost down to four minutes."

Jude's lips tilted at the right corner, and a hint of a dimple played peekaboo with Felix's heart. Damn, he'd loved those adorable divots that appeared whenever Jude smiled. There hadn't been much for his nemesis to grin about during their past half dozen encounters. This wasn't a full-blown smile, but Felix still felt it in his loins.

"What?" Felix asked.

Jude's eyes glittered and dark pink circles bloomed on his cheeks. "Your friend's guesstimate was probably too generous."

Since when? Luckily, Felix hadn't voiced his thought out loud. "That's nothing to boast about."

Jude took a deep, shaky breath and returned his hands to Felix's hips, trapping Felix's hands between their chests. Jude leaned forward and put his lips against Felix's ear. "I was referring to how long I'd last inside you the first time. We both know I'd make you come hard for me before we ever arrived at penetration."

Jude's hot breath tickled his flesh, and the urge to melt into Jude's embrace nearly overpowered Felix's common sense. Only his grip on Jude's lapels kept him upright and rigid, but his grasp on his self-control was tenuous at best.

"By the time I flooded your ass with my spunk, you'd be fully erect and ready for round two. Do you remember what would happen next?"

Of course, he did. Jude would offer up his ass for Felix.

Jude bit down on Felix's earlobe and dragged his teeth over the flesh until it popped free. "You're the only one I've ever given myself to like that." Felix had known the truth back then but was stunned to hear Jude hadn't bottomed since. The confession was nearly the straw that broke his restraint.

Felix relaxed his grip and released Jude's lapels. He took a step back, attempting to break the embrace, but Jude only tightened his fingers.

"Any harder and you'll leave marks," Felix warned in a teasing tone that contradicted the emotions riding him hard. *There's that damn phrase again.*

Jude rubbed his nose along the sensitive flesh beneath Felix's ear. "Good."

Felix shivered and Jude chuckled.

"Less than four minutes," Felix said.

Jude released Felix's hips and headed for the same door Rocky had exited through. Felix waited a heartbeat before turning and following Jude. The corridor on the other side of the door was illuminated by cobalt blue diamond sconces on the wall and tape lighting in the same hue running along the edges of the floor. The club music piped through the hidden speakers was heavy on the bass. Excitement crackled and popped along his spine as Felix's heart tried to match the tempo. They'd only made it a few feet before Jude stopped suddenly and shoved Felix against the wall.

"Why are you really here?" Jude asked.

Felix raised his chin and stared defiantly into Jude's eyes. "The same reason you are."

"Yeah?" Jude asked, pushing his knee between Felix's legs until Jude's thick thigh rested just under Felix's taut balls. "You're looking to fuck?"

"Someone who isn't you," Felix countered.

Jude dropped his gaze to Felix's throat. Could he see Felix's pulse pounding beneath his skin, or could he hear Felix's heart trying to beat its way out of his chest? Jude met Felix's eyes once more, smiling broadly so the dimples were on full display. *Tricky bastard.* Jude leaned forward, and Felix thought he was going to kiss him. He stopped just shy and whispered, "Liar." Jude's breath ghosted over his lips, and it was as hot as the accusation.

Felix was lying, but he was only willing to admit it to himself. "Three minutes."

Jude pouted playfully. "I don't think my five minutes should start before I get you someplace private where we can talk."

Felix shook his head. "That wasn't the deal we struck."

Jude pressed tighter against Felix's body, feeling every inch of him. "You're a *hard* man."

Felix refused to take the bait. Yeah, Jude could feel the way Felix's body had reacted to his bold moves and his dirty talk. So what. Felix still had a firm grip on his heart, and that's what mattered the most.

Jude heaved a sigh, then shoved off the wall. "Come on."

There was another door at the far end of the corridor. Jude opened it, and they stepped inside the jack of diamonds area. The layout and look were similar to the first section, but everything was elevated here, starting with the presence of a dance floor where several people danced seductively to the music. The servers wore fewer clothes, and the people in the booths weren't eating food as he and Rocky had in the jack of clubs area. Felix caught glimpses of lap dances and make-out sessions. So far, everyone had remained fully clothed in this area of the club.

And there was no sign of Rocky anywhere.

"This way," Jude said before Felix had a chance to really scope out the place. Felix was torn between curiosity to see the club and hearing whatever bullshit line Jude would deliver.

A server who looked more like a dark-haired Adonis smiled at Jude as he approached. Jude stopped and chatted briefly with the man, and Felix wondered how intimately Jude knew him. Jealousy burned through Felix, followed by anger for allowing himself to care.

Jude Arrow was nothing to him. He never really was. It had all been an illusion built on a bedrock of deception. Felix caught up to Jude in a few steps. "Two minutes."

Jude peeled his gaze off the sexy server and smirked at Felix. Maybe his tone had given away his baser reaction to seeing Jude flirt with the other man. "I'll catch you later, Alejandro."

"I'm looking forward to it," the man replied silkily.

Jude led him to a door with a glowing red heart above it. The corridor to the jack of hearts was the same setup as the one leading to the diamonds, only with red illumination and music with a slower, sexier tempo. Felix's cock throbbed to the beat until he thought he might come in his pants. Wouldn't that be humiliating?

He thought he was prepared for the sights and sounds in the jack of hearts, based on their chat with Mercedes, but he was wrong. Half-naked bodies were everywhere, and they weren't playing Monopoly. Still no Rocky.

"We're not in Kansas anymore, Toto."

Jude chuckled, then grabbed Felix's hand. He didn't have to drag Felix away like an unruly child; Felix went voluntarily. He'd never considered himself a prude, but there was no denying that he felt extremely uncomfortable. Felix could tell Jude was guiding him to the door with a platinum spade above it. Once in the corridor, Felix tugged on his hand to stop him.

"Is your membership to the club the reason the news station ran you out of Atlanta?" Felix asked. It was a low blow, but he needed to feel like they were on even footing again. Jude being here and demonstrating his familiarity with the club had knocked Felix off-kilter.

Jude repeated his macho move from the first corridor. He pinned Felix to the wall with his body. "No one ran me out of Atlanta." There was a ghost of something in Jude's expression that told Felix he wasn't being truthful. Who was he lying to? Felix or himself? "I told you why I came to Savannah. You just don't want to believe it."

"You only have a minute left," Felix said. "Do you really want to waste it by trying to convince me that you came to Savannah for me?"

Jude inhaled deeply, his nostrils flaring. "No," he said seconds before dropping his mouth to Felix's.

Felix moaned—first in surprise, then in ecstasy at the familiarity of Jude's warmth. Jude licked Felix's bottom lip before biting down on it. Because it felt as natural as breathing, Felix parted his lips invitingly. Jude slid his tongue inside, rasping it against Felix's and fanning the desire even more. Felix tangled his hands in Jude's hair, intending on yanking his head back, but instead, held him in place. Felix rose on his tiptoes seeking a deeper connection, sucking on Jude's tongue until he elicited a deep moan from the bigger man.

Jude slid his hands down from Felix's hips to cup his ass, grinding their hard-ons together. Oh, fuck. He really was going to come in his pants from dry humping in a sex club. *Christ.* The thought should've been like a bucket of ice water to his libido. Instead, it was as if the devil was riding shotgun on his shoulder, jabbing his pitchfork into his psyche and twisting it.

"Just this once won't hurt anyone," the devil whispered in Felix's ear.

Liar. He knew it was wrong, but he still lowered a hand between their bodies to yank Jude's dress shirt free. Felix pushed his hand beneath the fabric and ghosted his palm over the rigid, washboard abs. Lust and desire crackled and thickened the air around them. Felix kept his hand moving upward until he coasted over one deliciously defined pec. He scraped a fingernail over Jude's hardened nipple, triggering a deep groan from the bigger man. Felix was fast approaching the point of no return but felt powerless to stop himself.

"No, Felix," his conscience hissed.

Felix ignored it, sliding his knuckles back down Jude's torso. He'd just reached Jude's belt when he heard it again.

"No, Felix."

Jude groaned and ripped his mouth away from Felix's, then snapped his head to the left. Felix followed Jude's line of vision to see what put the scowl on his handsome face.

Rocky was barreling toward them as if the hounds of hell were snapping at his heels. His friend plowed into Jude hard enough to make him stagger backward a few steps. Seizing the momentum, Rocky gripped Felix's bicep and propelled him down the corridor toward the jack of hearts section.

Felix knew something bigger had occurred than Rocky catching him sucking face with Jude. "What's wrong?"

"Besides me catching you about to give The Straight Arrow a hand job in the hallway?"

"I was not." Felix had actually planned to drop to his knees and suck Jude off. Rocky didn't need to know that.

"Hey," Jude hollered from behind them. "Who the hell do you think you are?"

Rocky stopped abruptly and released Felix so fast that he stumbled. He just righted himself in time to see Rocky punch Jude square in the mouth. Jude's head snapped back, then his hand flew up to cover his mouth.

"Major," Felix said.

Rocky ignored Felix and pointed a finger at Jude. "Stay the fuck away from Felix."

Jude lowered his hand, revealing a tiny cut at the right corner of his bottom lip. "Or what?" he asked.

Felix wanted to know the same thing.

"You don't want to find out, Arrow. I promise you," Rocky said, then took Felix's arm once more and guided him back through the club.

They didn't utter a single word until they reached the Lincoln.

"I found it," Rocky said triumphantly from the passenger seat.

Felix's brain cells still weren't firing on all cylinders. Hell, most were still back in the hallway with Jude. Whew. Rocky had saved him from making a huge mistake. "It?" Felix asked.

"Proof that Cameron Spencer is a no-good son of a bitch."

CHAPTER 12

A different kind of thrill spread through Felix's veins like lava, shoving all thoughts of Jude aside. Well, almost all. Felix let himself briefly imagine the fiery liquid pulling Jude under its current. He pivoted his body toward Rocky. "Show me."

Rocky shook his head. "We gotta get out of here. He's coming."

A loud thud sounded against Felix's window, making him jump. Rocky only looked annoyed, so Felix had a good idea who stood outside the SUV. He twisted his torso and confirmed Jude was staring at him through the window. His nemesis looked angry, roughed up, and so fucking hot. Felix turned back around to Rocky. "Ignore him. I'll run over his foot."

"He wasn't the one I was talking about," Rocky said. "Spencer wasn't too far behind me, and I didn't want him to exit the club and recognize the vehicle."

Jude pounded against the glass. *Thud. Thud. Thud.*

"Goddamn it," Felix said as he shoved open the door hard enough to propel Jude backward a few steps. Too bad he hadn't knocked the nuisance on his delectable ass. Felix stepped onto the asphalt but left his door open for a quick escape. "Not now, Jude," Felix said.

"When?" Jude asked.

"Felix, we really need to go," Rocky said from inside the SUV. "You and this piece of shit can have a conversation when we don't have somewhere to be."

"Where are you going?" Jude asked.

Felix closed the distance until he was practically in Jude's face. "None of your fucking business."

Jude stood tall, proud, and as immovable as a statue. "I want it to be my business."

Felix searched for the words that would make Jude's insides quake hard enough to crack his cool façade. He needed his nemesis to rage and burn from the inside out like Felix was.

"Damn it," Rocky said. "Too late. Both of you idiots get in the vehicle right now."

Felix turned to get back behind the wheel, but Jude shut the driver's door, then gripped Felix's bicep and shoved him toward the back seat. Felix was momentarily too stunned to resist until he felt Jude sliding into the rear of the SUV with him.

"I don't think so," Felix said, trying to pivot so he could shove Jude out of the vehicle.

"Get down," Rocky said.

Felix could hear his friend sliding down in the front passenger seat as Jude eased the door shut before tackling Felix to the floorboard. Felix lay on his right side, and Jude covered him, pinning Felix tightly against the carpet. The back seat looked like it had a lot of legroom until you tried to cram two grown men between the rows of seats. Jude's bulk made it hard for Felix to breathe, or maybe it was the hard-on pressing against Felix's outer thigh.

"What's happening?" Felix whispered.

Jude replied by grinding his dick against Felix.

"I wasn't talking to you," Felix whisper shouted.

"Shh," Rocky replied.

Jude's weight momentarily eased when he lifted up enough to peek over the dashboard. A dry chuckle rumbled low in Jude's chest when he lowered himself back down on top of Felix. He pressed his mouth to Felix's ear and whispered, "Now I know why you're here." Felix didn't take the bait. "Walk away before you get hurt, Felix."

Felix's body stiffened at the tenderness and concern he heard in Jude's voice. He wiggled his arm free enough to elbow Jude in the side. The big man made an *oomph* sound but didn't budge.

"There's a reason I didn't pursue Molly Gregg's allegations, Felix."

"You're lazy," Felix hissed.

"Both of you shut up right now. The men stopped directly in front of the vehicle," Rocky said. "I'm going to lower the window an inch to see if I can hear what they're saying."

Felix heard the soft whir of the power window motor followed by distant male voices, but he couldn't make out what the men were saying.

Jude's body tensed, but he didn't argue with Rocky. He slid his hand under Felix's chin, turning his face enough for Jude to press his mouth against Felix's. He felt Jude wince for a second and remembered the cut from Rocky's fist. Rather than pull back, Jude angled his head and teased the seam of Felix's lips with the tip of his tongue. And, like an idiot, Felix parted his lips and met Jude halfway. It was awkward at best, and Felix would probably feel the crick in his neck for days, but he couldn't care less at the moment. The only thing that mattered was Jude's lips and tongue and the reverent way Jude kissed him.

No one could make Felix feel seen and wanted the way Jude could. He'd tried replicating their connection over the years, but he only felt worse when each of his attempts had failed. So, he'd stopped trying and just focused on physical pleasure. It had been enough.

Until tonight.

The yearning Felix had denied for so long came roaring to the surface. Right then, he would've sacrificed anything or anyone to continue kissing Jude. With both his arms pinned, Felix couldn't reach for Jude. He couldn't caress the man's face or fist his hair or relearn every inch of Jude's skin. Felix couldn't stifle his whimper of frustration and need. Jude recognized his acquiescence. He slid his hand from Felix's chin to cradle the back of his head and cupped Felix's cheek with the other one.

The rasp of Jude's tongue against his drove Felix's need higher and higher until he thought he'd combust. Jude thrust his hips forward, rubbing his erection against Felix's thigh. Fuck. They had too many clothes on, and Felix needed to touch bare skin right now or—

"Okay. The coast is clear," Rocky said.

Jude broke the kiss and sat up suddenly. He looked around the vehicle like he'd forgotten where they were. Felix certainly had until Rocky shattered the moment. This was the second time his friend had saved his ass from making a big mistake. Jude hoisted himself up and flopped on to the bench seat, melting against the buttery leather. Felix unfolded himself and dragged his body up to sit next to Jude but was careful to keep space between them. He was dangerously tempted to straddle Jude's thick thighs and pick up where they left off.

Peering outside the windshield, Felix confirmed no one else was outside before facing Jude. "Get out."

A cocky grin spread slowly across Jude's face. "That wasn't what you were saying a second ago."

"I didn't say anything a second ago," Felix countered, even though he knew what Jude meant.

Jude leaned toward him but abruptly stopped when Felix raised his hands and pressed his palms against the solid wall of Jude's chest. "Body language says a lot."

"Yeah, that's what most sex offenders say too," Rocky said snidely from the front seat. "Get the hell out of here, Arrow, before I drag you out of this SUV and fuck up your pretty face some more."

Jude never tore his gaze away from Felix's, nor did his expression register the insult Rocky had landed. "Felix, you can search high and low for the connections you're dying to make between Cameron Spencer and a criminal element. You won't find them. If you do, you'll end up dead. Walk away."

"But you know, don't you?" He'd heard the real fear in Jude's voice. Fear for who? Felix?

"I know some things, and now your friend has a good idea too. He's going to share it with you as soon as I get out of the vehicle. You're going to get excited because you'll think you know the truth, but you won't. No one knows the full story." Jude tipped his head to the side. "No one living, I should say."

"Bullshit," Felix bit out. "What's really going on? Are you investigating Spencer? Is that it? You told Molly Gregg you wouldn't pursue it but did anyway. Now you're pushing me away because I've gotten too close to the truth. I've always been a better investigator than you."

"Yes, you have."

Jude's agreement momentarily staunched Felix's tirade, but he recovered quickly. "Oh, so now you're trying to distract me with flattery."

"No. You stated a fact, and I merely agreed. You are a better investigator and always have been. Your quest to learn the truth consumes you, and you won't relent until you uncover every last detail. It's admirable in a reporter and sets you apart from all others. But, Felix, this time…" Jude shook his head. "I'm begging you to let this go. Walk away while you still can."

The tremor in Jude's voice triggered alarm bells in Felix's brain, but why? Was it because Jude sounded genuinely worried about him, or was it just Felix's bullshit detector going off? He couldn't decide, at least not right then. Felix needed peace and quiet to center himself and regain his equilibrium.

Jude nodded. "I see that you don't believe me. With our history, I even understand why."

"How big of you," Rocky chided.

Jude tore his gaze from Felix's to look at Rocky. "Stay out of this," he snarled.

Rocky turned in his seat, meeting Jude's stare. Felix had never seen his friend look so menacing. "I will not."

Jude didn't back down. "When Felix's blood is on your hands, how will that make you feel? Are you prepared to live with that, because I'm not?"

Rocky flinched but didn't cave. "I got his back, Arrow."

"Your best won't be good enough to save him." Jude turned back to Felix. "You'll try to make the connections on your own, but you'll run into a brick wall. Come find me when you do."

Felix snorted. "First, you warned me away, and now you're offering to help me?"

Jude reached up and cupped Felix's face. The tender gesture caught Felix off guard, and he didn't flinch away fast enough. Jude's touch seared his skin. "If I can't save you, I might as well join you."

Jude pressed his lips against Felix's once more but didn't linger. He released Felix, got out of the car, and disappeared into the night, taking another chunk of Felix's heart with him.

Felix remained sitting in the back seat for several moments before climbing out of the car and sliding behind the wheel. "I want to see the footage."

Rocky was silent for so long that Felix turned his head to make sure he was still awake. His friend worked his bottom lip between his teeth as he stared pensively through the windshield.

"Did you hear me, Major?"

"I heard you," he replied without looking at Felix.

"Why aren't you complying?" Felix knew why. Jude's warning had gotten to Rocky. Felix snagged the glasses off Rocky's face and pushed the button on the arm to stop recording. "Give me your phone."

Rocky heaved a heavy sigh. "I think the putz might be right." Rocky knew who Cameron Spencer was talking to, and he might've even overheard what the men had discussed in the parking lot.

"He's not," Felix said with a surprisingly firm voice. "Give me your phone, or I'll come over there and get it."

"I don't want your blood on my hands. I want you healthy and safe." Rocky turned his head and looked at Felix with soulful blue eyes. "Meeting you and Jonah has been…" Rocky briefly closed his eyes. "You guys don't realize it, but your friendship saved me." The words hung heavy between them, expanding until they almost sucked all the air from the vehicle.

"From boredom?" Felix probed.

Rocky reached over and patted Felix's cheek. "You saved my life. I'm not going to lose either one of you. So as much as I hate agreeing with Arrow, I think we need to back away. Spencer is honoring his obligation to replace your transmission. Maybe it should be enough."

Enough. The word was the root of Felix's problem, the reason he never let up. Nothing ever felt like it was enough—not his accomplishments, not his possessions, and certainly not himself.

"Okay." For Rocky, he would try.

Rocky narrowed his eyes and studied his face. Felix figured Rocky was looking for signs that he was lying. Felix had meant what he'd said, or at least he had at the time. He even held on to his conviction during the drive back to the hotel.

"I'm too wired to sleep," Felix said when they got back to their room. "I'm going to swim laps in the hotel's pool to see if I can work off some excess energy. Care to join me?"

Rocky threw his suit jacket onto a club chair, then sat down on the foot of his bed to remove his shoes. "Nah. I'm beat. You go ahead."

Felix changed into his swim trunks and a T-shirt before sliding his feet into a pair of flip-flops.

"Don't go to him," Rocky said just as Felix reached for the door handle. "He's a sexy motherfucker, so I understand the attraction. You deserve better, Fee."

Felix chuckled at Rocky's use of the nickname. "I have no intention of going to Jude, Major. I'm simply going for a swim."

"Okay."

Felix left their room and headed down to the indoor pool, hoping he would find it relatively quiet since most guests would be enjoying the one outdoors. He was relieved when he opened the door and discovered he was the only person there. Felix tugged his T-shirt over his head, then dropped both it and the towel on a chaise. He jumped into the pool and discovered the water was cold enough to be refreshing without shocking his nervous system.

The pool wasn't quite fifty meters long, so he counted strokes until he reached the other side. He did a turn beneath the water, kicked off the wall, and started back toward the other side. He focused on his form and technique, and it didn't take long before the tension in his body eased. Cutting through the water always silenced the chaos inside his brain.

The irony wasn't lost on Felix that his favorite form of managing stress and anxiety was something he'd learned from Jude. Prior to college, Felix had been terrified of swimming pools. Kelly didn't have the extra cash for Felix to go to the public pool, so he and a few other kids from the trailer park snuck over the fence after the pool closed one night. Felix had jumped right into the deep end, which wasn't much different than how he behaved today. He'd nearly drowned back then, and he was suffocating on his feelings now.

Jude had been a competitive swimmer before college, and he'd patiently taught Felix how to swim in the university's pool. At first, Felix's attention to form and function came from a place of fear, but then he realized the concentration stymied his anxiety. Soon after, Felix noticed the changes in his body—physically and psychologically. After their breakup, the activity that had brought him so much joy became a method of survival.

But tonight, swimming wasn't giving him the much-needed reprieve from his internal battle. Felix replayed the words he'd exchanged with Jude and relived each touch and every kiss. Had Jude really been worried about the trouble he'd find if he pursued the investigation into Spencer's connection with—

Who?

No matter how fast or how far he swam, Felix couldn't get the question out of his head. What secret was Cameron Spencer willing to kill to protect? For the last fifty meters, he tried to convince himself that Jude and Rocky were right. Spencer was honoring his contractual obligations, and Felix didn't really want to die. He could let it go.

Except he couldn't. Not because the story called to him, or maybe not just because of it, but because a truth so deadly needed to be exposed.

No one knows the full story. No one living, I should say.

Jude's words taunted Felix, challenged him. Rocky's eyeglasses would've captured a chunk of the story. Whatever he saw was enough to convince Rocky to side with Jude. Felix just needed a few minutes alone with Rocky's phone, and he'd know what he was dealing with and could decide on how to proceed.

Felix continued swimming and debating until his body was too tired to keep up with his brain. When he rose from the pool, he saw Rocky lounging in the chaise he'd thrown his towel over.

"I thought you were tired," Felix said as he roughed the towel over his head to wick away the excess water.

"I'm even more tired after watching you swim all those laps."

"Why'd you come down here? Did you think I was going to sneak away to meet Jude?"

Rocky chuckled, then moved over to make room for Felix. He patted the chaise, and Felix dropped down beside him. "No. Not tonight anyway," Rocky teased. "I figured you'd try to break into my phone to watch the video from the club if I fell asleep. I thought I'd save you the hassle."

"I thought you said I should let it go," Felix said.

Rocky leaned his head against Felix's damp shoulder. "I did, but I know you won't. You'll try, but there's no way you can resist the lure. It's who you are."

"An inquisitive asshole?"

"An honorable man who can't stand injustice," Rocky said. "Big and Sexy Jude Arrow only succeeded in waving the red flag in front of the bull with his dire warning."

Felix laughed. "You're right."

"I'm also hoping you'll change your mind once you see the video." Rocky pulled his phone out of his pocket, turned the volume down low, and hit play. He fast-forwarded the recording until he reached the part he wanted Felix to see.

There was a black half-moon shaped sofa with three men sitting on it. The blond man on the far right was Cameron Spencer. The dark-haired man on the far left was someone Felix had never seen. The white-haired man in the middle receiving a blow job from a curvy, naked redhead was none other than Jack Mercy, the alleged crime boss of the Southern mafia.

"Did you know Mercy was a member of the club?" Felix asked.

"Mercy is Gentleman Jack."

"Christ," Felix said. Why hadn't that occurred to him? *Because Jude Fucking Arrow has thrown you off your game.*

Rocky snorted. "Pretty sure that's what Mercy is saying too."

Felix didn't care about Mercy's reactions or thoughts; he only had eyes for Spencer. The Auto King wasn't touching the leggy blonde woman sitting on the arm of the sofa beside him, nor was he watching the tableau. Spencer stared down at the tumbler in his hand, a slight frown marring his brow. What was he thinking about?

Felix turned his attention to the man he hadn't recognized. He was dressed as elegantly as Spencer and Mercy, but something set him apart. Maybe it was the naked hunger in his eyes as he watched the woman blow Mercy. Or perhaps it was the rough edges that no amount of fine fabric could soften. Whatever the reason, Felix hated him on sight. The intensity only grew when the man fisted the redheaded woman's hair and shoved her head farther down Mercy's shaft. Rough Guy laughed as Mercy's head lolled back against the sofa, and Spencer abruptly stood up.

He handed his drink to the leggy blonde and started walking toward Rocky. He'd only made it a few steps when Mercy called out. Spencer stopped but didn't turn around. Mercy cupped the woman's chin and lifted her head. He dropped a brief kiss on her mouth before whispering something in her ear. The woman nodded before scooting over a few feet and reaching for Rough Guy's belt.

Mercy tucked his spent dick away, then rose to his feet. Rough Guy started to move the woman aside to follow, but Mercy held up a hand and gestured to the redhead at his feet. Rough Guy relaxed back against the sofa and smiled down at the redhead. Mercy caught up to Spencer, and the two men started walking toward Rocky together. That's when he spun around and started retreating through the club.

Felix knew what Rocky's video captured next, but he let it play on. On the screen, Rocky entered the corridor outside the jack of spades area. The sight of Felix and Jude kissing so passionately stole his breath. He let the recording play until the moment Rocky punched Jude in the mouth.

"I think I might love you a little," Felix teased.

"You love me a lot," Rocky countered. "Just not the same kind of love you feel for that doofus."

"I'm not in love with Jude."

Rocky's laughter vibrated the chaise and echoed throughout the pool area.

A smile tugged at Felix's lips, but he fought it off. "I'm serious."

"About as serious as your hand was when reaching for his belt," Rocky countered.

Felix waved a dismissive hand. "That was lust, not love."

"Don't even get me started on the make-out session you two had in the back seat of the Lincoln."

"I was keeping him busy so he didn't blow our cover," Felix said defiantly.

Rocky laughed harder for several moments. Then he took a deep breath before turning solemn eyes on Felix. "Well, it worked. I picked up enough bits and pieces of Spencer's conversation with Mercy in the parking lot to know something is going down at the dealership on Monday night."

"Which dealership?" Felix asked. "Spencer owns several. They don't call him The Auto King for nothing, you know."

"Mercy mentioned port authority agents, so I'm figuring it's the one in Savannah."

Felix better understood Jude's dire warning. Jack Mercy, ironically named since he reportedly showed no leniency to his enemies, had evaded the FBI for decades. The federal arm of the law had gotten close to busting him a few times, but their key informants as well as the evidence against Mercy always vanished into thin air. No bodies were ever found, but it was a safe bet to say the witnesses were dead.

No one knows the full story. No one living, I should say.

A shiver of excitement snaked through Felix's body. He knew he should back off and let it go, but it just wasn't his nature. "You know what this means?"

Rocky smiled wickedly. "We're going on a stakeout."

CHAPTER 13

Sleep was as elusive for Felix as Jack Mercy was for the FBI. Swimming laps in the pool had exhausted his body, but Felix's brain was too amped up to give him peace. If he were at home, he would've started reading every article he could find on Jack and Cameron Spencer, then looked for similarities and connections. Rocky deserved to sleep, so Felix lay in the darkness and thought about his next steps. Occasionally, his brain would veer back to the club, and he'd recall the way Jude had pressed him against the wall and kissed him as if his life had depended on it.

Felix wouldn't allow himself to linger there long because it would stir a different kind of problem he didn't want to address when sharing a hotel room with Rocky. Yes, he could sneak off to the shower and rub one out, but it was unlikely he'd do it without waking his friend. It was bad enough Rocky witnessed him behaving like a weak fool at the club.

"I'm ready to give up pretending to sleep if you are," Rocky whispered in the dark.

Felix sat up and switched on the lamp on his nightstand. "Deal."

The two men powered up their laptops and divided tasks. Rocky chose Cameron Spencer, and Felix took Jack Mercy.

"Let's start with potential family connections," Rocky said. They'd each written down as much information as they could find about parents, siblings, spouses, aunts, uncles, cousins, and children.

"Jack Mercy doesn't have any children," Felix said after they'd crossed off all other avenues.

"Not legitimate ones at least," Rocky countered. "Okay, so the link between Spencer and Mercy isn't familial. What about education? Jack Mercy is old enough to be Spencer's father, but maybe they met at an alumni event."

It didn't take them long to rule that out too. Jack Mercy was born with a silver spoon in his mouth and attended the finest private schools and universities. Cameron Spencer barely graduated high school after getting bounced from foster home to foster home. He'd enrolled in vocational high school his final two years and trained to be an auto mechanic. Spencer turned wrenches for years until a salesman's position came open at the dealership that employed him. Selling cars eventually led him to much bigger and better things—none of which they could trace back to Jack Mercy.

"I'll call Jude on Monday," Felix said sometime around dawn when it became apparent the answers they sought wouldn't be found by a simple internet search.

"The hell you will," Rocky said.

"Jude knows something vital."

Rocky chuckled. "Listen, if you want to scratch that itch, then do it. You don't need an excuse."

"I'm serious, Major."

"I am too, Fee. Maybe it's what you need to do. Fuck him out of your system, so you can concentrate. Your pheromones are clouding your judgment."

"How do you figure?" Felix's voice rose along with his irritation.

"Everything Jude knows is probably from what he's witnessed at the club. Do you really think he's smarter than the FBI? If he does know details they don't, then you need to consider it's insider information."

"Insider? As in Jude is part of the mafia?"

Rocky shrugged. "Jack Mercy has avoided incriminating himself because he has the right connections."

"A news anchor is the right connection? Come on, Major."

Rocky set his laptop on the nightstand before turning his body to face Felix. "Look me in the eye and promise me you can be objective when it concerns Jude Arrow."

Felix took a deep, steadying breath to calm down. Getting pissed at Rocky for stating the obvious was just an exercise in futility. "Okay, so you have a point. What do you suggest?"

"The two of us might not be able to find connections or similarities with basic searches, but our partner has a supercomputer who can find patterns in the most minute details."

"True, but as an officer of the law, he's obligated to act on anything he finds," Felix said. "What if his search alerts someone in the GBI who's on Mercy's payroll? I don't want to put Jonah's life at risk."

"That's up to Jonah to decide, not us. Remember, we're in this together. I say we chat with Jonah when we get back to Savannah tomorrow."

"You're right."

"I usually am," Rocky said, punching his pillow. "In the meantime, we better try to get some sleep. I want to be sharp when I meet Reanna."

"I'm starting to have second thoughts about introducing the two of you."

Rocky laughed as he lay down on his bed. "It will be epic."

Felix managed to catch a few hours of sleep, but it only made him feel worse.

"Take your cranky ass to the shower while I go find us something to eat," Rocky said. He was freshly showered, dressed, and looked way more alert than he should.

"How do you know I'm cranky? I haven't said anything yet."

"It's written all over your face, Fee. Just listen for once instead of arguing. Not everything has to be a battle."

"We could always order room service."

Rocky nodded. "We could, or I could walk down the block and get us better food and coffee at a fraction of the cost the hotel would charge." He blew Felix air kisses on his way to the hotel door.

Felix didn't rush through his shower. He wasn't paying the water bill, so he lingered and let the hot water stir his senses alive, including the ones he didn't have the time or energy to indulge. Felix felt almost human when he stepped out of the bathroom fully dressed sometime later.

Rocky sat on his bed, eating a croissant breakfast sandwich and drinking a cup of coffee. "I wasn't sure what you were in the mood for, so I got a variety to choose from."

Felix crossed the room and peeked inside the bags. Rocky hadn't been joking. He'd picked up a few different pastries, a yogurt parfait, fresh fruit, another croissant sandwich, and an order of golden hash browns. Felix's stomach growled and his mouth watered. "Who are the hash browns for?" he asked.

"You. I ate mine on the walk back to the hotel."

As much as he wanted to tear into the breakfast sandwich, Felix decided to take the safer route with the yogurt parfait, fresh fruit, and a blueberry muffin. The hash browns were his only exception, and Felix hoped he wouldn't regret it later.

Felix had managed to clear all the cobwebs from his brain by the time they reached Reanna and Stephen's new house in John's Creek. They'd recently sold their condo downtown and moved to suburbia. The change had surprised Felix until Ree mentioned she wanted to start a family. He had to admit, her new digs were gorgeous, and he could easily picture her and Stephen pushing a stroller down the sidewalks.

"Welcome to suburbia," Ree said when she opened the front door. She launched herself into Felix's arms, and he spun her around. "I've missed you so much."

Her warmth and love seeped into Felix, reaching him at a level most people couldn't. Felix pulled back just far enough to look at her. "I've missed you too. You look good, Ree." She looked better than good. Radiant.

Ree narrowed her eyes, and said, "You look good too. Maybe a little tired. Did you boys stay out too late last night?"

"Later than I should have, I guess," Felix said. "It takes so much longer to recover as you get older."

"Wait until you hit your forties," Stephen said. The corporate attorney was seven years older than his wife and Felix.

"Oh, hush," Ree said, patting her husband's chest.

"It's good to see you, Felix," Stephen said, hugging him. "It's been too long."

"It has," Felix agreed.

Stephen wrapped his arm around Reanna's shoulder and pulled her close to his side. Felix would never forget the day Ree called him and said she'd met the man of her dreams. She rambled on for at least forty minutes about his ginger hair, brilliant green eyes, and adorable freckles. Felix had pictured some older version of Opie from *The Andy Griffith Show*, but Stephen looked nothing like the awkward little boy.

"Guys, this is Rocky. Rocky, this is Reanna and Stephen."

Stephen shook Rocky's hand, but Ree skipped the formalities and went in with a hug.

Then she looped her arm through Felix's and led them inside the house. "He is as pretty as you promised," she said.

"I heard that," Stephen teased. He and Rocky were a few feet behind them.

"I wasn't trying to hide it," she fired back.

Ree showed them around the house while Stephen made them drinks. They met poolside when the tour was over.

"Does anyone want something stronger than tea or lemonade?" Ree asked.

It was much too early for Felix to consider alcohol, plus he was driving. "Lemonade sounds perfect. What about you?" Felix asked Rocky. "I bet Stephen knows how to make a mean Manhattan."

"You know it," Stephen said. "It's my granddaddy's favorite drink. Would you like one?"

"No, thank you," Rocky said. "Sweet tea is perfect."

"What's it like working on the podcast with Felix?" Reanna asked Rocky.

"At first, I wasn't sure how it would work out," Rocky admitted. "I thought Felix was a cutthroat attention whore who wouldn't play well with others."

"Ouch," Stephen said, rubbing a hand over his chest like he'd been the one insulted.

"And now?" Ree asked.

Rocky chuckled and said, "Now, I know only two of those things are true."

"Nice, Major. Thank you."

Rocky hooked an arm around Felix's neck and pulled him closer so he could kiss the top of Felix's head.

Reanna threw her head back and laughed.

"Which two?" Stephen asked.

"Felix stops at nothing to get to the truth, and he doesn't play well with others. But it's what makes him so amazing," Rocky said. "Turns out, he's not an attention whore."

They swam, drank twice their weight in non-alcoholic beverages, and lounged in the sun. It was the most relaxed Felix had felt in ages. He hadn't planned on drifting to sleep, but one minute he and Ree were telling Stephen and Rocky stories from college, and the next, Ree was waking Felix to tell him dinner was ready.

"Are you battling insomnia?" Ree asked, her dark eyes filled with worry.

"No," Felix replied honestly. "I'm just working on a story that kept me up late."

"I can't help but worry about you."

Felix pulled her into a hug. "I'm in a good place." And he was. Mostly. Then, as if fate wanted to mock his bravado, Felix's cell phone buzzed with an incoming text. It could've been Kelly reaching out to give him an update on Pulitzer. Perhaps it was Minerva letting him know that the biggest story of all time was about to break in Savannah, and she needed him to come back and cover it. It wasn't how his luck ran, so Felix wasn't at all surprised when he saw a text from an unknown number asking if he was still in Atlanta.

He didn't need to ask their identity, but he tapped out a quick response. *Who's this?*

The reply was immediate. *Like you've been able to stop thinking about our kiss. I want to see you.*

Felix stared down at his phone while trying to come up with an adequate response to surmise the emotions rioting throughout his body. How'd Jude get his number? He nearly snorted out loud. Jude didn't have to be an ace investigator to track it down, so Felix didn't waste energy on silly questions. Instead, Felix slid his phone back inside his pocket and smiled at Ree, who was observing him. "I smell charred meat. Let's eat."

Felix could see in Reanna's eyes that she wanted to probe deeper and ask questions, but she didn't. She knew Felix would talk when he was ready.

Dinner was a fantastic feast of grilled steak, shrimp, twice baked potatoes, and roasted asparagus.

"I think I need another nap," Felix said, leaning back in his chair and patting his stomach.

"I'd sink to the bottom if I jumped into the pool right now," Rocky teased. "That was the best meal I've had in a long time."

"I love to cook," Stephen said.

"Thank goodness," Ree said. "I didn't inherit my mama and grandmama's culinary talents." She leaned over and kissed Stephen on the cheek before stacking his plate on top of hers. "You cooked, so I'll clean up." Felix started to reach for the dishes in front of him, but Ree stopped him. "Guests are exempt."

"Not this one," Rocky said, picking up his and Felix's plates. "I'm helping, and that's final."

"Well, I guess it's okay, Pretty Boy," Ree said.

Stephen leaned back in his chair when it was just the two of them. "I'm glad we have a few minutes. There's something I want to discuss with you. Two things, actually."

"Okay."

"I golfed this morning with some friends, and your podcast came up in conversation."

"Are these lawyer friends?" Felix asked.

Stephen smirked. "Of course. We have to stick together because no one else will have us."

Felix laughed. "Do I want to know what was said?" While most people agreed with their podcast's view, the dissenting voices were thunderous. It'd been much easier to believe Bo Cahill killed in cold blood than to accept that their justice system is rife with systemic racism.

"They were impressed with both the investigation and the way you presented the facts. One of them is an extremely successful criminal lawyer, and he asked me to pass along an offer."

Felix sat straighter in his chair. "I'm listening."

"I'm sure you've heard of Jose Ramirez."

"Of course." Not only was he one of Georgia's top defense attorneys, but he'd also worked on many high-profile cases throughout the country. Ramirez rarely lost. If you were going to prosecute one of his clients, you had to bring your A-game.

Stephen nodded. "He thinks Bo Cahill is an excellent candidate for a posthumous pardon and would like to assist the family pro bono if they're interested."

"Oh, man. That's awesome," Felix said. He didn't need to ask why Ramirez would volunteer his time and effort. "Ride the Lightning" continued to gain worldwide attention, so it made sense Ramirez would want a piece of the spotlight. "A pardon is something the Cahill family wants to pursue."

Stephen nodded. "The process is pretty straightforward and begins with filling out an application. It wouldn't hurt to have a lawyer onboard to ensure things go smoothly and to apply pressure if needed."

"Wow. That's wonderful news."

Stephen pulled his phone from his pocket and started tapping away. Felix's phone buzzed a moment later. "I've just forwarded his contact information to you."

"This is incredible. I can't wait to tell the Cahills. Thank you so much."

Reanna and Rocky returned to the outdoor dining area to clear more plates. Ree stopped long enough to kiss Stephen, and Rocky rubbed his knuckles on the top of Felix's head.

Once they were alone again, Stephen said, "Ree told me about your generous offer to help pay for IVF."

"I meant it," Felix said. "There's nothing I won't do to see her dreams come true."

Stephen smiled. "I was hoping you'd say that."

"How much do you need? I can call the bank and—"

Stephen raised a hand to cut him off. "I'm not worried about the money. We've paid off most of our debts and we have a lot of equity in our house." He picked up his wineglass and took a big drink. Felix wasn't accustomed to seeing Stephen rattled. He was the epitome of calm, cool, and collected.

"What's wrong?" Felix asked.

"If I can't... If I'm the reason..." Stephen groaned and scrubbed a hand over his face. "Would you be willing to donate sperm if, for some reason, my swimmers won't cooperate?"

Felix's breath whooshed out of him as if Stephen had punched him in the gut. His stomach churned, and then his breathing accelerated. Felix's body burned hot all over, but the sweat covering his skin felt cold and clammy. He opened his mouth to speak, but no words came.

"Felix, are you okay?" Stephen asked. He stood up and moved to sit in Rocky's vacated seat.

Felix took a drink of lemonade. "Why me?"

"Why not you?" Stephen asked calmly.

"Fuck," Felix said, rubbing a hand over his tight chest and willing the anxiety away. "I don't even know who my father is. Hell, I'm not sure Kelly knows either."

Stephen cupped the back of Felix's neck. "I know who you are, and that's more than enough for me. I want Reanna to have everything her heart desires, so I have to set aside my foolish pride. Who better to help create this miracle than the person who loves her as much as I do?"

Now that the initial panic was ebbing, Felix could think more clearly. "We don't know what I could pass on to a child through my DNA."

Stephen smiled and held up a finger. "Intelligence." Two fingers. "Persistence." Three fingers. "Strong principles." Stephen smiled. "Do you need me to keep going?" Felix didn't respond, so Stephen held up a fourth finger. "Good looks."

Felix scoffed at the last one. There were better-looking guys out in the world. Felix heard Ree and Rocky laughing from inside the house. Rocky would make some pretty babies for sure, but Felix was the one Stephen wanted. For once, he was enough. "I'm humbled and honored, and…"

"Overwhelmed?" Stephen asked.

Laughing, Felix said, "Just a little."

"I don't need an answer right now. With any luck, I won't need you to pinch-hit at all."

"When will you know?"

"We go in for physicals and testing soon," Stephen said. "Then we'll discuss all the options available to us. I'm just so afraid of letting her down, Felix." The tenderness and fear in Stephen's voice made Felix's heart swell.

Stephen wasn't asking a tiny favor. Felix wouldn't be lending him a cup of sugar; he'd be helping to create a life. But this was Reanna, his safe place, and Stephen, a man Felix loved like a brother. Did he really need to think about it?

"Of course, I'll be the donor if that's what you want and need."

Relief washed over Stephen's handsome features, and his grip tightened on Felix's neck. "I could kiss you."

"But your wife might not like it," Ree said as she approached the table carrying a cake platter in one hand and wielding a cake knife with the other. Rocky held a stack of dessert plates.

"What'd we miss?" Rocky asked, looking curiously between Felix and Stephen.

"Stephen knows Jose Ramirez," Felix replied. "Mr. Ramirez is offering his legal services pro bono to assist us with the posthumous pardon application."

"That's amazing," Rocky said. "It explains why you'd want to kiss Stephen, but not why he'd want to smooch you up."

Felix grinned wickedly. "All the boys want to kiss me."

Rocky's blue eyes twinkled with mirth, and Felix knew he was thinking about the passionate exchange he'd witnessed the previous evening.

Ree walked over and kissed the top of Felix's head. "Some girls do too." Ree set the cake platter down in front of him.

Felix inhaled deeply. "Lemon chiffon cake."

"I would take credit for baking it, but Pretty Boy witnessed me removing it from the bakery box," Ree said.

"I'm good at keeping secrets," Rocky teased.

"As am I, Major," Felix said.

Felix had already revealed enough things he would have preferred to remain hidden, and he was pretty sure Rocky felt the same way.

"I sense one hell of a story," Ree said as she sliced through the cake. The piece she served Felix was big enough for three people, but he planned to eat every single bite. He might even follow it up by licking the fork and plate.

"One that's best told another day," Felix replied. *If ever.*

"Spoilsport," Ree teased. She didn't push, because it was likely she knew the source.

"What's next for the podcast?" Stephen asked as he returned to his seat so Rocky could sit down.

"Honey, you've known Felix for how long?" Ree inquired, handing her husband a dessert plate. "He never talks about what he's working on."

"That's right," Stephen said, forking a big bite full of cake. "He's superstitious."

"Some might call him paranoid," Rocky teased.

"He has good reasons for protecting his story and his sources," Ree said, coming to Felix's defense.

"I do," Felix said. The most significant justification was keeping his friends out of the mafia's crosshairs.

CHAPTER 14

Cameron Spencer had built his sprawling auto mall along a busy four-lane highway, ensuring thousands of people saw his shiny new vehicles each day on their way to and from work or school. Many travelers would see the cars as a symbol of success. If they just worked hard enough, they could attain one of the sleek beasts for themselves. They could go anywhere and do anything. Driving meant freedom, which was the life-blood pulsing through their veins. That made Cameron Spencer a bona fide hero. All he needed was a spandex costume, boots, and a fucking cape.

Felix nearly saluted the dealership from where he parked at Billy Rae's Carpet and Flooring Emporium. It was located on the road behind the dealership, which gave Felix an advantage point to observe Spencer's backlot, as well as some of the auto repair bays. Felix's white, late '90s cargo van fit in well with Billy Rae's service vans. He'd bought it from the newspaper for dirt cheap when they replaced some of the vehicles in their fleet. It had a shit ton of miles and smelled like ink and paper, but it enabled Felix to blend in almost everywhere. There were so many white delivery and service vans on the road that they escaped most people's notice, which was precisely what Felix counted on whenever he pulled it out of the barn behind his house.

"Daphne to murder van. Come in, Fred," Rocky said through Felix's earpiece.

Felix groaned. "Not the *Scooby-Doo* shit again."

Avery and Jonah had decided the podcast partners closely resembled the Mystery, Inc. gang. They dubbed him Fred since he was big on setting traps, Rocky was Daphne because his pretty face distracted people, Jonah declared himself as Shaggy, which left Avery, the smartest one, as Velma.

"For the record, you're not *that* pretty, Major," Felix said.

"Felix prefers to call it his shaggin' wagon instead of the Mystery Machine," Jonah corrected.

Of course, Jonah had wanted a piece of the action when Rocky and Felix filled them in on everything after returning from Atlanta. Jonah, through his supercomputer Marla the Magnificent, also provided essential pieces of the puzzle. Felix was confident it was the link between Mercy and Spencer that Jude had dangled over his head. The new knowledge had almost made it easier for Felix to ignore the texts and emails he received from his nemesis throughout the day. He could've replied no to Jude's suggestions, but it was so much more fun to make the man stew. Then again, when had anyone ever told Jude Arrow no? Felix was willing to bet it didn't happen often.

Felix would be lying if he didn't admit to the little thrills coursing through him when each of Jude's invitations got racier, going from an offer to meet for lunch, followed by a dinner date request, and finally Jude provided a detailed accounting of where he would like to stick his tongue for dessert. The last one had kept arousal buzzing through Felix all day long. He remembered the first time Jude had run his tongue down Felix's spine and hadn't stopped at the top of Felix's ass crack.

Wowzah.

Rocky's laughter snapped Felix out of his fantasizing. "When the van starts rocking, don't come knocking," the private investigator suggested.

"Fuck both of you," Felix groused.

"At the same time?" Rocky asked. "You think you got it in you, Freddie?"

"I object," Avery said, making everyone laugh.

"I'm not after your man, Velma," Felix said. "And I've never used this van to pick up guys."

Rocky snorted. "He rolls up to the clubs and lures the twinks into his van. Bet he's got carpeted walls and a waterbed in the back."

"Do they even still make those?" Felix asked.

"How the hell would I know?" Rocky replied.

"If you're going to accuse me of procuring one to seduce the twinks, then you must know if it's a feasible thing. Are you talking to us from your waterbed right now?"

"Hardy har har," Rocky said. "I'm at the Port of Savannah as we discussed."

"I bet there's a mini-fridge in the van for snacks," Avery added. The newcomer still wasn't sure how to take Rocky and Felix's dynamic. He frequently mistook it as real hostility instead of friendly banter and often steered the conversation to safer topics. It was endearing and sweet.

"Now that sounds like a damn fine idea," Felix said. "Stakeouts can be tedious and long."

"So tedious," Rocky agreed. "You have any movement at the dealership, Fred?"

Felix lifted his binoculars and scanned the entire rear of the compound. He saw the overflow of new cars that wouldn't fit on the front lot, as well as a selection of used vehicles, varying in age and conditions. Some were probably awaiting minor repairs or detailing before resale while others would be hauled off to the scrap yard or an auction.

When setting up their mission, the guys had discussed the limitless possibilities of how Spencer's dealership could be useful to Jack Mercy. Aside from the apparent transportation needs, trafficking was their number one guess. What was Mercy moving?

Drugs? Guns? People?

The last one made Felix physically ill every time the thought crept into his mind. A successful crime boss changed with the times to keep the money flowing and elude capture. It was possible Mercy dabbled in all of them.

"Everything is quiet here so far," Felix said. He glanced at the clock and saw it was almost nine. It would be a while longer before they'd need to switch to the night vision goggles. Rocky had provided them along with the swivel earpieces with built-in microphones they were using. "How about you guys?"

"My end of the port is still pretty busy," Rocky said. "Crews are still loading cargo onto the ships with cranes. What about you, Jonah?"

"Activity has died down a lot on my end," Jonah replied.

"Sounds like I got the best assignment," Avery said. They'd placed him at a truck stop midway between the dealership and the port. If Felix tailed someone, Avery would intersect them and take over to prevent Felix from getting spotted. "I've seen a couple of drug deals go down and witnessed a truck driver get trick-rolled by a sex worker. I took down license plate numbers for the police. I'll call it in to Crimestoppers once we're finished with our stakeout."

"Maybe we should switch places," Jonah said. "If you're parked there too long, people might start to get suspicious."

"I'm fine," Avery said. "I'm tucked out of the way."

"I think Jonah is right," Rocky said. "It's better to be safe than—"

"I got activity," Felix said, cutting him off. "A semitruck pulling one of those double-decker car hauler trailers has pulled up behind the dealership."

When they'd worked out the ways Spencer could be aiding and abetting the mafia, they had to decide which part of the dealership they'd stake out. Providing transportation to Mercy's muscle would most likely occur in the showroom with a handshake. Nothing to see here, folks. Just another happy customer. Trafficking would happen in the back.

Rocky had recalled that the auto mall had recently run one of those push-pull-drag promotions. The ones where the dealership promised to give you a couple thousand for all trade-ins, regardless of the car's condition. It explained why there were so many clunkers in the back lot. Felix figured they were destined for scrap metal, but maybe not. It could be smoke and mirrors for criminal activity.

"Here we go," Rocky said excitedly.

Felix trained his binoculars on the cab of the semi. After a few minutes, the driver's door opened, and a familiar-looking man got out. It was the tow truck driver who'd picked up his car. Skeeter? *Something like that.* Skeet!

Skeet walked around the front of the truck and stopped. Bracing his legs shoulder's width apart, the greasy man crossed his arms over his barrel chest. Tension and obstinacy radiated off the man's stiff posture. Due to the placement of the semi, Felix couldn't see who Skeet had squared off against. After a few moments, two figures emerged from in front of the cab.

"I'll be damned," Felix whispered.

"What?" Jonah, Rocky, and Avery asked at once.

"The truck driver is the same asshole who picked up my Fusion. And he's currently having a conversation with Veronica, who's Spencer's personal assistant, and the rough guy Rocky and I saw at the club with Mercy on Friday."

"Veronica's presence erases Spencer's deniability," Rocky said.

His video footage from the club would never be admissible in court. Even if it were, Rocky had ducked down in his seat to keep from getting spotted, and the audio capabilities of the glasses weren't as high-tech as the video. When setting up their stakeout, they had relied on what Rocky overheard, which was only enough to know that something was going down tonight.

"Not necessarily," Jonah cautioned. "It depends how long she's worked for him and her access to Spencer's schedule, computer, and several other variables. We still need to catch them doing something illegal."

Felix watched the trio through the binoculars. While Veronica and Skeet looked tense and hostile during their brief exchange, Mercy's goon seemed relaxed and at ease. Veronica must've landed a verbal blow because Skeet lunged toward her. Rough Guy darted between them, facing off against Skeet. The unflappable woman held her ground and smirked at the big, greasy ape trying to get past Rough Guy. She'd wanted to get under Skeet's skin and had succeeded. *Score one for the lady.*

"What's happening now?" Jonah asked.

"Rough Guy stepped between Veronica and Skeet. Now he's

pointing to clunkers in the parking lot. Looks like he's telling Skeet to load them up on the hauler."

"We'll know soon if our suspicions are correct," Rocky said.

"We'll know half of the facts," Felix countered. "We'll know cars from Spencer's lot are going on cargo ships. We won't know if they're trafficking anything illegal unless we get to look inside them."

"Don't take stupid risks, Felix," Jonah cautioned.

"Me?" Felix asked.

"Oh God," Jonah, Rocky, and Avery groaned at once.

It was dark by the time Skeet loaded up the vehicles and climbed inside his cab.

"Here we go," Felix said as Skeet drove off.

"Don't tail him too close," Jonah said.

"Yes, Dad," Felix said.

Adrenaline pumped through him until he was nearly twitchy from it. He knew Jonah was right. Traffic wasn't as heavy this time of night, and Skeet might get suspicious if a van pulled out of Billy Rae's parking lot hours after the business had closed. From his vantage point, Felix could see which direction Skeet took and gave the guy a decent lead before shifting his van in drive.

Felix caught sight of the semi as soon as he merged onto the highway. Confident of Skeet's destination, Felix kept a minimum of three cars between them. "We're coming at you, Velma," Felix said, backing off to put more distance between him and the semi.

"I'm in position," Avery replied.

Up ahead, Avery pulled out of the truck stop and eased into traffic a few car lengths behind Skeet. Felix checked his mirror to see if the left lane was empty, then merged over. He drove past Avery and the hauler so he could get into position at the port when Skeet drove in. Avery's only job was to make sure the hauler continued toward the port. If not, he'd continue tailing it until the rest of them could relieve him.

The port was a vast expanse of commerce stretching along the Savannah River, which was deep enough and wide enough to allow ships on both sides. Huge corporate conglomerates vied for space among the global shipping and logistics companies. With its close proximity to the Atlantic Ocean and access to major highways and railways, the Port of Savannah had become the fastest-growing container terminal in the US.

Felix would've felt overwhelmed by all the cargo ships, cranes, and heavy equipment if they hadn't spent hours researching and looking at aerial maps to formulate a plan. One of the other puzzle pieces Marla the Magnificent found was Jack Mercy's connection to a few companies who operated at the port. He wasn't listed as an owner or financial backer, but he sat on the board of these companies, which meant he'd potentially have access to the ships anchored along Berth Road.

Georgia Ports Authority operated several gated checkpoints and restricted access to some areas more stringently than others. Rocky had produced barcode stickers for their windshields to grant them access when he handed out the electronic surveillance gear.

"Where'd you get those?" Felix had asked.

"I called in some favors," Rocky had replied slyly. "People don't forget when you save them from paying out millions of dollars in a divorce settlement by proving their spouse broke clauses in their prenup."

"Ah," Felix had said.

As they'd discussed, Felix chose one of the "employee only" entrances that used an electronic scanner instead of one operated by a person who might ask questions or demand to see additional credentials. He pulled up to the stop sign and held his breath while a blue laser scanned the windshield sticker. The red light above the gate turned green, and the arm swung up, granting him entrance.

"I'm in," Felix said.

Rocky, Jonah, and now Felix were all at the port. His partners were at the opposite ends, and he'd hidden in the middle. Each of them had a good view of one of the potential companies Mercy could be using to move drugs or guns. Or people.

Please don't let it be people.

If their information was wrong or insufficient, they'd possibly lose Skeet and not know which ship he delivered the cars to. Their mission needed a little bit of luck to go with their skills and Rocky's connections.

"Got eyes on the hauler," Rocky said. "He's heading your way, Felix."

Nervous energy flowed through him, and Felix bounced his knees as he waited impatiently as the minutes ticked by. Skeet could've stopped anywhere along the immense expanse between Rocky and Felix. He contemplated getting out of the van and walking in Rocky's direction. With his dark gray coveralls, he'd fit right in with one of the other workers. No one would question his presence. Unless he was stupid enough to run into good ole Skeet, who would definitely recognize Felix. The voice of reason won out over impatience, and Felix stayed put.

"Do you see him yet?" Jonah asked.

"Not yet," Felix replied.

"Stay cool, everyone," Rocky cautioned.

Lady Luck must've been smiling down on them because Skeet eased past Felix a few moments later and stopped in front of the loading dock near him. "Got eyes on the hauler," Felix said, sinking lower in his seat.

The parts of the port buzzing with activity were well lit, but there were pockets of pitch black in the areas where crews had finished for the day. He'd backed into an opening in a darker spot, so it wasn't likely Skeet saw him behind the wheel.

"What's happening?" Jonah asked.

Felix watched through the NVGs as Skeet climbed out of the truck and strolled toward an office that wasn't much bigger than a shed. The sign above the door identified it as JWM Logistics, one of the companies they traced to Mercy. He relayed the information to the gang, and followed it up with, "Sure would love to know what's in those vehicles."

"No," the others said collectively.

"Felix, don't you dare," Rocky said.

"It's not safe," Jonah warned.

"I agree with the other two," Avery added.

Felix kept his gaze locked on Skeet and debated what to do next. Spencer shipping old clunkers on a cargo ship was odd, but was it criminal? There was only one way to find out. Skeet's entire demeanor shifted once he started talking to the lady inside the office. His stance was loose, and he used his hands to gesture when he spoke. Whatever he said must've been funny because the woman laughed heartily as she flipped her long brunette ponytail back over her shoulder. Skeet leaned forward and said something else. The lady looked at the clock for a second before nodding. A moment later, they both stepped out of the small office, and she locked the door behind them. Linking her arm through his, the two of them walked away from Felix before disappearing into the encroaching darkness.

"You guys, Skeet and a lady friend just took off on foot down the dock," Felix said. "Now's my chance to get a closer look." He'd love to take a look at the paperwork in the little shack, but it would be too risky.

"A guy named Skeet probably doesn't have much stamina," Rocky said. "You probably have two minutes tops."

"Not enough time," Jonah said.

"I have to try," Felix said as he eased his van door open and slipped out as quietly as he could.

"Be careful," Rocky groused.

Felix checked both directions to make sure no one was approaching on foot or by vehicle. The coast was clear, so he ran as stealthily as he could to the hauler. Felix could hear feminine giggles followed by a deep groan and knew Rocky had probably been generous with his lead time. Felix went around to the far end and climbed through the steel bars until he was on the bottom level of the hauler.

He checked the driver's side door of the car closest to him, which was a late '90s Pontiac Bonneville. The vehicle was unlocked, so he performed a quick search of the center console, looked under the seats, and rifled through the contents in the glovebox. He found nothing besides lip balm, a compact umbrella, a stack of napkins from fast-food restaurants, as well as several different condiment packets. The night vision goggles gave everything a greenish tint. Felix found no guns, smoking or otherwise, and no stash of drugs. He pulled the lever under the dashboard to pop the trunk.

The moaning echoing from the shadows got louder, and Felix knew he was running out of time. He shut the door just enough to make it latch, but soft enough that it wouldn't give his presence away. He eased around to the rear of the car and pushed the trunk open so he could get a closer look. It was empty.

His heart sank, but Felix refused to give in. He didn't expect Mercy to make his job easy. Felix pulled back the carpet in the trunk, intending to search the emergency tire well, but froze when he heard gravel crunching beneath someone's feet.

"Fuck! Someone's coming," he whispered.

"Get out of there," Jonah said.

"Oh, dear," Avery whimpered.

"You fucking dumbass," Rocky groused.

The footsteps were approaching from the front of the semi cab, which meant Felix hadn't been spotted yet. His choices were to hide or get caught. Since he had no idea who was coming toward him, Felix climbed inside the spacious trunk of the Bonneville. The car came equipped with one of those emergency handles a person could use in case they got locked inside. Felix pulled the lid closed but stopped just shy of latching it. Emergency handle or not, he couldn't stand the thought of being shut away inside the trunk. Maybe the release wouldn't work, and he'd be forced to give himself up unless he wanted to take a boat ride to only God knew where.

Felix's heartbeat thudded loudly in his ears as the footsteps got closer. Who was it? Port authority patrolling? A crew member returning from a dinner break? Whoever it was stopped suddenly, and Felix held his breath. The next noise sent fear spiking through him. Rubber soles squeaked and bounced against metal as someone climbed onto the hauler.

Felix wished like hell he'd thought to grab something he could use for protection. He could pull off his NVGs and swing them like a weapon. *Please let it be Major. Please let it be Jonah.* The lid opened suddenly, and Felix stared in shock at the last person on earth he wanted to see.

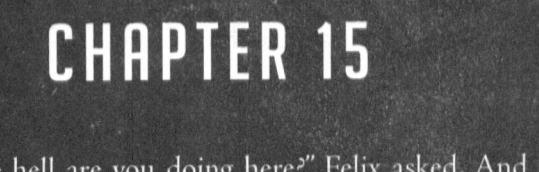

CHAPTER 15

"What the hell are you doing here?" Felix asked. And why the hell did Jude look hot even when the NVGs gave him eerie, glowing eyes and turned him a Hulk-ish shade of green?

"Who?" his friends asked but not at the same time. The question came out in a staccato burst from three different people. Who? Who? Who?

"We sound like a demented owl," Rocky said.

"Or a broken record," Jonah teased.

"Guys," Avery said, sounding frustrated. "Felix could be in trouble."

"Are you, Fee?" Rocky asked.

Felix ignored them all.

Jude scowled down at him, utterly oblivious to the conversation going on in Felix's ear. "I'm saving your stupid ass," he snarled.

"Saving me from who?" Felix asked Jude. "You're the reason I ducked inside the trunk in the first place."

"Trunk?" Rocky repeated.

"Who the fuck is Felix talking to?" Jonah asked.

"I bet I know," Rocky answered.

"Who?" Jonah and Avery asked at the same time.

Jude gripped Felix's bicep and hauled him to a sitting position. "We're getting out of here before you end up dead."

"Is that Arrow?" Rocky asked. "Answer me, Felix."

"Yeah," Felix said. "It's Arrow."

"Goddamn it," Rocky groused. "You okay?"

"I'm fine, Major," Felix said, wrenching his arm free from Jude's grasp and scrambling out of the trunk before closing it quietly.

"If not, I'll drive down there and punch him again," Rocky offered.

"You're too eager. You guys meet me at the rendezvous point," Felix said as he looked left and right to make sure the coast was still clear.

Felix took off the goggles and pulled the earpiece free as he jogged toward the safety of his van. Unfortunately, he could hear Jude right behind him. Felix yanked the driver's side door open and got into the vehicle. His nemesis climbed in on the passenger side.

"You should lock your doors," Jude said.

Felix scowled at him, but Jude didn't budge. "Get out."

"No."

Felix took a deep breath to calm his racing heart. He couldn't start his van and drive off because he didn't want the noise to draw Skeet's attention. Shouting at Jude would also give them away.

"What the hell are you even doing here?" Felix whispered angrily.

"I followed you. I knew you were up to no good when you ignored my texts and email messages. If you'd taken a few seconds to tell me to fuck off, I wouldn't have gotten suspicious."

The hair stood up on the back of Felix's neck. Could Rocky have been right about Jude's involvement with Spencer and Mercy? "You followed me?"

"Isn't that what I just said?" Jude asked. "You were so caught up in getting answers and didn't even notice I was tailing you once you left the newspaper. Felix, you can't afford to make these kinds of mistakes."

"The only error I've made tonight was not kicking you in the teeth when you started to get in the van. How'd you get through a security gate?"

Jude grimaced. "Thank you for sparing my teeth. My parents paid a lot of money to give me this pretty smile, which along with my journalism credentials, got me through the gate. I'd ask how you got back here, but I don't want to know. I'm already furious enough with you as it is."

He had some fucking nerve. Felix bristled as frustration morphed into rage. "Tell me what Mercy is trafficking in Spencer's clunkers or go home."

"Not going to happen."

"Which are you saying no to?" Felix pressed.

"Both. I'm not leaving until you do, and I never claimed to know intimate details about Mercy's operation, Ace. I only said I knew the connection between them."

"Don't call me that," Felix said vehemently.

It triggered intimate memories he wasn't prepared to face when tucked away in a dark van without someone there to stop him from doing something stupid. Jude had a predatory gleam in his eyes, which spelled big trouble.

"Why not?" Jude asked. "Does it remind you of happier times?"

Felix tried to form words that would shatter the smug look on Jude's face, but he couldn't. To deny Jude had once made him deliriously happy would just be a bald-faced lie. So, he changed the topic. "Maybe you didn't come right out and say you knew what Mercy and Spencer were up to, but you implied it."

Jude's lips twitched because he recognized Felix's patented deflection moves. "It's not my fault if you read more into my remarks and drew the wrong conclusions."

"Do you ever listen to the bullshit spewing out of your mouth? That's exactly what you wanted to happen. You think you're smarter than I am and didn't plan on me figuring out that Cameron Spencer's wife, Brigitte, is Jack Mercy's illegitimate daughter."

Not only was she Jack's daughter, she was his only child.

Technically, Marla the Magnificent connected the dots. Jonah had entered everything they knew about the key players, including their families—blood relatives and the connections gained through marriage. It only took her a few hours to scan the data and find the association. Brigitte Spencer's mother had been Jack Mercy's secretary. Lillian Sullivan was a redheaded eighteen-year-old beauty whose tenure with Mercy, a married man, abruptly ended about seven months before

Brigitte was born. Lillian married a man named Edgar Stevenson soon after leaving Mercy's employment, and he was the one listed as Brigitte's biological father on her birth certificate. Marla was a genius, and Felix would have given her full credit if he weren't too busy basking in Jude's wide-eyed, slack-mouthed stare.

"You were just trying to insert yourself into my investigation by claiming to have valuable information. Why? Do you want a chunk of the notoriety when Mercy gets taken down?"

Jude closed his mouth and narrowed his eyes. "You're a damn fool, Felix."

"Me? Why? Because I want to stop guys like Spencer and Mercy?"

Jude shook his head. "No. It's a commendable trait, even if it's delusional." His voice was sad and tinged with regret.

"Then, why?"

Jude reached over and cupped Felix's cheek. The move was so unexpected and tender that Felix flinched. Jude didn't retract his hand though; he doubled down by stroking Felix's flesh with his thumb. Felix wanted to moan and lean into his touch, but he couldn't—wouldn't.

"Why?" Felix prompted again.

Jude swallowed hard, and Felix could see the internal struggle raging in Jude's gaze before he closed his eyes. Jude took a deep breath, then reopened them. Felix only saw determination in his midnight irises. Whatever conflict Jude had wrestled was settled. The sexy tilt of Jude's lips promised trouble.

"It would've given me an excuse to be around you," Jude said.

The words knocked the wind from Felix's sails, and he nearly folded in on himself. It felt like Jude's caress was the only thing holding him upright. No matter how hard Felix tried to convince himself otherwise, Jude still had the power to knock him for a loop.

Felix wrapped his hand around Jude's wrist and forcibly removed Jude's hand from his face. "Are we back to this again?"

Jude looked down at his hand, then made a fist like he was holding on to something. "We never left it. If you'd give me five uninterrupted minutes to explain, I—"

"We tried that Friday night. You didn't use your time wisely."

Jude snorted. "I spent most of it hauling you through the club to find a private spot. Have lunch with me tomorrow."

"No."

"Dinner? I'll fix all your favorites."

Felix shook his head. "Hell no."

Jude chuckled. "What are you afraid of, Felix?"

Felix's bark of laughter was sharp enough to cut glass. "First, you try to bribe me and now you appeal to the part of me that can't resist a challenge."

"Did it work?" Jude asked.

"Other than to remind me what a manipulative bastard you are?" Felix asked. "No, it didn't."

Jude's nostrils flared, and his eyes glittered in the dark van. He wasn't mad; he was aroused. Felix wasn't the only one who loved a challenge. The air around them thickened, turning heavy and cloying. "That's too bad. How else will you know if I'm involved in sordid activities?"

Felix quirked a brow. "Are you?"

"You think I'm just going to confess my sins in your van because you ask?" Jude briefly glanced toward the cargo area before locking his hungry eyes on Felix once more. "You might be able to drag me back there and coerce some answers from me. We're kind of stuck here until the slimeball returns from exchanging pleasantries with the lady from the office."

Felix leaned forward until his lips were almost touching Jude's. "Unlike you, there are lines I won't cross to get a story." Felix started to retreat back to his seat, but Jude's hand snaked out and grabbed the back of his neck, holding him in place.

"We'll just see about that. My place tomorrow night. Six o'clock. I'll text you my address."

Jude released Felix and exited the van. Felix kept watching long after Jude disappeared into the night until metal clanking against concrete penetrated his foggy brain. Turning his head, Felix saw that Skeet had returned and lowered the ramp on the hauler.

He slid the NVGs back on and tucked the earpiece back in. "Hey, guys, I'm going to be pinned down for a bit."

"I bet," Rocky replied, making Jonah and Avery snicker.

"Smartass," Felix replied dryly. "Skeet is back and unloading vehicles. I can't leave without tipping him off, so I'll record the activity instead. Maybe the hull ID on the ship will give us some answers."

"Or you could just ask Jude tomorrow when you go to his house for dinner," Avery suggested.

Felix groaned. "You guys heard that?"

"You pulled the piece out of your ear but didn't power it down, so your microphone still picked up the conversation," Rocky replied. "You were holding your own. I'm proud of you."

"Christ," Felix groused. "I'm not going to Jude's house for dinner."

"Uh-huh," Jonah said.

"Sure, you're not," Rocky said.

"Don't do anything I wouldn't," Avery teased.

Felix removed the earpiece again but powered it off this time. "Smug smartasses think they know me. I'll show them. There's no way in hell I'm going to the bastard's house to talk or anything else."

Felix's phone buzzed with an incoming text a few minutes later. He expected one of his friends wanted to give him more shit, but it was from Jude providing his address.

I have a pool. Bring your swim trunks. Or not.

CHAPTER 16

At 5:45 the next evening, Felix's phone buzzed on the table beside his lounge chair. Then it sounded again and again, one right after the other. And without looking away from his laptop, Felix knew two things: it was a group text, and the senders weren't some random persons who'd included his phone number by accident. He could ignore the messages, but it would only encourage or mislead his smartass friends.

Felix set his laptop aside and picked up his phone. Sure enough. He had messages from Rocky, Jonah, and Avery.

Good luck on your date, Jonah said.

Hope you trimmed your pubes, Rocky added.

How do you know he has them? Avery asked.

Every adult has pubes. Some just choose to shave or wax them off, Rocky replied.

Yes, but your message implies you have firsthand knowledge of whether Felix waxes, trims, or shaves his pubes, Avery responded.

Stop saying pubes. It's a gross word, Jonah admonished them.

Felix laughed loud enough to scare the birds out of a nearby tree. He tapped out a single reply. *I'm not going to Jude's.* He'd told them twice already, but he could see how little they'd believed him. Then Felix added, *My pubes aren't up for discussion.*

Come on. Not you too, Jonah replied.

It's not too late to go to Jude's, Avery said.

It's fourteen years too late, Felix replied.

Rocky replied with a fist bump, and Avery sent a sad face emoji. He was such a cutie. It was no wonder he had Jonah wrapped around his pinky. Felix figured it wouldn't be long before Jonah took up real estate on Avery's ring finger too. He was happy for his friends and a little envious also.

They exchanged a few more jabs before each of them claimed to have something to do. Rocky had super-secret PI stuff to attend to, and Jonah and Avery got to do each other.

Yep. Envious. Not because he wanted Jonah or Avery for himself. That smarmy bastard Jude had Felix so worked up lately that even masturbating didn't ease the ache for long. He could've gone to The Cockpit or another club to find someone to ease his loneliness with, but it would only make him feel worse, not better. The need pulsing through his veins wouldn't be sated by physical release alone.

Felix hadn't connected with anyone the way he had with Jude Arrow. Part of it, he chalked up to chemistry and physical attraction, but most of it was due to emotional stimulation. Jude had been the first person to make Felix feel seen and valued, at least romantically. Jude had never looked at him with disdain; he'd expressed genuine curiosity about Felix—first as a person, then as a lover.

It had stirred a longing within Felix that became addictive. For the first time in his life, Felix had understood why his mother had sold her body to get her next high. Every day had revolved around getting a fix of Jude. Felix had known to limit his exposure to drugs and alcohol at college, but no one warned him about the impact love and lust had on a person.

But Jude had used the knowledge he'd gained to humiliate Felix in front of his peers.

Poof.

Just like that, the temptation to drive over to Jude's house downshifted from a throbbing, aching need to a low-level hum he could swat away like a pesky mosquito.

Felix picked up his laptop and hit play to continue watching the video he'd paused when the group messages started. Marla the Magnificent might have linked Brigitte Spencer's mother to Jack Mercy through employment records, but it alone wasn't enough. Felix needed to find other connections between Cameron Spencer and Jack Mercy he could exploit.

He'd uncovered two videos which looked promising. The first one was recorded ten years ago. An anchor from Atlanta interviewed Cameron and Brigitte Spencer for their morning show program. It was aired on Valentine's Day, so the featured couples had all discussed true love and finding their soul mates. Felix had started feeling nauseated a few minutes in, so he'd fast-forwarded to Cameron and Brigitte's interview. The anchor, Tanda Rinehart, had just introduced them when his friends had started their shenanigans.

"The two of you have an interesting story," Tanda said on screen. "Why don't you tell us about it."

Brigitte Spencer—petite, stunning, and poised—smiled at her husband and said, "Do you want to go first, or shall I?"

Cameron's expression was so sappy that Felix rolled his eyes. "I saw you at the sex club, pal," he said out loud to no one. Just because Spencer hadn't been participating in a particular sex act when Felix was there didn't mean he never partook. His membership was enough to cast doubt on his fidelity.

"You go ahead," Cameron told his wife. "You tell the story so much better than I do."

Brigitte giggled as she faced Tanda. "I was traveling home from college late one evening and experienced some car trouble. One of my tires blew, and I barely avoided having an accident. There I was, stranded along the side of the road in the dark all by myself. I was terrified. We didn't have cell phones back then, so my options were to flag down someone to help me or start walking."

"Which did you choose?" Tanda asked.

Brigitte smiled. "I decided to walk, but I hadn't made it far before my knight in shining armor came along."

"More like a grease monkey driving a rusted-out clunker." Cameron chuckled, and his cheeks turned pink. He'd already mastered the art of self-deprecation. "Here was this stunningly beautiful woman marching down the road with her head held high."

"I must've looked like a hot mess. My sweaty hair was plastered to my head, my clothes were rumpled, and one of my sandals broke before I got a mile down the road."

"You were still the most alluring woman I'd ever met. Still are," Cameron added.

"Damn, he's smooth," Felix said as Brigitte swatted at him playfully.

Cameron refocused on Tanda and said, "She wasn't in the best of moods, you see. I asked if that was her disabled car I just passed, and she replied with something sarcastic."

"Do you remember what she said?" Tanda asked.

Cameron smiled at his wife again. "Every word."

"Would you like to share?"

Cameron chuckled. "She stopped, turned to face me, and put both hands on her hips. She gave me a look that would've made most men wilt and said, 'Nope, I'm just bored and out looking for trouble.'"

"To which you replied?" Tanda prompted.

The Spencers looked deep into one another's eyes for several moments before Cameron answered. "I told her that trouble had arrived."

The couple spent the next few minutes talking about the rest of the events that evening and how it had unknowingly shaped their futures. Cameron had replaced Brigitte's tire with the emergency spare, then followed her to make sure she arrived home safely. The next day, Brigitte showed up at the small dealership where Cameron had worked as a mechanic.

"I baked him cookies to thank him for helping me and also to apologize for being so sarcastic and hateful."

"You were scared," Cameron said.

Brigitte leaned into him. "He was even more handsome than I remembered, so I was a little flustered."

"She stole my breath the previous night on the side of the road, but

I was fully prepared to offer my heart to her in the middle of the show-room floor. Only one thing stopped me."

"His silly pride," Brigitte said. "Cam didn't think he was good enough for me."

"I wasn't good enough for you. An educated young lady from a good home didn't belong with a man who could never quite get the grease out from beneath his fingernails no matter how hard he tried. I decided right then and there that I would be worthy of her someday."

"And I ensured I'd get a chance to knock him off his feet at least once more," Brigitte said.

"How?" Tandy asked.

"By making sure I put his cookies in my mama's favorite Tupperware container," Brigitte replied.

"And making sure I knew the proper etiquette would be to return it promptly," Cameron added.

"I looked for him every day for a month. I took extra time putting on my makeup and fixing my hair. I bet I tried on two or three outfits each morning until I found the right one," Brigitte said. "By the end of the month, I'd given up on him turning up with Mama's Tupperware in hand."

Cameron chuckled. "I was busy improving my situation so I could impress her folks. A sales position came open at the dealership, so I was turning wrenches during the day and selling cars in the evenings and on weekends. By the end of the month, I was selling enough cars to do it full time. I bought my first suit, a bouquet of flowers for Brigitte and her mother, and a bottle of whiskey for her father."

"Except my father didn't drink, and my mother was allergic to the flowers."

"And I returned the Tupperware with crumbs in it." Cameron shrugged. "I was off to a great start."

"Mama still teases him about the Tupperware to this day," Brigitte said.

The Spencers talked for a while about overcoming their differences and learning to compromise.

"Nothing was good enough for Cam," Brigitte said. "He was too hard on himself and kept pushing and pushing. Selling the most cars wasn't enough. He wanted to learn other parts about the business. Being promoted to sales manager didn't satisfy him. He wanted to go into business for himself."

"My desire to provide the life I thought she deserved meant I was never home to share it with her," Cameron said.

The more Felix watched them interact, the more he was convinced Spencer's devotion to his wife, at least then, was genuine. Brigitte was the most important person in his life.

The screen went black when the video ended a few minutes later, and Felix caught his scowling reflection on the computer screen. He hated that he could relate to Cameron's drive and ambition.

Felix closed the link and pulled up the second interview from a year ago. He'd put off watching it because the interviewer was Jude. Felix wished he could skip it altogether, but the subject matter was one he couldn't ignore. Felix hit play and was immediately assailed by emotions when Jude's handsome face appeared on the screen.

"Let's talk about your Second Chance Program," Jude said.

When the camera panned to Spencer, Felix realized he'd been holding his breath.

"Stupid. Stupid. Stupid," Felix mumbled.

He tamped down his attraction to Jude to focus on the conversation.

"The Second Chance Program is geared to help non-violent felons have a second start at life once they're released from prison. In addition to work opportunities, I make sure they have access to other resources, such as counseling. I can relate to these people more than they realize. I also had two strikes against me at birth, but I got lucky early on and found a mentor. I want to be that rock for others."

"That's commendable," Jude said. "Are there circumstances where people blow their second chances?"

"Of course," Spencer said. "You and I both know the cards are stacked against some people, and others will choose the path of least resistance, which is the life they know. Some of the enrollees do end up going back to jail, but the Second Chance Program has an eighty-five percent success rate. I'm extremely proud of that."

"As you should be," Jude said.

As the interview continued, Felix's irritation grew. Not once did Jude probe deep enough to find out how the parolees were chosen or what happened to them after they completed the twelve-month program. He just let Spencer spew the facts he wanted to share.

"Fucking lazy reporting," Felix grimaced.

He shut the laptop and set it aside. He stared out over the wooded expanse of his backyard and let his mind wander. Could there be a link between Mercy and the program? He felt like he was on the verge of connecting some significant dots when the sound of tires crunching on gravel caught his attention. It was too close for it to be someone pulling into his neighbor's driveway.

Gee, I wonder who it could be?

Felix wasn't lucky enough for his visitor to be a nice church lady who wanted to convert a sinner like him, nor would it be someone hoping to sell him steaks, a vacuum, or a set of encyclopedias.

Fuck me.

Felix got up and started walking toward the corner of the house when an ungodly shriek erupted from the front of the house.

"Holy fuck!" Jude yelled.

More earsplitting shrieking bounced off the trees.

"Get back," Jude said. "Don't you dare bite me. Felix! Get these demonic birds away from me."

Felix took his sweet time rounding the front corner of the house where his neighbor's peacocks had Jude pinned up against the garage.

CHAPTER 17

"I see you've met Pete and Pearl," Felix said casually.

Pete was a teal-colored male with stunningly beautiful plumage, which he showed off when he was horny or pissed. Felix wasn't sure which emotion Jude stirred within the feathered beast until Pete tried to chomp the man's crotch. Pearl was a white female who was more mild-mannered than her mate. She bumped Pete out of the way and took aim at Jude's crotch too while Pete shrieked his outrage. Okay, sometimes she was just as wild as Pete.

Jude held a large storage box in one arm and tried to cover his cock and balls with his free hand. "A little help here, please."

Felix stuck two fingers in his mouth and whistled like Tracey had shown him. Pete and Pearl turned their heads in his direction, then sauntered over. Felix petted the top of their heads while they cooed happily.

"You have attack peacocks?" Jude asked.

"I don't own them, so I can't be sure what kind of training they've had. Pete and Pearl live at the property next door, but for some reason, the birds seem to like me."

He'd never forget the first time Pete shrieked outside his window in the middle of the night. It had scared him so much that Felix had rolled out of bed and landed on the floor with a jarring thud. They'd had a rough introduction, but the birds grew on him.

"They don't seem to care for you, though." Felix looked away from the birds and met Jude's gaze. "What are you doing here?"

"We had dinner plans."

"No," Felix said, shaking his head. "You made plans and expected me to abide by them."

"The guy I used to know could never resist the offer of a pulled pork dinner and swimming."

"I'm not the guy you knew, Jude. I'm not sure what it's going to take for you to realize how much I've changed."

Jude heaved a heavy sigh and took a few steps away from the garage door. "I catch an occasional glimpse of the boy I adored before you tuck him away again. It's why I can't give up."

"Get him, Pete," Felix said, pointing at Jude. The male peacock looked between Felix and Jude before taking a few steps toward his uninvited guest.

Jude flattened himself against the garage door once more. "Fine. I'll leave the food and get out of here." Jude's voice was resigned, and defeat clung to him like a cloak. Felix had won.

Then why did he feel so hollow inside?

Would Felix spend the rest of his life wondering why Jude had betrayed him? Would he regret not letting the man say whatever it was he needed to get off his chest?

"Come, Pete and Pearl," Felix said, turning and retracing his steps to the backyard. "You can come too, Jude."

I'm a fucking fool.

Jude followed him around to the back patio. His property probably paled in comparison to Jude's, but he loved it. Felix didn't have a pool, but he had a gorgeous koi pond with a soothing water fountain. The brightly colored orange and white fish fascinated the peacocks, and although they were omnivores, they never tried to eat any of the koi. Pete helped himself to a tadpole every now and then, but he and Pearl preferred to eat bugs and small reptiles.

"You have a pretty home."

"Thanks. I'm really happy here." Felix opened the sliding patio door and gestured for Jude to enter ahead of him.

Jude set the box down on the farmhouse table Felix had fallen in love with at a flea market. He released a shaky breath, then locked eyes with Felix. "I never told a single soul about your mom."

"Okay, we're doing this now. I'll play along," Felix said, even though it was difficult with those delicious aromas wafting out of the cardboard box. He detected smoked meat and cheesy potatoes, and it was almost enough to derail his focus. "If not you, then who did?"

"Bobby Cooper," Jude said.

"Coop? Your roommate? He was hardly ever there." That's why they'd been able to fuck like rabbits pretty much anytime they'd wanted.

"Seldom isn't the same thing as never," Jude said. "He was in the dorm at one point that night because some of my things were moved the next morning. He loved playing stupid little mind-fuck games. He either purposely spied on us or overheard our conversation."

"Why would he blab about my personal business?" Felix asked, even though he knew the answer.

"To cause trouble for us," Jude replied. "Coop wanted me for himself."

"Oh, wow. Arrogant much?"

"He hit on me before we started dating, several times during, and again afterward. Coop wanted to break us up in such a horrible way that you wouldn't give me the time of day, let alone allow me to defend myself."

Jude sounded so sincere, and Felix had been aware of Coop's crush on Jude. Bile surged upward, but Felix swallowed it back down. He'd had his own suspicions about Jude's roommate. He'd shoved them aside every time they crept into his psyche. It was safer for Felix to believe Jude had betrayed him than to doubt himself.

Or maybe it was just easier.

Had he played so willingly into Coop's plan? Had it worked? Did Jude turn to his roommate after they'd broken up? Felix's mouth went as dry as the Sahara, and his throat burned like he'd chased a shot of moonshine with a flaming marshmallow. It hurt to breathe. Felix took a long drink of sweet tea, the ice-cold liquid momentarily extinguishing the hellish fire.

"Did you take Coop up on it?"

"Hell no. Even if I hadn't been hung up on you, I wouldn't have turned to Coop. I got a different roommate after my freshman year."

"No," Felix said, shaking his head. "It's too convenient."

"Are you saying that because you'd prefer I was the enemy, or do you actually believe I intentionally hurt you?" Jude moved around the table and took Felix's face in his hands. "I didn't betray your confidence, but I still failed you because I hadn't earned your trust. The man standing in front of me now would demand more evidence, but the boy I worshiped hadn't discovered his worth yet."

In such proximity, it was impossible to dodge the emotional grenade Jude lobbed at him. Felix could step back and break their physical link, but fourteen years apart hadn't severed their emotional bond. What would a few feet of separation do for him now?

Felix opened his mouth to respond, but the only thing passing through his lips was a ragged sigh. Jude must've taken it as a sign that he was getting through to Felix because he pushed on.

"I'm sorry I didn't fight harder back then. I never should've given you three years to shore up your defenses against me. If I could go back in time and do it all over again, I would. I'd give us back the years we lost. Felix, I..." Jude briefly closed his eyes and took a deep breath. When their gazes collided again, all Felix saw was the same kind of longing he felt deep down in his soul.

Fuck, I want to believe.

Jude hadn't been the only one to take the path of least resistance. Hurting and doubting was easier than trusting and trying. Felix's lonely heart urged him to have faith and lean toward Jude. That's all it would take on Felix's part—a mere inch of forward momentum, and Jude would do the rest.

"I let my broken heart and wounded pride steer the ship back in college," Jude said, his yearning resonating with every syllable. Jude gently pressed his lips to Felix's but didn't linger or attempt to deepen the kiss. "The man standing in front of you realizes he should've fought harder for you back then. I'm prepared to wage a fierce battle now."

Felix swallowed hard. Many people had taken him head-on, a few had battled beside Felix, but no one had fought *for* him.

"No one I know has better instincts than you do, Ace. Listen to them." Jude dropped his hand and took a step back. "I think my five minutes are up. Shall I stay or go?"

Everything Felix had wanted and denied himself was right there for the taking. Which instinct should he call upon at this moment: fight or fuck? He'd been fleeing from his feelings for this man for far too long.

Felix fisted Jude's dress shirt and dragged him the few feet separating them. He slammed his lips against Jude's sinfully beautiful mouth. Felix wasn't capable of the tenderness and finesse Jude had just exuded. Lust raced through his veins, heightening his awareness into a symphony of senses.

Jude's gasp of surprise turned into a moan of pleasure when Felix pushed his tongue between Jude's parted lips. Jude met his aggression head-on by closing his lips around the invader and sucking it deeper.

They reached for each other at the same time. Jude slipped his hand beneath Felix's T-shirt while Felix tore Jude's shirt open, sending buttons skittering across the hardwood floor.

Jude broke the kiss to glance at the damage. "This is my favorite shirt," he said, his voice thick with arousal. When their eyes met again, Felix saw the blown pupils and knew they were on the same page.

"I'll buy you two more just like it," Felix said, shoving the shirt off Jude's broad shoulders and down his arms. He reached shaking hands out to touch Jude's hard chest but was derailed when Jude yanked Felix's T-shirt up and off.

They crashed into each other, bare flesh to bare flesh. Felix melted into Jude's heat. Their hands and mouths started roaming, each of them knowing where to touch the other to draw out whimpers and moans. Jude scraped his fingernails over Felix's sensitive nipples before pinching and rolling them between his thumbs and index fingers. Felix trailed kisses and bites along Jude's neck while getting two handfuls of Jude's muscular ass.

Felix burned hotter with each suckle, kiss, nip, and touch. Much more of this and his organs might liquify, turning him into jelly at Jude's feet.

"Tell me you haven't been able to stop thinking about that kiss," Jude whispered.

"I haven't." Then Felix latched on to the spot on Jude's neck that made him insane. He sucked hard, knowing he was going to mark Jude. Felix relaxed his lips and pulled back, admiring the angry flesh. He ran his tongue over it to soothe, then continued licking a path upward until he reached Jude's earlobe. He bit down before pressing his lips to Jude's ear. "Nor could I stop thinking about what I wanted to happen next."

"What was that?"

Instead of answering, Felix dropped to his knees and reached for Jude's belt.

"Felix," Jude moaned, fisting Felix's hair.

Felix continued leaving love bites on Jude's abdomen while he released the belt and opened Jude's pants. He felt the arousal thrumming through Jude's body, and when he pressed his nose against Jude's briefs, Felix smelled it. He couldn't wait for a taste.

"Felix, wait," Jude said, pulling his head up to meet his gaze. "As much as I want to feel your mouth on me, I don't want you to regret it afterward. There's more we should talk about."

Felix nodded. "Okay, fine. You didn't steal my idea for your senior project. We'd all tossed out ideas during a round-robin session. I mentioned ethics in journalism as an option but ultimately didn't select it for my final project, which made it fair game. You took the idea and ran with it and deserved the praise Professor Alexander heaped on you."

Felix tugged Jude's pants and underwear down enough to expose the head of his dick. He inhaled deeply, breathing in the scent of Jude's arousal. He tore his gaze off Jude's mammoth dick to look up into his eyes. "You were getting too close again. I had to grasp on to anything that would give me an excuse to push you away."

Jude ran the back of his hand along Felix's cheek. "I didn't mean—"

Felix turned his head and nipped Jude's thumb hard enough to make him suck in a sharp breath. "Weren't you the one who told me to follow my instincts?" Jude nodded. "That's what I'm doing."

Felix leaned forward and swiped his tongue over the swollen head of

Jude's cock, capturing the pearl of precum gathered there. Fuck, he tasted even better than Felix remembered. It encouraged him to yank Jude's pants and underwear down to his knees and deep throat him until Felix choked.

"Fuck," Jude growled, gripping Felix's hair tighter. "I won't last."

Felix ignored the warning and bobbed his head up and down Jude's shaft, applying the perfect amount of pressure to make Jude's muscular, hairy thighs tremble beneath Felix's hands.

"My balls," Jude urged. He'd always been the dominant and bold one, bordering on bossy. Jude parted his legs as far as they'd go within the confines of the dress pants at his knees.

Felix released Jude's cock with a wet plop and sucked a taut orb into his mouth. Then paid equal attention to the other before licking Jude's taint.

"Get up here," Jude growled. "I always make you come first." He hooked his hands beneath Felix's armpits, but Felix sank his teeth into Jude's meaty thigh before Jude could drag him to his feet.

Jude released his grip and surrendered. Felix sprung his own cock from his jeans, then resumed sucking Jude's cock as if he might never get another chance. Felix stroked himself, his fist keeping pace with the rhythm his mouth set. Sensing Jude was a powder keg ready to explode, Felix reached between Jude's thighs with his free hand and massaged Jude's balls until the big man's entire body tensed. When the first spurt of cum landed on his tongue, Felix pulled back. The rest painted Felix's face and chest. He continued stroking Jude's throbbing dick until he'd milked the last drop.

Felix's orgasm was only a few strokes behind. He splattered his release onto the floor as pleasure blasted through his entire body like a starburst.

Jude stumbled back against the table as if his legs could no longer support him. He still had one hand fisted in Felix's hair. Jude used it to tilt Felix's head back. Cupping Felix's face with his free hand, Jude smeared his cum into Felix's skin. "Christ, you're sexy," Jude growled.

"And a little messy."

Jude helped Felix to his feet, then pulled him into his arms for a deep, hot kiss. Just as it had all those years ago, the first climax they shared hadn't sated the hunger. It had always been the appetizer in a sexual smorgasbord. The aftershocks of the orgasm hadn't even left Felix's body yet, but he still craved the next one.

A loud pecking came from the glass patio door, startling the men apart. A million and one thoughts floated through Felix's mind in the nanosecond it took for him to turn his head. It was a neighbor borrowing sugar. His lovable but annoying friends had shown up to prove him wrong about meeting Jude for dinner. Bigfoot had wandered out from the woods and was looking for beef jerky. Nope. It was two judgmental-as-fuck peacocks staring at them.

"Are you sure those aren't your birds?" Jude asked. "Pete looks like he wants to know what my intentions are."

Felix laughed. "I hope they're exceptionally dirty."

"Downright filthy."

The interruption, although hilarious, dispersed the sexual fog that had commandeered Felix's brain. An awkward silence fell over the room.

What have I just done?

Something in Felix's expression must've betrayed his thoughts because Jude pulled Felix back into his arms. He leaned forward until their foreheads touched. "Please don't overthink this," he urged. "I know there's a lot of baggage between us and many unanswered questions, but we can work through them."

Felix nodded. "Why don't we eat first."

"Good idea," Jude said. "I outdid myself tonight."

"Arrogant ass."

Jude chuckled. "You'll see for yourself."

They tucked themselves away and refastened their pants. Felix cleaned off his face, chest, and mess on the floor with his discarded T-shirt. He tossed the dirty garment into the laundry room on the other side of his kitchen, then retrieved plates and silverware. When he returned to the dining room, Jude was still bare chested but had unpacked the containers of pulled pork, scalloped potatoes, green beans, and cornbread from the cardboard box.

"Damn, that smells incredible," Felix said. Jude's gleaming chest was just as appetizing.

"Wait until you taste it."

The food was as delicious as Jude promised, but the conversation was stilted and clumsy at best.

"How do you like living in Savannah?" Felix asked.

"I wasn't sure if I'd like it. I'd always heard the city was a little weird. I think she's more eclectic than strange."

Felix nodded. "Do you like the slower pace in a smaller market, or do you miss the hustle and bustle of a big city?"

Jude set his fork down. "The Felix Franklin I know doesn't dance around a subject. Why don't you ask what you really want to know?"

"If you really moved back to Savannah for me, why did you stay away so long?"

"I drove by your house three times my first night in town. I couldn't work up the courage to pull into your driveway." Jude took a deep breath. "I expected you to show up at the news station and try to run me out of town, but you didn't."

"I sure as hell thought about it," Felix admitted. "Those fucking billboards infuriated me." He narrowed his eyes. "Is that why you started investigating Earl Ison's murder once I released the article? You hoped I would confront you about stealing my work?"

Jude nodded. "Every day I stayed away made it harder to explain why I hadn't sought you out. I've never considered myself a coward, but you're fucking scary, Ace."

"I only bite a little," Felix murmured.

"I knew I'd only have one shot to do it right, so I asked Jed to contact your editor for the Crime Prevention Month crossover. I'd heard about the other successful mergers and thought it made a perfect ice breaker."

"Except the Rotary Club president usurped you by inviting us both to address the club." Felix quirked a brow. "Or was that also your doing?"

Jude chuckled. "I was just as surprised as you were."

"I hate surprises, but I guess not all of them are bad," Felix admitted, although it pained him.

Jude's cell phone rang, and he checked the caller ID. "Speak of the devil," he said before answering it. "Hey, Jed. What's up?" Jude straightened in his chair as he listened to his station manager. "Yeah, I'll be there in about twenty minutes." He disconnected the call and set his phone down. "I have to go back to the news station. There was a train derailment at the port. Jed said there's a large fire and potential chemical spill. He has a reporter heading out to the scene, but he wants me on set to do the breaking news alerts."

They both rose at the same time. Jude retrieved his shirt from the floor and shrugged into it.

"You can't go back to the station wearing that. What will people think?"

"I have extra shirts in my office," Jude said.

"What about the people you encounter on the way to your office. You're just going to parade through the building half-naked?"

Jude put his hands on Felix's hips and drew him near. "Jealous?"

Felix refused to admit it. He stepped out of Jude's arms and headed toward his bedroom. "You can borrow one of my shirts," he called over his shoulder. "It might be a little small, but it will at least cover all the marks I left on your body."

"Bummer," Jude said.

Felix opened his T-shirt drawer and picked up the first one he saw. He returned it, then rifled through the folded shirts until he found the one he was looking for. It was old, faded from many years of use, and held a special meaning to both of them.

When he returned to the dining room, he caught Jude waggling his fingers at Pete. It looked more taunting than friendly.

"Your peacock is trying to call me out."

Felix looked over in time to catch Pete peck the glass door again. "I think you're right." Felix handed the shirt to Jude and waited with his heart in his throat while he unfolded it.

Jude's head snapped up after he recognized the faded crest from his private high school. "You kept it all these years?"

Felix nodded.

Jude ran his fingers over the thin, navy blue fabric. Jude's smirk spread into a full smile, showcasing those adorable dimples. "Looks like someone has worn and washed it about a hundred times since they stole it from me."

More like a thousand. "Don't make me regret this."

Jude's laughter was muffled as he pulled the shirt over his head. It was about three sizes too small and clung to every inch of his muscled torso and his biceps.

"I'm not sure that's any better," Felix said.

"It'll have to do for now. I'll return my shirt to you later," Jude said. He eyed the angry birds at the back door. "Mind if I go out the front door? I'm kind of partial to keeping my cock and balls."

Felix was a big fan of them too. He walked with Jude to the front door. They stopped on the front porch, and Jude pulled Felix to him for a long goodbye kiss.

Then Jude walked away, leaving Felix's lips tingling and his emotions reeling. He'd almost made it to his car when Pete and Pearl came shrieking around the side of the house.

"Get him, Pete," Felix yelled.

Jude sprinted to the safety of his car, then flipped Felix off before driving away.

Felix whistled, and the birds followed him to the back yard. He plopped down into the chaise, then stared at the trees surrounding his property until his eyes lost focus and the colorful landscape became an impressionist painting. Pete and Pearl made their way home at twilight as the fireflies lit up the woods surrounding his house like tiny fairies dancing on the wind.

A question played through his head like a broken record, but the hunt for answers had changed. He'd stopped asking *why* and started wondering *what if?*

CHAPTER 18

A few days later, someone lightly tapped on the frame of Felix's open door. When Felix didn't stop what he was doing, the person cleared their throat. Felix kept working.

"Excuse me, Felix. Can I have a minute?"

Felix had known who his visitor was without looking up from his computer screen. Shy knock, awkward throat noise, and a timid voice equaled Jimmy.

"What can I do for you, Jimmy?" Felix asked, but he didn't stop typing. If the rookie wasn't confident about interrupting him, then Felix had no qualms about giving the kid only part of his attention. When the pause stretched beyond awkward and became weird, Felix finally looked up.

Jimmy was as pale as a ghost and worrying his bottom lip between his teeth hard enough to draw blood.

"For fuck's sake," Felix groused. "Come in here and sit down before you pass out. I'm all out of smelling salts."

Jimmy's shoulders tensed, and his face turned a mottled pink as if his skin couldn't make up its mind about being angry. Felix was just happy to see a spark of life. "I'm not going to pass out like a damsel in distress."

"Convince me," Felix challenged, gesturing to the empty chair in front of his desk. "Show me that you want to be a reporter for *Savannah Morning News*. Scratch that, Jimmy. Show me you deserve to be here."

Jimmy swallowed hard, his Adam's apple bobbing almost cartoon-ishly. If this had been one of Felix's beloved childhood Saturday-morning shows, Jimmy's heart would be knocking against his rib cage.

"Spit it out, kid. I don't have all day. Wow me."

Jimmy laughed nervously. "My first article is due next week. Would you consider reading it and providing feedback?"

"Me?" Felix asked. People rarely caught him by surprise, but Jimmy just had. Felix had been nothing but caustic and rude to him. Why the hell would the younger man seek him out? "Why?"

"Because you'll be brutally honest, and it's the only way I will reach my full potential."

Felix nodded. "I won't hold anything back. Are you sure you're pre-pared for it?"

"No," Jimmy admitted. "But it's what I need."

Felix had never seen himself as the mentoring type. Correction: he'd never wanted to be a mentor. That hadn't changed, but Jimmy had piqued his curiosity. "Email it to me. Be sure to include the deadline for me to provide my feedback." With that, Felix turned his attention back to his computer without so much as a goodbye to the young reporter. He was such a dick sometimes.

At three o'clock, he powered down his computer and left for an im-portant appointment. He'd called Veronica the morning after watching Spencer's interviews and requested a meeting with The Auto King. She'd assumed Felix wanted to inquire about the status of his Fusion and re-ferred him to the service department.

"Making assumptions is your specialty, isn't it?" Felix had asked her. He hadn't waited for her to answer; he'd saved them both precious time by stating the reason for his call. "I'd like to interview Mr. Spencer about his Second Chance Program."

"Oh. Is this for the paper?"

"Either the paper or the podcast," Felix had replied. "I'm not sure where it fits yet, but I know it's a critical conversation to have. If I'm going to showcase the more sinister parts of our fair city, then I should also highlight her best attributes."

"Isn't that contradictory?"

"Isn't that life?" Felix had countered. "Seldom is a person, or a city in this case, all good or all bad."

"True. I'll talk to Mr. Spencer when he arrives. One of us will get back to you sometime today."

"I'd appreciate it."

Spencer had called him a few hours later. "I'd be delighted to discuss our Second Chance Program with you, Felix. How does Thursday at three thirty work?"

"Perfect." He'd replied without looking at his calendar. Getting a face-to-face meeting with Spencer would take precedence over everything else. "Would you like to see my interview questions in advance to prepare?" It was an offer he made to no one.

"That won't be necessary, Felix." Spencer had passed the test.

When he arrived at the dealership, Felix repeated the steps from his first meeting with Spencer—dodging overeager salesmen, getting buzzed back into the corporate office, and facing down a fire-breathing dragon.

"Mr. Franklin," Veronica said. Her voice wasn't quite sharp enough to cut glass, but it didn't give him warm and fuzzy feelings either.

Spencer's greeting was as cordial as Felix's last visit but seemed less forced. Felix's aversion to the king's inner lair, however, was the same. Maybe more so after witnessing the man's golly-gee-aw-shucks routine during the two interviews.

"I won't keep you long," Felix said as he took his seat in front of the sprawling desk. "I know you're busy."

"No busier than you are, I'm guessing." Spencer leaned back in his leather chair and steepled his hands in front of his chest. "I talked to Bill a little while ago and confirmed your Fusion should be ready tomorrow. If so, he'll give you a call."

"That's great news," Felix said.

"How's the Lincoln been working out for you?"

Felix smiled. "Really nice. I could get used to driving a vehicle like that."

Spencer smiled happily. "I know several salesmen who'd love to help put you in the SUV. I can promise you a top-notch value for your trade-in."

"Yes, I believe I just met a few of the eager gentlemen on my way in," Felix teased. "I'm thinking the payments exceed a reporter's salary."

"You're going places. That podcast of yours is turning a lot of heads." Spencer tilted his head and studied Felix. "You remind me of myself when I was much younger. I was ambitious and determined. The word no wasn't in my vocabulary, and I didn't mind stepping on toes to get my way."

"It does sound quite familiar," Felix agreed. He doubted time had softened Spencer's edges. "But I can't claim all the credit for the success of the podcast. I have two skilled partners."

They were more than partners; Jonah and Rocky were his brothers. Letting Spencer know their significance would be the same as baring his throat to the older man. Not in this fucking lifetime.

Felix locked eyes with Spencer. "We're only as good as the company we keep, wouldn't you say?"

If Felix hadn't been watching closely, he would've missed the slight frown and narrowing of eyes. Felix had struck a nerve.

"I would," Spencer said, recovering quickly. "What would you like to know about our Second Chance Program?"

"I stumbled upon an interview you did with Jude Arrow a few years back, so I already have a lot of background information. I'd like to focus on the things he didn't ask you and maybe update some of the details."

Just speaking Jude's name reminded Felix of their shared orgasm in his kitchen two days prior, as well as the messages from Jude he'd ignored. He wasn't trying to be intentionally cruel, but what they'd shared had sent him into a tailspin of fear, doubt, and second-guessing himself.

Felix wanted to believe, but who would he be putting his faith in? While Felix didn't think Jude had outright lied to him about Spencer and Mercy, he suspected Jude was only telling half-truths. Why? Who was he protecting?

He'd expected Jude to get angry about Felix's avoidance, but he'd sent a text the previous night that nearly made Felix cave in. *I understand you need time, and I'll wait. You're worth it.*

"Sounds like a good plan," Spencer said, yanking Felix from his reverie. "Why don't you start with the missing information."

"Yes." Felix nodded as he pretended to scan over his notes. "Do you mind if I record the interview?"

"Of course not."

Felix turned on the recording device on his phone. "The most pressing question I have is how the enrollees are chosen for the program."

Spencer nodded. "Jude did ask me about it during the interview. The station must've edited it out due to time constraints."

"You weren't aware?" Felix asked.

Spencer laughed. "I don't watch my own interviews. It just feels weird." So far, his answers hadn't tripped Felix's bullshit meter, so he pressed on.

"This will be new information for the readers or listeners."

"Let's start with an overview of how the program formed and who oversees it because I think that's a good segue into how the enrollees are chosen," Spencer said.

"By all means," Felix said. He wasn't about to discourage Spencer from talking.

"I can't claim the credit for coming up with the Second Chance Program. It was my wife's suggestion after talking to our pastor. He spends much of his time ministering to inmates at the county and state facilities. Once she planted the idea in my head, I couldn't stop thinking about it. I'm sure you recognize the attribute."

"Absolutely," Felix agreed.

"I had the financial resources and the jobs to offer but wasn't sure where to start. The first thing I did was reach out to parole officers and ask who I should talk to and how I should best implement hiring practices."

Felix nodded. "Makes sense."

"I worked with the department of corrections and several branches of law enforcement to first determine the needs of the parolees when they get released. From there, they helped me formulate program eligibility guidelines."

"Which excludes violent offenders, correct?" Felix asked.

"Absolutely. Now, I know people are wrongfully convicted, but I have to put the safety of the auto mall employees first."

"I agree," Felix said.

Cameron's cell phone rang on the desk. "One minute, please." He checked the caller ID, silenced the ringing, then smiled at Felix. "We hired experts to ensure we met the parolees' needs. When we first started out, we only offered the program at the dealership in Atlanta. The parole officers would provide us with a list of eligible candidates, and we put them through an interview process like we would any other employee.

"As the program grew, I recognized the need for a full-time staff dedicated to overseeing it. I now have a board of ten members made up of law enforcement officers, mental health advocates, and social workers. They review the applications, oversee the interview process, and monitor each enrollee. My wife is the board director and does a wonderful job."

"What happens after the candidates graduate from the program? Do they keep their jobs with you or move on?" Felix asked.

"Some do take permanent jobs at one of my dealerships, and others move on."

Felix nodded. "Do they lose access to their mental health advocates and social workers?"

"They do not."

"How's that possible?" Felix asked.

"How is what possible?"

"Forgive me for being vague," Felix said. "Let's say a twenty-year-old man graduates from your program. Are you telling me that your foundation will continue to pay for the man's counseling for the rest of his life should he need it?"

Spencer chuckled. "No. You asked me if they lost their access to their mental health advocates and social workers. I told you that they didn't, and they don't. You didn't ask who picked up the bills for their services after graduating."

"Fair enough," Felix said. "Who picks up the tab for the twenty-year-old?"

"The hypothetical twenty-year-old," Spencer said, softening his correction with a smile.

"Yes, hypothetical."

"After he graduates, either his health insurance from his new job will cover it, or he will work out a cash payment plan with his therapist. The mental health professionals all agreed to continue working with the parolees beyond the program. My aim is to help them get back on their feet and give them a fresh start. I want to help as many people as I can, so I have to set limitations on how long I can cover expenses for one person."

Felix could be a dick and resume looking for inadequacies in the program or continue looking for ways to tie this program to Mercy's thugs. Wouldn't Jack want to reward the ones who kept their mouths shut and did time after getting caught? Or was this program a recruiting agency for Mercy? How could Felix make the connection?

"Do you provide a list of enrollees?"

"Publicly?" Cameron asked. "No, but their names appear in the board meeting minutes, and we keep extensive records in case law enforcement officers request them."

"Fair enough." He'd find another way.

Spencer's phone rang again, and he sighed. "I'm sorry to cut this meeting short, but I must take this call. We can continue another day if you need additional information. Veronica could also help you since she assists my wife with her board director duties."

The same woman who went toe-to-toe with Skeet and Jack Mercy's muscle. "Good to know. Thank you for your time," Felix said.

He gave Veronica a friendly finger wave as he exited the corporate offices.

Felix dialed Rocky's cell number. "Do you know any parole officers?" he asked when his friend answered.

"Several," Rocky replied.

"How about ones you're certain aren't tied to Jack Mercy?" Felix probed.

"I know a gal. Are you finished with the interview already?"

"Yeah," Felix replied before repeating his conversation with Spencer. "You think your gal could discreetly get her hands on the names of the parolees who came through or are currently in the Second Chance Program? I think it's important."

"I'll find out," Rocky said.

"If we get the list, Marla the Magnificent can work her magic and crosscheck to see if any are known Mercy associates."

"It would be an excellent breeding ground to choose muscle from," Rocky said.

"Or a way to reward the ones who'd kept their mouths shut when they were busted."

"You're fucking good at this, Felix."

"That's what he said."

"Oh, so you did go to Jude's house on Tuesday night."

Fuck. Felix stepped right into that one. "Wrong." Jude had come to his house, so it wasn't a lie.

"Uh-huh," Rocky said. "The Straight Shooter was sporting a hickey on his neck during his broadcasts on Tuesday night. Do you happen to know anything about that?"

Felix neither confirmed nor denied. He said, "Talk to you later, Major."

"Later, Fee."

Felix disconnected and drove out to Jonah's neighborhood. Neither he nor Avery would be home from work yet, but he wasn't going there to see them. Watching the video about the Tupperware container the other night reminded him of a beautiful lady waiting for him to return her cobbler dish. At least he was smart enough to wash it first.

Felix had called Marla at lunchtime to make sure she was feeling up to having company.

"Company?" she'd asked. "Baby, you're family."

Amos's old Cadillac convertible wasn't in the driveway when he arrived, but Marla was sitting on the porch with Betty, her precious French bulldog, on her lap. She held a hand up to shield her eyes from the sun and leaned forward to get a better look at him. He'd gotten so used to driving the big SUV that he forgot he'd only had it for a week.

"How are my prettiest girls?" Felix asked when he stepped out of the Lincoln.

"Felix? What are you doing driving a car that costs more than my house?" Marla teased.

"It's a loaner while the dealership replaces my transmission. Rocky is in love with it, and I have to admit I've become a little spoiled too."

"Let me check it out," Marla said, rising slowly from her rocker. She wore a lavender summer dress, a straw hat in the same hue, and sandals. Her makeup was impeccably applied, and not a hair from her shoulder-length wig was out of place.

Felix hated seeing the toll liver cancer was taking on her, but he admired her fighting spirit. Marla was his kind of people.

"Want me to take you for a ride?" Felix asked.

"If you think this beast can stop at the ice cream parlor. I'm in the mood for a mint chocolate chip cone."

"I could use a milkshake," Felix said.

He held Betty in one arm while assisting Marla into the passenger seat with the other.

"It's so tall," she said. "Lord, I feel like I can see all the way to South Carolina from up here."

"It was an adjustment from the Fusion."

Felix backed out of the driveway and said, "Which parlor?"

"Clem's. I want ice cream made with natural ingredients on site, and none of the crap that's pumped full of chemicals and hormones. No wonder everybody is getting cancer."

Felix drove five blocks to Clem's. He settled Marla and Betty at a table in the shade before going inside. He ordered two scoops of mint chocolate chip for Marla, an order of whipped cream for Betty, and a mojito milkshake for himself.

"Does it come with real rum?" he asked.

Clem laughed heartily. "I'm afraid you'll have to settle for rum extract."

His ladies were excited to see him when he returned.

"Miss Thing," Marla playfully admonished when Betty got whipped cream all over her face. "You're making a right mess of yourself. Felix won't want you in his pretty car, and I'm in no condition to walk home these days."

Felix covered her hand. "I'm not worried about it."

"Shh. Betty still needs to mind her manners."

"Are you giving cancer hell?" Felix asked.

Marla chuckled. "You know it." She leaned into him. "Thank you for the ice cream."

"Thank you for the peach cobbler."

Marla batted her eyelashes. "Come on and tell Mama. Was it the best you've ever had?"

"Yes," Felix replied honestly.

"I'll be happy to share the recipe with you," Marla said. "I like the idea of people using them after I'm gone."

Felix sighed. "I'm helpless in the kitchen."

"Only because it's not important to you," Marla countered. "What about a special fella who excels at cooking or baking?"

Felix thought about the dinner Jude had brought over Tuesday night. He'd been eating the delicious leftovers for days and still hadn't tired of them.

"Mmmhmm," Marla said. "There is. I recognize that face."

"It's complicated."

Marla threw her head back and laughed, the sound deep and rich. "Isn't that always the situation when a man is involved?"

"Touché."

"Is there hope for you and your complicated man?"

Felix quietly pondered her question, which reminded him of the what-if game he'd been playing the past few days.

What if he could believe Jude was telling the truth about Cooper?

What if Felix could trust Jude?

What if they could try again?

Marla's giggle snapped him out of his daydreams. She smiled knowingly at him.

"Yes, there could be."

"But?" Marla prompted.

"I'd have to believe, trust, and try. I'm not sure I can."

Marla squeezed his hand. "But you want to." It wasn't a question.

Felix released a shaky breath and nodded. "I do." Admitting the truth out loud lifted a heavy weight from his shoulders. He'd never gotten over Jude, and maybe it was time he investigated why that was.

"Can a dying gal give you some advice?"

The back of Felix's nose burned as tears filled his eyes. She'd come to mean so much to him, and they were running out of time.

"Don't you do it," Marla said sternly, waggling her finger. "What's the rule?"

"No mourning you while you're still living," Felix answered obediently.

"When I was your age, I thought time was a limitless resource. It was a well that never ran dry. A lady who never aged. I was famous for saying 'I'll get to it tomorrow' or 'there's plenty of time.' I took so many things for granted, including the love of a good man. By the grace of God, Amos never gave up on me. Time isn't limitless, baby. The well does run dry, and the lady not only turns old, but she gets fat and sings off-key. Who the hell wants to spend their last days stranded in Shouldacouldawouldaville? Not me. You shouldn't either. If you have a shot at happiness, take it. You are fearless when it comes to uncovering truths and righting wrongs. Be courageous in love, my friend."

Felix was too moved to speak, so he nodded and kissed her cheek.

Marla changed the conversation to lighter topics while they finished their frozen dairy treats. Amos's Cadillac was in the driveway when they returned. He scowled at the unfamiliar vehicle until Felix got out.

"Hey, Felix," he said. "I was wondering who the hell ran off with my woman."

"I just stole her away for ice cream," Felix said. He handed the cobbler dish to Amos, then helped Marla out of the SUV.

"Does that mean you won't have an appetite for the catfish dinner I've planned?" Amos asked his wife.

"Don't be ridiculous," Marla scoffed. "Don't be stingy with the potato salad either. I know how you like to hoard it all for yourself." She kissed Amos when they reached him on the porch.

"Felix, would you like to stay for dinner?" Amos asked.

Fried catfish and potato salad sounded delicious. "I don't want to inconvenience you."

"I wouldn't have invited you to stay if it was an inconvenience," he said. "Why don't y'all come in out of this heat and visit in the air-conditioning?"

"You twisted my arm," Felix said.

Felix and Marla settled in the living room. Marla sat in her recliner with Betty on her lap. Amos gave Felix a glass of sweet tea and Marla a glass of water so she could take some medication.

"I hate these damn pills," Marla said. "They dull my brain."

"Yeah, but they also dull the pain," Amos said before dropping a kiss on her forehead. "That's what counts. I'm going to start putting dinner together. Holler if you need me."

"I will, baby."

"Are you scared?" Felix asked when they were alone again.

"Of dying?" she asked.

Felix nodded.

"No. Living is much harder." Marla gave him a pointed look, reminding him of their conversation earlier.

Be courageous in love, my friend.

CHAPTER 19

Friday objectives at the office were always relatively simple: get the work done and go home. How Felix chose to spend his weekends was his business and often depended on his mood.

Once upon a time, aka before Jude's reappearance, Felix would hang out at clubs and flirt with cute guys. Sometimes, he took them home; other times, he didn't. More often than not, Felix worked on various projects like gardening or editing podcast episodes. Too much downtime was a bad thing for him. It allowed his mind to wander, which always led to trouble.

On this particular Friday, all he wanted to do was decompress on his patio next to his serene pond with a cold drink—alcohol was welcomed but not necessary. Felix didn't want to think, and he sure as hell didn't want to unpack the overstuffed suitcase of emotions taking up too much real estate in his brain.

Who was he kidding? He really wanted to drive to Jude's house, swim in his pool, eat his food, and get tangled up in his sheets. He wasn't done overthinking their situation yet, so he'd have to settle for a quiet night at his house.

It felt like the universe was out to derail him, first with Todd delivering his Fusion to him around three o'clock and collecting the keys to the Lincoln. The asshole had then insisted on a detailed inspection of the SUV, of course, to make sure Felix hadn't caused any damages. Felix hadn't trusted Todd not to scratch the paint or damage the leather seats if he turned his back for a few seconds, so he'd supervised the inspection while the sun baked him like a biscuit. Todd hadn't just walked around with a clipboard checking off boxes like at the car rental places. That would've been asking for too much. The annoying fucker had to get his digs in wherever he could. Felix had persevered, collected his copy of the clean inspection, and returned to his office where a Diet Coke and three Advil tablets waited for him.

Unfortunately, an email from Jimmy had been waiting for him too. Felix scanned the email, looking for the deadline for his feedback, and noticed he had until the middle of next week. Felix had every intention of putting it off until Monday, especially when his article submission deadline was only hours away.

Turning in his assignments at the last minute was a horrible practice, and one Felix had avoided for the most part. It was just lazy. Sometimes stories broke late, and he couldn't prevent last-minute submissions. That had been his only exception until recently. His head was everyplace it shouldn't have been, and his focus had turned to shit. So, Felix had started cramming errant thoughts and random worries into the suitcase to focus on the task at hand.

By five, he'd finished the last edits on his piece on upcoming changes to the FBI's Uniform Crime Reporting Program and sent it off. That was the good news. The bad news was that the Advil and caffeine hadn't put a dent in his headache. Felix had skipped lunch and his afternoon snack, then stood out in the heat for nearly an hour while Todd acted like an asshole. The latches on his bulging suitcase were groaning under the strain, and Felix felt like his brain was about to explode.

He'd had enough for the day. Hell, he'd had enough bullshit lately to last him a lifetime. Felix started to power down his computer and call it quits when he saw Jimmy's email.

You can read it next week. There's still time.

He recalled his conversation with Marla the previous day, which made his heart throb harder than his brain.

"Damn it."

Felix clicked on the attachment and began to read. It wouldn't hurt to do a cursory scan and see what he was dealing with. If it needed too much work, he'd save it for next week. That was a fair bargain.

Felix groaned out loud when he saw that Jimmy's piece was about antiquing. He was prepared to be bored out of his mind, but what he found was something entirely different. Jimmy's shy, meek personality disappeared when sitting behind a keyboard. The author of the article was witty, snarky, and endearing as he intertwined stories of antiquing with his grandmother around historical facts about Savannah. It was as much a story about love for one's family and pride for their city as it was a how-to guide on finding the best pieces for the lowest price.

Felix was thoroughly charmed by the time he finished reading it, which was such a rare occurrence that he reread the story. This time slower so he could make a few minor suggestions in the margins. The article was nearly flawless as it was.

He saved the altered document and attached it to an email to Jimmy. He debated what to say for a few minutes, then went with his instinct.

Jimmy,

If this is an accurate representation of your skill, you don't need a writing mentor. You do need someone to give you a swift kick in the ass. I have a feeling you've been mollycoddled your entire life. The result is a combination of low self-esteem and timidity which does not serve your talents well.

If you really want my help, be in my office on Monday morning at nine to begin your boot camp. Check your insecurities at the damn door. Shoulders back. Chin up. Look like you believe in your ability. By the time I'm through with you, there will be no need to pretend.

Consider yourself warned.

Felix.

He hit send, powered everything down, and turned off his light. The lights were off in the newsroom because everyone had already gone home. His footsteps echoed off the tile floor as loudly as Marla's advice bounced through his head.

Be courageous in love.

The flimsy latches on his abused suitcase broke, suffocating Felix beneath too many thoughts, memories, and yearnings. Before he could talk himself out of it, Felix called Jude.

"Have dinner with me," he said when Jude answered.

"I'd love to. Where do you want to go?"

"I was thinking pizza. I know a great parlor," Felix replied.

Jude chuckled. The low, rumbling sound did wicked things to Felix's insides. "Do you want to meet in public because you think I won't make a scene when you tell me to take a hike?"

"Nope. It's because I have a ton of questions I want answered. We both know what will happen if we go to either of our homes."

"Okay," Jude ceded with ease. "I'll answer every question you have."

"The whole truth or just enough to appease me?"

"I'll be an open book for you. Just tell me when and where to meet you."

Felix stepped out of the building and fished his key fob out of his pocket with his free hand. The remote start was his favorite feature on the car. He just had to hit the button twice. The lights would flash, the horn would sound two short beeps, and the engine would turn over. A running motor meant the air-conditioning would be blowing too. Since Todd had parked his car at the furthest point away from the front door, chances were the interior would be cool by the time Felix reached it.

He aimed the key fob at the Fusion and pressed the button twice. Nothing happened. He thought maybe he was too far away and waited until he walked another ten feet before trying again. This time, the lights flashed twice as usual. The first horn beep was weak, and the second sounded like a dying animal.

"Damn it," Felix said as he increased his pace. Had that fucking Todd sabotaged his car? Felix hadn't been smart enough to start it and make sure everything was kosher before letting the son of a bitch drive off.

"What's the matter?" Jude asked.

"I think there's something wrong with the starter."

"Where are you?"

"Work," Felix grumbled.

"I'm just around the corner. I'll come get you."

"This can't be happening." Felix pushed the remote start button two more times. The lights flashed weakly, followed by two metallic clicking sounds. "What's wrong with this—"

KABOOM!

CHAPTER 20

Felix's car erupted into a ball of fire. The deafening blast shook the ground and propelled him backward through the air like a ragdoll. Like an action scene in a movie, time seemed to stand still. No, it didn't stop completely; it downshifted into slow motion.

Felix's head bounced off the pavement hard enough to rattle his teeth. The asphalt shredded through his cotton T-shirt as his momentum turned the parking lot into a massive cheese grater and him into a block of cheddar. Black plumes of acrid smoke billowed through the air, catching on the wind and performing a macabre dance for an audience of one. Chunks of metal and slivers of glass rained down from the sky, cutting his flesh and burning holes in his clothes wherever they landed.

He should do something. Cover his head or protect himself, but Felix could only watch in muted horror as the fabric of his shirt smoldered and turned black in places. A high-pitched noise pierced his head. A smoke alarm? Then Felix realized it was his ears ringing. Every other noise was muffled and sounded like it came from a great distance, even the enormous ball of fire where his car had once been. What should've been a loud roar was barely a rumble.

Time upshifted to full speed once his body came to a halt. The drastic change had a dizzying effect, and his stomach pitched and rocked. Bile burned a path as it rocketed up his throat. Felix had just enough time to roll to his hands and knees before the putrid green foam spilled onto the asphalt, covering his shredded skin which looked like ghoulish confetti.

From a great distance, someone called his name. The voice was stretched out, so each syllable was drawn out cartoonishly long. "Feeeeeliiiiiiix."

He retched and heaved until there was nothing left, and even then, Felix's body quaked from the aftershocks.

"Felix!"

The voice. It was Jude. They'd been talking when the car exploded. The phone had fallen from his hand when he was thrown backward. Where was it now?

"Felix!"

Jude's voice sounded louder and frantic, or maybe the ringing had ebbed a little in his ears. Felix carefully looked around for the phone, but the world around him started spinning again.

His arms buckled, and Felix pitched forward, narrowly avoiding the puddle of bile on the pavement. The blacktop burned Felix's face, but he was suddenly too tired to care. This felt like an okay place to die.

"Felix!"

A pair of navy blue Chucks came into his line of sight. The color reminded him of Jude's eyes. Deep and bottomless. The shoes drew nearer as their owner ran toward him, not stopping until they reached his side.

"Felix." It was Jude. He was here. "Baby," he said in an anguished voice, his strong arms lifted Felix off the pavement.

Jude shifted Felix's body, cradling him against his chest. Felix cried out in pain when his tattered skin came in to contact with Jude's body.

"I got you, Ace," Jude whispered, pressing kisses in Felix's hair.

Jude carried him to a grassy area far away from the blast site, then gently sat down, continuing to cradle Felix in his arms. Water droplets splattered onto Felix's face. He squinted up at the sky but only saw fluffy white clouds. He looked at Jude's shattered expression and realized it wasn't raining. Jude was sobbing.

"Hey," Felix croaked, wanting to comfort Jude. This felt like an okay place to live.

Jude cried harder while cradling Felix against his chest and gently rocking him back and forth. After a few moments, Jude took a shaky breath and wiped his forearm over his face. "What happened?"

"Kaboom!" Felix croaked.

"I heard the explosion, then saw the inferno when I pulled into the parking lot. At first, I thought you were inside the car." Jude sucked in a shaky breath. "I thought I'd lost you."

Emergency sirens blared in the distance. Help was on the way, but Felix couldn't care about his car or even his injuries when Jude looked so distraught.

"I was so relieved when I saw you lying on the pavement until I noticed how still you were."

"Stunned," Felix rasped out.

Jude nodded. "I've never been so grateful to see someone get to their knees and vomit. There were times I wished I could puke. Remember the party we went to where they served mixed drinks that tasted like cherry Kool-Aid? I have never been so sick in my life." Jude spoke rapidly, his words tripping and stumbling faster as his composure slipped. "Well, there was this one time when my entire family got the flu. I was six and—"

Felix pressed his hand to Jude's lips, silencing him. He'd never seen this silver-tongued devil babble and ramble. That more than the tears made Felix realize how rattled Jude was and how deeply he cared. Maybe it wasn't fourteen years too late.

"Kiss me." Felix's voice sounded awful and not at all sexy.

Felix felt Jude's lips trembling beneath his hand, then the soft flesh stretched into a smile he wanted to see, to taste.

Lowering his hand, Felix said, "Kiss me." This time he sounded like he only smoked one pack a day instead of three.

"Talking sounds painful. I have a bottle of water in the car. Let me go get it for you," Jude said.

"Kiss," Felix demanded, sounding like a toddler on the verge of a tantrum.

Jude ran the back of his hand over Felix's cheek. "There will be plenty of time for kisses later. Besides, you just puked."

Time. Felix's eyes burned as he recalled Marla's dire warning. "A wise woman recently reminded me that time is not limitless. I could have internal bleeding. Do you really want to waste time arguing with me when you could be kissing me? No tongue," he offered as a compromise.

Anguish washed over Jude's face as the encroaching sirens grew louder. It sounded like every available unit was converging on them.

"Don't say that, Felix. I just got you back."

"Who says you got me back?"

Jude's mouth tilted upward on one side. "This does." He gently pressed his lips to Felix's, and for those few blissful seconds, the chaos quieted and the pain ebbed. The only sound Felix heard was his own heartbeat. His brain shut down every sensory neuron except for the one computing how good this kiss felt.

Jude broke their connection and stared down at him.

"Maybe it's not too late."

Jude grinned. "I'd prefer to hear you say that when you're not in shock."

Felix would've tried to argue with Jude, but the cavalry had arrived. Two patrol cars were the first on the scene. The officers had to assess the situation before allowing the firefighters and EMTs on site. Firemen went to work putting out the blaze, while Jude waved a male and a female paramedic over to start evaluating Felix's injuries. Their nametags read Barns and Nobel. Felix would've thought their names were cute if not for his discomfort.

"I'm just a little scraped up," he told them.

"Oh, honey," Nobel said, shaking her head. "You're more than a little scraped up. It's not quite as bad as the road rash you see on motorcycle crash victims, but it's close enough. Does anything else hurt?"

"My head, but it was already hurting before I bounced it off the asphalt."

Barns shone his penlight in Felix's eyes. "I don't think you have a concussion, but you need to have it checked out."

"I'll go to the hospital tomorrow if—"

"You'll go now," Jude said firmly.

More cops arrived on the scene. Some navigated the gawkers who'd appeared out of nowhere while others talked to the firemen spraying water on what remained of Felix's beloved Fusion. The first officers to arrive, Ramos and Hamilton, hovered nearby, waiting for an opportunity to question him further.

Felix had no intention of lying to the officers, but he also wasn't sure how much information he wanted to divulge right then. Obviously, Spencer was more dangerous than Felix had given him credit for, and he needed to rethink his investigation strategy going forward.

"Okay, I'll go to the hospital," Felix said. "But an ambulance isn't necessary."

"I thought you were worried about internal bleeding," Jude countered.

Felix grinned for the first time since... He couldn't remember. "I just wanted you to kiss me."

Nobel giggled while Barns shook his head.

"I'll drive you," Jude said.

Officer Ramos stepped forward. "We can take you," he said.

"No offense, but the back of your cruiser wouldn't be very sterile," Felix said. "I'd prefer if Jude took me." It would give them a chance to talk.

Hamilton tipped his head to the side. "We can get you into an exam room quicker."

"Not as fast as we can," Nobel countered. Felix was starting to like her a lot.

"I'll ride with Jude," Felix said firmly.

"We'll follow," Ramos stated.

Barns and Nobel didn't agree with Felix's decision, but he signed a waiver and followed Jude to his car. Each step sent a jolt of pain radiating through his body.

"I think I bruised my tailbone," Felix said.

"I think you've bruised everything." Jude helped him get settled in the passenger seat before getting behind the wheel. He started the car but didn't put it in drive right away. "I could've lost you."

"You didn't."

"I could have. There's so much I want to say." Jude turned his head and stared into Felix's eyes. "I don't know where to begin."

Felix wanted to focus on the tender expression on Jude's face and in his voice, but he couldn't afford to. One misstep and maybe the next accident would have deadlier consequences. "Let's start with what I should say to the police. Do I tell them Cameron Spencer is trying to kill me, or do I play dumb and pretend it has to be a mechanical malfunction?"

Jude quirked a brow. "Do I really need to answer that question?"

Jude's avoidance was Felix's answer. "Mechanical malfunction, it is." *Live to investigate another day.*

Getting Ramos and Hamilton to buy into his desired theory was easy. After all, the vehicle had just come back from the dealership. A leak of flammable fluids was highly plausible. Navigating the medical personnel who questioned his refusal of certain medications was tougher.

"No pain meds," he said for what seemed like the millionth time. This time it was to the ER doctor and not a nurse or PA.

"You're going to be in a lot of pain when the adrenaline wears off," Dr. Laurens said in her matter-of-fact voice.

"It will remind me that I'm alive," Felix countered.

A dark eyebrow went up.

"My mother is an addict."

Not was. Is. Addiction wasn't a hobby; it was a disease. Kelly told him the cravings would go away, and she'd celebrate turning a corner. Then she'd wake up one day, and they'd be back with a vengeance. The battle to stay on the right path would be harder. Once Kelly caught onto addiction's evil games, it got easier for her to manage the highs and the lows. Once she had accepted the road before her would never be easy, the twists and turns became easier for Kelly to navigate.

"A person can learn from someone else's mistakes." There was no scorn in Felix's voice, only open honesty.

"How do you feel about using anti-bacterial cream with lidocaine?" Dr. Laurens asked.

"That, I can do," Felix said. "Just no opiates."

The nursing staff began removing the glass and asphalt imbedded in his skin before cleaning and treating the cuts and scrapes. Afterward, Felix had a barrage of tests to clear him of a brain injury or internal bleeding. By the time they exited the hospital, Felix felt as shattered as his cell phone. Ramos had found it in the parking lot and returned it to Felix, but not before someone ran over it.

"I can take you to the cell phone store in the morning if you want," Jude offered.

Felix heaved a sigh. "It will certainly be easier to replace than the car." He mentally began ticking off the things he needed to do: call his insurance company about the car, replace his phone, and track down Todd Dartmouth to give him the beating Felix should've given the bully in high school.

Imagining plowing his fist in Todd's face started to reinvigorate Felix. With every imaginary hit and kick, Felix felt less like wilted lettuce disguised as a human. Felix might've been knocked on his ass, but he wasn't down for the count. He silently called to his fighting spirit.

Give me the strength to see this battle through to the end.

Felix suddenly noticed the direction Jude had turned when they exited the hospital parking lot. "This isn't the way to my house."

Jude briefly met his gaze, a slight smirk tilting at the corner of his mouth. It did more to boost Felix's energy than the fantasy ass-whooping he'd given Todd Dartmouth.

"No, but it is the way to mine."

Felix snorted. "You think my near-death experience has softened me toward an alliance with you?"

Jude stopped at a red light, then turned his full attention to Felix. "Hardly."

Despite everything, Felix smiled at Jude's play on words. "No more games, Jude." Felix couldn't risk them. "No more holding back." He wouldn't accept it. "All or nothing. Do you agree to the terms?"

The hint of a smile tugging at Jude's lips disappeared. "I do."

Jude's acquiescence was a victory. So, why did it feel like Felix had cut the wrong wire, and an invisible doomsday clock was ticking down?

Jude's house was everything Felix had imagined it would look like. It was modern, two stories, and beautiful—inside and out. He couldn't help imagining his rustic farmhouse style mingled with Jude's sleek modern furnishings. Oddly, the old-meets-new aesthetic really appealed to Felix.

Could the same be said for them?

"Are you hungry?" Jude asked when the tour of the first floor ended in his enormous kitchen. "I have some leftover soup I made a few nights ago. I can make a couple grilled cheese sandwiches."

"I'm starving," Felix admitted. "I haven't eaten since breakfast."

Jude narrowed his eyes. Was he remembering the first time he'd seen Felix's bare chest? Jude had sucked in a sharp breath, making Felix reach for the shirt he'd tossed to the floor. He'd always been underweight and hated changing around other people, especially in gym class. Fucking Todd used to count Felix's ribs out loud while the other boys laughed. What was funny about a malnourished kid?

But Jude, or maybe it was Felix's hormones, had made him temporarily forget his self-consciousness.

"No," Jude had said, grabbing Felix's wrist. "I like looking at you. I want to touch you." He'd had a silver tongue even back then.

"I'm too skinny," he'd said, crossing his free arm over his chest. Felix's scholarship came with a meal plan, but he only had enough for three meals a day. He didn't get care packages from home like the other kids, and he didn't have spare cash for pizza and junk food. Felix was always so fucking hungry. With Jude, he craved something beyond food.

"You're beautiful."

They hadn't had sex that night, but Jude had kissed his chest, teased and sucked his nipples, and made Felix feel as unique as Jude claimed him to be. Afterward, Jude had made them grilled cheese sandwiches. It took him a while to recognize the pattern, but Jude had taken every opportunity to feed him from that day forward. Felix was humiliated when it first occurred to him, and his youthful pride reared its ugly head. He'd chosen to view the gesture as a token of Jude's affection because feeding Felix had made Jude happy.

"Still trying to feed me, I see."

"Some things never change."

"Do you still make the best grilled cheese sandwiches?" Felix asked.

Jude's lips curved into a smug smile. "I do."

"Would you mind if I take a shower and maybe borrow a pair of shorts?"

"Of course not."

Felix followed Jude upstairs to the master bedroom. At no point did either of them reach for the other. The desire to do so pulsed between them, thickening the air. If they started kissing and touching now, they wouldn't get around to talking for a long time. As much as Felix wanted Jude, he needed answers more.

The master bedroom was an ample space decorated in calming hues of blues and gray. Jude walked to a tall chest of drawers and pulled out a pair of gym shorts. "Do you want my old T-shirt back? It will be much softer than the one we got from the hospital gift shop."

"I'd rather go without if you don't mind." Felix couldn't imagine any fabric would feel good against his ravaged flesh. He'd only sustained road rash to his shoulder blades. It could've been much worse.

"Of course not." Jude set the shorts on his bed and retraced his steps to where Felix stood near the door. "The shower is a little tricky. It took me a while to get used to it."

"One of those smart systems where you tell it to turn on or adjust the temperatures?"

"Sort of, but it's not voice-activated." Jude smiled at him. "I'll demonstrate it for you."

Felix quirked a brow. "How gallant."

Jude chuckled. "I meant that I'd show you which buttons to push."

"Well, you are filthy too," Felix said, gesturing to the dried blood and dirt staining the front of Jude's dress shirt. Felix had been too distracted by questions from the police and the medical staff to notice Jude's condition.

That was *his* dried blood smeared on the light blue fabric from where Jude had cradled Felix against his chest. A hard shiver rolled through Felix that had nothing to do with being cold.

The urge to request hands-on instruction temporarily obliterated all other thoughts. Jude leaned forward and pressed a soft kiss against his lips, but it didn't last long enough. He turned and walked toward the bathroom. "The quicker you shower, the faster you get your grilled cheese sandwich."

Felix smiled as he followed. "Are you going to feed me every chance you get? I've packed on quite a bit of muscle since our freshman year of college."

Jude waited for him by the shower. "It was never pity, Felix. Those big amber eyes just brought out my nurturing instincts. Sometimes, I think another chance with you is too much to wish for, but I do hope that someday you'll realize my affection for you is genuine." Is. Not was. "Shower. Food. Talk."

Felix nodded.

Jude showed him how to work the shower, then left him to his own devices. Careful to keep his back out of the spray, Felix washed himself as best he could. Jude's bodywash smelled, looked, and felt luxurious, and Felix relished smelling like him. After toweling off, Felix slid on the borrowed pair of shorts. They were a little large, but the drawstring ensured they stayed on his hips.

Felix padded barefoot downstairs. The hot water helped relieve his aching muscles, but his movements were stiffer than usual. The smell of butter, toasty bread, and melted cheese greeted him when he reached the first floor. He inhaled appreciatively and headed toward the kitchen.

Jude's face was in profile as he entered the room, but Felix could still see the intensity etched in his expression as he scrutinized the contents in the skillet. He was such a food snob. Felix wasn't sure what cheese or type of bread Jude chose, but it wouldn't be basic-bitch white bread or Kraft singles.

Jude's cell phone rang before Felix could tease him. Jude's body tensed when he checked the screen. He let it ring a few more times before moving the skillet to a cool burner.

"Hello," Jude said, his expression and voice were cold enough to freeze hell. Felix didn't recognize this side of Jude, but he was intrigued to know who could make him react so viscerally.

Jude turned and looked at Felix then. He jolted but recovered quickly, running his gaze over Felix's barely dressed body. The iciness in Jude's eyes melted a little as he listened to whoever was speaking on the other end of the connection. He looked no less dangerous or predatory, and the blood-stained shirt made him look like the sexiest action hero Felix had ever seen.

Felix felt frozen to the spot, barely able to breathe. What the hell was going on?

Jude closed the space between them. He cupped Felix's face with his free hand, running his thumb over Felix's lips. "Yes, I got your message. Now hear mine." Jude paused but never looked away from Felix's eyes. "Fuck you, Jack."

CHAPTER 21

*J*ack?

Felix's blood turned to ice, creating goose bumps all over his skin. He recoiled from Jude's touch, but the bigger man followed relentlessly. Jude's penetrative gaze ensnared him, preventing Felix's retreat. He didn't need to hear the caller's last name to know which Jack had called Jude.

Jude's nostrils flared with each inhale of breath. "If you come near Felix again, the FBI will be the least of your problems. I will kill you." His voice was hard, barely more than a whispered growl, but Felix knew Jude meant it.

But why? And how did Jude get tangled up with Jack Mercy in the first place? Memories played through his mind like a kaleidoscope. Running into Jude at the club. Jude crashing their stakeout. Rocky intimating that Jude's involvement could be deeper than his ex-boyfriend claimed.

Jude ended the call and tossed his phone on the counter without breaking eye contact with Felix.

Run, a voice inside Felix's head screamed. *But this is Jude,* another said.

And where would he go? How would he get there? His car had blown up. He didn't even have a phone to call his friends.

Another memory flashed in his mind's eye of Jude sobbing and cradling Felix in his arms.

I thought I'd lost you.

Jude had seemed so sincere. Was it all a lie?

Felix's confusion cemented him in place. He could run, but he'd never get answers to the questions zooming through his brain. They were coming fast and hard, one right after the other with no reprieve. Every time Felix started to analyze a piece of the puzzle, another would take its place. A solid picture couldn't form because Felix had only seen fragments of the danger facing him, including the man staring into his eyes so intently.

Hadn't he known there was more to Jude's story? Hadn't he known Jude was protecting somebody?

Run.

"Don't run," Jude said, reading Felix's mind. "I know you have questions. I'll answer every one of them, but not until after you eat."

Felix pulled free from his grip and crossed his arms over his bare chest. He felt naked and exposed, and so fucking cold without Jude's hands on him. "I j-just found out that Jack Mercy t-tried to kill me, and you expect me to c-calmly sit down and eat like nothing h-happened."

Jude reached for him, but Felix took two steps backward. "You also heard me threaten Jack Mercy if he came near you again."

"And you think it makes everything okay?" he asked, backing up two more steps.

Unfortunately, Felix's shoulder caught the edge of the archway between the kitchen and the great room. Searing pain fried his synapses, and Felix would've slid to the floor if Jude hadn't lunged forward to catch him. Once again, Felix found himself in Jude's embrace. This time, Felix was the one crying.

"You're safe with me," Jude told him. "Safer than you are on your own, especially when you get so busy that you don't take time to eat."

"Give it a rest, Jude. I'll eat your damn food after I get answers." Felix's stomach growled its protest, making a mockery of him. Maybe he didn't need all the answers before he ate.

Jude nodded. "Ask me anything."

"I need to know why," Felix whispered, sounding like a lost, little boy. He resented Jude for reducing him to a quivering mass of pitifulness more than any betrayal—past or present. He pulled free from Jude's embrace. The motion was clunky on wobbly legs. Felix saw the protest in Jude's compressed lips, but he remained silent. "Why would Mercy think killing me would send you a message?"

"Because losing you would hurt me the most," Jude said without hesitation.

"Don't take me for a fool. There's more to the story."

"Mercy ruined my career in Atlanta, but that didn't stop me from pursuing the truth. The son of a bitch upped the ante. Fuck," Jude roared. "I told you to stay away. Why couldn't you have listened?"

Felix opened his mouth to respond, but nothing came out. He was trying to process too much information without sufficient fuel. "So, you didn't move to Savannah because of me?"

He just found out Jude was connected to the mafia, and this was the part his brain chose to latch on to?

"Okay, maybe I could use a few bites of food."

Felix didn't care about having diminished physical functions, but he couldn't tolerate an impaired brain. It was his most potent weapon. His head got him into trouble, but it also found solutions to sticky situations.

"You'll eat an entire sandwich and at least one bowl of soup," Jude said.

Felix narrowed his eyes. "You're in no damn position to negotiate." Stepping around Jude, Felix intended to walk to the stove to claim a sandwich for himself but stopped when Jude gripped his forearm. He glanced over his shoulder and caught Jude's worried expression.

"I want to make sure you're not bleeding again."

"Maybe I should borrow a shirt so I don't ruin any of your furniture."

Jude made an indecipherable noise as he turned to face Felix. "I don't care about my stuff. I'm more concerned about you getting an infection. Do you promise not to snatch my car keys and leave when I go upstairs?"

"You could take them with you, or you could trust me. After all, you're asking me to believe you're not involved in a plot to kill me. Trust your instincts."

"Fair enough. I'll be right back," Jude said.

Felix glanced at the car keys and briefly debated running. Then he saw the grilled cheese sandwiches resting in the cast iron skillet. Just as he suspected. No basic-bitch white bread and Kraft singles. Jude had chosen sourdough bread, ham, and gruyere or another super melty cheese.

"Fuel before fleeing."

Felix picked up the spatula and put a sandwich on each of the plates Jude had set on the counter. Then he ladled soup into the matching bowls. The smell wafting from the porcelain dishes made his mouth water.

"Minestrone," Jude said when he returned.

"My favorite."

Felix turned and found Jude standing at the threshold of the room. Their gazes locked, and neither man so much as blinked until a grandfather clock chimed somewhere in the house.

Jude crossed to him, extending the shirt. "Do you want me to put more ointment on your wounds?"

Felix accepted the soft T-shirt. Jude discovering that he had kept it all these years felt different now. Tuesday night, the gesture came across as sweet and maybe a little like a peace offering. Now, Felix just felt foolish.

"Not right now," Felix said. His arms and shoulders were stiff as hell, but he managed to pull the shirt on without too much discomfort.

They carried their plates and bowls over to a small table tucked into the nook. Felix only planned to take a few bites of his soup and grilled cheese before interrogating Jude, but he couldn't stop shoveling food in his mouth once he started. He ate his sandwich, half of Jude's, and two bowls of minestrone.

"More soup?" Jude asked.

Felix shook his head and set his spoon inside the empty bowl. "No, but it's the best minestrone I've had in ages."

"I've tweaked the recipe a lot over the years, but I still can't get mine to taste as good as Del Rey's."

Felix felt a pang in his heart at hearing the name of the Italian restaurant where they'd had their first date. Felix had never heard of minestrone soup until Jude had taken him there.

"It's been so long I can't remember what Del Rey's soup tastes like, but this was amazing."

Jude stacked his bowl on top of his plate and started to reach for Felix's dirty dishes too.

"Huh-uh," Felix said. "I'm firing on all cylinders now. No more procrastination."

Jude leaned back in his chair and dropped his hands to his lap. "Jack Mercy killed my father."

"I thought you said he died of an aneurysm."

"Because that's what my mother and everyone else told me. I was a devastated kid, reeling from the sudden loss of my father. They didn't think it was a great time to tell me my dad's firm had direct ties to the Southern mafia, and the man I'd called Uncle Jack was the crime boss."

Jude picked up his glass with a shaking hand and took a long drink of water. He set it down, then picked up the napkin next to his plate. Jude stared off into space with a pained expression on his face while absentmindedly tearing strips of paper. He looked so distant and alone. Felix wanted to comfort him, but he was as immobile as if someone had glued him to the seat.

"Jesus, Jude. I'm sorry," Felix said.

Jude flinched, and Felix regretted saying anything. Then Jude looked down at the table and tilted his head as he studied the mess he'd made. His expression tightened, and he balled the paper strips in his fist.

"The longer my mom waited to tell me the truth, the easier it became to justify the lie. She needed to keep me alive. She wanted to stay alive to watch me grow. My mother limited my exposure to Jack after my father's death, but he was always in the periphery. Far enough that I wasn't privy to who he really was, but close enough so my mom would know Jack was watching."

"Why?" Felix asked. "I assume he killed your dad to silence him."

Jude looked up and met Felix's stare, then nodded.

"You said your father's firm was connected to Mercy. Was he a lawyer?"

Jude smirked. "Accountant. Remember, Al Capone was sent to prison for tax evasion and not because of the deaths he was responsible for. There's always a trail when it comes to money. Yes, you can launder it and slow the feds down, but they'll eventually find the right path and follow it to both ends."

Felix rubbed a hand over his face. "So, your father either stumbled across something he shouldn't have, or he knew Mercy was bad all along and had a change of conscience."

Jude winced. "It was the latter."

"How and when did you find all this out?" Felix asked. Then he remembered the interview Jude did with The Auto King last year. "Spencer."

"In a roundabout way, yes. The interview started off innocently enough, but I noticed Spencer's hesitation when I started digging deeper for information on the parolees taking part in his program. At the time, it was in its infancy, and he didn't have a board running the show as he does now. I offered to set up an interview so the enrollees could talk about what their second chance meant to them. He declined."

"And miss out on the good publicity? That's odd," Felix said.

"I told him the same thing, but Spencer just reiterated how the program isn't about him. He was adamant that profiting off the program was unethical. When I suggested he could pump the extra revenue back into the program, Spencer got defensive. I backed off. I quickly realized the avenue was closed to me, so I shifted my attention to the eligibility guidelines established for the program. The only thing Spencer could tell me was the parolees selected weren't convicted of violent offenses."

Felix rubbed his chin. "That's all I got out of Spencer when I interviewed him about the program."

"When?" Jude asked sharply.

"Yesterday."

"Damn it, Felix. Why didn't you stay away from Spencer like I asked you to? What did you say to tip him off?"

"Nothing," Felix said defensively. "I didn't push for information. I…" Felix slapped his forehead when he recalled how he'd triggered Spencer's red flag. "I made a remark that we're only as good as the company we keep."

"Felix." Jude's tone was a mixture of admiration and admonishment.

"We were talking about the *Sinister in Savannah* podcast, and I told him I couldn't take all the credit for its success. So, yeah, I used the opportunity to get a dig in, but the remark hadn't come out of left field."

"The interviews were the incendiary devices for both explosions that followed them," Jude said.

Felix's explosion was literal and obvious, considering the situation they'd found themselves in. He had a feeling Jude's bomb was more personal. "What blew up in your face?"

Jude took another long drink. This time Felix did get out of his chair and moved closer, taking the seat to Jude's right instead of sitting across the table. Felix didn't reach for him, but he was within touching distance.

"My whole world exploded because, of course, I didn't let it go. That's not what good reporters do."

Felix nodded. "We follow the lead until there's nowhere left to go." He snorted. "And to think I thought your interview was lazy."

Jude winced. "You watched it?"

"On Tuesday before you showed up."

"Wow. And you still sucked my dick?"

Felix smirked. "I followed my instincts."

"The abbreviated version they aired was lazy as fuck. A fluff piece that didn't come close to telling the whole story."

"They never do," Felix said. He reached over and covered Jude's hands. "I'm listening."

"Because you want to out-scoop me." Jude's sapphire gaze glittered with mirth. It was brief, but Felix was so relieved to see life sparking in Jude's eyes again.

"I'd planned to fuck it out of you anyway," Felix said with a casual shrug. He'd planned no such thing, but he loved the wry smile tugging at Jude's lips.

"Well, in that case, why should I divulge my secrets now? Bring on your wicked ways."

"I've had second thoughts. A near-death experience can have strange effects on a man."

Felix nearly swore when he saw Jude flinch. He released Jude's hand and cupped the back of Jude's neck, pulling him closer. Felix rested his forehead against Jude's.

"I want all the secrets aired *before* I take you to bed," Felix whispered.

Jude closed his eyes and shook his head. "Don't give me that kind of hope unless you mean it."

"Were you telling me the truth about why you moved here?" Felix asked. *Please say yes.*

Jude nodded. "I would've moved to Anchorage, Alaska, if that's where you were. Then I would've been battling attack moose instead of peacocks. I much prefer my odds against Pete and Pearl."

"They're not my peacocks."

"They are. You just don't realize it yet," Jude said.

"Walk me through the timeline, starting with your interview with Spencer."

Jude cleared his throat. "The station manager cut most of the interview due to time constraints, but I was shocked when he cut out every tough question I asked. He could've cut out some of the fluff, but he didn't. So, I confronted him."

"What did he say?"

Jude's phone rang in the kitchen. He started to rise from the chair, but Felix snaked out a hand to stop him. Jude's warmth seeped into Felix, and he reflexively tightened his fingers around Jude's wrist. "Unless you think it's Jed, let it go."

Jude sat back down, and Felix retracted his arm. "I talked to Jed earlier when I went to get your T-shirt from the gift shop. He'd heard about the explosion and asked me to come in and report on it."

"Why didn't you?" Felix asked. "Being on the scene so early, you had an advantage that no other news anchor would have."

Jude inhaled deeply. "You know why, Felix. You're more important to me than chasing a story. You always have been, and you always will be. No matter what happens after tonight."

Felix briefly closed his eyes as the heft of Jude's words settled over him like a weighted blanket. He wished he could wrap them around him, but it wasn't the right time. Felix's adrenaline was fading with each passing minute, and there was still so much he needed to know.

The phone stopped ringing when the call rolled over to voice mail.

"Let's go back to discussing your old station manager in Atlanta," Felix prompted. "You confronted him about the editing, and he said…"

"He accused me of being combative and accusatory, which wasn't the tone they'd wanted for the piece. They had wanted to highlight Spencer's Second Chance Program, and my line of questioning suggested Spencer was up to no good."

"By asking how eligibility is determined? By wanting to speak to the parolees who are benefiting from the jobs?"

Jude nodded. "I was already suspicious because Cameron dodged my questions, but my curiosity intensified with my station manager's behavior."

Felix ran a finger over his lips while he thought about it. "So, his reaction was unique?"

"Completely. I can't say Bob and I were in constant agreement, but he never silenced me either. Bob refused to even discuss the Spencer interview."

"Which prompted you to do some digging. Where'd you begin?"

"I reached out to one of my friends in law enforcement," Jude said. "They referred me to a parole officer who they'd heard was sending Spencer names for consideration."

"Did you meet this *friend* at Gentleman Jack's?" Felix's expression or tone of voice must've betrayed his jealousy.

"My membership to the club isn't what you think, Ace. But we'll get to that part later."

Felix rolled his eyes but gestured for Jude to continue. "What did you learn when you got your hands on the list of Second Chance enrollees?"

"As Spencer claimed, these were non-violent offenders. We're talking tax fraud schemes, illegal gambling, loan sharking, insider trading, money laundering, and forgery."

"White-collar crimes."

"Yep," Jude said. "It didn't immediately occur to me that the program could be used to find mafia muscle or to reward loyal soldiers who'd kept their mouths shut. I was focused on the fact that not a single one of the parolees was a person of color. That's what I thought Spencer was worried about."

"What happened next?"

Jude's phone rang again, but they continued to ignore it. "I started looking at every name on the list. I discovered they were middle- to upper-middle-class people who didn't need the program at all. They lived in nice houses in suburban neighborhoods. I started to wonder if they actually worked at the dealership at all."

Felix got a sinking feeling. "You called the dealership and asked to speak to one of them, didn't you?" It's what Felix would've done.

"Sure did. I was told a person by that name didn't work at Spencer Auto Mall. I don't know if it was my conversation with the parole officer or the phone call to the dealership that tipped somebody off, but the fallout from my probe occurred quickly."

"How quick?"

"Jack Mercy was waiting for me in my office when I returned from lunch the day after the phone call. I recognized him from media coverage and greeted him as Mr. Mercy. A hard expression washed over his features, and he said 'you used to call me Uncle Jack.' He didn't look like the smiling honorary uncle who used to show up for all my big occasions. His dark hair was snowy white, and there wasn't a trace of a smile to be found. His eyes were as black and as cold as a shark's. Do you know what I mean? Have you ever looked into the soleless eyes of a predator?" Jude asked, his voice shaking.

Felix thought of Franco Humphries, the serial-rapist-and-killer case that had brought Rocky and Jonah into his life. The three of them were asked to join an unauthorized task force to bring the man down, and they had succeeded. Felix had interviewed the man afterward. Looking into his eyes was just as Jude described.

"I have."

Jude swallowed hard. "I asked him what he wanted. Mercy told me he was in the neighborhood and wanted to drop by. Then he expressed regret for not looking in on me after my father died. Once I connected Uncle Jack to Jack Mercy, the crime boss, I was too stunned to say much. Before he left, Mercy sized me up and said, 'You're more like your father than I ever realized.' He didn't make it sound like much of a compliment. His parting words were to pass on his love to my mother."

"Son of a bitch," Felix growled.

"I confronted my mother, which is what he wanted the entire time. She tearfully explained that my father had been one of Mercy's accountants and he hadn't died of natural causes. The official police report says it was a botched carjacking, but there was a jack of hearts playing card tucked inside his suit coat pocket. Mom found it when the police returned Dad's personal belongings."

Felix covered Jude's hand on the table. "I'm so fucking sorry, Jude. It must've felt like losing your dad all over again."

"It was awful," Jude said. "Once I knew the truth, other memories became clearer, and a devastating picture formed. Someone had burglarized our house on the day of Dad's burial. Can you imagine coming home from the cemetery to find your house ransacked?"

"Christ. No, I can't."

"It didn't occur to me then, but the robbers didn't take any of our big-ticket items. Our appliances and electronics were still there, as well as my mom's jewelry. Our drawers were tipped out, and even our mattresses were cut open. My dad's office took the brunt of it. They'd even pulled the wainscoting off the wall in his room to make sure there were no hidden passages or rooms. His safe looked like someone had blasted it with a shotgun. I was too distraught to understand what the hell was going on, and from that moment forward, my mom did everything she could to shield me from Jack Mercy. I never saw the man again."

"Until he appeared in your office."

Jude nodded. "Dad had decided to turn Jack in to the FBI. She thinks Dad knew his days were numbered, and that's why we went to the Braves game." Jude's voice cracked, so he cleared his throat. "I'm so grateful for the experience, and I'll cherish the baseball for as long as I live."

"As you should. It's a wonderful memory."

"I went a little crazy after I found out the truth. My mother insisted Jack must've retrieved the evidence when his goons ransacked our home because he'd left us alone all these years. I figured she was right, but I just couldn't let it go. Remember the friend in law enforcement I told you about?"

Felix bit back a snarl. "I recall."

Jude leaned forward and kissed him soundly on the mouth. "You still have the most beautiful eyes I've ever seen. Your amber irises turn a darker shade of brown when you're jealous."

"Bullshit," Felix said.

Jude chuckled. "Pay attention. We're getting to the sex club part."

"I'm listening." Felix was wide awake now.

"My friend is an undercover cop who works at the club. That's how I was able to get my membership. He set me up under a false identity. I went there to scope things out and saw Jack Mercy talking to Spencer. I couldn't get close enough to overhear their information, but it was obvious they knew each other well. Since Cameron Spencer was close to my parents' age, I figured my dad might've known him. So, I asked my mom about him."

Felix grimaced. "I bet that didn't go over well."

"First, she yelled at me for continuing the investigation. Then she told me how the two were connected. According to my mom, Brigitte Spencer has no idea her biological father is Jack Mercy. He kept a close eye on Brigitte from afar and provided for her. When she started show-ing interest in Cameron Spencer, his choices were to kill the young man or bring him on board."

"Spencer was hungry for money and prestige to be worthy of Brigitte, so he didn't think Mercy's offer through," Felix said. "He just took the money. Now he's looking the other way while Jack Mercy uses his vehicles for illicit purposes. What do you think he traffics?"

Please don't let it be people.

"Ace," Jude said tenderly. Felix's gaze dropped to Jude's sensuous mouth. "Ask me what you really want to know."

"It's not really my business," Felix said. He'd broken up with Jude seventeen years ago and hadn't spoken to him for fourteen years. He had no right to demand answers, even though he wanted them.

Jude quirked a brow as he leaned forward until his lips nearly touched Felix's. "I had promised to be an open book."

"I shouldn't care," Felix amended. "But I do." He took a deep breath. "Did you take advantage of any of the services while you were there?"

Jude stared Felix right in the eye. "No."

"Why?"

"I remembered what you always said about consent and sex workers. How can it be consensual if their survival depends on the sex act? If they stood to lose their job for refusing a request, then it's not a consensual environment. At nineteen years old, you were smarter than most people twice your age."

"It's an extremely personal subject for me," Felix whispered.

He and his mom had discussed it several times during their journey of healing and growth. Kelly's ideas about sex and intimacy had gotten so warped over the years that she'd started seeing a therapist. Maybe it was an odd conversation for a mother and son to have, but Felix respected Kelly more for her honesty.

"I know, Ace."

Felix's eyes were tired and gritty, but he wasn't ready to wave a white flag yet. "What happened next?"

"The Monday after my club visit, my station manager called me into his office. He informed me there had been numerous sexual harassment complaints filed against me."

"What? The fucker couldn't have been a little more creative?" Felix asked.

Jude snorted. "It is a little funny now that you bring it up."

Felix tried to fight off a yawn but failed. "I'd say more ironic than humorous."

"You look so tired. Are you sure you don't want to do this in the morning? You can have my bed, and I'll sleep in the guest room."

No fucking way.

"Positive," Felix said around a bigger yawn. "On with the story."

"We argued. Bob showed me the complaints submitted to HR. My only options were to accept their decision or sue them."

"Which did you take?"

Jude smiled at Felix. "I chose door number one at first, then hired a good lawyer to help me navigate door number two."

"Best of both worlds," Felix said, blinking his eyes extra to keep the heavy lids from closing.

"I had the freedom to investigate Mercy further while my lawyer worked her magic. Luckily, the news station didn't have a leg to stand on. They agreed to expunge my record of the false reports if I dropped the lawsuit."

Felix scrunched up his nose. "Doesn't sound like much of a victory for you."

"It allowed me to find another job doing what I love. That's when I started evaluating the other aspects of my life. I'd met Jed at a convention a few months before getting fired. He'd just taken the job as station manager at Channel Eleven. He'd mentioned wanting to find an investigative reporter like myself, so I called and offered my services to him."

"Must've been one hell of a pay cut," Felix said.

Jude chuckled. "The cost of living is much lower than in Atlanta, so it's a pretty fair trade. Plus, you're here."

"If you weren't a frequent visitor at Gentleman Jack's, then how did you happen to be there the same night as us?"

"My undercover cop friend called me. He said he had something important he needed to tell me."

"Why you? What did he say?"

"I don't know because I never got a chance to speak to him. You saw me walk in, and we left at the same time."

"You could've gone back in after we left," Felix pointed out.

"I could have, but I didn't. I've tried getting back in touch with Alejandro since then, but he hasn't returned my calls."

"The dark-haired Adonis. The two of you seemed cozy. Was it an act, or were you more than friends?" Felix asked.

"I thought you didn't have the right to ask those questions."

Felix narrowed his eyes. "Answer it anyway."

Jude leaned forward and brushed his mouth against Felix's. "We dated for a while. We didn't love each other, and the chemistry fizzled out pretty fast."

"Could've fooled me," Felix groused.

"You should see your eyes. They're getting darker by the second and burning hot enough to spark a fire."

Felix rolled said eyes and noticed how dry they felt. He rubbed both hands over them.

"Let's get some sleep," Jude said as he stood up. He collected the dirty dishes and headed into the kitchen. He set the dishes in the sink and retrieved his phone.

Felix rose to his feet and stiffly followed. "Anything important?"

Jude slid the phone in his pocket and started turning off lights. "Not sure. It was an unknown caller, and they didn't leave a message."

Jude placed his hands on Felix's hips. "Do you want me to sleep in the guest room, Ace?"

"Shut the fuck up and take me to bed."

CHAPTER 22

Once upstairs, Jude pulled Felix into his arms and gently cupped his face. He slid his hands up into Felix's hair and massaged his scalp. "I want you more than my next breath," he whispered against Felix's lips.

Felix nipped Jude's plump bottom lip, then tugged it until it plopped free. "Good thing I'm not asking you to choose."

Jude chuckled. "I'm trying to be chivalrous here."

Felix slid his hand between their bodies and ran the back of his fingers over Jude's lengthening dick. "Who asked you to be?"

"Ace, you've had a traumatic experience and are trying to process a fuck ton of information I dumped on you. It wouldn't be right if I—"

Felix silenced him with a kiss. Jude tensed but didn't pull away. His lips trembled beneath Felix's, reminding him of their first kiss when they were still clueless kids. This kiss felt like coming full circle. Felix boldly ran the tip of his tongue along the seam of Jude's lips. The bigger man groaned and opened for Felix, relaxing into his touch. Felix rotated his wrist and stroked Jude's cock through his dress pants until he was fully erect.

"I want to feel this monster inside me," Felix said between kisses along Jude's neck. The big man shuddered in his arms, and Felix wanted to drop to his knees again. "It's all I've been able to think about."

Jude lowered his hands to Felix's ass and massaged the globes. "Fuck, I've missed you, Ace. Not just the passion we share, but the way you challenge me and make me want to be a better man."

Jude's words were as intoxicating and arousing as his touch. Felix made fast work of Jude's belt and was reaching for the zipper when Jude stopped him.

"I'm filthy. Let me take a quick shower. Then we'll find a comfortable position—"

"I know just the one," Felix said, cutting him off. "Will you help me take off my shirt?"

"Don't you mean *my* shirt?"

"Possession is nine-tenths of the law. I have the shirt in said possession. Therefore, it's mine. Again."

Jude chuckled as he gingerly lifted the shirt up and over Felix's head. "I'll remember that."

Felix gritted his teeth to keep from gasping as the fabric rasped over his injuries. Jude wasn't fooled. He walked around Felix to get a look at his skin.

"Ace," Jude whispered brokenly. He placed tender kisses on the uninjured skin around the wounds. "I'm so fucking sorry. I could've lost you, and it would've been my fault. If I'd told you the whole story sooner—"

"I'd have investigated harder to get justice for your family," Felix said, his voice resolute and sincere. "And I might've wound up dead instead of just scuffed up."

Sliding his arms around Felix's waist, Jude pressed his forehead to the back of Felix's head. "Promise me you won't go after him alone," Jude pleaded. "You might be a better investigator than I am, but two are stronger than one."

Felix didn't work alone anymore, but he wouldn't hang Jude out to dry either. "I come as part of an army of four." Avery was part of the team, even if he didn't fully believe it yet. Felix turned in Jude's embrace. "There's room for one more."

Jude smiled. "Shouldn't you ask your friends first? Rocky hates me."

"He'll come around when he gets to know the real you and not the awful picture I painted."

Jude groaned. "How bad did you make me out to be?"

"I told him the truth as I knew it," Felix said, adding a careless shrug, sending pain screaming through his body.

"You told him the truth you found easier to believe," Jude countered.

Felix quirked a brow. "Are we going to fight or fuck?"

Felix had his answer when Jude stepped back and started unbuttoning his stained shirt.

"Looks like I owe you two new shirts." A part of his brain was already picking out the colors.

"You owe me nothing," Jude countered, slipping his shirt down his shoulders and arms, letting it fall to the floor. He quickly divested himself of his shoes, socks, and pants while Felix just stood there gaping at Jude's masculine beauty.

"Forgot something," Felix said, pointing to the boxer briefs with the noticeable bulge.

"I'll take them off when I'm out of reaching distance."

Felix snorted and thought Jude changed his mind when he closed the distance between them and yanked Felix's gym shorts down his legs. He'd chosen to go commando instead of putting his dirty underwear back on.

"Get in my bed and make yourself comfortable. I won't be long." Jude turned and headed into the bathroom with a purposeful stride.

God, the man had an incredible ass. Round and firm. Felix wanted to sink his teeth into both cheeks. He turned down the sheets and got into bed. He'd always been a belly sleeper, so lying on his stomach to avoid agonizing pain was a no-brainer. Exposing his ass to Jude for the taking was a bonus.

Felix's hard-on was sandwiched between his stomach and the soft bed. It wouldn't take much friction for him to blast off, so he lay still and watched Jude showering through the open door. The sound of trickling water was so relaxing, and watching Jude run soapy hands over his hunky body was mesmerizing. The remaining tension in his body drained, and Felix sank deeper into the mattress and pillow. His ten-ton eyelids fluttered once, twice, and finally slammed closed.

A shrill sound woke Felix from a deep sleep. What was it? The neighbor's vicious peacocks shrieking in the bushes outside his window again? No, that wasn't the right noise. By the time it sounded again, Felix was wide awake and fully aware of what had woken him.

A phone.

To most, a ringing phone in the dead of night was a bad thing. To a reporter, it was the sound of opportunity and possibility. Would this be the story that brought them fame and notoriety? Any reporter who claimed not to want those things was full of shit. They either were lying to themselves or just everyone around them. Felix was many things, some of them unpleasant, but self-delusional wasn't among his attributes or flaws. He knew who he was, what he wanted, and what it took to make it happen. He didn't lie to himself or anyone around him.

It was the only way to live.

Felix retracted his right hand from beneath his pillow. He reached for his phone but connected with a second pillow where his nightstand should've been. Wait a minute. He was on the wrong side of the bed. That alone wasn't enough to induce panic, but the sleepy voice answering the phone from his normal side of the bed was.

Oh God.

The events of the evening assailed him—one earth-shattering, technicolor image after the other. It wasn't *his* phone ringing. He wasn't even sleeping in *his* bed.

Fuck. Oh fuck. What have I done?

Felix had fallen asleep before Jude came to bed, and instead of waking him, Jude had covered his body, turned off the lights, and gotten in bed beside Felix. He'd slept through it and lost precious time.

"Yeah, he's here." Jude's sleep-roughened voice interrupted Felix's pouting.

Felix could hear a male voice coming from Jude's phone, but he couldn't make out who it was. Fear momentarily spiked through him. Was it Mercy calling again? Felix nearly laughed out loud at his silliness. Mercy wouldn't warn them before striking again. He'd just do it. *Gulp.*

Jude made a snarly sound. "Kiss my ass, Jacobs."

"That's my job." Felix's protest was ignored while Jude continued to argue with Rocky.

"Of course, you can talk to him. I don't have him tied and gagged in my dungeon, asshole."

"Oh, kinky," Felix said breathlessly. "Is that an available option?"

Jude snorted, finally acknowledging Felix's sidebar conversation. Jude extended the phone to him. "It's for you, dear."

Felix accepted the phone from Jude, who then sat up and turned on the bedside lamp. Soft light flooded the room, but it was bright enough to make Felix blink.

"Hey, Major," Felix said.

"I was going to ask where the fuck you've been all night, but I guess I know. Why the fuck couldn't you have at least answered the fucking phone?" Felix had never heard Rocky sound so angry and drop so many F-bombs in succession.

"I—"

"This is typical Felix behavior. You claim to be part of the team, yet you leave us to worry about you."

Warmth spread through Felix when he realized Rocky's anger was from being scared out of his mind. "You've heard about the explosion, then."

"Felix, I'm going to drive over there and throttle you."

"Can you wait until after I heal?" Felix asked.

Rocky swore again. "Are you okay? How bad is it?"

"A little bit of road rash on my shoulder blades and some sore muscles. I'll heal in no time," Felix assured his friend. "My cell phone was destroyed in the aftermath of the blast, so that's why I didn't call you."

"You could've borrowed the asshole's phone before you started playing house together," Rocky countered. He blew out a puff of air. "Jesus, I sound like such a jerk right now. You could've been killed, so of course you jumped his bones."

"Jude took me to the hospital and brought me back to his house so we could talk through some things," Felix explained. "I might've been a little wrong about Jude, Major." The man in question quirked a brow. "Okay. I was a lot wrong about Jude."

"Is he making you say that?" Rocky asked. "Blink twice if you're okay."

"Blink twice? How would you see it? Please tell me you're not watching us through night vision goggles or something."

Rocky laughed. "No. I'm a fucking mess and talking out of my ass."

"I'm fine, Major. I promise."

"I tracked down one of the EMT workers who responded to the incident, and he described the man who was with you. How did Jude arrive on the scene so quickly?" Rocky asked suspiciously.

"I know what you're thinking."

"I don't think you do," Rocky said. "I went to the hospital and charmed some answers out of a nurse too. I knew you were with Jude, but fuck me, it was hard to breathe a sigh of relief when he has such a large cloud of suspicions floating over his head."

"We do have a lot to tell you guys."

"We?" Rocky asked. How'd he pack so much disdain in one little word?

"Yeah, we," Felix said. There was no way in hell he'd air Jude's secrets behind his back. "I need to get a new phone first thing in the morning. Then I'd—"

Jude cleared his throat.

"We'd like to meet with you, Jonah, and Avery."

Rocky sighed heavily. "Fine. I'll text Jonah now and let him know you're not dead."

"Come on, Major. Stop being a drama queen. You already knew I wasn't dead."

"You weren't when you left the hospital, at least," Rocky replied, getting the last dig.

"I'm safe, and I'm where I want to be," Felix said. Jude reached over and brushed a knuckle over his cheek. "Your concern means a lot to me."

"You've grown on me."

"Like a hairy mole?"

Laughing, Rocky said, "Slightly better than that. Text or call when you have your replacement phone. We'll figure out when and where to meet."

"Will do. Good night, Major."

"Night, Fee."

Felix handed the phone to Jude, who disconnected the call and set it on the nightstand. Jude reached over to turn the light off, but Felix gripped his bicep to stop him.

"Leave it on. I remember how much you love seeing your dick moving in and out me."

Jude's mouth fell open on a soft gasp, and a deep pink blush stained his cheeks. Felix slowly spread his legs wide beneath the covers, and Jude broke their eye contact to watch the action.

"Are you sure you want this?" Jude asked.

God, yes. "I'm sure I want *us*," Felix replied. Old insecurities and doubts clawed their way to the surface like skeletal hands reaching up out of a grave. Felix's fear of never being good enough was the rotting skin clinging to the brittle bones of his past. "Do you?"

"So goddamn much." Jude's voice shook with emotion. "If we do this, I will not let you push me away again. I will follow you to the ends of the earth if that's what it takes. I won't stop fighting for us."

Felix pushed up on his elbows and leaned toward Jude, answering him with a kiss. The angle prevented a deep exchange, but the men tangled and twisted their tongues together as best they could.

"Fuck, yes," Felix said. "I need you more than air."

Jude's lips quirked up. "It's a good thing I'm not making you choose."

"Funny guy." Felix crooked his finger. "Come over here."

Jude obliged and began kissing a trail on the back of Felix's neck, around his wounds, down his spine until he reached the top of Felix's ass. Jude shoved the blankets down before repositioning his body to lie on his stomach between Felix's legs. He resumed kissing, starting with Felix's right cheek before moving to the left. Afterward, he spread Felix's ass apart and went to work on his puckered entrance. Jude licked and sucked the sensitive flesh, then took his time working his tongue inside the ring of muscles. Felix moaned and pushed his ass up higher, seeking more friction.

Jude snaked a hand beneath him to grip his shaft. "Remember that possession is nine-tenths of the law. This bad boy is all mine now."

"You're calling dibs on my cock during sex?" Felix asked.

Inside, he was thrilled to his core by Jude's show of possessiveness. This man had been the only one to willingly lay claim to Felix and mean it. The law hadn't required Jude to as it did with a parent, and fate hadn't forced his hand. Jude had wanted and chosen Felix—then and now.

I am enough.

Jude sank his teeth in Felix's ass while stroking his shaft.

"Fuck," Felix moaned.

Jude circled his pucker with the tip of his tongue before speaking again. "So, I'm asking you again. Are you sure you want this?"

Felix's entire body trembled with need, but nothing quaked as hard as his heart. "Yes."

Jude slid his hand lower to massage Felix's balls and sank his teeth into the back of Felix's thighs.

"That's right," Felix moaned. "Mark me."

Jude chuckled. "Like you did to me the other night before I had to go on air?"

"Not my fault you didn't spend enough time in the makeup chair." Felix sounded needy and greedy. "Want you inside me."

Jude released him long enough to retrieve supplies from the night-stand drawer. Knowing what was about to happen had Felix's hips moving on their own volition, rubbing the head of his dick against Jude's super-soft sheets. Felix's eyes rolled back, and he let out a long groan.

Jude smacked his right ass cheek. "Not yet."

Felix started to protest, but it died a sudden death when Jude pressed a lubed finger against his pucker. "I'll be good."

"I'll believe it when I see it."

Jude worked one slick finger inside Felix until he relaxed enough to accept a second, then a third. Jude had reduced Felix to gibberish by the time he deemed Felix's ass sufficiently stretched. Jude rolled on the condom and smeared more lube down his steely length before straddling the outside of Felix's hips and thighs. He leaned forward, placing one hand on the headboard to support his weight and keep him from falling onto Felix's ravaged back.

Pressing the tip of his cock to Felix's quivering hole, Jude said, "We're taking this slow." He guided the engorged head inside Felix, stretching him what seemed impossibly wide. "Relax for me, baby. Let me in," Jude urged. "You were made for me."

Felix breathed through the initial sting because he knew what would come next.

"That's it," Jude said, feeding more of his big cock inside Felix.

Felix's nerve endings sang as the stinging discomfort turned into immense pleasure. The more he relaxed, the more dick Jude gave him until he was buried to the hilt.

"I won't last long," Jude warned. "Not this first time."

"I'm right there with you."

Jude released the headboard to grip Felix's ass with both hands and spread his cheeks apart. "So fucking sexy. Your greedy ass can't get enough of me. Just like always."

Felix knew Jude got off on watching his possession. They'd often fucked in front of mirrors or anything with a reflective surface because it drove Jude crazy. Jude shifted his thighs a little, changing the angle of his penetration. Felix cried out in ecstasy.

"Harder."

Jude released a guttural groan that resonated in Felix's soul like one primal beast answering the mating call of another. "You feel so good. I can't hold back much longer."

"Then don't."

Jude placed both hands on the headboard, then snapped his hips forward with a savage roar, driving deep inside Felix. "I need you."

"Prove it. Give me everything."

"Don't. Want. To. Hurt. You." Jude punctuated each word with a deep thrust.

"That the best you got?" Felix asked. Never one to back down from a challenge, Jude pegged his prostate masterfully, reducing Felix to a series of grunts and single-word demands like "more" and "again."

Jude hammered him hard, driving Felix's dick against the bed. Felix cried out as he came all over the sheets. The headboard creaked beneath Jude's unrelenting grip as he rode Felix's ass even harder. Jude roared as his body bucked and jerked while he flooded the condom.

Felix lay shattered against the sheets as Jude panted above him.

"How the hell are we supposed to forgo cuddling after sex like that?" Jude said.

"Who said we can't snuggle?" Felix said. "We'll have to do it on your side of the bed because mine is a mess."

Jude chuckled as he eased his weight off Felix. He slid off the bed and headed to the bathroom to dispose of the condom. Felix carefully sat up when Jude returned with a warm, wet washcloth. Jude kissed him hungrily while he ran the cloth over Felix's abdomen and pelvis. When he finished, Jude broke their embrace and returned the soiled washcloth to the bathroom.

Once Jude returned to bed, Felix said, "Lie down on your back." He did, and Felix slid over and lay on his left side next to him.

"I wish I could hold you in my arms."

Felix wished Jude could too, but it would hurt too much to have Jude's arms draped across his shoulder blades. "We'll have to improvise until I heal." Felix draped his thigh over Jude's pelvis and an arm over Jude's chest. Beneath his hand, Felix felt Jude's heart beating steadily. Fuck, this felt so right. Felix was afraid he'd wake up to find it had all been a vivid dream. If it were, he'd be sure to make it a reality.

Jude turned his head and looked into Felix's eyes. His expression was sated and sappy. "So, you don't regret what happened?"

"I only regret it took fourteen damn years for us to get back to where we belong."

"We're smarter people now," Jude said.

"All we need to do is outsmart the Southern mafia and stay alive."

Jude grinned. "Easy peasy."

CHAPTER 23

Since his cellular provider didn't open until ten, Felix and Jude had plenty of time to reacquaint themselves with one another's bodies the next morning. They carefully shared a joint shower before making breakfast.

"Can I borrow your phone and make a few calls?" Felix asked once they finished eating.

"Of course."

"I doubt the explosion made news in Atlanta, but I want to talk to Reanna just in case."

Jude pulled his phone from his pocket and handed it to Felix.

"Thanks," Felix said, leaning into him for a kiss.

He took the phone outside. Rather than sit in a lounge chair, Felix sat at the edge of the pool, dangling his legs in the water. It would be a while before Felix could swim again, but he could enjoy this much.

Felix dialed Kelly first because it was the right thing to do. He felt horrible that he hadn't thought to call his mother the previous night.

"Hello?"

"Hi, it's Felix."

"How's my favorite son?" Kelly cheerfully asked. It was apparent she either hadn't heard about the explosion or hadn't connected it to him if his name was kept out of the press. "And why are you calling me from a different number?"

"I'm good," he said. "I had an incident with my car last night. My phone got damaged, so I borrowed a friend's."

"Were you in an accident?" she asked worriedly.

"My car was the victim of an accident, but I wasn't in it at the time." He kept his explanation brief and made it sound like there was a short in the wiring that had ignited the fire. "I need to call my insurance company after I get a new phone."

"I'm so glad you weren't hurt. Is there anything I can do to help you get this straightened out?"

Felix wanted Kelly as far removed from the situation as possible. Regardless of their past, she was his mother. Felix would be crushed if someone hurt her because of him. "Nah, but I appreciate your offer. Love you, Mom."

Her breath caught in her throat, and Felix knew she was crying. "I love you too. I can't remember the last time you called me mom. Still not sure I deserve the title."

If Felix had learned anything from this week, it was that life was too short, no matter how long you lived. Might as well do it without regrets. Shouldacouldawouldaville, as Marla called it, was overcrowded and didn't have good restaurants.

"I think you do," Felix said.

They spoke for a few more minutes before hanging up. Felix dialed Reanna next but wasn't in any way prepared for her greeting.

"Jude Arrow, have you kidnapped Felix? I've been calling and texting him for hours. He doesn't answer, won't return my messages, and now the calls go straight to voice mail. What is going on? He better be tied to your bed and sleeping off some epic sex hangover."

"Why the hell do you have Jude's number saved in your phone?" Felix demanded.

"Felix! Where the fuck have you been? I was worried sick about you. I didn't get a moment of sleep."

"You have to answer my question first," Felix said stubbornly.

"Fine." He imagined the dramatic eye roll which had probably accompanied Ree's exasperated tone of voice. "The two of us had lunch a few times over the years since we both lived and worked in Atlanta."

"Did you talk about me?"

"That's two questions," Ree said. "I can't believe you have the audacity to ask me that." Okay, so they hadn't talked about him. "You should be glad you're not within slapping distance."

"I'm sorry I missed all your calls. My phone was damaged in the fire." Ree gasped. "Fire? What fire?"

Uh-oh. Felix had assumed her frantic calls were due to the explosion, but he'd thought wrong. He gave her the same spiel about the shorted wire and subsequent fire. He left out the explosion part, neglected to mention the Southern mafia connection, and didn't tell her he was hurt. "Jude is going to take me to the cell phone store when it opens."

"So, you and Jude, huh?" Felix heard some shuffling, then Ree spoke away from the phone. "Babe, you owe me twenty bucks and a foot massage."

"Attaboy, Felix," Stephen said in the background.

"Okay, you have my full attention," Ree said. "Tell me everything and do not leave out a single detail."

Felix laughed. "Why were you frantically calling my phone?"

"You have to answer my question first," Ree said.

"Jude and I have been talking and working through things."

"With or without clothes on?" she asked. Had they been face-to-face, Ree would've been leaning forward and waggling her eyebrows. Nothing was off limits between them. They told each other everything.

"Both."

Ree let out a delightful squeal and followed it up with a lengthy giggle. "It's about time," she said breathlessly.

"For you to tell me what upset you last night," Felix said.

"Oh, Fee. I was calling you because I have exciting news. The absolute best news." Ree sniffled, and Felix knew she was crying.

Thank God they were happy tears, or he'd be driving to Atlanta to fuck somebody up. Ree was a badass and didn't need men fighting her battles for her, but he'd happily stand beside her.

"What is it, Ree?" There was only one thing left in this world Ree wanted. Felix was terrified to hope.

"I'm pregnant," she said before squealing again. "We went in for our physicals and were expecting the results to tell us how difficult it would be for us to conceive together. When the doctor walked into the room with this big smile on her face, I assumed the outlook was good. Then she said, 'I have great news. You don't need my services.' I told her we most definitely did and reminded her that we'd been trying to get pregnant for eighteen months. The doctor smiled and said, 'And you finally did it. Congratulations.'"

Felix's heart swelled and tears stung the back of his eyes. "This is the best news ever. I'm so happy for you and Stephen."

"Felix," Ree said, her voice thick with emotion. "Stephen told me about the conversation he had with you during your birthday dinner. Do you have any idea how much I love you?"

"As much as I love you," Felix said as tears spilled down his face.

"Well, if you and Jude finally stop dicking around—" Ree laughed. "Okay, maybe I have that backward. If you and Jude start dicking around and build a life together, I would happily be your surrogate if you want to have a baby."

"Ree, I don't know what to say." He'd never thought of himself as father material before, but he could easily picture Jude cradling a newborn against his chest.

"Thank you is a good start," she said.

"Thank you."

They talked about all the baby plans they were making even though she was terrified. Ree spoke of relying on her faith to get through the anxieties. Felix wasn't the praying type. Maybe it was because he never considered himself worthy of God's love or His mercy. He would pray for her, Stephen, and the baby.

Ree moaned on the other end of the connection. "Oh, yeah, right there, baby."

Felix snorted. "Um, should I let you go?"

"Stephen is paying up the foot rub he owes me for betting against me. I told him it was only a matter of time before you and Jude found your way back to each other. Haven't I been saying this since our freshman year?"

"I think you've mentioned it once or twice."

"Ree is all-knowing."

Felix laughed so hard he nearly dropped Jude's phone in the pool. "Ree is also talking about herself in the third person."

"Gross. Oh, not you, baby. Dig your thumb in my arch again. Oh! Ohhhh. Felix, I gotta go. These pregnancy hormones are intense." She lowered her voice. "Some of them make me happy, and Stephen even happier, if you know what I mean."

Felix laughed. "Attagirl."

They said their goodbyes, then Felix set the phone on the concrete next to him. Jude joined him a few moments later, carrying two cups of coffee. He handed them both to Felix to hold while he sat down and dangled his legs in the pool too. Felix passed the cup with creamer and sugar to Jude and kept the black coffee for himself.

"Your house is beautiful, but this is my favorite part." Felix looked at the lush landscaping surrounding the pool. "It's so peaceful."

"Maybe too peaceful. Attack peacocks would add a nice flair."

Felix laughed. "I could bring Pete and Pearl over for a visit."

"What a sight that would be. You driving your pet peacocks around town."

"They're not my peacocks," Felix said.

"So you say."

"So I know."

They bantered back and forth for a bit before Jude set his cup of coffee down and jumped into the pool.

"You're so mean," Felix said, not bothering to hide his pout. Then Jude made his intentions known when he slid his hand up Felix's thigh. Felix quickly changed his tune when Jude stripped his borrowed shorts off and took Felix's dick in his mouth. Felix loved the feel of Jude's firm lips working his shaft up and down, bringing him to a shattering climax, which Felix repaid on his knees in the outdoor shower.

The trip to the cellular store was quick but costly. Usually, that kind of unexpected purchase would cause Felix a fuck ton of anxiety. What if he lost his job down the road? It could be money he'd need someday. The questions would typically play out endlessly, causing bouts of insomnia. Today, he was calmer. Maybe it was because of the man beside him, or the mind-blowing orgasms received from said man. Or, perhaps it was from Felix's conviction that Cameron Spencer would pay for all the damage he'd caused—one way or the other.

Felix was shocked by the volume of missed calls, voicemail messages, and texts. There were several calls from a number he didn't recognize, but the caller didn't leave a voice mail. Felix read his texts and listened to all his messages before replying or returning calls in the order of priority, starting with Minerva. He assured her he was fine and didn't mention anything about the real cause of the explosion. He gave her the same song and dance as everyone else; the fewer people who knew the truth, the better.

The frantic messages from Rocky triggered reactions in Felix, ranging from humor to astonishment that this man was his friend. It made his insides feel like a glass of Sprite—bubbly and refreshing.

The messages that surprised him the most were from Royce Locke, a Savannah detective in the Major Crimes Unit. His partner and boyfriend, Sawyer Key, had gone to Emory with Felix and Jude. The guys were the ones who pulled Felix, Jonah, and Rocky into the Franco Humphries investigation. If Royce was calling, did it mean SPD had already figured out the car fire wasn't accidental?

Felix called Royce as soon as they were back in Jude's car.

"Who have you pissed off now?" Royce asked once greetings were exchanged.

Felix bristled. "What a rude assumption."

Royce laughed. "Come on. You know the effect you have on people. How are you feeling?"

"As good as can be expected," Felix replied vaguely. He wasn't sure how much he wanted to tell Royce without discussing the facts with Jonah and Rocky first.

"When and where is the posse meeting this morning? Sawyer and I want to be there."

"Posse? Are Butch Cassidy and the Sundance Kid up to no good again?"

"Cut the bullshit," Royce groused. "I got the truth out of Rocky last night when he was frantically looking for you."

"Then why did you ask who I'd pissed off if you already knew?"

"I wanted to see how much you were willing to tell me."

"Not much," Felix admitted.

"And yet, I'm surprised and hurt."

It was Felix's turn to scoff. "Were you assigned to my case?"

"Yep, so I started calling you. Then I called Jacobs since I couldn't get in touch with you. He found out you left with Arrow, and I tried calling him a few times, but I guess he was busy tending to your injuries."

"You could've left a message," Felix countered. "You could've driven over to Jude's house if you were anxious."

"Rocky told me not to," Royce said.

"And you listened?"

"Jacobs might be an annoying asshole, but the man has excellent instincts, and they've served him well as a PI. He was worried about your injuries but seemed relieved once he found out who you were with."

"I'm only a little roughed up and feeling pretty grateful at the moment," Felix said. "I have to call Rocky and figure out when and where we're meeting. One of us will text you."

"See that it happens. There will be hell to pay if I have to exude any effort in tracking your asses down."

Felix snorted. "Royce, your threat might've worked if I haven't personally seen you baby talk to your enormous cat. One of us will call you." It wouldn't be him, but he'd be sure to pass along Royce's message.

Felix disconnected the call. "Speaking of cats, can we run by my place so I can change my clothes and beg my cat's forgiveness."

"You have a cat?"

"The cat has me," Felix countered. "Pul came with the house."

"Pull? As in you're pulling my leg."

"One L. It's short for Pulitzer."

Jude laughed.

Felix scowled. Did Jude think Felix's dream of being awarded the prestigious journalism prize was hilarious? "What's so funny?"

"I have a terrarium in my home office. Guess what my turtle's name is."

Felix tried to think what a broadcast journalist's equivalent to a Pulitzer was. He grinned when it came to him. "Peabody."

"Yep."

They headed to Felix's house, where he phoned his claim into his insurance company before searching out his feisty feline. Pul was stretched across Felix's bed like he didn't have a care in the world, but he glared at his human with eyes that promised revenge.

"You still have food and water in your bowl," Felix said. If the cat could roll his eyes or flip him the middle claw, he would've done it. "I've replenished your supplies, my king." Felix curtsied, but Pul yawned as if Felix was boring him.

"That's some cat," Jude said.

Felix smiled. The cat was missing half a tail, a chunk of one ear, and only had one eye. He'd been through hell and back before Felix arrived on the scene. Felix spent a fortune getting rid of his fleas, ear mites, mange, and even his testicles. The last one was still a sore subject, no pun intended. Now Pul was a spoiled house cat who lived a lavish life. "He's a little rough around the edges like me, but we have an understanding."

"This is his house, and you live in it?" Jude asked.

"You're familiar with cats, then?"

Jude laughed. "I've had a few over the years." He approached the bed with his hand out.

"Careful," Felix cautioned. "You might lose a digit. I have plans for all of them later."

Jude grinned impishly over his shoulder before returning his attention to the beast on the bed. "I think you're a magnificent boy."

"Thanks."

Jude laughed at Felix's antics but continued making nice with Pulitzer. The cat sniffed his fingers before looking up at the big man's face. Felix would swear on a stack of Bibles that the feline narrowed his eyes and assessed Jude. Pul must've liked what he saw because he rubbed his head against Jude's outstretched hand and emitted a rattling, rumbly sound.

"That's some purr," Jude said.

"My boy didn't have a lot to be happy about until we met. His skills got rusty."

"Gives you character, doesn't it, handsome?" Jude said, scratching behind the cat's ears with skillful, strong fingers. Pul closed his eyes and leaned harder into the touch. "Too bad. I couldn't win over your human this easy."

"Which time? Then or now? I was pretty much an eager puppy when we met in college. I rolled over and begged you to pet my belly."

Jude laughed. "If only it were that easy." He smoothed his hand a few times over Pulitzer's head before turning to face Felix. "You were suspicious and prickly, and I had to work hard just to get you to speak to me."

"You smiled at me the first day in class, and I was a goner."

"Really?"

Felix nodded. "I turned to see who had entered the classroom behind me."

"I remember." A smiled tugged at Jude's lips.

"I was certain there had to be somebody because why would a guy like you waste those dimples on someone like me?"

Jude pressed his lips against Felix's for a quick kiss. "There was only you."

"I never allowed myself to believe it for long."

"You were stingy with your smiles," Jude said, lowering his hands to Felix's hips. "You were more guarded than anyone I'd ever met."

"I made you work harder than anyone you'd ever met too."

Jude smiled. "True. It's why I respected you so much. You just couldn't see it."

"Hope, faith, and trust were luxuries I couldn't afford back then."

"And now?" Jude asked.

Their conversation had taken a melancholy turn, but they couldn't hide from their past. It would always be there, waiting to throw a wrench in the cogs, unless they took the time to repair their tattered relationship properly. Felix took a deep breath and took a giant leap.

"I'm a man who's no longer afraid to want the finer things in life. *You* are the finest of them all."

"You're late," Rocky said when they arrived at Jonah's house ninety minutes later.

"I'm injured," Felix said but did a horrible job of keeping the smirk off his face. Was it his fault Jude couldn't keep his hands to himself when he helped Felix change shirts? No. He didn't know how they'd ended up naked in bed and had lost all track of time.

Jonah and Rocky scowled, Avery laughed, and the two detectives looked like they heard the punchline but not the joke. Then Avery got up and crossed the room to shake Jude's hand and make introductions.

"What's going on?" Rocky whispered once Jude was engaged in a conversation with Royce and Sawyer.

"What does it look like?" Jonah countered.

"Not what's going on between Felix and Jude, dumbass. I'd have to be blind not to notice how relaxed Felix is."

"Standing right here," Felix said.

His friends ignored him and kept bantering back and forth.

"I don't think we should trust Arrow," Jonah said.

"I trust Felix's judgment. No way he bangs someone who just tried to kill him."

"Thanks, Major," Felix said.

Rocky either didn't hear Felix or just ignored him. "I'm sure Jude wants to choke Felix a little, but kill him? Nah."

Felix rolled his eyes. "Fuck you, Major."

"If not Arrow, who? Spencer?" Jonah asked.

"Jack Mercy tried to kill me," Felix said loud enough to get everyone's attention.

"Start from the fucking beginning," Sawyer said. "Don't leave a damn thing out."

So, they did. Felix did most of the talking, but Jonah, Rocky, and Jude injected bits and pieces to enhance the big picture.

"Let me get this straight," Royce said once they were done. "Your father was on the verge of turning evidence over to the FBI twenty-plus years ago but was executed before he could do it. Either that, or the person he'd given it to at the FBI was dirty and had alerted Mercy."

"I don't think it was the latter because someone ransacked our house while we were at my father's funeral," Jude said.

"Talk about adding insult to injury," Jonah remarked.

"If they'd waited to kill my dad until after he handed over the evidence to the FBI, then they wouldn't have needed to search our house."

"There are a few exceptions to your logic," Sawyer said. "The evidence might've been encrypted, and your father kept the key as an insurance policy, or he didn't turn over all the evidence. Mercy still would've wanted to silence your dad."

"Since they left you and your mother alone all these years, it's safe to say they either found what they were looking for or decided it never existed," Jonah said.

Jude nodded. "I agree."

"Once you started digging around in Mercy's business, he showed back up and warned you away," Royce said. "Why? The man doesn't show leniency to his enemies."

"My mother said there's a code of honor they must abide by. No kids or families are to be harmed."

Avery tilted his head. "I'd always heard that but didn't know if it was true."

"It is, at least in my situation," Jude replied.

Royce tapped a long finger over his lips before lowering his hand. "Hear me out. What if the evidence does exist, but your dad squirreled it away so good that they couldn't find it? Once you started asking questions, Mercy got worried you might've found it. You move back to Savannah, and not long after, Felix picks up the same trail and follows it."

Jude heaved a deep sigh. "It's possible, but I don't know where my father would've hidden it. My mother never received a bill for a storage unit or a safe deposit box from her bank. I can't think of any place that would've allowed my dad to pay for storage for nearly two decades in advance."

"There were no hidden safes or rooms in your parents' home?" Sawyer asked.

Jude shook his head. "I can't even prove Mercy was responsible for me losing my job or was the one who blew up Felix's car."

"I thought you said he called and taunted you," Royce said with a scowl.

"He asked if I'd received his message," Jude replied. "The man is no fool."

"Our only hope at this point is to tie the person who set the car bomb to Mercy," Sawyer said. "We're pulling CCTV and video footage from the surrounding businesses. Hopefully, they caught something."

"We'll interview everyone from Spencer Auto Mall who touched your car," Royce added.

"Start with Todd Dartmouth," Felix said. "He's the person who drove it when he dropped it off and picked up the loaner."

Felix doubted Todd had the skill to make a car bomb. He recalled how the guy couldn't make the simplest dishes in home economics and bumbled his way through their various science classes. Besides, Todd didn't have the balls to drive a car he knew was a ticking time bomb. Not many people would take that chance. Still, it made Felix happy to know Sawyer and Royce would make the bully squirm as he'd done to so many other people.

"Jude, I'll make some discreet calls to see if I can find out what happened to your friend Alejandro," Sawyer said. "It's not uncommon for undercover officers to lie low for a while."

"Thanks," Jude said. "I appreciate it."

Royce looked up from the notes he'd taken and pinned Felix with a dark look. "Now, tell me the parts you're leaving out."

Felix held up his hand in surrender. "I've told you everything I know."

"Me too," Jude said.

"Fucking reporters," Royce groused as he shook his head. "Listen, guys. I know how exciting this investigation must seem to all of you, but it's obviously dangerous. Leave it to the professionals to investigate."

"Isn't he GBI?" Jude asked, pointing at Jonah.

"He is," Sawyer said. "He's not assigned to work on this case. If that changes, he won't be able to share the details of the investigation."

"Right, Big Guy?" Royce asked.

"Yep," Jonah said with an easy smile.

"What about you, Jacobs?" Royce said. "You have anything you want to share with the rest of the class? You've been awfully quiet."

"It's never a good sign," Sawyer said.

"Both of you are so annoying," Rocky replied. "If you're not making kissy faces at one another, you're tag-teaming some unsuspecting schmuck who's only trying to do his job."

"You're laying it on a bit thick, don't you think?" Royce asked.

"He does sound like a private eye from an old movie."

Rocky smirked and flipped them off.

Royce and Sawyer stood. "Don't investigate this any further. There must be dozens of other cases you guys can look into for your podcast that won't result in your death."

"Of course," Felix said.

"They're not going to listen to us," Sawyer said to Royce.

Royce looked around the room, making eye contact with each of them. "Nope."

After Royce and Sawyer left, Felix looked at Rocky, Jonah, and Avery. "Well, are we going to walk away from this or keep digging?"

Rocky's wicked grin was Felix's answer. "I got the names of the Second Chance Program enrollees working at the Savannah dealership."

"Marla the Magnificent is processing them now," Jonah said. "We'll tell Royce and Sawyer if she uncovers anything pertinent to their investigation."

"What are you going to do about your car?" Avery said.

"I reported the claim to my insurance company this morning. My agent said my policy will cover the loss and even provide a rental car until they make an offer. There's more to consider here than just the car. What about my injuries and destroyed phone? Why should I have to eat the cost?"

"You shouldn't," Rocky replied.

"If I'm going to continue spouting the cover story about my car catching fire due to mechanical malfunction, then I would logically contact the dealership and insist on restitution."

"Naturally," Jonah said.

"I have to decide if I do it in person or through an attorney. Which would make a bigger impact?"

"A letter from a lawyer," Avery said. "Even Spencer would have to take notice."

"It might cost a lot of money," Jonah said.

"I have money tucked away if that's the option I choose," Felix replied.

"You won't have to pay," Jude said. "I know a great attorney who'd represent you pro bono."

"Who?" Felix asked.

"Jillian Sharkey."

"You know The Shark?" Jonah asked.

"I do," Jude replied proudly.

Jillian Sharkey was one of the fiercest attorneys in the country. She'd made a name for herself by filing the most significant class-action lawsuits against American corporations whose gross negligence caused people to become sick, severely injured, or had resulted in their death. Sometimes her enemies were conglomerates that tainted water sources by dumping toxins into the ground, and other times, it was automotive manufacturers who put the almighty dollar before recalling vehicles with defective safety equipment. Her latest target was the Catholic Church for failing to protect children from predatory priests.

Felix had watched an interview with her the previous week where the talk show host said she was either the devil or a democrat. Lisa Loren, the host, made it clear she didn't like either one.

Jillian had smirked and said, "One of those is true. I'll let you figure out which one." Then she doubled down. "My next target will be any religious institution that has participated in or encouraged conversion therapy."

Once Lisa had picked her jaw up off the ground, she said, "So, you're going to war with Christianity."

Jillian gave Lisa a look that shouted "you poor pitiful soul." Her words had been much more eloquent though. "I *am* a Christian, Ms. Loren. I'm looking to take down fake Christians who twist words and phrases from the Bible and use them to cause great harm, especially to children. No one is above the law. I will not allow rapists and abusers to hide behind a pulpit."

Felix studied Jude's smug face. "Why would an attorney of her stature have time for such an insignificant issue?"

"Because she's my mother, and *you* are very significant to *me*."

CHAPTER 24

Felix paused midway through the newsroom on Monday morning when he realized everyone was staring at him.

"What? You've never seen a man who was nearly blown up before?" he asked.

"We've never heard you whistle before," Sanja said. She slid her glasses higher up her nose to see Felix better.

"Or smiling," said Jerry Symon.

"Sanja, I'm sure you have a new restaurant to rip apart," Felix said before turning his attention to the other brave soul who spoke up. "And you, Jerry. Wasn't there a Little League tournament this weekend that needs your attention?"

Both of them continued to stare at Felix like he'd grown two new heads, so Felix continued to his office without further comment. He screeched to a halt when he saw Jimmy waiting outside his closed door.

"Oh, hi," Jimmy said, straightening away from the door. He held a notebook against his chest. "I wasn't sure you still wanted to do this after the weekend you had. Are you okay?"

Do this? It took Felix a minute to remember the email he'd sent the rookie reporter before leaving the office on Friday evening. So much had happened since then, it was hard to believe only a few days had passed.

"I'm fine, Jimmy. Thanks for asking."

Felix opened the door and gestured for Jimmy to enter the room.

The younger man hesitated on the threshold. "I can come back later if this isn't a good time."

Felix sighed. "Jimmy?"

"Yes?"

"Do you want my help or not?

"Of course. Your email made my weekend. It quite possibly made my entire year so far." Jimmy's face fell and he squirmed a little. "God, I sound pathetic. You must think I'm a loser."

"No, but I can see I have my work cut out for me." Felix clasped the man on his thin shoulder. "Are you ready to hear rule number one?" Jimmy nodded eagerly. "It doesn't matter what others think about you. They don't get to decide who you are or where you belong. They sure as hell don't decide your capabilities."

Jimmy's smile was tenuous and timid. "That's where I want to be, but how do I get there?"

"You fake it until you believe it. One day you'll wake up, and you won't be pretending any longer."

"You make it seem so simple."

Felix grinned and gave him a good-natured shove into his office. "It's harder than it sounds. The biggest obstacle you'll face along the journey is yourself. I have some tips."

Felix coached Jimmy for the next half hour by sharing personal stories with him about Felix's triumphs and failures. The young reporter listened carefully and asked the right questions.

"You're great at writing and even interviewing people when you forget about your insecurities."

"Writing comes naturally to me."

"It shows," Felix said.

"Thanks." Jimmy's blush was kind of cute. He broke eye contact and looked at the notes he'd made.

"Your homework is to write an article about our training session. It will be for my eyes only, but I want you to pretend as if it will go on the front page of the paper. I want to know what you've gleaned from my wisdom and the steps you'll take to achieve more confidence."

"Easy enough," Jimmy said as he wrote down his assignment.

"I want you to include your observations about me."

Jimmy jerked his gaze upward. "Um…"

"I'm fully aware of how I come across sometimes. You cannot write an honest piece if you're afraid to hurt my feelings."

"But I r-respect you so m-much though," Jimmy stammered.

Felix met Jimmy's timid gaze until the man stopped shaking. "And you'd like mine in return. Am I right?"

"Well, I know it's a lot to hope for, but—"

"Yes or no, Jimmy."

The reporter's cheeks blushed even darker. "Yes. Someday."

"Rule number two. No caveats." Felix pointed to his notebook. "Write it down, Jimmy."

"No caveats," Jimmy repeated as he wrote it down in his notebook.

"I am a person who respects honesty, even when it's not something I want to hear. The harsh reality is that life doesn't come tied up in pretty bows. It's gritty, sometimes ugly, but those things make the beauty so much more vibrant when it shines through."

"Like a rainbow after an ugly storm?"

"Yes." *Or like spending the weekend in the arms of the only man you've ever loved.* Felix kept that tidbit private. "You have your marching orders. Your journey to confidence begins now."

"Yes, of course." Jimmy rose from his chair. He took a deep breath, then began to morph right in front of Felix's eyes. The young reporter stood taller, squared his shoulders, and lifted his chin a few notches higher, and met Felix's gaze.

"Attaboy, Jimmy."

Not long after Jimmy left, Minerva knocked on the doorframe. "How are you?" she asked, stepping inside his office.

"Stiff and sore, but I'm on the mend."

Minerva handed him a flash drive. "This is a copy of everything I emailed over to the police. I wanted you to have a copy since we're fast approaching the time when the system will start recording over it."

"Thanks," Felix said, looking at the hot pink piece of plastic. "Did you look at it?"

"I'm a reporter first and an editor second. Of course, I did."

"And?"

Minerva sat down and crossed her legs. "A panel van pulled up from the west side of the parking lot and stopped in front of your car at about five thirty. It had tinted windows, so you couldn't get a look at the driver."

"And since he came from the west, the passenger side of the van would've faced the camera," Felix said. "So he was able to use the van as a shield to get out, set the explosives, and leave without getting caught on film." Felix knew it was too much to hope for anything less. "Was everyone gone by then?"

"The parking lot was mostly empty," Minerva replied. "I hadn't left yet and neither had a few other staff members. Detective Key said he will interview each of us today. The van wasn't there when I left, and I didn't spot it in the vicinity. The tinted windows make it stand out, and I think I would've noticed it hanging around."

Felix thought it was more likely the tinted windows looked more ominous because she knew what happened next. He held up the flash drive. "Thanks for making a copy for me. I'll take a look at it tonight." Felix didn't expect to find anything useful, but he wasn't willing to throw it in the bottom of a drawer and forget about it either.

After Minerva left, Felix had a hard time sinking into his work. It was something that rarely occurred, but could anyone blame him? He figuratively grabbed himself by the scruff and forced himself to focus on his outstanding tasks. Jude sent a text around eleven asking what he wanted to eat for lunch. They had a teleconference with Jillian Sharkey, aka Jude's mom, planned at one o'clock. This was one of the moments when Felix was sure the events from the previous few weeks were nothing more than a dream.

He'd known Jude's mom was a lawyer, but he had no idea she was The Shark. He'd been so intimidated when Jude called her over the weekend to give her an update. Jill, as she'd insisted he call her, morphed from concerned, to angry, to outright furious by the time they told her everything.

"Jude," she'd said. "Why couldn't you have let this go as I asked you?"

"This sounds familiar," Felix whispered into Jude's ear.

"Because I'm your son," Jude responded.

"Flattery will not save your ass, young man," she'd replied, but the fury in her voice ebbed a little. "Why didn't you tell me at least?"

"I didn't want to tarnish your reputation," Jude had explained. "My goal was to handle this in a way that kept your name away from it. You shouldn't pay for Dad's mistakes."

"Nor should Felix sacrifice his life for them," Jill had said. "Give me the names of these potential shell companies, and I'll start working on it. We'll regroup on Monday."

Monday had arrived, and Felix was just as nervous as he'd been over the weekend. He wanted to make a good impression on Jill, and not because she was a kickass attorney. She was Jude's mother, and he adored her. Of course, Felix wanted Jill to like him. But if she didn't, it wouldn't change anything. He'd try his best to meet her in the middle, but he wasn't giving Jude up again. Not for anyone, including the woman who'd given him life.

Felix smiled as he read Jude's text. He told Jude to surprise him, then set the alarm on his watch to go off at noon. He tended to get lost in his work, and he didn't want to be late.

The receptionist at Channel Eleven perkily smiled when he arrived. She handed him a visitor's badge and started to give him directions to Jude's office.

"I know the way," he said.

Stopping outside Jude's office, Felix took a few deep breaths before knocking. The door opened before his fist could land against the wood. Jude tugged him inside, shut them away in his lair, and kissed Felix until he was breathless.

"Hiya," Felix said. "Miss me?" It hadn't been that long since they'd crawled out of his bed and got ready for the day.

"Terribly." Jude kissed Felix again until another knock interrupted them. "Lunch has arrived." Jude smoothed a hand over the front of his shirt and readjusted his semi-erection before answering. He accepted the food, tipped the delivery man, and shut the door. "Steak hoagies, French fries, and Sprite."

It had been Felix's favorite meal in college, and it warmed his heart that Jude still remembered those little details about him.

"Perfect."

They enjoyed their sandwiches while getting caught up on their morning so far. Jude wasn't surprised to hear the guy who'd set the bomb was wise enough to do it without getting caught on camera.

"He set the damn thing during broad daylight," Jude said. "Either his balls are bigger than his brain, or he'd taken the time to scope out the security camera situation beforehand."

"He also knew how to avoid CCTV." The security measure didn't encompass the entire city, mostly just the touristy parts.

Jude shrugged. "They might pick him up elsewhere in the city. All they need is a quick glance at the license plate."

Felix held up crossed fingers.

They'd just finished tidying up their lunch mess when Jude's mom called. He put her on speakerphone but kept the volume as low as possible.

"Hi, honey," Jill said to Jude. "I hope you're having a good day so far."

Without looking away from Felix, Jude said, "It's going great."

His lusty gaze made it clear Jude was thinking of the way they'd started off their day and the kisses they'd exchanged at lunchtime. It should've seemed weird considering Jude's mom was on the phone, but he only felt desired.

Jill laughed, breaking their trance. "I bet," she said wryly. She wasn't the least bit confused about the source of Jude's good mood. "I'm about to make it even better."

"Impossible," Jude countered.

Jill responded with an indecipherable sound.

"Mom, are you giggling?" Jude asked.

"The Shark doesn't giggle," Felix said.

"She does when her son is happy," Jill told them.

Felix tried to dig deep for some kind of comeback, but he'd melted like ice cream in August.

Jude leaned forward for a quick kiss. "Wow, Mom. You've rendered Felix speechless."

"I'm just getting started too." Jillian laid out all the reasons she thought The Camelot Corporation was a front for illegal activity. "One of the best ways to launder money is to create fake third-party service providers, like the gap insurance and extended warranty companies in this case. They'll have all the appearances of a legitimate business and will often obtain real tax ID numbers. Spencer didn't cut corners here like many do, which enables him to fly under the radar. The websites for the third-party service providers and The Camelot Corporation, although basic, are fully functioning. The only obvious flags are the lack of phone numbers and the generic email addresses provided for their service and claims department. Did you ever get a response when you emailed the extended warranty company?"

"I didn't," Felix replied. "They weren't kicked back as an invalid email address either. I paid a visit to Peachtree Tower when I was in Atlanta but couldn't get upstairs to check out their offices."

"Luckily, I have a friend who works in Peachtree," Jill said.

Jude snorted. "Mom, it's okay if you admit Stedman is your boyfriend."

"I'm too old to have a boyfriend."

"You're never too old," Jude said.

"This isn't the time or place to have this discussion *again*," she admonished.

Jude's eyes glittered like sapphires. He was enjoying her discomfort. "Yes, ma'am."

"As I was saying, I visited my friend who works in the same tower. I veered off course to check out The Camelot Corporation's office."

"And?" Felix asked.

Jill laughed. "You're as bad as my son. I was getting there. The office was locked."

"Were there any lights on inside?" Jude asked.

"The door was solid wood with no glass inserts, so I couldn't tell."

Felix stood up and started pacing. He thought best on his feet. "That alone isn't enough to prove anything, I guess."

"I agree, which is why I stopped the mail clerk who was making his rounds when I was there. I noticed there wasn't any mail in the box by the door. He informed me that he's never seen anyone going in or out of the office, but someone collects mail from their box weekly. It usually occurs over the weekend when he isn't working."

"There's not a lot we can do with the information," Jude said.

"I could set up a toll-free number, then run an ad asking people to contact us if they've ever purchased an extended warranty or gap insurance policy through Spencer Auto Mall that wasn't honored," Jill said.

Felix halted his pacing. "I'd rather not tip our hand yet."

"I agree," Jill said. "The other option is to keep digging and look for concrete proof."

"Which takes time," Jude countered.

"It does, but the devil is in the details," Jill said. "But that doesn't mean we sit on our hands. We can focus on the immediate concern, which is making Spencer pay for reparations to Felix. I've drafted a letter for your approval, Felix. I'm going to email it to you as soon as we hang up. If you find it satisfactory, I'll send it out via certified mail this afternoon."

"I'll get back to you right away."

"I got to run, guys. I have a pretrial hearing this afternoon, and I need to go over some last-minute changes with my team."

"Thanks so much, Jill," Felix said.

"You're welcome," she replied warmly.

"Love you, Mom."

"Love you more."

Felix received an email on his phone as soon as Jude disconnected the call. He opened it up and read the personal note she wrote to him.

Felix,

Please let me know if you have any changes you wish to make. By the way, I haven't seen my son this happy since his freshman year at Emory. I'll never forget the joy in his voice when he spoke about you. I look forward to finally meeting you in person.

xoxoxo

Jill

Her words moved him so deeply that it took three attempts to open the attached letter to Spencer. The draft was professional, precise, and perfect, which is what he told her in his response. Felix ended the email by expressing his eagerness to meet her too.

When he finished, he glanced up just as he almost collided with Jude. Felix pulled up quickly but tripped and stumbled into the bookshelf hard enough to make the Chipper Jones baseball roll off the shelf and hit the floor with a thud.

"Oh shit," Felix said, quickly retrieving the ball. "I'm so sorry."

"Why are you sorry? You're not the one who broke my souvenir box," Jude said. "The cleaning staff accidentally knocked it off the shelf this weekend. They left an apology note on my desk."

Felix studied the box closer. The glass case was gone, and one of the metal prongs holding the ball was bent at an awkward angle, which was why it had fallen off just now. But there was something else off about it. The wood was sticking up weirdly at one corner.

"Hold this," Felix said, handing the ball to Jude. "I bet I can fix this box. I've gotten handy at rehab projects." The wood was smooth and faded from age, but it could be sanded and stained. Felix wiggled the metal piece that held the ball, and the entire top of the trophy box snapped off in his hand. "Oh fuck," Felix said. "Jude, I'm—" His voice died when he saw a three-and-a-half-inch floppy disk hidden in the bottom of the box. Felix jerked his head up and met Jude's gaze. "I think I know where your dad hid the evidence on Mercy."

Felix tilted the box to Jude.

Jude swallowed hard as he removed the dark blue disk. "I haven't seen one of these in forever. Who even has the capability of reading data stored on one of these?"

Felix smiled. "I know a guy."

CHAPTER 25

"I got a bad feeling about this," Royce said later that evening when he and Sawyer arrived at Jonah's house.

"It feels like we were just here, doesn't it?" Sawyer said, placing his hands on his lean hips. "If I remember correctly, these knuckleheads promised to keep their noses out of trouble."

"We kept our noses clean," Felix said. "Trouble found us anyway."

"Why am I having a hard time believing you?" Royce asked him.

Felix gestured for the men to join them in the living room. "Because you're stubborn and suspicious."

Sawyer sat down on the loveseat next to his boyfriend. He looked at Jude and said, "I found out your cop buddy is okay."

"Oh, good," Jude said.

"He did have to abandon his undercover persona and is lying low."

"I'm just glad he's safe," Jude said.

Sawyer looked around the room. "You guys asked for a meeting. Tell us everything."

Felix held up the floppy disk. "We found this by sheer accident."

Royce narrowed his eyes. "Why do you sound so defensive?"

"Because you're stubborn and—"

"Suspicious," Royce said. "Yeah, I get it."

"I haven't seen one of those floppy disks in twenty years," Sawyer said. "What is it?"

"We're pretty sure it's the evidence my dad planned to hand over to the FBI," Jude replied.

"Or a copy of what he turned over to them," Felix added.

Royce released a deep breath. "This ought to be good. How did you *accidentally* find it?"

Felix and Jude tag-teamed while telling the story. They left out Jill's involvement because Felix had no intention of actually filing a lawsuit against Spencer. He just wanted to keep up pretenses to buy them time.

"So, what's on the disk?" Sawyer asked.

Jonah handed him a stack of pages he'd printed. "It looks like ledgers and financial documents. I couldn't decipher it, but a forensic accountant could."

"The feds won't be able to charge him with a crime based on this information," Sawyer said. "The statute of limitations for financial crimes was up fifteen to twenty years ago, which was probably why Mercy didn't harass your family."

"If that were the case," Royce said, "why did Mercy turn up the heat on Jude after he interviewed Spencer about his Second Chance Program?"

"I think I know the answer," Jonah said. "This information can't be used to indict Mercy, but it could show a pattern the FBI could use now to infiltrate his current operations. That's why we're giving it to you."

They'd talked about it before Royce and Sawyer arrived. They all agreed that letting the proper authorities investigate Mercy and Spencer from here on out was in everyone's best interest, especially Felix and Jude's. Which brought them to their second reason for inviting the detectives over.

"Don't be mad," Felix said.

Royce groaned. "A conversation that starts out with that phrase never goes well."

"I feel like we're practicing for fatherhood," Sawyer added. "You might as well come clean now. We'll go easier on you."

Jonah cleared his throat. "We obtained a list of the parolees currently working at the Savannah dealership. I plugged them into Marla the Magnificent, and she drew some interesting conclusions."

"Which are?" Royce asked.

Jonah handed him another printout. Royce held it between them so Sawyer could read the report too.

"A document forger, a counterfeiter, and an embezzler walk into a bar," Royce teased as he read.

"Do you have lists of the program enrollees at the other dealerships?" Sawyer asked without looking up from the report.

Jonah nodded. "It's the same kind of offenses. White-collar crimes and con artists."

Sawyer finally looked up when he got to the supercomputer's assessment. "Spencer has put together a crew of individuals who could create a false identity for him."

Felix nodded. "And he's been skimming money off the dealership for who knows how long with his scams."

"Holy fuck," Royce said. "Cameron Spencer is going to disappear."

Sawyer blew out a frustrated breath of air. "And we don't have a single shred of evidence to bring him in for questioning."

Felix wanted to ask about the van and CCTV footage, but he didn't want to make trouble for Minerva. As much as he hated to sit by and do nothing, he trusted Royce and Sawyer to run down every possible lead.

"We'll take all this to Chief Mendoza and find out what he wants to do," Royce said. "We'll apprise you as best we can." He smacked the documents against his palm as he rose to his feet. "Thank you for turning this over to us instead of investigating it on your own."

"It's for the best," Felix said. So why did it feel so wrong?

After Royce and Sawyer left, Rocky checked his watch. "I gotta get going. I have overnight surveillance duties for a client, so I need to get in a nap or else risk falling asleep in my car."

"Overnight surveillance, huh?" Jude asked.

Jonah quirked a brow. "Do we know this client?"

"I bet they just happen to live in Spencer's neighborhood," Avery added.

Rocky winked. "Plausible deniability, gents."

"Be careful," Felix said.

Rocky held up a hand. "Always."

"What are you in the mood to eat?" Jude asked once they'd left Jonah's. "I have a couple of steaks and chicken breasts thawed out." When Felix didn't answer, Jude reached over and covered Felix's hand with his. He must've assumed neither option appealed to Felix because he continued to verbally roll through the alternate choices. "I always have ingredients on hand to make breakfast. I also have spaghetti noodles and a jar of sauce in my pantry." Still no response. "Felix, are you okay?"

Okay. It was such a generic word and didn't come close to describing how Felix felt. As a writer, words were his weapon of choice, and Felix wielded them mercilessly. Fighting wasn't his aim though. Felix found himself stumbling on how to express the emotion swelling inside him. He knew how to communicate fear and fury and a bevy of other feelings. But this was… This was love, and he was fucking clueless.

Felix turned his head and studied Jude as he drove. Jude's face was more angular now, having lost the rounded softness of youth. His mouth was firmer, and he smiled less. The most significant changes were in Jude's eyes though. His navy blue irises were achingly familiar when Felix glimpsed laughter and mirth dancing in them. Other times, Jude's gaze took on the hardness of a predatory bird stalking its prey. And with good reason. Jude's entire life had been turned upside down over the past year.

And who had Jude sought out for help? Who had he trusted with the truth? Felix. He would do everything in his power to help Jude get justice for his father, but it wasn't Felix's primary goal. He wanted to see Jude frown less and smile more. Felix wanted to coax those dimples out of hiding and see laughter return to Jude's eyes.

Jude glanced over at Felix, and his worry was etched in the

furrowed brow and fine line bracketing Jude's mouth. The boy who'd stolen Felix's heart still lived inside the brawny, beautiful man. It was time the two halves joined to form the whole. Felix just wasn't sure how to start the conversation.

Jude pulled over and shifted the car into park. "What's wrong, Ace?"

Felix parted his lips to say something, anything, but the only thing passing through them was a shaky breath. "You told your mom about me back in college." It wasn't a question or accusation. Felix spoke the words with as much awe as he'd felt when he'd read Jill's remark.

"Of course, I told her about you. She heard the happiness in my voice when I called home and saw it on my face when I visited. I wasn't ashamed of you or us."

"She must've thought I was a complete asshole for not giving you a chance to explain the situation with Cooper," Felix said.

Jude shook his head. "I never told her the full story. I just told her I messed up and ruined our relationship."

"Why would you take the full blame?"

"So many reasons. I knew Coop was a problem and should've insisted on a different roommate. I knew you were skittish, and I shouldn't have let things get physical between us until you trusted me."

Felix snorted. "You're analyzing the situation with an adult's brain and not the one belonging to a horny, teenage virgin."

"True," Jude admitted. "When things went tits up, I didn't fight hard enough."

"It wouldn't have worked no matter how hard you tried. I wasn't ready to hear it, let alone believe it." The realization didn't hit Felix between the eyes; it slowly unfurled in his soul like a rare flower that only blooms beneath a full moon during the summer solstice. In this case, it was rarer still and only blooms once in a lifetime. "I think I finally understand the crux of the issue."

"Yeah?"

Felix nodded. "We weren't in the right place in our lives to fully appreciate the connection we shared. We clicked intellectually and physically, but I lagged emotionally. I didn't like myself, so no matter what you said or did, I wouldn't have believed you capable of liking me. It was so much easier to accept betrayal."

Jude leaned forward, pressing his forehead to Felix's. "And now?"

Felix slid his hand into Jude's hair, loving the silky slide of the strands through his fingers. "I'll never fully banish doubt and insecurity, because I've used them as glue to keep the chip on my shoulder in place. But I do like myself, and I really like you."

"Just like?" Jude teased.

It was too soon to claim anything more profound. Just a few weeks ago, Felix refused to admit the truth even to himself. "I like you a whole lot," he said as a nod to compromise.

Jude chuckled, then flashed his dimples at Felix. "Good enough. For now." He gave Felix a quick kiss before straightening in his seat. After checking his mirrors, Jude shifted the car in drive and merged back into traffic. "About dinner? What are you in the mood for?"

"You. All I want is you."

Jude flipped on the turn signal and ducked down the next side street.

"This isn't the way to your house," Felix said.

"Your house is closer."

They pulled up in front of Felix's house a few minutes later. Felix expected Jude to jump out of his car right away, but he cautiously scanned the area.

"Looking for snipers or henchmen?" Felix asked.

Jude scoffed. "Killer peacocks."

"Tracey is still at work, so Pete and Pearl aren't roaming free yet."

Jude wasn't taking any chances. He kept his eyes peeled while they headed toward the house. Felix slid the key into the deadbolt and glanced over his shoulder at Jude as he turned the lock. Jude was braced for attack, and so fucking cute Felix couldn't stop himself from yelling, "Get 'm, Pete," just to watch Jude's reaction.

Jude didn't disappoint. He barreled them through the door and slammed it closed. Felix nearly doubled over laughing at the panicked expression on the big guy's face.

"You little shit," Jude said, lunging for Felix.

Felix had straightened up to his full height just as a muscular body slammed into his chest.

Jude smashed his lips against Felix's, claiming his mouth in a ferocious kiss. Felix reached for Jude's shirt but was careful not to destroy a third one. Jude wasn't nearly as judicious, whipping Felix's polo shirt up and over his head.

"I need you," Jude groaned before pressing hot, open-mouth kisses all along Felix's throat.

Felix pushed the last button free on Jude's dress shirt, then spread the fabric apart. He placed his palms on Jude's lower abdomen and slowly slid them upward until he reached his broad shoulders. Felix shoved the fine material down Jude's muscular arms, reveling in the electricity arcing between them.

"I need you too."

The clothes continued to come off as they made their way to Felix's room. Pulitzer was stretched across his bed when they walked in. The cat opened one eye, saw the men's current condition, and scrammed off the bed.

"He's going to make me pay later, isn't he?" Jude asked.

"Yep. Think you'll regret it?"

Jude slid his hand into Felix's hair, cupping the back of his head to bring his mouth closer. "Not even for a millisecond." Their kiss was long, wet, and breathtaking. "I want to feel you inside me again," Jude whispered once they parted.

Felix ignored the frenzied need spiking in his blood in favor of tempting and teasing Jude. They lay side by side on the bed, kissing and caressing one another as their desire built to a fevered pitch. Jude took both their cocks in his large hand and stroked them together. Felix rolled and massaged Jude's balls because he knew how much the bigger man loved it.

"Playtime is over. Fuck me." Jude rolled to his back and spread his legs, exposing his pucker to Felix. "Lube and condom, Ace," he said when Felix just continued to stare.

How many times had Felix thought about having Jude under him again? Too many to count. No pressure though. He knew exactly how to please this man. Felix grabbed the supplies from the drawer, then kissed a path down Jude's torso, stopping to lave both nipples and nip Jude's navel. Felix lapped the dripping precum from Jude's stomach before he licked and sucked Jude's cock, balls, and taint. Felix blew a stream of air across Jude's pucker and relished the way it quivered in response.

Jude fisted his hand in Felix's hair and lifted his head. "Fuck me."

Felix nipped Jude's inner thigh. "So bossy."

"So bitchy."

Felix crawled up the length of his body. Lust rode him hard, making his aches and pains barely noticeable. Rather than position himself between Jude's thighs, Felix straddled his hips.

"To frot or not to frot, that is the question," Felix said, dribbling lube over their cocks. Felix aligned their erections together, then began grinding his dick against Jude's. "We shared our first few orgasms together like this," Felix said, leaning over Jude.

"Until we got braver," Jude said, cupping Felix's face and pulling him down for a kiss so tender it made Felix lose his rhythm.

Felix opened the condom and rolled it down his shaft before pouring lube on his fingers. He worked Jude's ass until the big man's moaning turned into curses and kinky threats. After slicking up his dick, Felix pressed the head of his erection against Jude's pucker. He pushed past the first ring of muscles and stopped to let Jude adjust.

"Christ, you feel so good," Felix said, closing his eyes and breathing through the urge to plunge deep inside Jude.

Jude reached down and grabbed Felix's ass with both hands, drawing Felix in deeper into his clench until his balls slapped against Jude's taut flesh. Warmth enveloped Felix's cock, but it paled in comparison to the peace spreading through his body.

"So, this is what it feels like to come home," Felix said, pressing his chest against Jude's.

Jude smiled, and his eyes shone with promises Felix wanted to hang his hat on. Not just tonight. Every night. Felix battled through the frenetic urge to feast and devour in favor of sipping and savoring. He pushed them toward the edge, then pulled them back until avoiding the fall was no longer a possibility. They plummeted together, something they'd never done before.

Felix tried to ease out of him, but Jude tightened his grip around Felix.

"Stay. I like you right here," Jude said.

"Let me get rid of the condom and grab a washcloth. I'll be right back."

Jude unlocked his legs from Felix's lower back, and Felix nipped Jude's pouting lower lip. Felix kept his word, returning to Jude as quickly as he could. They lay together in a tangle of arms and legs, kissing and touching just like they had when they first got on the bed.

"Are you ready to talk about dinner yet?" Jude asked.

Felix chuckled. "What is with you and—" A loud screech cut Felix off.

"Help!" yelled a man from outside.

Jude stiffened and looked around the room as if the peacocks from hell were hiding under the bed. "What the hell is going on?"

Felix got off the bed as fast as he could, ignoring his protesting body. "We have a visitor."

Jude jumped off the bed too, and they quickly donned pants before running out of the room. By the time they reached the door, Pearl had joined Pete, so the screeching had doubled, and so did the panicked request for help.

"I don't fucking believe this," Felix said when he saw who the peacocks had pinned up against the garage.

"Who the fuck is that?" Jude asked.

"Todd Dartmouth. He's the douchebag bully who made my life hell in school. He's also the guy who delivered the car that nearly killed me when it blew up."

"Get him, Pete," Jude yelled.

Pete and Pearl both let out a battle cry before they took a swipe at Todd's crotch.

"I wasn't involved in trying to kill you, Felix," Todd said, trying to dance out of their way. "You gotta believe me."

"Why should I listen to you?" Felix asked.

"I think someone is trying to kill you."

Felix whistled, and the birds backed away a few feet. "Don't make any sudden moves," he cautioned Todd. Felix whistled again, and the birds slowly withdrew before turning and trotting off around the side of the house to ogle the fishpond.

Todd blew out a relieved breath, then started walking toward the house.

"Stop right there," Felix said before Todd reached the small walkway to his porch. "I'm not about to invite you in for tea and a chat. Say what you came to say and get out of here."

Todd nodded. "I didn't have anything to do with your car. I tried calling you Friday night as soon as it happened, but you didn't answer your phone." That explained the calls from the unknown number.

"My phone was destroyed in the explosion," Felix said. A slight exaggeration. "Why didn't you just leave a message?"

Todd shrugged. "I should have but decided I wanted to tell you to your face that I didn't set that car bomb."

"Who said anything about a car bomb?" Jude asked.

"I was told the fire was caused by an electrical short," Felix added.

"Neither of you are that stupid. Cops have been sniffing around the dealership all day. They think someone tried to blow you up. Detectives interviewed anyone who so much as looked at your car, including me."

"You were the last person to drive it before handing the keys to me," Felix pointed out. "Of course, they wanted to speak to you."

"Have you ever considered the police suspect the fire is an act of vandalism and not attempted murder?" Jude asked.

Felix wanted to kiss Jude for thinking fast on his feet.

"Whatever their reason, I didn't have anything to do with it. I just wanted you to know," Todd said.

"Why?" Felix asked.

"Look, I know I've acted like a complete asshole over the years, but I don't want you dead."

"Good to know. You can go now," Felix said. Todd had been sorely mistaken if he'd expected a sappy ending like in one of the Hallmark movies.

"I want to tell you something else. I think it's important," Todd said. "Have you ever heard about Spencer's Second Chance Program?"

"Vaguely," Felix replied.

Todd gave him a brief overview of the program, then said, "Half of the enrollees didn't show up for work today. Don't you think that's strange?"

He did, but Felix shrugged casually. "This is information you should tell the police, not me."

"Okay. I tried," Todd said, throwing up his arms and stalking back to his vehicle.

Jude and Felix went back inside once he drove away.

"None of the men currently participating in the program have a history of violent crimes," Felix said. "Why would they run?"

"Because they might be connected to someone who is more violent," Jude suggested.

"Or because they've lived out their usefulness, and Spencer no longer requires their services."

Jude narrowed his eyes. "He has the documents he needs and plenty of money tucked away offshore. He's about to make his move."

Felix nodded. "I'll call Rocky."

CHAPTER 26

"**A**t least this stakeout is more romantic than the last one," Felix said one week later as he leaned against Jude in the stern of an aluminum jon boat.

"Mmmhmmm," Jude said, nuzzling his nose against Felix's neck.

"Speak for yourself," Rocky grumbled from the bow. "In fact, don't speak at all. We're supposed to be sneaking up on the backside of Spencer's property under cover of darkness. The sound of you two making out is going to give us away."

Felix felt Jude tense against him and knew his big guy was about to go toe to toe with Major. *Again.* Felix had been confident that Rocky and Jude would get along once Felix set the record straight, but Rocky hadn't softened toward Jude much. Felix thought the stakeout would be an excellent opportunity for them to get to know each other better. Wrong again. Rather than referee another argument, Felix took one for the team and pressed his lips against Jude's. He hadn't planned to let his hands roam over Jude's sexy body but couldn't seem to help himself.

"I'm wearing night vision goggles, Fee. Maybe you halt your hand at his waistband unless you plan on giving me a really good show."

Rocky's voice broke the sensual spell Felix had been under. "Sorry, Major."

"God, I'm acting like a complete asshole," Rocky said a moment later. "I'm the one who's sorry."

"What's bothering you?" Felix asked his friend. "Besides the fact that we might've been way off about Spencer planning to leave town."

The Spencers lived in a gated community in Isle of Hope. The secluded location prevented Felix and company from watching the house for any signs of unusual activity. Not that they expected to see moving vans parked outside their estate or anything glaringly obvious. The team had settled for randomly tailing the couple when their work schedules permitted. If the Spencers' routines this past week were anything to go by, they lived a busy but dull life.

Cameron worked, played golf, and sat on committees. Brigitte spent most of her time chauffeuring their preteens, a twelve-year-old blond boy who was the spitting image of his father, and a ten-year-old girl whose red hair was a few shades lighter than her mother's. The kids had at least one activity a day, sometimes two or three. When she wasn't with her children, Brigitte was playing tennis or also serving on a committee. There were absolutely no signs that either of the Spencers planned to abandon their lives like snakes shedding their skin. Which is why Felix, Rocky, and Jude were in an aluminum boat with a small trolling motor on the Skidaway River at ten o'clock at night. It was the only way to get eyes on the property that backed up to the waterway.

"It's nothing and everything, I guess," Rocky replied. The man was such a curious enigma. "Whatever the cause, I shouldn't be taking it out on you and fuckface."

"Hey," Jude said. "Don't call Felix hateful names."

Rocky snorted, and it was the closest thing to a laugh Felix had heard all week. "Maybe you're not completely awful, Arrow."

"Aww, shucks."

"Felix obviously likes you, and I trust his judgment," Rocky added.

Jude chuckled. "You're too kind."

Felix more than liked Jude. He was head over heels in love and felt like a kid again. Each new day was a different discovery about Jude that entrenched the man deeper inside Felix's soul. Jude was determined to make friends with Pete and Pearl and researched ways he could endear himself to the peacocks. One night, he showed up with a box of live crickets he'd purchased from a pet store. Pete and Pearl went crazy eating the insects but still cornered Jude against the house the next morning when he'd tried to leave for work. Mostly, Felix loved how he could just be himself around Jude.

He was enough.

And he learned new things about himself, too, once he'd let his guard down. He liked making Jude happy and finding ways to draw out the dimples. He'd never be a chef, but Jude was turning him into quite a gourmand. Food had been a necessity for survival, but Felix loved trying new tastes and textures. They even started cooking most dinners together. Jude was a patient teacher, and Felix was burning himself and the food less these days. He especially liked spending every night in Jude's arms. They spent most of their nights at Felix's house because of Pul, but he'd stayed over a few nights at Jude's.

Neither man had confessed the depth of their feelings, but it was as apparent as the hard-on pushing against Felix's jeans.

"Kill the trolling motor," Rocky said. "According to the map, the Spensers' house is just around the bend. We'll paddle the rest of the way."

Jude shut down the motor and grabbed a paddle while Rocky picked up the other one. It took a few minutes for Jude and Rocky to synchronize their strokes effectively, so they floated in the right direction. Felix's heart sank when they rounded the bend in the river, and the Spencers' property came into view. He'd expected a well-lit, bustling home that mirrored the lives of the people who inhabited it. What he saw was a dark, lifeless structure looming ominously amidst a thick copse of trees.

"That's not good," Rocky whispered, echoing the dread pulsing in the pit of Felix's stomach.

They were too late.

"Maybe they go to bed early," Jude suggested.

"Doesn't explain the lack of exterior lights," Felix said. "They're gone."

"Only one way to know for sure," Rocky said, steering the boat toward the Spencers' boat dock.

"I don't think this is a good idea," Felix whispered as they neared the wooden structure.

"Of course, it's not," Rocky replied. "Since when has that stopped you?"

Rocky wasn't wrong. Knowing he shouldn't leave the boat, Felix still accepted Rocky's hand and climbed onto the deck. It took him a second to get his bearings on the floating structure, then Felix turned and assisted Jude. He didn't break their connection once Jude stood on the deck beside him. The strength and warmth of Jude's hand made Felix feel braver as they wordlessly crept over the lawn. The expanse of grass narrowed and was swallowed up by the trees as they neared the house. Various nocturnal creatures serenaded them along their journey, but Felix wasn't tricked into believing they'd been written into a Disney film. It was probably more like a Tarantino movie.

Overhead, the wind kicked up and whistled eerily through the trees, and it felt like a bad omen. Felix shivered but still persisted putting one foot in front of the other. The cloud cover shifted, as did the shadows all around them. Felix's heart sped up, but he didn't retreat. He started to feel less anxious when they reached the edge of the trees surrounding the Spencers' massive home and hadn't encountered booby traps or mafia henchmen.

"Should we split up?" Rocky asked.

"Hell no," Jude said. "We check things out together and get the hell out of here."

"Yeah," Rocky agreed. "Left to your own devices, there's no telling what the two of you would get up to."

"Absolutely no breaking and entering," Felix said. "I better not see a lock pick in your hand."

"I agree wholeheartedly," a deep voice with a hint of a Brooklyn accent rang out from the trees. It had to be one of Mercy's goons.

"Oh fuck," Rocky said.

"Hands in the air and turn around. Slowly. No sudden moves," the man commanded.

"Oh fuck. Oh fuck," Rocky repeated.

"He sounds like a broken record," Jude whispered. "Can I hit him and see if he plays a different song?"

"Maybe," Felix said. It had been Rocky's dumb idea to get out of the damn boat.

"He said to turn the fuck around," a second goon commanded. His voice was equally as stern as Goon One but not as deep.

"Okay," Felix said.

"Without talking," a third henchman said.

Felix, Rocky, and Jude slowly turned around to face the threat lurking in the shadows behind them. Their NVGs didn't help identify the men dressed in black from their ski masks down to the boots on their feet. Felix nearly pissed himself when he saw the guns in their gloved hands. A fourth man in black jogged out of the woods.

"No one else arrived with The Three Stooges," he said.

"Who the hell are you?" Felix asked.

Goon Four turned on a light, temporarily blinding Felix, Rocky, and Jude through their NVGs. Felix cursed and reached to rip his headset off but stopped when all four men yelled at him not to move. He closed his eyes instead.

"Get on your knees," One said.

Rocky laughed dryly. "Not until you buy me a steak dinner first."

Concern for his friend's mental state eclipsed fear for his own life. Felix looked over at Rocky, who was grinning like a lunatic.

"I think your friend has lost his mind," Jude whispered.

"Excuse me," Three said, pulling their attention back to the dangerous men with guns. "On. Your. Knees. Now."

Felix, Rocky, and Jude unceremoniously dropped to their knees. Four turned off the light once they complied.

"Bend your arms and lace your fingers behind your heads and keep them there," One said.

Felix complied without hesitation. It was better to live to fight his way out of this when the men didn't have scary-looking guns aimed at them.

"Now you other two do it too," Four commanded. "We don't have all night to be dicking around with you idiots."

"If you have someplace you'd rather be, we won't hold it against you," Rocky said.

"I'm not doing another thing until you identify yourselves," Jude added.

"Jude," Felix hissed. "Do what they say. I just got you back, and I want to hold on to you longer." Felix breathed a sigh of relief when he heard Jude moving. "You too, Major. You're my best friend."

"Fine, damn it," Rocky groused.

"This is so sweet," One said. Felix expected the man to taunt them, but he didn't say anything. Goons One, Two, and Three holstered their weapons and advanced on Felix, Rocky, and Jude.

Felix flinched when Two yanked his arms down and behind his back before securing his wrists with zip ties. Felix heard Jude struggling beside him.

"Get your fucking hands off him," Jude snarled.

"I'm fine, Jude," Felix assured him.

Two yanked Felix's NVGs off before tugging a hood over his head, pitching Felix into total darkness. That's when panic really started to set in. Blood rushed to his ears, making it hard for Felix to hear what was going on. A cold sweat broke out all over his body, and he found it hard to breathe through the cloth.

"Hey," Two said. "Focus on your breathing. Inhale a deep breath and push it back out through your mouth."

"Is this the latest trend in meditation?" Felix found himself asking.

"There you go, buddy. Get pissed. It helps calm the fear," Two said before patting Felix on the shoulder.

Felix tried to flinch away from Two's touch, but the bigger man hooked a hand beneath his armpit and yanked Felix to his feet like he weighed nothing.

"Who are you?" Jude asked again.

"Your worst nightmare if you don't shut up," Four said.

Next thing Felix knew, the henchmen were frog-marching them through the woods. Felix tripped over limbs and undergrowth and would've planted face-first in the dirt if not for the steely grip Two had on his bicep. He heard the familiar slide of a van door opening, and Felix dug his feet into the ground. People who were thrown into vans rarely escaped and lived to tell about it.

Jude and Rocky must've drawn the same conclusion because he heard them scuffling with their escorts too.

"Settle the fuck down, Ford," One said.

Ford?

"Who the hell is Ford?" Jude asked.

"None of us are named Ford," Felix said. Relief flooded his body, and he stopped struggling against his escort's hold. "This is just one big misunderstanding."

Rocky's laughter bordered on unhinged, and it ratcheted Felix's anxiety again. "Asher, is this your idea of foreplay?" Rocky asked.

Asher? Is that Goon One's name?

"Who the hell is Asher?" Jude asked. "Are you losing your shit, Jacobs, or are these assholes friends of yours?"

"Rocky?" Felix asked.

"Just relax, guys," Rocky said calmly. "Everything is going to be okay."

"So touching," Asher, aka One, said. "You guys can get in the van willingly with assistance, or we can throw you in. Your choice."

"Fine," Felix said. "I'll go peacefully." His captor helped Felix into the van. Since it was made to haul cargo and not people, there were no seats in the back. He propped Felix up against the far side of the van and stepped out.

"I'll go next," Jude volunteered.

The van rocked as two men climbed inside. Jude was placed on Felix's right side. The warmth of Jude's body seeped into Felix and chased away the chill that had settled in his bones. Felix scooted over until he was pressed entirely up against Jude's side and rested his head against Jude's shoulder.

"We're going out of town for a romantic weekend getaway as soon as this is over," Jude said.

Felix chuckled. He loved Jude's confidence, but Felix thought maybe he was being too presumptuous this time. Regardless of Rocky's nonchalance, Felix felt it would be a miracle if they survived the night.

If that were the case... *Be courageous in love.*

"Jude," Felix said.

"Hmmm?"

"I love you," Felix said. "I always have, and I always will."

Jude sucked in a sharp breath, and his body shuddered. "I love you too, Ace."

"What about me?" Rocky asked. The pout in his voice made Felix grin.

"You're my best friend, Major," Felix said. "Of course, I love you. I'm totally kicking your ass for suggesting we get off the fucking boat though."

"My bad," Rocky said.

"Aww. How sweet," Four said. "I was dead set against this mission, but I'm damn glad you guys talked me into it."

"Watch your hands, Asher," Rocky said as he was shoved inside the van and sat on Felix's other side. "I don't think you're supposed to be grabbing people there."

"Oops," Asher replied. "My hand slipped."

"So will my fist once you untie my wrists," Rocky countered.

"Kinky," Three said.

"More like ouch," Four remarked.

"Everyone get in the van and shut the hell up," Asher commanded.

Two men rode in the front, and the other two climbed into the cargo hold with Felix, Jude, and Rocky, although Felix didn't know which goon sat where.

Whoever was behind the wheel showed no concerns for their safety as he drove fast and braked hard. Felix had started out keeping track of the turns they'd made but lost track after a while. It was hard to tell if some of the changes in direction were due to sharp bends in a country road or an actual turn.

"Where are you taking us?" Jude asked.

"Would we have put hoods over your faces if we wanted you to know?" Two asked from a few feet away.

"Nice try though," Asher said. He was also in the cargo section of the van with them, which put Three and Four in the front.

They rode in silence for what seemed like hours before the vehicle finally came to a stop.

"Honey, we're home," Asher said.

"Fuck you," Rocky groused.

Asher emitted a growl that might've sounded sexy if Felix wasn't so scared. "Later, baby."

They were yanked out of the van, marched across a gravel driveway, and led into a building of some sort. The goons cut the zip ties and shoved them down onto metal chairs. Felix massaged his tingling wrists to get the circulation flowing. Someone yanked off his hood without warning, and bright light blinded him. Felix blinked a few times, bringing the room into focus as his eyes adjusted. He took in the concrete floors, unfinished drywall, and sliding doors and realized they were in a garage or outbuilding. The four goons from outside the Spencers' house stood in front of them again, but with one noticeable difference: they'd removed their ski masks.

Uh-oh. If the bad guys were showing their faces, then they weren't worried about Felix, Jude, and Rocky talking later. There wouldn't be a later.

"Oh, this can't be good," Jude whispered, echoing Felix's thoughts.

The biggest, scariest-looking goon stepped forward. The man's sweaty, coal black hair was plastered to his head and eyes as dark as midnight snapped with an intensity that stole Felix's breath. A scraggly beard drew Felix's attention to a firm mouth that slowly parted into a huge smile, showing perfect white teeth against a swarthy complexion. Big and Scary stopped in front of Rocky and squatted down until they were eye to eye.

"Hey, baby. Miss me?" he asked Rocky.

Baby?

Felix recognized his voice. It was the henchman that Rocky had called Asher.

Asher chuckled when Rocky didn't answer him, then he leaned forward and kissed Rocky on the mouth.

CHAPTER 27

"**B**aby?" Jude asked contemptuously. "Jacobs is dating one of Mercy's men?"

Asher and Rocky continued staring at each other in silence for a few seconds before Asher slowly turned his head and looked at Jude. The outrage in the man's eyes would've been hilarious if Felix hadn't been on the verge of wetting himself.

"You think we're Mercy's men?" Asher asked.

"Aren't you?" Felix and Jude asked at the same time.

Asher heaved a deep sigh and rose to his full height. Then as if on a director's cue, all four men lifted their black tactical shirts high enough to show badges clipped to their belts. The silver star was universally recognized.

"You're US Marshals?" Felix asked.

"You've got to be kidding me," Jude groused.

Felix turned to look at Rocky. "How do you figure into all of this?"

"Oh, this I can't wait to hear," Jude said.

Rocky turned solemn blue eyes on Felix. "Remember my Vegas problem?"

Vegas? Felix tried to remember a conversation they'd had about Vegas, but his brain had turned to sludge. Vegas? Oh. *OH!*

"This is your ex-husband?" Felix whispered while studying Big and

Scary again. Physically, he could see where the man ticked all of Rocky's boxes.

Asher broke eye contact with Felix to glare at Rocky. "*Ex?*" he asked, quirking a raven brow. "Is that what you're telling people, Ford?"

Rocky heaved a deep sigh, then met Felix's stare. "We're still legally married." He shifted his attention back to the bulky bear of a man standing too close for Felix's comfort, regardless of the shiny star on his belt. "For now," Rocky added for good measure.

"Are you planning on killing us?" Jude asked suddenly. "If so, I want to hear this story before I die."

A ginger-haired marshal with a crooked smile and penetrating blue eyes smirked at Jude. "Killing idiot reporters and a private detective who happened to stumble into trouble is not in our job description." Felix recognized the voice as belonging to Goon Two.

"We didn't ask for your help," Felix said.

A man with tawny hair the color of a lion's mane and soulful brown eyes snorted and shook his head. "You would've been killed if we hadn't." Felix matched his voice to Goon Three.

That meant the marshal with white-blond hair and green eyes was Goon Four. "I don't hear a thank you," he said.

"Hold your breath while you wait," Felix suggested. Blondie replied by flipping him off.

"Marshals don't investigate crimes, and none of us are fugitives on your apprehension list." Jude looked at Felix and Rocky. "Right?"

A man wearing pajamas, a robe, and a pair of slippers padded into the garage, holding a pint of Ben & Jerry's in one hand and a spoon in the other. All the puzzle pieces clicked into place and the picture crystallized, reenergizing Felix's tired brain.

"Was this really necessary, fellas?" Cameron Spencer asked.

Asher smirked at them. "Maybe not, but it sure was fun."

"Did I hear you say you're married to one of them?" Spencer asked.

"That one," Asher said, pointing to Rocky.

Spencer nodded. "Your transfer from Vegas makes sense now. I was worried you were dirty."

"What the hell is happening?" Jude asked.

"Witness protection," Felix replied. "You're helping the FBI take down Jack Mercy."

"I am, although you nearly ruined it with your investigation," Cameron said before turning his attention to Jude. "Both your investigations."

"So, you decided to get even by sending Mercy after us?" Jude asked.

"I did no such thing," Cameron said patiently. Then he looked at Asher. "Can I speak to them alone?"

Asher took turns studying Felix, Jude, and Rocky before nodding for the others to follow him out of the garage.

Cameron pulled over another folding metal chair and dropped down onto it. "I know you must have a ton of questions."

Felix wanted to knock Spencer out of his chair but had no desire to take on the four bruisers who would be loitering on the other side of the door. "I'm not even sure where the hell to begin."

"By now, you've figured out that The Camelot Corporation was a shell company, and the extended warranties and gap insurance offered at my dealership was a way for me to steal money," Spencer said.

"We have," Felix said. He couldn't believe Cameron would admit it upfront.

"You thought I was laundering money for the mafia, but I was socking it away so my family could start over fresh someplace else," Cameron said. "Mercy was never going to let me go. He'd been using my dealership to move drugs and guns for years."

"No people?" Jude asked.

Cameron shook his head vigorously. "Never. Even Mercy isn't that evil."

"I beg to differ," Felix replied dryly, rolling his shoulders to ease the tension. The marshals' rough handling had aggravated every ache he'd sustained the prior week.

"You wouldn't be alive to have this conversation if Mercy truly wanted you dead," Cameron countered. "He's had plenty of opportunities to take you out since the explosion." Spencer looked at Jude. "Mercy's attack on Felix was a lesson for you. Luckily, you both came out of it unscathed."

Felix couldn't find fault in Spencer's claim, because Mercy had made his position known to Jude. But something had been bothering Felix all week. "If I wasn't Mercy's target, then why did the attempt on my life come so soon after I interviewed you about the Second Chance Program?" he asked.

"Mercy has people inside my dealerships watching me and reporting back to him. When you started asking the same questions as Jude, Mercy must've assumed Jude had recruited your help in bringing his empire down."

Felix recalled Veronica meeting with Mercy's ruffian from the club before Skeet loaded the clunker cars onto the hauler. She'd helped facilitate the interview, so was she the mole?

"How would Mercy have known what questions either of us asked you?" Jude asked.

Cameron heaved a deep sigh. "I panicked and told him about Jude's interview questions. I didn't make the connection between them until it was too late."

"You son of a bitch," Felix snarled.

Spencer looked at Jude. "I swear I never meant for you to come to any harm, emotionally or physically. I simply told Mercy we needed to be smarter about the program going forward."

"So, your philanthropic gesture was nothing more than a lie?" Felix asked.

"No," Spencer said adamantly. "What I told you both about the origin of Second Chance was true. Mercy ruined it like he did everything. I realized I would never get out from under him. I'd repaid the loan he'd given me ten times over, but it was never enough. That's when I decided to exploit the program for my personal gain."

"What about Felix's interview?" Jude asked. "Are you saying your office was bugged?"

"Veronica knew about the interview," Felix said.

Spencer nodded. "She did, but she's not the one who tipped Mercy off."

"How do you know?" Jude asked.

The door opened again, and Veronica walked into the garage with Skeet. They both wore FBI badges on chains around their necks.

"Christ," Felix said. If Todd Dartmouth walked in next, he was going to launch his chair at someone. "No wonder you worked so hard to keep me away from Spencer."

Veronica smiled wryly. "You nearly wrecked two years of undercover work."

"You should've passed my messages along to The Auto King sooner," Felix countered. "Had he made things right with my transmission, I would've let it go."

"I realized my mistake too late," Veronica acknowledged.

"As for tipping Mercy off about your interview," Cameron said, "it had to be someone with easy access to my office. I suspected it was someone on my janitorial staff, but then Veronica recalled all the weird IT issues we'd had."

"So, the service records really were gone?" Felix asked.

"The systems upgrade was legitimate, but we continued to have issues which required IT technicians to come in almost weekly over the past few months," Veronica said.

"Let me guess, one of those technicians was in Spencer's office before my interview," Felix said.

"And the following day," Veronica said. "I swept Spencer's office daily for bugs, but they were able to circumvent me. We're taking a closer look at the software company itself, as well as the technicians they sent to the dealership."

"We've had to move up every single part of our takedown mission to keep it from backfiring in our faces," Skeet said. Felix was impressed the man could speak without spitting tobacco first.

"So, you're going to testify against Mercy?" Rocky asked. It was the first thing he said since acknowledging he was still married to the sexy marshal.

"I am now," Spencer said, "but initially, I planned to fake my family's death and use the new identities I procured."

"You're still going to do that, but now on the government's dime," Jude remarked.

"Also true," Spencer acknowledged.

"What happens to all the money you stole from your customers?" Felix asked.

"They will receive a full refund," Skeet said. "It will look like a class action settlement payout through a law firm the agency has partnered with to help provide cover."

Still unable to grasp the magnitude of the trouble he'd stumbled into, Felix asked, "So, how did we end up here tonight?"

Asher stepped back into the room. "We've been following you as you tailed the Spencers. We knew you weren't going to let your investigation go. I obviously have a vested interest in one of you, and Mr. Spencer is fond of the other two."

Rocky flipped him off, and Asher blew him a kiss.

"I wanted the opportunity to apologize to you, Felix," Spencer said. "You deserve to know the truth."

"You can't stop me from writing the truth about what I learned once the news of your deaths break," Felix said stubbornly.

"True," Veronica said. "But do you really want your reputation to shift from respected investigative journalist to a conspiracy theorist?"

"I'll be vindicated once Spencer reappears on the witness stand," Felix challenged.

"*If* he testifies," Skeet countered. "Right now, it looks like we have enough to lock Mercy away for the rest of his life without Spencer ever taking the stand."

Fuck. There was no good choice. Felix could tell the truth and risk getting shunned by the writing community or keep Spencer's secret and live with a nagging conscience.

Spencer chuckled. "You really do remind me of myself when I was younger. We're often blinded by our ambition and drive. I made a deal with the devil to ensure the future I envisioned. I should've had more faith in myself and Brigitte."

"This feels like making a deal with the devil," Felix countered. "Maybe you never personally shot anyone or sold drugs to kids, but you helped Mercy do it."

Spencer swallowed hard. "And I will spend every day trying to atone for the horrible decisions I've made."

"When Mr. Spencer dies, he will be reborn a much poorer man. He isn't taking his assets with him. The vice president of Spencer Auto Malls will take over the reins, and the Second Chance Program will continue after his death. All of the Spencers' personal assets will go to charities that address drug addiction, poverty, homelessness, and victims of gun violence," Veronica said.

"I'll live in a tent as long as my wife and kids are safe," Spencer said.

"We've planned slightly better accommodations than that, sir," Asher said.

Veronica quirked a brow. "You can keep your mouth shut for the greater good and help bring down the Southern mafia or run with your story and collect your fifteen minutes of fame. If you survive Mercy, then what?"

Felix scowled at her while he thought it over. He'd still have his job, his friends, his podcast, and Jude. Or would he? Would Minerva still look upon him favorably if he became a joke? What would become of Felix if he lost his job? He could bypass the paper and use the podcast to get the information out, but it came with the same peril of turning their investigative podcast into one that pushes conspiracy theories. That could also hurt Jonah's standing with the GBI. If people stopped tuning in to their podcast, how much longer would his friends be willing to give up their valuable time to record episodes? How long would his relationships last under duress?

There was a soft knock on the garage door before it opened. Brigitte Spencer poked her head in. "Is everything okay?"

"Yes," Spencer said. "Everything is fine."

She looked at each person in the garage. The expression in her cornflower blue eyes reminded Felix of the one he wore in his second-grade school photo. This was a woman who'd been knocked down, but she wasn't out. Brigitte had pulled herself up and dusted herself off. She was a survivor, and she was assessing the threat to herself and her family. When her gaze landed on Felix, he offered a smile, hoping to assure her that he wasn't a threat.

But was he? What would happen to them if he reported that the Spencer family was really alive? Jack Mercy would never give up until he found Cameron and killed him. Would he stop there? Would he kill his own daughter and grandchildren?

Brigitte returned Felix's gesture before shifting her attention back to her husband. "It's getting late. Are you coming to bed soon?" she asked.

"I'll be there shortly," Cameron promised her.

"If you're not coming now, can I have the ice cream you promised to get for me?" she asked sheepishly.

Cameron stared down at the pint and spoon in his hands as if he'd forgotten about them. He probably had, and who could blame him? Cameron chuckled as he crossed the room. Brigitte took the items but didn't immediately back out of the doorway. The couple had a private exchange of words that didn't reach Felix's ears. He didn't need to hear their voices to know what was said. He could read so much in their actions and expressions.

Brigitte looked up at her husband with big, worried eyes. Cameron smiled and brushed a hand over Brigitte's cheek before dropping a kiss on her forehead. The worry immediately faded from her expression, and the tension eased from her posture. Brigitte nodded, then ducked out of the room.

Spencer took a deep breath before facing Felix once more. "Be smarter than I was. Choose a better path."

It was odd how Spencer only addressed Felix, but maybe he rightly sensed the other two would quickly back down without a fight. Jude had his mother to protect, and Rocky... Well, he had a big, sexy husband who could abduct him as easily as plucking flowers from a field. If Jonah were there, he'd cede authority to the FBI. Avery wouldn't do anything to jeopardize Jonah's career.

Whatever Felix decided, he would make sure his friends stayed clean. That meant he'd have to choose the paper over the podcast, *if* he blew the whistle on Spencer.

"Anything else you want to know before we take you back?" Asher asked.

So many thoughts and questions ran through his mind, but Felix voiced none of them. He would kick himself in the ass for it someday, but all he wanted right now was to go home. He shook his head.

"No," Jude said.

"I'm good," Rocky added.

"Let's get you guys back," Asher said.

"Spencer," Felix called out when the man opened the garage door. "Don't blow your second chance."

Spencer smiled. "That I can promise." Then he was gone, and Felix knew he'd never see the man again.

"What about the person who blew up my car?" Felix asked Veronica. "Will you at least tell me if you have leads?"

"He's in custody," she said. "We traced the van's movement through the city via CCTV and ATM cameras."

"Is he talking?" Felix asked.

"We don't comment on active investigations," Skeet said.

Veronica looked at the man and rolled her eyes. "Really? What would you call this evening?" She faced Felix again. "He has confessed to setting the bomb but has denied the Mercy connection."

"For now," Skeet added.

The tension sparking off the two FBI agents reminded Felix of the exchange he'd witnessed between them in the back lot at Spencer Auto Mall. They might be playing for the same team, but they didn't like each other much.

"Let's head out," Asher said, picking up a hood from the floor. Two other goons, um, marshals did the same.

"Is that really necessary?" Jude asked as the tawny lion-like marshal approached him.

"We can't allow you to see the location of our safe house," Tawny replied.

"Fine," Jude grumbled.

Ginger Snap approached Felix with a crooked grin. Felix sat still while the guy draped the fabric over his head. Then he took deep, steady breaths to counter the anxiety building inside him. Guess he realized that bondage and blindfolds wasn't his kind of kink.

"Are you going to fight me on this too?" Asher asked Rocky.

"Would it make a difference?" Rocky countered.

Asher chuckled. "Nope."

"Fine," Rocky said, echoing Jude's irritation.

"Can we trust you to behave, or do we need to bind your hands again?" Tawny asked.

Felix, Jude, and Rocky were adamant they'd behave. The marshals escorted the men back to the van much more gently the second time around. They rode in silence for what seemed like forever, and Felix eventually drifted to sleep with his head on Jude's shoulder. The van door sliding open startled him awake.

"Rise and shine, sleepyheads," Asher said.

"This is not how I prefer my husband to wake me," Rocky grumbled.

"Then maybe you shouldn't have given up on me so easily," Asher countered.

Felix heard Rocky mumble something that sounded like "prick."

"Keep going back to the damn sex club, and you'll see just what kind of prick I can be," Asher said.

Felix had been in the process of scooting to the edge of the van but froze at Asher's remark. "How'd you know about that?"

"You think the FBI doesn't have undercover agents working inside Mercy's club?" Ginger Snap asked as he gripped Felix's bicep and pulled him out of the van. He snorted. "Bruce Wayne and Clark Kent."

"Mercy has facial recognition software for members and guests," Tawny said. "You think he's going to settle for fake names when he can wield his membership list as a weapon to keep politicians and cops in his corner?"

"So, that's how he knew I was in the club both times," Jude said. "It should've occurred to me."

"I hate to sound like Cameron," Ginger Snap said, "but all three of you were blinded by ambition and drive. Noble, but stupid."

"Thanks," Felix grumbled.

"So, Ford," Asher said once they were walking, "how'd you get into the club?"

Rocky heaved a deep sigh. "My cousin is a member. He pulled strings."

"The kissing-cousin variety?" Asher wanted to know.

"Fuck you, Yankee," Tawny said. "We don't all kiss our cousins down here in the South."

Asher laughed and let the subject drop.

Felix heard water slapping against wood and caught a whiff of the fishy river smell as they neared the wooden dock where they'd left their boat. Once they stepped onto the floating platform, the marshals removed their hoods. It was still dark out, but the sun was flirting with the horizon. Tawny, Ginger Snap, and Blondie retreated into the woods, leaving Asher behind to talk to Rocky. Asher stood with his hands on his hips while Rocky crossed his arms over his chest. His friend looked utterly closed down, and Felix didn't like it.

Jude pulled Felix into his arms and kissed him softly on his lips. "What a crazy night."

Felix burrowed tighter against Jude, letting the bigger man's warmth seep into him. "It feels like a nightmare."

Jude softly said his name, so Felix looked up at him. "The whole declaration... It's okay if you want to take it back. We were under duress, and I can't expect you to—"

Felix shut Jude up by kissing him hard on the mouth. It was brief, but it got his point across. "I won't take it back. I love you."

Jude's lips curled into a smile, flexing his dimples. "I love you too."

The wood beneath Felix's feet vibrated as footsteps echoed against the planks.

"Ready?" Rocky asked warily.

Felix pulled Rocky into an embrace and kissed his forehead. "You okay, Major?"

"No," Rocky said honestly. Then he leaned into Felix and sighed. "I will be though."

Asher narrowed his eyes as he watched them, and Felix flipped him the middle finger.

"Let's go home," Jude said, clasping Felix on the shoulder.

Felix released Rocky and stepped back. They took turns climbing into the boat bobbing in the water.

"Thank goodness for the trolling motor," Rocky said. "I'm too knackered to row."

Jude and Felix returned to the stern, and Rocky sat in the bow, facing them instead of Asher, who'd remained on the deck. Jude yanked the pull string, firing the engine to life while Felix untied the rope tethering them to the dock.

Jude turned the boat around and steered them back to where they'd left Rocky's truck and boat trailer. The change in direction made it possible for Rocky to watch Asher until they rounded the bend. Felix couldn't tell what his friend was thinking. Rocky had always been an enigma. A man who flirted shamelessly but never acted on it. Someone who camouflaged their quick wit and brilliant mind behind good looks and a laidback personality. There was so much Felix didn't know about Rocky, but Felix trusted the man implicitly and would wait patiently for his friend to open up.

"Why does everyone call you something different, Jacobs?" Jude asked, breaking the silence.

"Most people call you Rocky, Felix calls you Major, and US Deputy Douchebag calls you Ford."

Rocky threw his head back and laughed. "US Deputy Douchebag. I'm totally stealing that."

"Go right ahead," Jude said.

"My full name is Major Rockford Michael Jacobs."

"What a mouthful," Jude said. Felix was too tired to jump on that opening.

"Asher is the only one who shortens Rockford to Ford instead of Rocky like everyone else."

"Except me," Felix said proudly.

Rocky grinned. "Just don't call me late to dinner." He looked at his watch. "Or breakfast in this case. Anyone interested in a bite to eat?"

Felix just wanted to go home and sit in the quiet of his home office. He had a big decision to make. Skeet, or whatever his name really was, mentioned the timelines had moved up, so Felix expected the news about the Spencer family's death to break later in the day. If he was going to expose Cameron, he'd need to have a story ready.

"We're in," Jude said, pressing a kiss to Felix's temple.

"Always trying to feed me," Felix grumbled.

"Because I love you," Jude murmured in his ear.

Felix's answering shiver had nothing to do with the air temperature. He nestled closer to Jude and returned the sentiment. Felix wanted to start each new day wrapped up in Jude's arms and love. Decisions could wait. His people came first.

"Yeah, I could eat."

CHAPTER 28

The food was awful, but it was worth the indigestion to see Rocky's smartass nature return over a stack of rubbery pancakes and greasy breakfast meat. They hadn't discussed the events of the evening other than agreeing to bring Jonah and Avery up to speed later. There was no need to wreck their sleep too. By the time the trio parted ways, Jude and Rocky had found a peaceful coexistence in Felix's world, for which he was eternally grateful.

Felix initially climbed into bed with Jude and Pul when they got home, but his brain wouldn't shut off. He replayed the conversation with Cameron Spencer on an endless loop, analyzing every spoken word and the silent clues hidden in the man's body language and expressions. Felix's brain felt like an overstuffed suitcase again, and he could hear the hinges creaking. They were about to surrender to the laws of physics just as Felix gave up any hope of getting sleep. He crept out of his bedroom and went to his office down the hall. Felix sat at his desk and powered up his computer because his keyboard was the best tool for unpacking a cluttered mind.

Felix wrote for hours, stringing together the timeline of events as well as his thoughts and feelings on each. Like he'd instructed Jimmy, Felix wrote the piece as if he planned to publish it. After he finished, he returned to his room to crawl back into his bed but discovered it was empty. Felix heard the shower running and stripped down on his way to the bathroom.

Felix was grateful for the glass shower doors when he got an eyeful of Jude standing beneath the spray, rinsing soap out of his hair. He watched the suds glide over Jude's sexy body and swirl around his feet before going down the drain.

Damn, I'm a lucky man.

"Are you going to stand there like a perv or join me?" Jude asked, snagging Felix's attention.

Felix chuckled as he opened the glass door and stepped inside.

Jude greeted him with a hot kiss. "I missed waking up beside you," he said once they parted.

"I missed it too." Felix felt calmer after writing his mock story, but the gravity of the situation still weighed heavily on his shoulders. "I still don't know what I'm going to do yet."

Jude cupped Felix's face. "I do. You're going to take a shower with me, then we're going to drink some coffee."

Jude grabbed the shampoo bottle and squirted some into his palm before working it into Felix's hair. Felix moaned and leaned harder against Jude, who pressed his fingertips into Felix's scalp, easing the tension from his body.

"You know I wasn't talking about morning activities, right?" Felix asked.

Jude turned Felix around and tilted his head to rinse the shampoo out of his hair. Once he finished, Jude nuzzled Felix's neck, turning him into complete mush. "You'll do the right thing, Ace. You always do."

"No solution feels a hundred percent right," Felix admitted.

His ambitions were at war with his conscience. Felix had made a career out of exposing people like Cameron Spencer, who used their advantage and privilege to avoid getting punished for their evil deeds. Keeping quiet made him feel like a hypocrite. But Felix couldn't dismiss the sacrifices Spencer was making to get his second chance. Spencer would be looking over his shoulder for the rest of his life, even if the feds were able to make a case against Mercy without his testimony. He'd had to humble himself in front of his wife and children, and that couldn't be ignored either.

"You'll pick the option you can live with the easiest," Jude said, squirting bodywash into his hand. "And I'll support whatever you decide."

They took turns washing each other in between kisses, sighs, and moans. Felix ran his thumb over the spot where he'd left his love bite on Jude's neck. The mark had faded since then, but Felix loved the memory of seeing it peeking above Jude's shirt collar while he was on air. Felix pressed his lips to Jude's neck and swirled his tongue over tender skin, feeling Jude's pulse dance in response.

"Do it," Jude growled, sliding his hand into Felix's hair.

Felix chuckled. "You going to cover it up with makeup this time?"

Jude reached down to grip Felix's ass with his other hand. "Maybe."

"I think maybe we should take this into my bedroom where we have enough room to do it right."

Jude shut off the water while Felix grabbed two towels off the rack. Neither of them spent much time drying off before falling onto the bed in a tangle of limbs and a symphony of moans.

Jude pinned Felix to the bed before he remembered Felix's back. "Ace, I'm sorry."

"Huh-uh," Felix said, tightening his legs around Jude's waist when he tried to roll off. "I want you just like this."

Jude started to protest until Felix latched his mouth on to the spot that drove the big man nuts. Felix continued to suck, lick, and bite Jude's neck while Jude stretched Felix's ass with lubed fingers.

Then Jude rolled on a condom and repositioned himself between Felix's legs. He paused after breaching the first ring of muscles to allow Felix time to adjust. Instead of kissing him like he normally would, Jude hovered over his mouth.

"Say it again," Jude whispered.

Felix smiled. "I love you."

A shiver rolled through Jude's body. "I love you too. So fucking much." Jude fully joined their bodies with one deep thrust. Brushing his fingers over Felix's cheekbones, he said, "You're more important to me than any scoop. Your heart is more valuable than any award."

"Jude," Felix whispered thickly, as tears formed in his eyes.

"You're my home, Ace. That's what I should've told you all those years ago."

Before Jude, Felix hadn't realized a person could be a home. Now he understood. Once Jude started moving inside him, the time for talking ended. Felix communicated by touching and kissing. He held on to Jude as if the man were his lifeboat in a riptide of chaos, and they clung to one another afterward like shipwreck survivors washed up on the beach. Jude nuzzled his neck, sending warmth throughout Felix's body.

"I could stay like this all day," Jude whispered in his ear.

"Me too," Felix said sleepily.

He debated calling in sick to catch up on sleep but decided to go in after all. It was unlikely he'd get any real rest until he made a decision on what to do about Spencer. When Felix wasn't thinking about his article, he was wondering when the news about the family would break. And what about the subsequent raids and arrests at Mercy's home and businesses, as well as those of his associates? It was better to keep his mind busy so he didn't drive himself crazy. Like Jude had said, he'd know the right thing to do when the situation presented itself.

Felix refilled his travel mug in the break room before continuing to his office. The familiar sounds of a bustling newsroom eased his tiredness, and he was glad he'd decided to work. He was even happier when he saw an email from Darnell Cahill in his inbox.

Felix,

My family met with Jose Ramirez last night and began the process for a posthumous pardon for my father. I think my mother has a little crush on the gentleman, which I thought you'd find cute. Please don't tell her I said so. Even though I spent two hours in his company, I still find it hard to believe a lawyer of his stature wants to help us. By us, I'm including you, Jonah, and Rocky. We consider the three of you as part of our family, which is why we have insisted Mr. Ramirez include the terrific trio, which we've dubbed you, in any public appearances his office sets up. Maybe you want to appear on camera, and perhaps you don't. We wanted you and your podcast partners to have the opportunity to choose your level of involvement since none of this would be possible without you.

The truth is, I've become a cynical man over the years, and the current climate has done nothing to allay my concerns for my children's future. But then Sinister in Savannah *comes along and reminds me that we do have allies. People really do care about injustice and suffering. As grateful as I am for all you've done to restore my family's name, I appreciate my rejuvenated faith most of all.*

My mom's birthday is in September, and we'd love for the three of you to attend her birthday celebration. I'll send information once we have everything set up.

Our regards,
The Cahill Family

Felix blinked to clear the moisture gathering in his eyes. Then he re-read Darnell's message and didn't bother to fight off his tears the second time through. He forwarded the email to Rocky and Jonah before replying to Darnell, thanking him for the update and the birthday invitation.

"Oh," Jimmy said from the doorway. "Maybe I should come back later."

Felix snapped his head up to meet his gaze. He rubbed his hands over his face and sniffed. "What's up, Jimmy?"

The reporter lifted a sheet of paper. "I was just going to turn in my boot camp assignment."

Felix quirked a brow and waved him into the room. Jimmy took a seat and Felix smiled when he noticed the young reporter's improved posture. "You could've emailed it to me."

Jimmy's chin notched a degree higher. "I could have, but it would've defeated the purpose of the exercise. You wanted me to write my observations and feelings about my first boot camp lesson to build my confidence and also toughen my skin a bit, right?"

"Yes."

Jimmy nodded. "I'm delivering the assignment in person so I can gauge your reaction as you read it."

Felix figuratively tipped his hat to the man. "That's a bold move."

"It is," Jimmy agreed. "I can come back later if this is a bad time. Looks like seasonal allergies are giving you fits."

Felix appreciated the out but wouldn't take it. "The red, puffy eyes are from lack of sleep, and the tears are from reading a touching email." He held out his hand for the assignment, and Jimmy gave it to him. Felix studied the man over the top of the page for a few seconds before dropping his gaze to the document. He'd titled it: The Reluctant Mentor vs. the People Pleaser.

There was something I admired about Felix Franklin from the moment I met him, which says a lot because he's as prickly as a cactus at times, as sly as a fox, and more perceptive than any one person should be. It's an intimidating combination he wields like Thor's hammer. He pulls no punches, gives no fucks, and demands the best from everyone in his purview. I always know where I stand with him. No false pleasantries and insincere platitudes. Some might find it caustic, but I find it refreshing.

You see, this man told me I've been coddled too long, and he was right. I was a sickly child, so my mother and grandmother overcompensated when I couldn't do things other children could. As I grew older, I got physically stronger but weakened emotionally, feeling as if I couldn't do or say anything without getting their approval. Don't get me wrong, these wonderful women meant well, but sometimes children need to fall and get a little bruised and banged up. It's how we learn and grow bolder with each success and failure.

What happens when we don't get back on the bike after falling? We never learn the exhilarating pleasure of soaring down a hill on a warm sunny day. If left up to my mother and grandmother, I never would've ridden a bike after the first tumble, and I never would've experienced the rush first-hand. Of course, I wouldn't have broken my arm in two places, either. You know what? It made me stronger. I just didn't realize it until now.

Felix might be reluctant about mentoring me, but I have no doubt he's the right person for the job. His style of coaching is direct but not cruel. He is patient when it's warranted and reminds you he doesn't have time for your bullshit when it's not. He is both hard to please and generous with his praise. I thought those things were mutually exclusive, but they're not.

Here are a few things I took away from my first day in boot camp.

1. *Pleasing others is great, but it shouldn't come at the expense of my own happiness*
2. *Words are weapons that should be wielded responsibly*
3. *Believing in myself is paramount to what anyone else believes*
4. *Dreams are easy, achieving them is hard*
5. *I am enough, even if I don't always realize it*

I think Felix is a better mentor than he realizes, and I look forward to learning more from him. Someday, I hope to call him a friend.

Felix glanced up and met Jimmy's gaze after he finished reading the report. The younger man had maintained his proud posture, but Felix caught him chewing on the corner of his bottom lip, and a light blush tinted his cheeks. Felix quirked a brow, and Jimmy released his abused mouth.

"This is impressive, Jimmy."

The rookie blushed adorably. "Thank you."

"There's not a single comma out of place."

Jimmy groaned. "Will I ever live that down?"

"Nope, but how does tomorrow at nine sound for lesson two?" Felix asked.

Jimmy smiled. "I'll be here."

After Jimmy left, Felix pulled up the story he'd feverishly written just hours before with the intent to edit and have it ready to publish when the news broke. He noticed halfway through the story he had switched from relaying the timeline events to laying out the reasons he should keep Spencer's secret as if it were a foregone conclusion. The last line hooked his gaze and held it.

I could spend my energy wrecking Spencer's second chance, or I can focus on the one I've been given with Jude.

When phrased like that, was there really a choice? Felix deleted the file, messaged Minerva that he was taking a personal day, then powered off his computer.

On his way to the parking lot, Felix sent Jude a quick text. *Today would be a perfect day to lounge naked by the pool.*

Jude's response was immediate and resolute. *Meet you there in twenty minutes.*

CHAPTER 29

"Lord, how the times have changed," Marla said. She shook her head. "It wasn't so long ago that I would've spent my Saturday afternoon getting ready for the club."

Felix laughed. "And now you're stuck teaching a knucklehead like me how to make your peach cobbler."

Marla swatted his ass with a spatula. "I didn't say anything about feeling stuck. I just remarked on how the times have changed."

"How many more peaches do I need to slice?" Felix whined.

"Until I tell you to stop."

"Why can't we use canned peaches? Wouldn't it be easier?"

Marla gasped and covered her heart as if Felix had mortally wounded her. "Baby, no self-respecting Southerner uses canned peaches in their pies or cobblers. It just isn't done. Do you want to impress your man or not?"

"I do."

"Then shut up and do what I say."

"Yes, ma'am," Felix replied.

Marla looked toward the hallway Jude had disappeared down when his mother called him. "Lord, honey, your man is so yummy."

"I heard that," Amos said from the barstool at the kitchen island.

"He's nothing compared to you, darling," Marla said, leaning forward to kiss her husband.

The couple had arrived at Jude's early so Marla could teach Felix how to make the cobbler for the pool party Jude was hosting to get to know Felix's friends better. The week had been a whirlwind of activity. First, the abduction, then the breaking story about the Spencer family perishing in a boat accident off the coast of Mexico, which hogged the headlines until the FBI arrested Mercy and his men. There were two dozen arrests, but Felix expected the number to go up. No one in the media made a connection between the Spencers and Mercy, and it was a bitter pill for Felix to swallow on some days, even though he knew he'd made the right decision.

It felt like they'd barely had any time to breathe, and Felix was looking forward to spending a relaxing evening with friends.

"So, what's next for the podcast now that the pardon process is underway and Mr. Perfect didn't pan out."

Felix chuckled. "Well, The Auto King investigation ended abruptly, but I still found *my* Mr. Perfect."

"I'm so happy for you, Felix," Marla said.

"Thank you. A wise woman advised me to be courageous in love."

Marla kissed his cheek.

"It's Rocky's turn to pick our next investigation, and he wants to pursue Tess Hamilton."

"She's the one they suspect killed her three husbands?" Marla asked.

Felix nodded. "That's her."

Marla checked Felix's progress and motioned for him to keep working. "What are you going to call the episodes? Wicked Woman? The Black Widow?"

"Rocky chose Pretty Poison," Felix replied.

Marla let out a deep sigh. "If only I can live long enough to see the pretty one settled too."

Felix thought about the standoff he'd witnessed between Rocky and his husband earlier in the week. He bit his lip to keep from laughing, but it slipped out anyway in the form of a ridiculous giggle snort.

"What the hell was that noise?" Amos asked.

"It's the sound of a man who knows a secret," Marla told Amos. She turned her attention to Felix. "You better tell Mama everything."

Felix set the knife on the counter. "It's not my secret to tell."

Marla arched a brow, then looked heavenward. "I've often wondered these past weeks why you haven't called me home yet, Lord. Now I know. There is much work to be done still." She leveled her dark, impish gaze on Felix. "I don't think it's too much to ask for a hint about what I should expect. How hard is my task?"

"Rocky has a husband. A super sexy one and sparks fly when they look at each other," Felix blurted out before darting from the room before Marla could ask more questions.

"Felix, you get back here," Marla yelled after him.

He kept heading for the sanctity of Jude's office but pulled up short before reaching the door when he heard Jill's voice.

"Jude, you promised to bring Felix home to meet me. Why are you hesitating? Do I embarrass you?" Jill asked.

Felix's heart sank. *Do I embarrass him?*

"Don't be ridiculous, Mom. I crazy love you, and I can't wait to introduce you to Felix."

Oh, thank fuck!

Realizing it was rude not to make his presence known, Felix continued into Jude's office. He casually made his way to Peabody's terrarium and watched the turtle do...absolutely nothing.

"Mom," Jude said, "I promised Felix a romantic getaway. I think you and I have drastically different ideas on what that means."

"Bring him to me or else," Jill said before disconnecting the call.

Felix turned and caught Jude staring at his phone in disbelief. Then he jerked his head up and met Felix's gaze. "She hung up on me."

"The Shark has no time for bullshit. Looks like we're going to Atlanta next weekend."

Jude scowled. "Atlanta isn't romantic."

"Says you." Felix crossed the room, took the phone from Jude's hand, and set it on his desk. He looped his arms around Jude's neck, while Jude settled his hands on Felix's hips. "What if we visit all our old haunts?"

Jude pressed a brief kiss on Felix's lips. "Relive some of our big moments, perhaps?"

Felix laughed. "I'm not sure how Emory would feel about us breaking into your old dorm."

"True," Jude conceded. "I was referring to the moment on the quad when I watched you walk away. I want a redo."

Felix tipped his head to the side while he thought about it. What if Jude had persisted and Felix had backed down? Would they have shared these past fourteen years together? If so, Felix wouldn't have moved back to Savannah and landed his dream job. He might not have repaired his relationship with his mom. Felix would never have met Jonah, Rocky, Avery, and Marla. More importantly, Felix wouldn't have learned to stand on his own. He was stronger for the hardships and heartaches. They'd made him wiser, bolder, and braver.

"I think things turned out how they were supposed to," Felix finally said. "Rather than a do-over, let's call it a second chance tour." Felix winced because the name was too close to Spencer's program.

Jude pulled Felix tighter against his chest. "Fresh start?"

Felix shook his head. "That sounds like we're trying to rebuild our credit after bankruptcy." Then the answer hit him. "I say we call it our happily ever after."

Jude smiled, showing off those adorable dimples before he lowered his head and kissed Felix until he was breathless.

So long for now…

The Sinister in Savannah series will continue with Rocky and Asher in Pretty Poison.

Want to be the first to know about my book releases and have access to extra content? You can sign up for my newsletter here: eepurl.com/dlhPYj

My favorite place to hang out and chat with my readers is my Facebook group. Would you like to be a member of Aimee's Dye Hards? We'd love to have you! Go here: www.facebook.com/groups/AimeesDyeHards

OTHER BOOKS BY
AIMEE NICOLE WALKER

Only You

The Fated Hearts Series
Chasing Mr. Wright, Book 1
Rhythm of Us, Book 2
Surrender Your Heart, Book 3
Perfect Fit, Book 4
Return to Me, Book 5
Always You, Book 6
Any Means Necessary, Book 7

Curl Up and Dye Mysteries
Dyeing to be Loved
Something to Dye For
Dyed and Gone to Heaven
I Do, or Dye Trying
A Dye Hard Holiday
Ride or Dye

Road to Blissville Series
Unscripted Love
Someone to Call My Own
Nobody's Prince Charming
This Time Around
Smoke in the Mirror
Inside Out
Prescription for Love

The Lady is Mine Series
The Lady is a Thief
The Lady Stole My Heart

Queen City Rogue Series
Broken Halos
Wicked Games
Beautiful Trauma

Zero Hour Series
Ground Zero
Devil's Hour
Zero Divergence

Sinister in Savannah Series
Ride the Lightning

Standalone Novels
Second Wind

Coauthored with Nicholas Bella
Undisputed
Circle of Darkness (Genesis Circle, Book 1)
Circle of Trust (Genesis Circle, Book 2)

ACKNOWLEDGMENTS

First, I need to thank my husband and children for their constant support and encouragement. It's not easy living with a writer who often disappears into a fictional world for long periods of time. They do so many things to help me out so that I can realize my dream. I love you guys more than words can ever express.

To my creative dream team, thanks seem hardly enough for all that you do. Miranda Turner of V8 Editing and Proofreading, thank you for your tireless work, feedback, and many laughs while editing. Jay Aheer of Simply Defined art is an incredible artist, and I love how she brings my words to life. Stacey Blake of Champagne Formats is also an amazing artist who does incredible interior formatting, illustrating, and designing for e-books and paperbacks. It truly takes a village to whip me into shape. Judy Zweifel of Judy's' Proofreading, Jill Wexler, and Michael Beckett did a great job of proofreading and polishing to make my manuscript shine.

To my lovely PA, Michelle Slagan. I'm not sure how I ever did this without you. I love you to the moon and back!

I want to thank the Brittany for being a wonderful critique partner and Racheal and Melinda for being amazing alpha readers. And to my betas, Kim, Michael, and Laurel, I appreciate your honest feedback. I love working with you all.

ABOUT
AIMEE NICOLE WALKER

Ever since she was a little girl, Aimee Nicole Walker entertained herself with stories that popped into her head. Now she gets paid to tell those stories to other people. She wears many titles—wife, mom, and animal lover are just a few of them. Her absolute favorite title is champion of the happily ever after. Love inspires everything she does, music keeps her sane, and coffee is the magic elixir that fuels her day.

I'd love to hear from you.

Want to connect with me? All my links are in one nifty location. Click here:

linktr.ee/AimeeNicoleWalker